Deadly Messengers

SUSAN MAY

DEDICATION

For Franco. You know why.

A SPECIAL THANK YOU
TO MY EARLY READERS

A special thank you to my wonderful early readers who encouraged me with their kind words and early reviews. Without you, these are just words on a page. Thank you for coming along for the ride.

"Susan May is sure to become one of the great suspense writers of our times!" **Lisa Bailey** *(Good Reads USA)*

"This is honestly one of the best thrillers I have ever read, I couldn't put it down." **Kirsty Ward** *(UK) Kirstysreviews.wordpress.com*

"At times it is more or less impossible to put the book down. I expect nothing less than great offerings from Susan May in the future." **Thomas Strömquist** *(Good Reads Sweden)*

"The only author I can think of who can still surprise me is Mr. Stephen King himself. Australia just might have their own female King!" **Amanda Jane** *(Good Reads Australia)*

"I've stayed up most of the night and lost sleep and put housework off just to read this great book because it was that good." **Jane Culwell** *(Good Reads USA)*

"If the TV show *Criminal Minds* ever creates a movie or mini-series, this would be the perfect plot." **Robyn E. Lee** *(Good Reads USA)*

"I am a genre snob. I pretty much stick with YA without fail. This may be one of my top 10 favorite books." **Amanda Gillespie** *(Good Reads USA)*

"Wow! Susan May you know how to pack a punch! It was like riding a roller coaster reading it!" **Sandy Jones** *(Good Reads New Zealand)*

"Real page turner for me. I found myself caught up in the story and suspense and how it would all turn out." **Carrie Glover** *(Good Reads USA)*

"Suspenseful, maintaining it's pacing as I turned pages furiously, finishing the book in a day and a half." **Doris** *(Canada) Bleep50.wordpress.com*

"In my top 5 of the year, that's saying something since I've read 150 books." **Sandy** *(Good Reads USA)*

"One of the best novels I've read in a long time" *Peg McDaniel (Good Reads USA*

"Deadly Messengers has to be one of the best mystery, thrillers I have ever read." *Ilakiya Selvakumar (Good Reads Canada)*

"A unique story line that made an excellent thriller." *Diane Kasperski (USA) 2readreadandreviewed.blogspot.com.au*

"Grit, tension and horror are laced the entire way through." *Brenda Telford (Good Reads Australia)*

"This book is a bona fide thriller. *The twists and turns kept me reading the book way into the night." Chris French (Good Reads USA)*

"Impressed at the ingenuity of plot. I read A LOT of books and she offered up something very unique." *Deborah Cook (Australia) Debbish.com*

"This book was awesome and it reminded my of the TV show X-Files. The major plot twist hit me like a freight train!" *Sage Alberhasky (Good Reads USA)*

"This book was mind blowing !!! I've read some thrillers but this was one of the best." *Ginanusha Gnaneswaran (Good Reads Canada)*

"I found it very difficult to put down" *Irene Adam (Good Reads)*

"Very compelling read" *Shilpi Goel (USA) shilpigoel.blogspot.com*

"Riveting and suspenseful novel" *Evie Harris (Good Reads USA)*

"A very fast read...plot twists that came out of nowhere" *Connor J. Bedell (Good Reads USA)*

"A sophisticated mixture of storytelling with violence and suspense" *T.C. Stevenson (Good Reads USA)*

"WOW WOW WOW ... this book was brilliant." *Lynn MCarthy (Good Reads Australia)*

"A quick, suspenseful read." *Beth Lee (Good Reads USA)*

"A truly intelligent suspense/thriller novel!" *Dominique Fort (Good Reads Canada)*

"I found the premise extremely original and refreshing." *Melissa (Australia)* Booksbabiesbeing.com

"This is a page turning book which I found hard to put down." *Louise Wilson (Good Reads UK)*

"I was busy turning the pages like crazy, curious to know how it all would end." *Sandra C. (Good Reads Suriname, South America)*

"An exciting fast paced thriller! My only regret is the fact it ended," *Cynthia Gunnels (Good Reads USA)*

"A unique idea with well-developed characters and a lot of tension." *Brian Switzer (USA) The Belated Wordsmith*

"May has a way of taking a real-life fear and bringing it to life." *Christy Davis (Good Reads USA)*

"A great book, thrilling and also thought provoking." *Sophie David (Good Reads UK)*

"From the first chapter I was hooked." *Josh Cormier (Good Reads Canada)*

"A captivating page turner." *Annika (Good Reads Germany)*

"I really enjoyed this different take on a serial thriller." *Shelby (USA)* Flyingmonkeyreads.wordpress.com

"For most of the book I had no idea what was going to happen." *Alicia (Good Reads UK)*

"Filled with suspense, compassion … murder" *Victoria Schwimley (UK)* www.victoriaschwimley.com

"Giving this one 5 stars…held my complete interest from start to finish." *Linda Strong (Good Reads USA)*

"A thriller with a heart-thumping climax" *M. (Good Reads Australia)*

"If you enjoy crime thrillers this book is for you." *Mark Schafer (Good Reads USA)*

"One of the best books I've read in a long time!." *Ansley Wright (Good Reads USA)*

"A quick-paced (dark) thriller which ratchets up the tension as you read." *J.L.Sutton (USA)* *www.jlsutton.com*

"I started this book and could not put it down!" *Mayra (Good Reads USA)*

"The writing was amazing, the plot flowed beautifully and the character development was spot on." *Gaynor (Good Reads Wales)*

"Diabolical! A sinister and refreshing twist on the mass/serial killer genre." *David (Good Reads USA)*

"The tension was literary unbearable. I didn't know whether to scream or cry." *Mish Farrugia (Good Reads Australia)*

"Just reading to find out HOW it happens is worth the read." *Jean Coldwell (Good Reads USA)*

"The development of the characters is very well done as are the surprises and suspense building throughout the book." *Rhonda (Good Reads USA)*

"Quality thriller from start to finish, straight and true. *Mike Rice (Good Reads UK)*

Susan May made me feel what the bad guys were going through and that is rare. *Bill Craig (Good Reads USA)*

"The plot is amazing; some serious research must have gone into this." *James Hayward (Good Reads UK)*

Whodunnit? Susan May has done it in Deadly Messengers! Read this great and gory thriller at your risk!" *Ashok* Chennai *(Good Reads)*

"Very well written with a fast-paced plot and compelling characters. It is not for the squeamish." Lissa Johnston *(USA) Lissajohnston.com*

"A haunting message 'straight and true,' that I will not forget." *Sue Leonhardt (Good Reads Canada)*

"It felt like I was in the story with the characters. A must read for all who like thrillers." *Britney Wilkins (Good Reads USA)*

"The plot of this story was very intriguing. Thank you, Susan, for a very well done storyline." *Darlene Abrahamson* (*Good Reads USA*)

"Such a great read! Just when I thought I had guessed what would happen, I was surprised." *Ashley* (*Good Reads Canada*)

"Thrilling, tense, interesting and topical. If you like your thrillers with meat on their bones get into Deadly Messengers." *Jo-Ann Duffy* (*Australia*) *Duffythewriterblog.com*

"I didn't want to put this down once I started reading." *Meghann Sherman* (*Good Reads USA*)

"I found it a real page-turner and read in no time." *Jesena Đurović* (*Good Reads Serbia*)

"Fast-paced, well-written, and everything moves at a terrific pace, the kind of book I might even be tempted to read in one sitting." *Dan Sihota* (*UK*) *Dansihota.blogspot.com*

"I loved reading this brilliant well written masterpiece by Susan May." *Danielle Urban* (*USA*) *Urban Lit Magazine*

"This book is a lurching ride through every person's worst nightmare." *Janis Milford* (*Good Reads Canada*)

"A very well written Crime Mystery book. 1 book you must read to the very end. A very easy rating of 5 stars." *Tony Parsons* (*Good Reads USA*)

"OMG One of the best books I have read in 2015. I highly recommend it." *Samantha Curtis* (*Good Reads UK*)

"Susan May pulls no punches with this page turning thriller." *Julie McBride* (*Good Reads Australia*)

"I spent my entire study period, afternoon and English class in twelve hours, reading through this unforgettable book." *Rebecca McNutt* (*Canada*) *Author of Smog City*

"If you liked Gillian Flynn novels or "The Girl on the train" by Paula Hawkins, you are going to love Deadly Messengers." *Jorge* (*Good Reads-Germany*)

"A great job taking us along for the ride; I enjoyed trying to figure out "just what exactly is going on here?!." *Candi Horihan* (*Good Reads USA*)

"POWERFUL! Ms. May is definitely an artist of her craft. Not too many authors, especially unknown ones, can leave me with the feeling of amazement." *Jan E. Klein* (*Good Reads USA*)

"A fun read and very fast-paced". *Riana Barbara* (*Malta*) *Thelivesofabookaholic.blogspot.com.au*

"Gripped the imagination at the first page and held it until the last when it left you gasping for more… I couldn't put it down." *Pippa Willis* (*Good Reads UK*)

"I really, really enjoyed this book. It's fast paced, exciting, has great characters." *Cynthia Corral* (*UK*) *Lostbookmark.wordpress.com*

"Brings our fears home to us with "Deadly Messengers," a tense tale of mayhem by design." *Jay Cole* (*USA*) *www.amazon.com/author/jaycole*

"The book doesn't wait for you to settle down as it hits you with a brutal mass killing from page 1" *Ishita Choudhary* (*Good Reads India*)

"It's my first book of dear Susan 'n I love it. It's amazing" *Neha* (*Good Reads India*)

"Susan May is responsible for my un-hoovered house and my growing ironing pile. I started this book and finished it in a day." *Karen Male* (*Good Reads UK*)

"Grabbed me at the start and by the time I got to the last 100 pages or so, I couldn't put it down and I had to finish it." *Terri* (*Good Reads Australia*)

"Filled with wonderfully descriptive passages and well constructed characters, this book was a thrilling read from its first word until its last." *Sharon Berge* (*Good Reads USA*)

"A very gripping, gritty thriller that will keep you on the edge as you try to work out what is driving normal, sane people to kill." *Carolyn* (*Good Reads USA*)

"Creepy, unnerving and leaving you on the edge of your seat wondering what is about to happen. One of the best books I have read in a long time." *Chelsea* (*Good Reads UK*)

"A unique twist on the crime that I've never seen before and was very cleverly plotted out." *Lisa* (*Good Reads USA*)

"It's a gripping, entertaining, eye-opening and well-researched novel. What I liked best about this book is its highly social and moral significance." *AJ The Ravenous Reader (Good Reads Philippines)*

"Fast read, exciting, too! A page-turner." *Jeri (Good Reads USA)*

"Easy to become so trapped inside the book that the world around you becomes lost. So good, I didn't want to sleep until I'd finished." *Natasha (Good Reads UK)*

"Deadly Messengers by Susan May is described as a "can't-put-it-down thriller" and most definitely lives up to its reputation." *Jan (Good Reads UK)*

"Describing everything in such detail that I could imagine myself right beside the killer." *Hannah Haines (Good Reads USA)*

"Recipe for Compulsive Reading: One cup each of horror, crime fiction, science fiction/science fact. Add a dollop of incredibly well written, fast paced, action packed narrative. Guaranteed to produce a satisfying outcome!" *Carol Seeley (Australia) Readingwritingandriesling.wordpress.com*

"This is a great book, very fast paced and full of action." *Emma J. (Good Reads UK)*

"Deadly Messengers is a total mind rush and real page turner that has mystery, suspense, and lots and lots of murder." *Vanessa Vallejos (Good Reads USA)*

"I was literally feeling very anxious, heart racing, pulled in, and wanted to get to the end of this." *Suzanne Robinson (Good Reads Australia)*

"A good thrilling book that definitely many would enjoy." *Amanda Weidensjö (USA) www.AmandaWeidensjo.ca*

Sweet are the uses of adversity,
Which, like the toad, ugly and venomous,
Wears yet a precious jewel in his head;
And this our life, exempt from public haunt,
Finds tongues in trees, books in the running brooks,
Sermons in stones, and good in every thing.

William Shakespeare
(As You Like It Act 2, scene 1, 12–17)

CHAPTER 1

T OBY BENSON PAUSED AT THE alley's entrance to hoist the ungainly blue sports bag higher on his shoulder. Traveling here, the awkward, precious cargo had caused the bag to slip down his arm, forcing him to stop several times to rebalance the weight.

He stared up the dark corridor of gray shadows and fractured shapes, the towering buildings only allowing the barest slip of light to enter from the full moon overhead. Wall lights hung above the back entrances to the establishments illuminating a collection of trash containers, sentinels to the doors. A perfect location to film a horror movie; just add haunting music and the audience would be clued something terrifying was about to happen.

Toby didn't notice these things. Somewhere deep inside, perhaps, he registered them on a subconscious level, understood he should be afraid or this wasn't the place for him. If he did, though, the thought didn't make it through to that part of his brain controlled by self-preservation.

He saw nothing except a strange mist settled over his vision like a swirling film on the surface of a pond. He heard nothing except the voice in his head, which he imagined came from God, spoken with such authority he couldn't resist. The voice knew him, wanted to help him and guide him toward his destiny.

At the end of the brick corridor a doorway lay, guarded on either side by two tall commercial waste containers. Pieces of trash dotted about their bases as though rejected competitors that hadn't made the cut—scattered bottles, empty cardboard fast-food containers, plastic bags, paper, and even what looked like a woman's shirt. Wasteful. Thoughtless. Humanity's flotsam discarded to become someone else's problem.

Human beings were filthy creatures.

He noted the fleeting thought, but decided it was unimportant and unrelated to his future. To the mission.

The back door glowed a fluorescent green as though it were showing him the perfect entry. A signal he was on the right path.

Green meant go to him, but he didn't fully understand why.

On the opposite side of the building would be the front door to Café Amaretto. Toby knew this area well, the entertainment section of the city, populated with myriad restaurants and clubs, ranging from small cafés to silver service establishments.

As he neared the doorway, the green intensified, the light piercing his eyes, making his brain feel as though it were pulsing. The alley, which had been dark upon his entry, now appeared bathed in green. This radiance, like colored breadcrumbs, gave him assurance this was his mission path.

This way. This is for you.

He'd followed the markers for the past hour, and they'd led him here. A streetlight, a car, a crosswalk sign—they were all just like the door. At first they would shimmer softly with a gentle hum of color against the darkness of night, then intensify as he neared, so he never doubted his path.

The voice buzzed again in his brain. He stopped and listened, tilting his head to the left, then the right, stretching his neck. The sound of his joints cracking like a sharp snap, felt like a mini-explosion in his skull.

Then he was moving again. The voice wanted him inside that door. *He* wanted to be inside that door.

Ten more steps and he would be inside and then—

Wait.

Toby stopped, his feet felt suddenly magnetized to the ground. He stared at the door a few steps away. Inside the door lay his future, the rest of his life, the thing he was born to do, an act to change the world. *So said the voice.*

Doubts slipped into his mind, a million ideas and images circling simultaneously as the gray film covering his eyes disappeared.

Why did it matter? Why was he really here?

An urgent idea swept over him. He should be home asleep, or watching television, his girlfriend snuggled against him.

The word *desperate* hung before his eyes, ferociously demanding his attention, with the same fierceness the door beckoned. He *should* be home. Not here. Not in this alley. Not ten steps from that door.

Toby wanted to turn and walk away. His legs wouldn't move, wouldn't allow him control. His desire to move forward greater than his desire to back away and abort the mission.

Mission?

Where did that come from?

He didn't go on *missions*. He went to work. He came home. He made plans for the weekend. Plans for dinner. Plans for the future. He thought about his past, only twenty-seven years in the making. He didn't walk down dark alleys. Not like this.

Toby began to turn, to walk away, but the sight of the door caught him. The deep green flashing: *Enter me. Enter me, now!*

He did want to enter. *Yes.* Be inside, on the other side of the door. The need, strong, intoxicating, overpowering him like a drug. The thought wended through his synapses, drilling into his subconscious until thoughts of his girlfriend and his life disappeared, until it became him and the door, and the thing stowed inside his bag.

Ten steps, he now took, the sound of his boots echoing in the hollow of the alley, the reverberations, earthquake loud in his skull. All doubts evaporated, his steps, the sound of destiny as he approached the door.

He shrugged his shoulders and stretched a hand across his chest to yank the bag from his shoulder, allowing it to drop to the ground at his feet. Bending to it, he pulled back the zipper and reached inside, his hand electrified as he found the prize he sought.

Toby drew the axe up, the smooth weight soothing to his palm, his skin melding with the wood as though an extension of his body. This axe had served him well. Last autumn, when he'd removed the tree whose roots insisted on invading the front pathway, its blade swung true and straight. Now it would serve another purpose. Just as true. Just as straight.

He reached for the door's metal handle. As he turned the knob, he felt the click of the enabled lock resisting him. He took two steps back, examining the impediment. The gray film swimming before his eyes had returned, blurring his vision. Still he saw what needed to be done.

It would take two hands. He knew this from chopping the tree. He moved his left hand to the axe and swung the weighty and powerful tool over his shoulder. Then back at the door. As the blade slammed just left of the handle, the crack of splitting wood sounded sharp and loud.

A fracture appeared in the door, jagged splinters protruding from the dull, white surface.

Again.

He repeated the action, this time swinging with even more conviction. This time his aim was true. The blade sliced through the wood, hitting the internal lock. The door instantly sprang open as if relieved to be free of constraint.

Toby shifted the axe to his left hand and reached down to pull open the door. Coming from behind the entry, he heard voices and the sound of shattering plates and glasses.

The light from within spilled out, enveloping him in a pool of brilliance. He blinked rapidly, momentarily blinded, the light painfully piercing his eyes. Then, as though an automatic recalibration was made, he could see again.

Inside lay a small kitchen, fifteen feet by ten feet wide. Two men, dressed in t-shirts and jeans, wearing white aprons from chest to knees, stood staring at him. To the side, a ponytailed woman, wearing a white shirt and black skirt, covered her mouth with her hands. At her feet lay the shattered mess of an unserved meal and drinks.

Toby looked toward the men, then to the woman. Behind her, he noted another door. The door to Amaretto Café's dining area filled with patrons enjoying a meal; laughing, drinking, eating, never thinking in the next five minutes their destiny would change. Soon something would enter their lives and they would be part of changing the world. Part of the message.

Those who survived.

"What the hell?" The speaker was a burly man with a carefully groomed three-day beard and blue bandanna tied about his head. His hand clasped a fryer basket submerged in bubbling oil. He hadn't moved, still standing in the same position since Toby had entered. His eyes were as white as the dinner plates laying on the counter.

"Listen, buddy, we don't want no trouble. Whatever you're thinking, we just don't—"

The third person in the kitchen, a scruffy teenager, skinny, with a pimple-peppered face, stepped back toward the sink. Dishes and pans overflowed the suds as though the sink was some kind of birthing incubator.

The three smelled of fear and confusion, vulnerable human beings now part of something they'd only imagined in nightmares. They didn't understand. This was a good thing. Soon they'd see. Just like Toby, who didn't fully understand, but still knew what needed to be done. Thanks to the voice, he was getting the picture, slide by slide, word by word, command by command.

Take the axe.

The voice was inside his mind, commanding his body. He sensed it wasn't his own thoughts, but he didn't care anymore. He didn't need direction on what to do with the axe, so hefty in his hand. He'd never done this before, never seen it done before, yet he knew. He knew to move fast. In seconds, they'd rally. It'd be the waitress, who decided to move, to leave the other two. It was in her eyes, the realization she couldn't help them. She could only help herself.

She wasn't quick enough—not for Toby on his mission.

Move quickly forward. Eight, maybe nine steps, is all. Swing now.

Toby accepted the commands firing in his brain, pulled back the gate inside his mind, the guard of all things sane, and allowed the impulses to travel from his head to his body. His arm twitched as the energy flowed through his being, down his arms and his legs, through his hands and his feet. Blue ice travelling at light speed.

A crazy kick thwacked in his mind like a detonator releasing an explosion in his synapses, and he was on the woman. She couldn't escape. That wouldn't do for the mission if she alerted the patrons. He couldn't have that. He didn't know why. He just knew.

The speed of his forward movement gave him momentum, as he firmed his grasp about the handle and swung the axe behind his shoulder.

Striking distance was three feet, and it was all in the timing.

The woman had expected to only fetch a table's order; fried calamari and chicken pesto pasta, now lying at her feet. It was in her eyes. The revelation had arrived. She should have run, but she'd wasted time evaluating, thinking *this can't be real*, thinking *this is some kind of joke*. Her hands flew to her face, instinctive and pointless.

As Toby swung it was as though his cognizance slipped outside his body. He saw where he was, saw her, and recognized he had no reason for this, no reason to take another step or do another thing, except put down the axe and run back out the door, leaving these people to their evening and their lives.

Then the thought was gone like a car fishtailing down a street, glancing off parked cars before careening away, without leaving a note—it's not *their* responsibility.

It's not his responsibility.

Toby let go of everything that *was* him, everything except the arc of the axe as it swung from behind his shoulder and the swish of air sliced like it was a solid thing.

The blade landed square in the woman's chest, the sound like the thick thud made when a basketball slaps against a wall. The axe stayed there, wedged, as though in a block of wood. She looked down at her front like she'd spilled coffee that could be wiped away with a cloth.

Add some soda to that and it'll be good as new, sweetheart.

Blood, rich and red, sprayed out at crazy angles. Some landed on him, thick and warm. Blood streamed down her body and legs, to run to the floor and begin to pool. The woman looked up at him again, before collapsing, her life gone.

The axe came away easily, her fall's momentum loosening it, so it required only a tug on the handle to retrieve. Back, in his control, resting between his legs, he gripped his weapon with both hands like it was a macabre walking stick.

Toby turned his head toward Fryer Guy, who still held the handgrip of the metal basket like it would be his salvation. Toby's neck stiffened. A sudden dull throb made itself known. *A muscle pulled when he swung the axe?*

He stretched his neck, twisting it sideways, left, toward his shoulder and then to the right.

"What the fuck, man?" said Fryer Guy, taking a step toward Toby, then moving like a world-class athlete, hurling the basket toward him. The metal container only made it halfway, landing between them; the smell of oil and half-fried chips bloomed in the air.

The woman's body lay crumpled to the left of the dining room doorway. Her eyes stared blankly at the ceiling as though examining a mark up there as her sprawled corpse blocked that avenue of escape. Fryer Guy appeared reluctant to pass near her, perhaps fearing he'd slip on the blood—there was a lot of it now. The only other exit was through the door Toby had entered. That meant moving by him, the intruder. A lost look crossed over Fryer Guy's face as he scanned the room, and probably realized there were only bad options.

Toby, also, calculated his next move.

A metal island stood in the center of the room, and it would be five strides to Skinny Kid round the right or three to the left to Fryer Guy.

He trusted his instinct. *Straight and true.* The phrase, embedded in his head, powered every command, the words like background music to his thoughts.

Skinny Kid cowered by the sink, barely breathing, his hands gripped together as though in prayer, his knuckles white and curled like mini rocks. Not a word or a cry had passed the kid's lips since Toby's entrance.

He would be easy.

The bulk of Fryer Guy made him more of a threat; he appeared more aggressive, more of an adversary ready to fight, as he stretched to his full height, his chest expanding as he drew in deep, readying breaths.

Fryer Guy had worked it out, weighed up his options. Trapped, yes, but not going down without a fight. Maybe he thought he could win. How could he believe anything else? What creature does when facing death?

Toby saw the thoughts in his eyes. *If he could throw this intruder off balance just for a second, he might have a chance. Too bad for Skinny Kid—he was on his own. When death visits, it's every man for himself.*

Fryer Guy lunged for a knife on the counter. A good size blade, too—a blade used for dicing carrots and onions the way cooks do, with machine-like fingers. An axe wasn't made for chopping onions. No, it was destined for greater things. It's blade came with a weight of conviction you just don't get with a knife.

Fryer Guy didn't understand this.

"You motherfucker," Fryer Guy screamed, lunging toward Toby, the knife held high as though he were flying a kite. Toby was ready, his thinking clear, as though he was an automaton with only one function. He sidestepped the spilled oil, moving with grace and instinct—and purpose. Purpose is a powerful thing.

Straight and true.

Toby swept sideways, swinging from waist height, instead of bringing the axe across his shoulder. Fryer Guy wasn't expecting that. The blade caught him in the gut—really more of a paunch—before he'd even come close with the knife. Wounded, he waved the knife in the air for the seconds it took him to glance to his waist, to see the parting of the muscles and skin, now incapable of holding his life within. Released, internal organs gushed out to mingle with the oil and the chips. Blood *is* thicker than oil— they don't mix. The evidence lay on the wet, red soaked floor.

Toby swung the axe again as though felling a tree; this time the blade connected with his adversary's neck. That did it grand. The knife dropped from Fryer Guy's hand and bounced on the floor before disappearing beneath the cooker and grill. Seconds later, his victim joined his knife to marinate in the blood and oil.

Gurgling sounds filled the room, as Fryer Guy's mouth opened and closed as though he had words to speak but just couldn't find them. Then he grew still, just his feet and hands twitching a flicker. A few jerks and he was done.

Toby took a moment to stand over the man and look at his handiwork. *Straight and true, my friend. Straight and true.*

"That's better, now, isn't it?" he wanted to say, but he couldn't speak the words. The voice in his head wanted him moving. So move he must.

Two down, one to go.

Slowly he looked up, tilting his head left then right. Toby scanned the room, his attention now focused on Skinny Kid. He stepped over the body of the felled man that he'd never met before this night.

No matter who, no matter what, you keep on going, so said the voice.

He wandered toward the boy, sitting slumped on the floor, his face pressed against the metal cabinet that held plates and utensils he'd never wash again. Five paces and Toby was over him, staring down at the cowering adolescent. The boy's hands were above his head, flattened against his skull, as though they offered some kind of protection.

A pain blossomed in Toby's head like a vice clamped round his brain. With each breath, it squeezed tighter, the ache growing sharper. The pure agony stopped him; halted his movement. He needed to readjust. He needed to fight past it.

Skinny Kid, perhaps sensing Toby's hesitancy, turned his head to look up, his body shaking as though the temperature of the room had dropped to a minus ten wind chill factor.

"Ple. Plee— pleeease."

Please won't help him.

Today was the day, and Toby was here to deliver a message to change the world. If only he knew the full message, maybe he'd deliver a meaningful speech, but he didn't get that memo. He still couldn't truly remember why he was here. All he knew: he was exactly where he was meant to be.

There was no hesitation as he swung the axe, because actions spoke louder than words.

Chapter 2

K ENDALL AWOKE WITH A SPLITTING headache. Waking up with pain in her head was becoming a regular occurrence. Her brother Marcus had suggested she probably needed her eyes checked. Like most brothers, he took loving delight in teasing her, which occasionally annoyed her. Without him, though, she'd have never survived her teenage years or that night they lost their mom. So she took his teasing and listened to his silly jokes. In an uncertain life at least, occasionally, she could count on him.

In regards to the jibe about glasses and her age, well... *Thanks, but no thanks.* Ignoring his advice instead, she continued her habit of swallowing two little codeine numbers from the packet she kept stashed in the drawer in her desk.

The idea her body was aging wasn't something she wanted to face just yet. When she looked in the mirror, it was only to enable the necessary maintenance chores of brushing teeth, washing her face, and the application of moisturizer. She didn't spend much time examining her appearance. Details such as wrinkles, heralding that she was exiting her prime years, were not high on her priority list.

She was attractive, so she was told, but she rarely gave it much thought. Admittedly, she'd been lucky in the hair department. With just a quick brush and a flick, her shoulder-length, golden-brown hair curled and bounced into place just below her shoulders as though styled for a Pantene commercial. She didn't fuss. She didn't primp. More important things concerned her, like ensuring she won enough article approvals to pay the rent.

Today, she wouldn't win any beauty contests. Her eyes felt red-raw, as though she'd weathered a sandstorm. Headaches like this one always caused her complexion to drain to a tone just above vampire white. Probably a cold was attacking her. It wasn't eyestrain or old age, and that was that. Seriously, she was only thirty-six!

Last month she'd written an article on fantastic foods for your eyes. Popular wisdom was that eating carrots was good for your eye health. Through her research, Kendall discovered oranges were better. Kale and black-eyed peas, too. Next time she shopped, she'd stock up on oranges. *Glasses not necessary.*

Kendall made a mental note to track down a chef to interview for recipes using black-eyed peas—a trick she used when wanting to know something for her own benefit. She'd come up with an article idea then research who she needed to track down for the answer. In this way, asking questions that *she* wanted answered also paid her.

Throwing down the codeine, she swigged from the water bottle she always kept on her bedside table. She picked up her partner in crime—her iPhone—lying beside the bottle and began her ritual of first-thing-upon-wakeup tasks.

She lived on the phone. Emails and messaging mainly. While her friends used theirs for Facebook, Twitter, and Candy Crush, hers was an all in one secretary, coach, and timekeeper.

"What's happening today, buddy? What's on our schedule?"

She opened her mail app. Within a few seconds her inbox filled with thirty-two messages. Many were junk. That's your reward for signing up at too many websites in the name of research. The others were from business acquaintances, friends, and daily Google alerts on subjects she followed for possible articles.

This morning, she was looking for particular messages, ones with the heading: "Article Needed Urgently" or "Yes—go ahead" or "More Work."

Anything that was income creating with a capital "I."

Work had slowed lately. She'd pitched dozens of articles in the past few weeks, but this month, being the end of the fiscal year, meant budgets were mostly exhausted. Urgent last-minute articles were all she was being sent. Work had dried up to only an article or two a day. This happened every year at this time, and every year Kendall panicked. It was silly, really. By the end of March her inbox would fill with so much work, she was awake until one or two in the morning to meet deadlines.

After checking all the emails, she found only two article requests. One she'd pitched months ago and was only for three hundred words, hardly paying anything. Another was from a women's magazine she only wrote for when desperate. They always paid late and their editor had no sense of humor, removing any witty asides in her articles.

"House style, please, Kendall!"

Kendall closed the email app, relieved she at least had *some* work, but downhearted it wasn't enough to even cover her weekly expenses. The next few hours would be spent coming up with pitch ideas. Not as easy as it sounds when you've freelanced for eight years.

She checked the time on her phone—seven fifteen. Fifteen minutes before she needed to get up. Technically, she didn't need to physically be anywhere. She treated her weekdays, though, as if she needed to be at an office by eight thirty. She'd learned a long time ago freelancing required the discipline of a job. Like any job, you needed to turn up.

Her commute was the thirty steps from her bedroom to her study via a small, combined kitchen-dining area. On the way, she'd get a strong, black coffee and some toast.

Kendall threw on her work clothes—casual, thank you. A tracksuit in, winter with scarf and wooly socks. In summer, shorts, tank top and flip-flops.

Her first task, once at her desk was to check the news sites, a necessary business ritual that occasionally supplied her with good material to spin into a story. Having an eye for an angle was her greatest skill.

"Something interesting, please," she prayed as the news site loaded.

When the lead heading came up, she gasped. The word for the news wasn't *interesting*.

Horrifying. Terrifying. Those words sprung into her mind. Then: *How could this happen?*

CHAPTER 3

WHEN KENDALL FIRST READ THE bolded heading on the "Breaking News" web page, she gasped. When she'd prayed for interesting news, she didn't mean anything like this.

**Café Attack in Lygard Street
Seven Dead. Three Critical.**

Lygard Street was very nearby her apartment block. As she read the article, Kendall realized it was Café Amaretto. Occasionally she'd grab a coffee there; they had the best tiramisu this side of the city. Reading on, she suddenly lost her taste for tiramisu; in fact, her appetite was gone, period.

A crazed psycho had entered the restaurant through the back door and killed several staff, unlucky enough to be in the kitchen. Then he'd headed into the dining area and attacked diners. Kendall's hand went to cover her mouth. My god, he used an axe to kill them. *An axe!*

That was *too* barbaric. What was happening in the world when things like this occurred in such a peaceful place? This neighborhood was home to mostly thirty-something professionals like her and retired the-kids-are-gone-and-we've-downsized people. It wasn't home to axe murderers.

She Googled Café Amaretto looking for more information on the killings, but all the links were just copies of the same article with no new information. Involuntarily, her body shivered at the thought of the crime's proximity.

Kendall stood and walked back into the kitchen to make a herbal tea. Something to calm her nerves, like chamomile. She wished she'd stayed in bed instead of waking up to this. Forget the lack of work. This trumped everything. A terrible tragedy in her neighborhood that, if not for fate, might have found her involved.

What a way to start a day.

CHAPTER 4

LANCE O'GRADY LOOKED OVER AT his partner, Trip Lindsay, and said, "This is not the way to start a day.

They hadn't been to bed yet, so technically this day had started yesterday. They'd attended the Café Amaretto murder scene late last night. The last time he'd checked, thirty minutes and two strong black coffees ago, it was still only around seven in the morning.

Since this had begun, they'd spent four hours at the crime scene, answered over twenty inquiries and phone-in leads, and had two update meetings with their sergeant, with more to come. By Lance's estimates, they would still be here until six tonight with everything they needed to do to keep the police commissioner and the mayor happy.

Everything they'd learned so far, made the crime cut and dried to him. Lunatic walks into a popular Italian restaurant and goes berserk with an axe. Out go seven bodies, with at least one survivor currently in intensive care probably about to make it a tally of a neat round eight. To say that he'd never seen anything like the bloody scene he'd walked into last night was not just an understatement, it missed the spot by a million miles.

So far, they understood little of what set the guy off. All they knew was bank clerk Toby Benson decided to hack his way through the rear entrance of Café Amaretto. Once in, he sliced and diced three of the staff in the kitchen, then took to patrons in the dining room simply enjoying a meal. No provocation and, so far, no claims of association with any terrorist groups.

Police arrived at the café approximately six minutes after the event began, thanks to several mobile calls from terrified patrons. Benson then decided to take a swing at the officers. Of course, the size of his axe was irrelevant. Guns trump axe pretty much every time. So their *Friday the 13th* wannabe ended up as the repository of a dozen bullets and just as dead as his unfortunate victims.

Everybody from O'Grady's boss to the mayor to the goddam president (if the already churning rumor mill could be believed) wanted to know how this could happen. This not-easily-answered question landed on his and Trip's plate to figure out. The police commissioner demanded answers yesterday because the PR minions wanted everything tied up in a neat little bow for the six o'clock news.

Even though there was an investigating team, the responsibility for managing the investigation fell on Trip's and his shoulders. As senior detectives of the city's smallish major case unit—small because these types of crime didn't usually happen in their city—it was expected they pull all-nighters. Only a few hours in, those responsibility-carrying shoulder were already weary.

With the killer as dead as his victims, the only urgency O'Grady saw was in giving the mayor something to calm the public. If the mayor had a little patience and foresight—which he clearly lacked—he'd find the next bad news story blowing in, would cause the public to quickly forget this.

It never took Joe Public long to move to the next news sensation. Downed airliners, earthquakes in China, tsunamis killing tens of thousands, or myriad of disasters that trotted across the news bulletins regularly, all of them were always replaced by the next big headline.

"Are you ready?" said Trip. "The sooner we get out door knocking, the sooner we get some sleep. I've gotten hold of Benson's boss at the bank. He'll see us just after eight. Then I think a visit to Benson's apartment in case CSI missed something."

O'Grady stood, pulling his jacket from the back of his chair.

"As ready as I'll ever be on no-hours sleep. Did you see one of the vics was celebrating his birthday? Some birthday present, right?"

O'Grady shook his head.

Trip sighed at the comment. His mouth sagged as he ran his hand over his sleek, shiny head, adorned with nothing but moisturizer.

"The guy had to be psychotic, or schizophrenic, or something with crazy in the subtitle. If we don't find out which, we're not getting the weekend off. Like the Sarge said, *Average Joe needs a reason for these things to feel safe at night.* I need the reason cause I got plans for the weekend. And they don't involve work."

O'Grady actually didn't mind if he worked weekends. What else would he do? Outside of the job, he had little to occupy his time. No wife, few friends. What was left of his family were all out on the coast.

Trip continued to muse aloud on the case and why Benson would go crazy in *that* particular restaurant. O'Grady's partner talked a great deal, most of the time speaking out loud what seemed was every idea that floated through his mind. The fact O'Grady only responded every now and then didn't seem to faze Trip.

O'Grady preferred to keep his thoughts to himself. After what happened to his brother, he'd learned zipping it was a safer way to live. The less people knew about you, the better. After three years as partners, Trip knew only as much as O'Grady cared to reveal. His partner seemed content with that. More opportunity for Trip to talk, O'Grady figured.

As they exited the building, they passed the arriving day shift staff. O'Grady threw out a few hellos and nodded to others. Mostly he kept his head down to avoid engagement. Trip smiled and greeted everyone who passed them.

Already O'Grady's thoughts were focused on Toby Benson. Something didn't sit right. Something itched in that place in his mind where the bullshit net was positioned; a mild flaring he just couldn't settle.

CSI had done their preliminary sweep of Benson's apartment. They discovered nothing. Hard to believe. Nothing, no evidence, was wrong. Unexpected. When someone commits a crime, even less savage than this, there are always indicators in his or her life pointing to issues that spun out of control. Big red, flashing signs blinking: "This person is dynamite just waiting for a match."

So far, this Benson seemed like just an average guy. Had a girlfriend; several smiling pictures of her and him dotted his apartment, CSI had informed. Had a stable job at a bank—a check of the website LinkedIn told them he'd been employed there five years. He'd lived in Danbridge all his life. Plenty of friends. From Facebook they'd gleaned his interactions and attitudes appeared normal.

Yet on a cool early-winter Sunday evening, he left his home prepared with a weapon, drove into the city, targeted a restaurant—for what reason, they were yet to ascertain—and had a swing-the-axe party.

As much as O'Grady wanted this to be a suicide-by-cop show, his itch told him it might turn out to be something quite different. He didn't know what, and he didn't know why. That bothered him.

O'Grady climbed into the front passenger seat next to Trip, who had launched into a dissection of a recent baseball game where his home team—according to him—was robbed by the umpire. Things like this mass killing didn't seem to invade his head. He treated the job like a *job*.

Not O'Grady. He needed to solve the crimes. In doing so it temporarily filled something missing in him, which no amount of women—whom he soon forgot—or phone calls home could satisfy. The emotional impact of the scene last night had left him drained. He looked ahead to when he could clock off, hit the sack, and get some dearly needed shut-eye. Hopefully, today would end better than it started.

But this damn itch in his gut still bothered him. Maybe sleep might reveal the answer. He hoped the answer would be simple and obvious and happen soon. One thing about Lance O'Grady, he didn't like loose ends.

CHAPTER 5

KENDALL SHOWERED AND CHANGED INTO her work gear—tracksuit pants, a t-shirt, and fleecy sweater. The chilly winter wind seeped inside, and the heater couldn't compete, even on full blast. The dilapidated thing, on its last legs, only warmed the air within a few feet.

After filling her bowl with her usual cereal, Raisin Bran topped with Cheerios, she nestled into the chair at her desk. Kendall surveyed the mess piled there: scraps of paper, books, and an assortment of dirty coffee cups ranging from one to four days old. She vowed to work on mustering the energy to tidy up. Once she'd booked a few jobs and removed the money stress, she'd attack it. The time had better be soon, though, or she'd be drinking coffee out of jars.

Tomorrow.

Right now, she needed to check her email again, and Twitter and Facebook. She'd found social media a handy way to gauge public mood. Beyond short on filling her twelve-story quota for the week, besides sending out queries, she would need to write pieces on spec in the hope an editor might have last-minute space to fill.

Slurping her coffee from the very last clean cup, she scanned the home page of *The Western*. Horrific pictures of the Amaretto Café massacre, complete with upturned tables and a blood-streaked floor, were spread across and down the page. Three victims' pictures were front and center, with the names of other casualties still to be released.

Looking at devastating photos of a place she'd visited often made her skin prickle. She looked over the main article again, which proclaimed it the worst mass murder in the city's history. A picture of the killer Toby Benson was front and center. He looked like an average guy. Dark, short-cropped hair and the type of smile that said *I'm friendly and I'm kind to my grandma.*

Kendall hypothesized he'd lost it because either his mother had neglected him or his girlfriend had just dumped him. Or box number three: he'd forgotten to take his meds.

The news article gave no information about him, except that he worked at a bank and his family and girlfriend were in shock, finding it impossible to believe he could kill anyone or anything.

Kendall noticed an email subject header flash at the bottom of her screen. The message was from Stef, the editor of *Healthy, Wealthy & Wisdom* magazine. She'd built a good relationship with Stef over the past few years by always turning work in on schedule and never, ever saying "no" to a commission, no matter how much she had on her plate. The articles were sometimes internationally syndicated into several small newspapers, the syndication payments being a nice little cash-flow bump when they came.

She flicked from the news page to Outlook, after glancing again at the photo of Toby Benson's smiling face. *You sure couldn't judge a book by its cover.*

The email was short and to the point.

Kendall,

Need urgent 1,000-word rush piece on survivor guilt. Work to fit this lead: "How to live with not dying." Mass killing from last night already covered by majors. This angle, good. Get interviews with any witnesses who'll talk. Morning papers quoted a survivor. Beverly Sanderson. Get her and quotes from a psychologist. Will need within 24 hours to make deadline.

Stef

Kendall replied with a, "Yes, I'm on it" message. As she hit send, her mood lifted. Rush jobs rarely meant rush payments, but a thousand words with this mag would cover a chunk of the month's rent if it scored syndication.

What didn't thrill her, though, was possibly hearing the terrible details of the murders first hand from witnesses. Violence made her squeamish. Even those slasher-horror films made her feel sick. Usually, she would close her eyes while sticking her fingers in her ears; the sound of the viciousness and the screams almost too much. The only reason she even watched them was her brother; Marcus was a big Quentin Tarantino over-the-top-violent film fan. He kept telling her if she watched enough of them, she would "toughen up." She still awaited that occurrence.

If Marcus actually took the time to read some of her articles, he'd see she was tough enough to write real horror—terrible heartbreaking articles. She'd covered everything from teen suicide to a baby boy killed by a drunk driver plowing through his bedroom wall. True life terror.

When it came to deliberate violence against others, she drew the line. Accidents she could handle, but it seemed too much like a slippery slope, flooding her mind with memories of ten years ago and her mom. Every time she thought about that night, her heart hardened against allowing herself to feel for anyone the love she felt for her mom. She felt empathy for people, but she didn't desire closeness. She didn't want to love someone and suffer having them torn away. She began to think about that night; she could smell the night air, hear the sounds in the darkness, feel the fear, the despair; her heart quickened.

No, she wouldn't think about it now. Maybe one day, if the right person came along, she might trust herself to feel something again. *Allow* herself to feel something again. Right now she had bills to pay and a job to do.

Most of her work *was* puff pieces. Marcus was right about that. She wondered if his occasional nagging about them was his way of testing her, see if she had grown stronger without having to come right out and ask the question.

What was wrong with writing about banal things like how to get your start in business; ten things airline hostesses don't want you to know; and interviews with best-selling novelists and comedy film stars? People enjoyed reading them or she wouldn't keep winning the commissions. These articles were magazines' bread and butter, and they always seemed to be the ones she was working on when Marcus asked what she was doing. The Pulitzer Prize-winning articles were never given to freelancers like her. She was fine with that, too. From the first few articles she wrote twelve years ago for *Seventeen, Family Fun,* and *Entertainment Weekly,* her career had pretty much travelled down the fluff-piece path.

Kendall opened up a fresh browser and Googled Toby Benson. He was on Facebook, Twitter, LinkedIn, and a website called ListenFM (the last being just someone with the same name as his).

When she clicked through to his Facebook account, she found he had 232 "friends." Over the past twenty-four hours, dozens of posts had been left on his page. Most were from real friends, sharing an outpouring of shock and horror, all messages of condolence, the presiding sentiment being there must be some mistake, that Toby Benson was no killer.

> "Good buddy, tell me this is a mistake. This can't be true."
>
> "Toby, you will be loved and missed."
>
> "God bless you and condolences to the Benson family."

Toby's account settings must have allowed anyone to post to his page. Comments from people who clearly weren't his friends shared the feed.

> "You fu*&!@# lunatic. Shooting was too good for you."
>
> "You should have been hacked to pieces or hung."
>
> "Hope hell is hell!"

Many more continued in that vein. Arguments had sprung up between his friends and these posters. His friends continued to defend the impossibility they knew someone who'd become a cold-blooded killer. Twitter had a similar mix of sentiment among Toby's 332 followers. When

Kendall read back over Toby's comments and tweets of the previous few days, there did appear no indication he harbored any thoughts of randomly venturing out hell-bent on murder. In fact, he seemed very normal, sharing snippets of weekend activities: a party, a lunch, and an evening watching Netflix. Just like everyone else, he was gorge-viewing *Breaking Bad*.

Somewhere, at this moment, a freelancer was probably writing a story on violent TV shows inciting murder.

Another twenty minutes of checking the first few pages of Google results for Toby Benson, and Kendall began to feel as surprised at Benson's actions as his friends. She'd found no comments about him hating the world or being unhappy; no pictures of him holding a rifle, *à la* Lee Harvey Oswald before he assassinated President Kennedy; not even an Instagram account picture of him holding as much as a bread knife, let alone an axe.

It was weird that a guy who looked *so* normal could do something *so* abnormal. Kendall was no investigative journalist, but surely there should be *something*. Maybe it was drugs or a broken relationship? Or was there a *crazy switch* in people's heads? And Toby Benson's crazy switch simply got flicked?

Now there was an article title: "*The Crazy Switch: How to keep yours turned off?*"

She made a note on the 'pitch' pad by her computer. It was stuffed full of ideas and thoughts with potential to become stories.

Really, though, she was procrastinating, delaying getting out there and talking to someone who'd experienced *crazy*. She was truly a wuss. Hearing the gory details, and asking the questions surrounding death and violence was probably her worst nightmare.

"*How does it feel to know you came this close to death?*"

"*Does this make you appreciate your loved ones?*"

Even thinking about it, the back of her neck suddenly felt clammy.

Kendall navigated back to *The Western's News* page, to find it updated with further information. Now they had a quote from Toby Benson's sister.

"My brother was the sweetest, kindest man you would ever meet. Our family is shocked and devastated."

This new article contained pictures of survivors. Beverley Sanderson—mid-forties, shaggy blonde hair, well-groomed eyebrows, and over-pink lipstick—was one of three people whose photo was subtitled "survivor." Kendall read the entire article, but found no quotes from any of the witnesses.

Something about the smiling persona of the polished looking Mrs. Sanderson made Kendall think she might be the person to approach, that she might be willing to talk. After years of interviewing people, Kendall had a feel for who was a talker and who wasn't. Time was the issue. In order to get to these witnesses before a big media outlet pulled out an equally big checkbook, she needed to move.

Searching through the online phone directory, Kendall immediately found Beverley Sanderson. The listing read *B & R. Sanderson.* "R," no doubt being the husband, Roy, who was, also, mentioned below the photo. If this was the same woman—and Kendall was pretty certain it was—she lived only a few blocks away.

Kendall scribbled down the address, quickly changed her clothes—tracksuit and slippers just didn't give her the right air—and headed out the door. The address was close enough to walk. She decided not to call first and give the Sandersons a chance to say "no" to an interview. Most interviewees found Kendall's enthusiastic and easy style relatable. Complete strangers found themselves opening up to her about the most intimate and personal experiences.

Her stomach filled with stone at the thought of hearing gruesome details. *You need this commission.* This would also prove to Marcus she was tough, that she'd grown up. She imagined the look of pride on her brother's face as he read the article.

Kendall hurried out the door, grabbing her laptop bag and an apple as she did. Today hadn't started well, but it was getting better by the hour. Even her headache had faded. This massacre *was* a horrific event, but a girl's gotta do what a girl's gotta do to pay the rent. Even if that meant dealing with the nightmares that would invariably follow.

CHAPTER 6

O'GRADY STOOD IN THE KITCHEN staring at the pools of dried blood. Trip was out in Café Amaretto's dining room among the ruins of what had only hours before been a bustling eatery.

He wondered what would become of the place and if it would ever recover. Eventually the murders would become folklore, but it might take several reincarnations of the business for people to forget. At the very least they would need to re-staff their kitchen. Basically the premises was screwed as any type of food establishment in the near future.

Forensics had already been over the place. The remnants of their visit— dozens of little numbered a-form placements littered around the kitchen and dining room—told of the hive of activity in the preceding hours. It would take days to process the scene. Not that it mattered hugely. There wasn't going to be a trial. Benson had seen to that.

Lesson one for mass killers who want to survive: when police arrive, put down your weapon. No guarantees even then, but if you wave the weapon you've just used to slaughter innocent people, don't wave said implement at armed human beings, police or not. The result rarely goes your way.

Trip and he planned to run interviews today with the witnesses—thirty-four freaked out patrons, four wait-staff, one female owner who ended up in hospital overnight under sedation, and several passers-by who witnessed something they would never forget. By night they should have a clear

27

picture of events.

Preliminary interviews puzzled O'Grady. Toby Benson was unknown to the wait-staff as far as they could remember. Arriving around nine-thirty, he'd smashed in the kitchen door, then proceeded to go crazy with an axe.

Normally these situations turned out to be an ex-employee, a spurned ex-husband of an employee, or at least someone with an axe to grind (excuse the pun). They still hadn't found any connection. Nada. This Benson character had simply flipped out—O'Grady's bet was a mental illness—and his victims were simply in a "wrong place, wrong time" scenario. O'Grady's experience told him if it looked like a crazy fish, smelled like a crazy fish, then that's what you were cooking … a crazy fish.

Examining the damaged kitchen door, O'Grady ran a cautious finger over the lock's remnants. The door was badly splintered; thin, jagged pieces of white wood stuck out at haphazard angles.

He pushed gently with his right hip to force the door open, keeping his hands in the air so he didn't touch anything and contaminate evidence the CSI team hadn't already noted.

Out in the alley, he carefully scanned the area. More yellow evidence markers littered the narrow laneway. Several forensic officers wearing thin white suits from head to toe moved slowly around, bending every few feet to examine something that had caught their eye. Down the end of the alley, where the entrance opened into the busy early morning street, yellow police tape flapped in the breeze. Just behind the tape, an officer stood, arms folded, staring out at the gathered crowd of curious onlookers.

O'Grady turned back to look at the door. Splinters of wood hung from around the lock. If nothing else, the guy was determined. Why had he picked this door, in this lane, when there were countless other restaurants and bars? The million-dollar question.

The detective took one more glance down the very ordinary-looking access lane and walked back in. He regarded the kitchen from the point of view of the killer upon first entering. The blood on the floor where the waitress had died drew his eye. The coroner had removed the body a few hours earlier. Poor girl. She was only twenty, waitressing to pay her college tuition.

Over by the kitchen sink they'd found the kid. O'Grady would never forget *that* image. He'd seen a lot in his eighteen years on the job, with twelve as detective, but what that freak had done to the kid was horrendous.

One of the beat police first on the scene had lost his lunch *and* his dinner within twenty seconds of walking in. Fortunately, he'd made it to the lane, so he hadn't polluted any evidence. O'Grady had taken a moment, too.

The boy's body had been nearly hacked in two. The first strike caught him full in the right shoulder, cutting through down to the armpit, severing the appendage from his body. Still alive after the first blow, he had tried to escape but looked to have fallen on oil spilled on the floor.

While he lay there defenseless, the killer had swung his axe with such force it took only a few blows to tear the kid apart. All Benson left were two halves of the kid's body—upper and lower torso, joined by small threads of muscle—and his arm back by the sink.

The kid was seventeen. *Jesus Christ. What the fuck was that?*

O'Grady didn't envy the coroner's job. At least his conclusion wouldn't be *cause of death: unknown*. This was an open and shut case. *Death by lunatic.*

You caught one of these cases rarely. If you were lucky—or unlucky, depending on your viewpoint—it could be considered a bonus. Another type of personality might dine out for a lifetime on a case like this. There might even be accolades or a promotion for closing it swiftly and putting the public's collective mind at rest.

O'Grady preferred to keep a low profile. He didn't like tributes. He didn't talk about his job. He was haunted enough by past events without rehashing the unsettling violent aspects of his career. Those memories he compartmentalized for his own sanity, only bringing them out if a case required it of him.

In this case, where he and Trip were there to simply mop up evidence and do the paperwork, "tying bows" was all he would focus on. Let the profilers sift through the life of Toby Benson and come up with the reasons, to give everyone a better night's sleep.

He glanced at another pool of blood near the boy's. The chef, a hefty man, bled out quickly. For him, at least, death was quick. O'Grady stared at the mottled dried stains of sticky, rust-brown, clotted with black globules. Of all the "make you, break you" cases he could snag, this one he'd have happily missed. Even with his mantra of leaving work at work, he didn't think the images would leave him for a long while. Italian was off the menu for the near future, too.

When he closed his eyes tonight, exhausted, he knew his mind would continue to circle one question: *what would possess someone to massacre these people?* If you wanted to make a case for evil, there was the confirmation, pooled in vivid red on this kitchen floor.

CHAPTER 7

KENDALL HAD NEVER AMBUSHED SOMEONE for a story. She wasn't one of those hard-nosed journalists who ran down the street after people shouting, "What do you have to say about ripping off old people?" Anyway, she probably wasn't fast enough to pursue anyone more than ten feet while holding a microphone. What she did have was a natural curiosity and, after all these years, a good instinct for people and stories.

She stood on Beverley Sanderson's doorstep wondering if her knock would bring anyone to the door, forcing herself to breathe deeply to calm her nerves. She'd managed only about two breaths before the sound of footsteps inside sent her heart racing.

The door swung open, revealing a woman in her mid-forties, her blonde hair held back by a bright purple scarf. She wore an unnaturally white smile. Kendall thought at first she must have the wrong address.

"Yes?"

"Beverley Sanderson?"

"Yes."

"My name is Kendall Jennings, and I'm working on an article for *Healthy, Wealthy and Wisdom* magazine."

The woman stared at her. In her nervousness, Kendall continued to talk, uncertain whether she was seconds away from the door being slammed in her face.

"Perhaps you've heard of it? They're sold in all the supermarkets. Very popular. Over three hundred thousand copies sold."

Still the woman stared.

"I thought you might speak to me about your experience at Café Amaretto last night."

Beverley Sanderson continued to hold the edge of the door. Her stare revealed nothing. Kendall imagined *it* coming any moment: the get-off-my-property-scum-newsperson retort. It surprised her the woman had even come to the door. Surely, she'd already had approaches by dozens of news outlets vying for her story.

Well, nothing ventured, nothing gained. Kendall smiled her biggest, brightest, you-can-trust-me smile.

"A lot of people want to know what it's like to survive what you went through …" Still nothing from the woman. She quickly added, "And Jennifer Aniston was on last month's cover."

Beverley Sanderson's face suddenly came to life. Her countenance lit up as though a spotlight was focused on her for a close-up. "Oh, you want to interview me? Is that what you mean?"

"Ah … *yes* … if you have time. It's just a few questions."

"Yes, yes. I'm fine. Come in. Jennifer Aniston. Wow!"

Beverley pulled the door further open, then stood back to allow Kendall to move past her into a mid-seventies style living room, complete with dark brown leather couches and orange flock wallpaper. Most extraordinary were the china dogs. They were everywhere. On every surface, they sat, lounged, heeled, and lay on their stomachs. Bookshelves, on top of the coffee table, and on several purpose-built ledges dotted along the room's walls.

"You like dogs, Beverley?"

"I love dogs. But I can't have a dog. Allergies. I've tried all types of dogs and medications. I just sneeze and sneeze. This is the next best thing."

Standing this close to Beverley, Kendall realized the woman was older than she looked in the newspaper picture. She was mid-fifties, and even at ten in the morning her face was plastered with a full complement of makeup. Her hot-pink lipstick combined with dark red lip liner gave her a clown-like appearance. The hair poking out from beneath her scarf was teased to a bushy bouffant.

"Coffee, Kelsey?"

She didn't bother correcting Beverley's mistake with her name. Something told her no matter how many times she corrected her, Beverley would never get it right.

"Fantastic, thanks."

Kendall glanced around the room, taking care to show an interest in the dogs.

It surprised her how together the woman was—hardly what she expected after what Beverley had witnessed the previous night. Most people would be distressed for days, even months. If they were like Kendall, years.

She couldn't decide if Beverley's stoic behavior was oddball or admirable. Although, now Kendall thought about it, the woman's calm perspective would certainly provide great counterbalance to other eyewitnesses—if she could get interviews with them—who *weren't* dealing well with the horrific event.

"I won't be a moment. I've just boiled the kettle."

Beverley bounced out of the room. Now alone, Kendall walked slowly around the cluttered space, checking for further insights into the woman. Alongside the dogs were scattered faded photos of children wearing clothes dating them as growing up in the eighties. On the wall behind the three-seater lounge hung a large frame containing variously sized professional portraits of a still overly made-up younger version of Beverley. In her youth she'd been quite striking. Beverley and her husband obviously liked to cruise; many other photos depicted the pair aboard a liner or posing on exotic beaches, a cruise boat in the background.

"Here we go," Beverley announced, as she walked back into the room carrying a tray with two mugs, a gilt coffee pot, a matching milk jug and a plate of cream cookies. She fussed over the coffee, pouring two cups and held out the cookies to Kendall with "Have one. I baked them this morning."

She smiled at Kendall as though she were a long lost relative and they were about to catch up on lost years. Her demeanor was bizarrely congenial, considering what they were to discuss. In her mind, Kendall began crafting the opening to her article.

"Sometimes survivors carry on without a hitch."
No, that didn't work.

"Everybody deals with death differently."
Yes, better.

"Some survivors cope, carrying on as if nothing ever happened."
Yes, that would fly.

Then, add a quote from a therapist and another professional who specialized in trauma. Oh, yes, and then thinking of trauma, she could speak to a psychologist who dealt in returning soldiers of war and add something about post-traumatic stress disorder.

Kendall *had* imagined she would need to console the woman, play the role of a confessor, but Kendall's confidence now grew by the second. This could turn out to be no more difficult than her usual stories.

There was an air of affectation about Beverley's movements as she positioned herself on the couch, her coffee cup held carefully in her lap. Clearly she enjoyed the attention.

Beverley lifted the hot drink to her mouth and took a long sip before returning it to her lap and wrapping both hands around the mug.

"Now, what did you want to know? It's all very exciting, isn't it? How long before you print the interview? What magazine is it again? I read *Cosmopolitan* every month. Have done since I was sixteen."

"No, it's not *Cosmopolitan*. It's for *Healthy, Wealthy and Wisdom*. I'm not sure how long. They've given me a tight deadline on the story, so I imagine it will be in the next issue out next Friday."

Beverley's brow creased. ""Hmm, I haven't heard of that one." Her frown then turned to a wide smile. "But it's all very exciting, isn't it?"

The woman suddenly glowed as though she'd won the lottery. Kendall gave an acknowledging smile to convey she agreed that it was *all very exciting*, though she failed to comprehend Beverley's enthusiasm.

Kendall held up her iPhone. "Is it okay if I record our interview?"

"Oh, yes." Beverley vigorously nodded her head. "What a good idea. Record away."

Kendall opened and pressed the button of the recording app, then placed the phone on the coffee table between a border collie and a particularly ugly Chihuahua. (To her, a non-animal lover, they weren't good looking dogs in life, and even less so in china.)

"So, you and your husband were at Café Amaretto last night just enjoying an evening out, right? How long had you been there before *he* arrived and *it* all began?"

Kendall didn't want to call *it* what it was, a massacre. She, also didn't want to call Toby Benson what *he* was—a murderer, a killer, a psychopath. Despite Beverley's non-plussed demeanor, Kendall was uncertain of her interviewee's reaction if it suddenly dawned on her what she'd actually experienced. That the murders weren't a scene from a TV show or whatever thought process she used as a coping mechanism. If she could avoid it, Kendall preferred not to sit here with a hysterical woman.

"Now, let me see. We were up to dessert. I'd just asked Roy—that's my husband—*how long does it take to cut a piece of cake?* It was getting near nine-thirty. We like to be in bed by ten these days."

Beverley smiled a crow's-foot smile, though her forehead remained unnaturally smooth.

"Then we heard the sound of glasses and plates breaking. Oh my! It was a dreadful racket. So loud. At first—and I said this to Roy—I thought the waitress—and she was actually our waitress, by the way—had slipped and dropped a tray in there, in the kitchen. She was the girl, you know, the one in the paper, the waitress that died. Young thing, too. Quite pretty. Just breaks your heart."

Beverley tilted her head to the side and looked toward the ceiling as though she were reexamining the memory for the finer details. Kendall leaned in toward her, putting her untouched beverage back on the coffee table as a subtle message to keep talking.

Beverley tut-tutted before continuing.

"Yes, terrible thing. She'd served us all night. We had the ravioli. They do a great mushroom ravioli."

Kendall was about to suggest Beverley focus on what had *actually* happened on the night, when she looked back at Kendall, her lips tight, the fond-memory look she'd worn moments before gone.

"Then we heard such a strange noise, I couldn't understand what I was hearing. Oh, my God, it was terrible. I actually heard the sound of the axe as it chopped into one of them. From another room, would you believe? That's how loud it was. Of course, I didn't know what the sound was—he killed a young boy in there, too. Seventeen. God, seventeen! When I heard that thumping, I just knew something was wrong. Really wrong. That's not a sound you hear from a kitchen."

She paused, raising her cup to her lips, then immediately lowered it to her lap again and continued.

"I don't know how I knew, but I said to Roy, 'I don't like this. I think we should forget dessert.' So we were up and standing at the register near the exit when *he* came through the door from the kitchen."

"That must have been terrifying, Beverley. Lucky you moved. What did he look like?"

Beverly straightened her back, placed her coffee cup on the table with a flourish, and raised her chin as though she were about to give a speech on molecular biology.

"That was the strange, *strange* thing. I said this to the policeman after. If he didn't have that axe, and if he weren't covered in blood, you would think he was just a nice, run-of-the-mill, everyday young man. Someone who'd carry your groceries from your car to the door. He didn't look like a murderer. He had nicely styled neat hair. In fact, I told Roy later, I thought he was quite handsome."

"Did he look like he knew someone in the room? Like he was after someone in particular? Revenge maybe?"

"No. He just stood in the kitchen doorway and looked around the room as if he was looking for a table. Like he was joining friends. That's why some of those people didn't move. *That's* how he got them. He looked so ordinary people didn't give him a second look. Mind you, on second look the blood on him should have rung bells. Then he went for the nearest table. I couldn't believe how quick he was with that axe. They didn't stand a chance. Within seconds, it was a mess. Blood everywhere. A man. A woman. Then another man. He smashed into them as if they were pieces of wood."

Kendall gagged. Something thick and nasty had lodged in her throat. She didn't need that image in her mind. She'd honestly expected Beverley would be too distressed to talk, and she would give Kendall a few quotes along the lines of being grateful to be alive and that she now had a new perspective on life. Beverley's gusto in sharing the events was almost as disturbing as the images conjured.

Beverley actually laughed. "For just a second, I thought, *This is one of those show setups. Someone's going to leap out from somewhere and yell 'You're all punk'd.'* Then I thought, *No, this blood looks too real. The screams are too real.* Then Roy grabbed my arm and yanked me toward the door. He's such a quick thinker. By then, everyone had the same idea. Even though we were near the front at the register, we couldn't get out. Everyone was trying to get through one little door. I fell over. When I looked up, Roy was gone."

"Oh, no. How awful."

"Oh, yes. It *was* awful. Roy's quick thinking rubbed off on me, thank goodness. I managed to clamber behind the reception desk. There was just enough room for me to hide. I thought, *If I try to get out now, well, he could be behind me.* You know what they say? When being chased by a lion, you only need to run faster than the other guy. More coffee, Karen?"

Call me what you want. Karen, Carmel, whatever. Just keep talking. She hated hearing the gruesome details, but already the story was written in her head.

"Um, no … thank you. I'm good."

As if she could eat or drink after hearing this story.

"Cookie? Have another cookie." Beverly picked up a cookie for herself, then leaned forward and pushed the plate toward Kendall.

Surreal, that was the word for this moment. Maybe it was Kendall being punk'd. Cookies and mass murder. Coffee and killings. *Wow.*

Kendall reluctantly took one of the proffered cookies and bit into it, eliciting a satisfied smile from Beverley. The sickly sweet cream cookie felt disgusting in her mouth. She wanted more than anything to spit it out. Instead, she swallowed and palmed the remainder, hoping Beverley wouldn't notice.

"Now where was I?" asked Beverley, after munching on another cookie and vigorously swiping the crumbs from the corner of her mouth, so that they fell like grains of sand into her lap.

"You were hiding?"

"Oh, yes, *hiding.* Well, you can imagine, I was thinking there was me, done for. In that moment, I even thought ahead and hoped Roy would find someone else after I died. Go on with his life. Honestly, that's what I thought. Then I heard them."

Beverley stopped, looking off toward a wall to the left of Kendall. When Kendall follower her gaze, she saw that Beverley stared at a poster-sized wedding photo of her younger self and presumably Roy.

"Heard who?"

"The police, of course. Thank God for the police. They were so ... so ... You know a lot of people don't like the police. It's hard to believe what they did. Don't you think?"

"Ah ... yes ... haven't had a lot to do with them."

Kendall searched for an ambiguous answer. Was Beverley impressed or disgusted by the police actions? "But, yes, they certainly were incredible from what I hear. What did they do, exactly?"

"They shot him. So brave. Otherwise, who knows? He might have got me."

"Did you see them shoot him?" Kendall ventured.

"Oh, yes, I saw everything. Soon as I heard them arrive, I popped my head out to see what was happening. See if I could run. They were just normal police, you know. The ones you see on the street every day. Not the

SWAT ones. They came later, in case he had accomplices. But it was just the one guy and his axe."

"Do you think they *had* to shoot him? Or do you think they panicked?"

"That's a good question, Karen. A really good question, because I had a very good view of him. If I hadn't been there, I would have thought they did the right thing when they shot him. After all, he killed all those people. You know, I saw him chop four people with that axe. But the more I think about it, I'm not sure."

It was an odd statement considering the brutal events Beverley had just, described, even with the woman's peculiar attitude.

"What do you think they *should* have done, Beverley?"

"Well, I've thought about this a lot since, because it was so strange. I think maybe they should have waited, because, well … because the axe man *did* ask for help."

"Help?"

"Yes. When the police called out to him to stop, he did stop, as if he recognized that they *were* the police and he was in trouble. He stood there, staring at them, a weird look in his eyes. That was the other thing … his eyes. He blinked a lot, as if the light hurt. Then when they yelled at him to put down the axe—no, that's not right. 'Weapon,' they said. 'Put down your weapon.' When they said that, his face changed. It was like, you know, a mask coming off. Oh, what do they call it? How they do it in the movies? Starts with *M*."

Kendall shrugged.

Beverley's eyes sparked. "I know. I've got it … morphing. Yes. *Yes.* His face morphed. For a few seconds he looked like a desperate person, someone trying to get out of somewhere they've gotten stuck. Then he said, 'Help me.' Funny way to ask for help, I thought."

"Help me? Are you sure he said *help me*?"

"Yes, he said it twice. Then he looked down at the axe like he'd never seen it before in his life. The two police just stood there, guns out in front of them. You know, they were all ready to shoot him, but it looked like he was giving himself up. Realized the terrible thing he'd done. Then he morphed again. The killer face came back: blank, with those horrible, blinking eyes. A woman lay at his feet, who wasn't dead, who started to move. Poor thing. He looked down at her and suddenly pulled back the axe. That was that. Awful."

Kendall put her hand to her mouth, dropping the concealed half-eaten cookie into her lap. Beverley was too engrossed in her storytelling to even notice.

"They shot him?"

"So many times I couldn't count. Both of the policemen just went for it. The noise was so loud it hurt my ears, even with my hands covering them. They're still ringing today. The guns clicked when they ran out of bullets. I really don't know how witnesses can count bullets. In *Law and Order*, when they say the criminal fired so many times. I don't know how you keep count of the bullets. It's so fast."

"How horrifying, Beverley. You must be very distressed to have witnessed that."

"Oh, yes, it was *aww-ful*. I couldn't find Roy for a long time. He thought I'd died. The poor darling."

Beverley's expression changed—in her own words, morphed—from wide-eyed horror storyteller to a smiling belle of the ball.

"All the TV show people are calling me now. I don't know how they got my number, but they want to know what happened. Like I told Roy, 'cause he doesn't *want* to talk about it, I need to be strong, so everyone can see how violence hasn't affected me. For the victims, you know."

Kendall listened for another fifteen minutes to Beverley discussing her excitement at her picture in the paper and now, thanks to Kendall, a magazine. Kendall finally extricated herself from the woman's company despite being kept on the doorstep another five minutes, while Beverley asked if she could read the article first and did they need a picture of her. Kendall took a few shots with her phone, not having thought to organize a photographer. She hadn't actually expected to even get an interview.

On her walk back home, Kendall felt as though she were wading through mud. Beverley's descriptions whirled in her mind. She couldn't help but place herself in the shoes of the victims, the police officers, and the survivors. That kind of experience—unless you're Beverley Sanderson—must scar you for life, invade your nightmares forever.

It wasn't until Kendall was almost home, waiting at a crosswalk, that she realized she'd forgotten the most important question, the one she'd been sent there to have answered. How sloppy of her. That was her inexperience with these types of stories for you.

She didn't ask Beverley if she felt any survivor's guilt. As she began to cross the road, she realized, she already knew the answer.

Chapter 8

B OSS17 WATCHED THE NEWS REPORTS.
It had begun.
He smiled at the thought.

CHAPTER 9

BENITO TAVELL STARED AT THE match. The tiny piece of wood felt loud in his hand, as though it were pulsing on the skin of his fingertips. He knew this was the wrong description, but they were the best words he could find. When he struck it, he wondered if the feeling would change into something else, become louder, sharper? Even hurt like a throbbing bruise when pushed? The longer he paused, the more the pulse grew, until it began to travel from his fingers into his palm, through his wrist, then up through his arm.

He would have waited to discover what would happen once the feeling reached the top of his arm, but he had an insatiable urge, an itch that needed to be scratched. The match demanded to be struck.

He ran the head against the side of the matchbox, the sound like a roaring jet. The flame flared, then settled into a burn, the yellow and white intensely bright even against the overhead fluorescent lights.

Interesting.

Benito imagined the unnatural white light would wash out the intensity of the flame. The flame had taken on properties of supernatural power. He watched it flicker and hold, flicker and hold, moving in tiny increments down the stem of wood. It took an hour, maybe, or so it seemed, before a thin, black end of burned wood formed.

Beautiful. A work of art.

He wanted to climb inside the white-yellow glow. Beckoning with warmth and a fiery life force. Feel the burn on his skin. Maybe later. Right now, things needed doing. He and the match had a destiny to fulfill. He held the half-burned match over the wastebasket carefully stuffed to overfull with toilet paper.

Now. Do it now.

He stretched his neck to the side until he heard a slight crack sounding like snapping, burning wood. Left. Then right. The joints popped as the action stretched the tendons and pulled them to release. His body flooded with a feeling of euphoria, of utter and total bliss.

Yes, I will do it now.

The thought rushed into his head as though pushed by the hand of God. He obeyed and dropped the match into the basket with a flick of his fingers. The paper caught instantly.

Wonderful. Truly wonderful. Even magnificent.

He'd accomplished the first part of his mission.

Within seconds, little licks of orange and yellow climbed over each other, consuming the fuel he'd gathered. He was feeding a pet. He wanted to reach in and touch it, feel the burn on his cool, fragile skin. Watch his skin peel back and wither to black. Instead, he moved back toward the doorway, a better vantage point to take in the scope of his good work.

In thirty seconds the curtains above the wastebasket ignited. The flames licked up the wall, eager to travel along the path he'd constructed, consume the meal he'd prepared. The bed he'd pushed against the other side of the window would alight shortly. He was proud of his assembly order. Wastebasket, curtains, bed. The room would succumb quickly.

Nobody would come in time. He knew this because he'd worked the skeleton-staffed two-to-ten shift many times. Early morning, events rarely happened. Nurses would only attend to patients when called or during their rounds every ninety minutes. If they even bothered with the rounds. Sometimes they didn't, falsifying the activity sheets.

This room had been empty. Empty no longer, now filled with color and life, beautiful to behold.

Benito reluctantly turned from his work, the sound of the growing flames music to his ears. Closing the door, he walked down the empty hall. The pale green walls needed paint; scuff marks crawled along and up their surface, giving the appearance of pale tiger stripes. Soon, the wall would require *more* than paint.

He walked to the very end of the hall and turned toward the fire escape, pushing open the door, which complained loudly in the silence of the hour. He took the stairs, two at a time, downward to the first floor, the sound of his steps unnaturally loud, like tap shoes on the concrete.

Exiting on the first floor, he turned left. The cafeteria lay to his right, but someone could be in there at the food dispensers or the coffee machine. He'd leave there until last. Left would do for the moment.

The matches felt heavy in his pocket; tiny pieces of innocuous wood, which held such potential. Just like him. He was ordinary, but he would change the destiny of the world. Even though he couldn't remember why, that knowledge was within his soul. He knew it as a certainty.

He entered Mr. Jacob's room. Age eighty-two. Dementia.

Yes. Mr. Jacobs would do very well.

He moved through the darkened room to the bathroom, switching on the overhead light as he entered. The light flickered alive, the sound of buzzing electrons filling the air.

Minutes later, he'd gathered the wastebasket from the bathroom and filled it with paper. He spilled lighter fluid over it from the small tin he'd carried in his jacket pocket. Back in the room, the sound of Mr. Jacobs' loud snores rhythmically breached the black silence like a homing beacon.

He placed the wastebasket on the floor near the bed and held a match above it. Now, the match must do its work; the sound of the strike, a thrill to his fingertips. A sizzling flare filled his sight, causing him to squint, until it settled to a bright white flame.

He casually dropped the match into the receptacle. To him, it took forever to fall. Once among the paper, it began to quickly consume the waiting fuel. Benito moved the crackling, flaming, metal bucket beneath the bed. Better this way. Mr. Jacobs wouldn't understand, though he felt certain the elderly man would be happy knowing his death would have meaning.

Turning back toward the door, a twinge shot through his neck. Again he stretched the muscles, turning his head, as he extended them first to the left, then to the right.

At the exit he paused, watching the flames lick hungrily beneath the bed of the sleeping man. To Benito it appeared a work of art, a beach bonfire, good memories, distant and untouchable, as though they were no longer part of his history. Something blocked them, held them hostage.

The voice urged him: *Complete the mission, stay straight and true.*

He pulled the door shut and walked across the hall to Mrs. Simpson's room. She was blind. He pitied her. The flames were really something to see. He had a vague memory of helping Mrs. Simpson with flowers and changing her bedclothes. Then the images vanished.

This time, he wouldn't use the electric lights; he knew the layout of the room. A sliver of moonlight marked the floor allowing just enough light to see. He walked through the gray darkness, his body slicing through the space as though *he* was made of sharp edges. She had no light, so neither would he. He honored and respected these people who would shortly die for a noble cause.

One foot after the other. One match after the other. One victim after the other.

Benito opened the bathroom door, but the wastebasket wasn't there. Frustratingly, this forced him to flick on the lights. *There* was the basket, behind the door.

He picked up the wastebasket and rifled through the contents. Yes, enough fuel there. Inside, a folded newspaper and scrunched up toilet paper with fruit peel scraps scattered between.

Now where?

He'd used curtains; he'd used a bed; where else could he place his work of warm art? He moved to the bathroom doorway and stood at the threshold between the small, lit room and the darkened bedroom.

Reaching into his pocket for the matches, the resonance of his hand against the fabric of his pants was of a rushing wind before a storm. The sound meant he was on the right path.

"Who is it there?"

Mrs. Simpson's dry, raspy voice stopped him. Her eyes would be open but unseeing. A shame this beautiful sight stolen from her.

"Is that you, Sophia? What time is it, dear?"

Benito left the bathroom to stand by her bed, the wastebasket clutched in his hand along with the matches. They itched in his palm to be struck.

One moment. One more moment.

He stood, listening to her struggling breath.

"What are you doing there? I can't see." Her voice was cracked and hesitant from age and sleep.

The dark felt pleasant on his skin, creeping inside him, filtering through his pores and into his cells, filling him with desire to strike the match and illuminate the room.

Benito placed the basket at the end of the bed, nestled between the folds of the bedcovers. Mrs. Simpson's frame, so shrunken from age and decay, took up only half the bed. Her mind was good but cell-by-cell time had whittled away her body.

Her voice, more urgent now: "What's going on? I was asleep. You woke me!"

Somehow she sensed this wasn't normal, that something was wrong. If he spoke, she would recognize Benito's voice, the cadence of his accent, although he'd lived here all his life. His father was from India; his mother met her husband there on a sabbatical in her twenties.

Now the match.

Oh, God, the match would be such a blessing. He struck the beautifully shaped wood, so perfect for the task, the design unaltered for centuries. The sound came again, the stinging hiss, a roar, then a warm glow. Magnificent. A tumult of beauty licking into the darkness, wearing away at the darkness. So small. So delicate. So perfect.

He dropped the glowing match into the basket to meet its paper partner. They began their mating dance. The flame rushed along the paper's edges, digging in deep, looking for more, its hunger for fuel insatiable.

"What's that s-s-sound?"

Mrs. Simpsons' voice came out a hiss. She smelled it now and began to understand. This wasn't a visit to check her vitals or tuck in her bedclothes. This was a visit by a friend, come to take away the pain, take away the blindness. The view was achingly beautiful. Tiny shreds of golden-white and orange licked gently upward.

Benito pulled the bed cover across the basket, careful to leave a gap, so as not to stifle the flames. He dipped the material's edge in so it could catch like the wick of an explosive. The fire liked the bed cover. Cotton breathes and burns. *How it burned.* In magnificent, leaping flames, travelling quickly up the bedclothes, it burned. Benito backed away toward the door, never taking his gaze from the vision.

Mrs. Simpson began to scream, so he couldn't stay.

One more.

The thought traveled through his mind. *One more.* Just to be sure. Just to seal the deal. Four people dead meant something important. A necessary number.

He exited the room. A squealing fire alarm suddenly filled the air, earsplitting and annoying, a relentless rhythm. As though the sound was suddenly muted, his focus returned to the mission, and it became just a sound in the background.

Someone was in the hall. Andrea almost slammed into him hurrying past.

"What's going on?" she yelled, through the screech of the alarm. "Is that Mrs. Simpson screaming?"

Andrea, two kids, a single mom always volunteered for night shift, because it suited her lifestyle. *"What life?"* she often said, to which Benito always nodded, not truly understanding her meaning.

She stared at him, awaiting a reply. When there came none, she shook her head and hurried past him into Mrs. Simpson's room.

Before entering, she stopped and turned back. "Benito, are you okay?"

He couldn't answer, wouldn't answer anyway, because the need for *one more* pulled him away. He needed to keep moving. Strings of thoughts attached to his will. He couldn't resist them. Didn't want to resist them.

Benito turned from Andrea to travel up the hall, as he imagined her running toward Mrs. Simpson in her room, running toward the screams. It would be too late. Even these few minutes would have given the flames all the time they needed to find their way. The flaming bed in the deep darkness would greet her with its beauty and life. And death.

Someone else ran past: a middle-aged nurse. He didn't look at Benito, didn't stop. The man was new, only starting last week. Benito couldn't remember his name. Now he would never know his name.

The buzz sizzled into his spine, travelling through him, under his skin like a wave. It was a vibration in his teeth and in the membranes of his eyes. This time it hurt. He stopped and gathered himself, resting his palm flat against the cool, smooth wall. Then, in the beat of a second, the buzzing and sound were gone. He looked around, his head swinging from side to side, suddenly surprised. His gaze fell on his hands as he held them up. They didn't look as though they belonged to him as if he was an alien inside his own skin. Fear shimmied through him. Something was wrong.

Should he be here?

How had he gotten here? And why? He couldn't remember. His last memory, a wisp of a thing, was of the end of his shift, saying goodnight to co-workers, then heading off for a meal before home.

"Goodnight Mr. Berry," he'd said to a long-term resident in the lounge playing solitaire. Mr. Berry always had a game or two before bed. "Helps me sleep," he would say.

"Goodnight, Carol." He liked working with her. She *got* his jokes; her laughter brightened his day.

"Goodnight, Jack Backer," he'd said, as he passed the octogenarian's room. A sweet old guy. WW2 veteran. Always good with a story. Man, those guys suffered.

"See you tomorrow, Alan," he'd said, after handing over the shift's charts to his colleague, high-fiving him on the way out. He'd reminded Alan who to check on and who to leave sleeping. There'd been talk of promoting him to assistant supervisor, so he showed even more care than usual.

"Goodnight—."

They were gone. All thoughts of *before* vanished, as though a veil came down like a theatre curtain. He couldn't see, couldn't hear them anymore.

Goodnight everyone. Goodnight.

He knew every one of their names, Jack Backer, Mr. Berry, Mrs. Wales, Fred Day, all of them, the sixty-two people in his care—joint-care with the other nursing home workers. They all worked diligently to ensure their charges were comfortable. *Comfortable and happy until they died.*

He couldn't feel them anymore. Suddenly all he felt was alone. The voice and him and the mission that must not fail. This was all he had. *Straight and true* was all he had.

The supply room was to the right. He jiggled his key in the lock and the door sprung open. Five wooden shelves, beginning at waist height, worked their way up the three walls. Below, standing at attention, were three buckets with mops. He wondered if the metal in the handles would color the flames.

He pulled the mops from the buckets, resting them against the opposite wall. From the shelves, he pulled cloths and paper towels, scrunching them together into small balls and shoving them into the buckets.

They would be here soon. He must hurry. Benito shoved his hand into his pocket and pulled out the matches. He would never use all of them, the shame that it was. The muscles in his neck screamed at him again. He tilted his head, attempting to ease the burn now inside his tendons. Ten more minutes were all he needed.

Plastic containers of blue and green liquid perched in neat rows, along the shelves. Would *they* burn a different color? He pulled one of the three methylated spirits bottles from the shelf and twisted open the lid. He moved the container to his nose, drawing in a deep, long breath. The noxious smell sharpened his anticipation.

Quickly, he upended the bottle into the first bucket. Fumes filled the room, hitting his olfactory glands with the sweet smell of peril and possibility, sweeter than if roses filled the room.

Afraid he'd lose himself in the exquisite potency, he covered his mouth and poured the remaining two bottles into the buckets. The liquid turned the balls of white paper dark vanilla.

Reaching for one of the mops, he shoved it inside the bucket and pushed down the paper. The bucket's wheels gave way with the pressure, skidding the container against the door.

Benito leaned forward to pull back the bucket as though it were an eager dog he needed to heel. He was ready to go. Clasping the silver metal door handle, he pushed the door ajar, allowing the bucket to move to the edge of the threshold and nestle there. It would hold the door open.

Benito turned and reached for another bucket. With the mop sticking out, it looked like a potted tree, naked of foliage. He stepped behind it, grasped the handle tightly, and pushed against it, wheeling it forward. Benito passed by his little metal partner still holding the door and swung his bucket into the middle of the hall.

Since he'd entered the closet, people had filled the hall. Cries of help came from all directions. Elderly, bewildered patients wandered lost as though they'd never before traveled outside their rooms. Confusion and fear filled the air, along with the scream of the alarm.

Benito ignored them as he wheeled the bucket along the scratched, shiny floor. To everyone he would be simply an employee sent to clean up another resident's bodily fluid mishap.

Next stop, the lounge, two doors down. A coffee table in there perfectly suited his needs, calling to him through the building's walls. The room would be empty thanks to the alarm.

A few minutes later, he was proved right—indeed empty and waiting for him. He didn't hesitate, trundling the bucket to the table; where he' discovered a problem. The bucket was too high to fit under the table as he'd originally envisaged.

Straight and true.

The thought echoed in his head.

Then: *Let nothing stop you.*

Yes, nothing *would* stop him. He understood his destiny. His mission.

Benito moved to plan B, upending the contents of the bucket onto the floor. He shoved the pieces under the table with the mop; the smell intoxicating, a sensory overload of perfume joy. A magazine rack by a threadbare, blue, sofa, overflowing with ancient reading material and two-week-old newspapers, caught his attention.

That would work. Dual action.

He hurriedly pulled out the contents of the wooden rack, bundled them onto the sofa, and began stuffing them between the cushions and around the curved wooden legs. The sofa now resembled a giant pincushion. The few remaining newspapers he crammed in the remaining space beneath the coffee table.

The matches prickled in his palm. For the fourth time tonight, he tore along the coarse side of the small cardboard box and watched as the match flamed to life. Standing over the sofa, he held out his hand as though he were a maestro conducting an orchestra. Steady and careful, he touched the flame to several rolled up pieces of paper, wanting to clap as each one flared alight. Now the chair was a *glowing* pincushion.

Benito turned to the coffee table with its decoration, above and below, of soaking wads of paper. With a flick, the match leaped from his fingers to land squarely amid the mix. This time, the paper did not come gently to life, but erupted, in what seemed to Benito a sonic boom. Circles of blue-green light spread quickly from the epicenter.

The sofa was now fully alight; already the flames reached several feet in the air. He stood, gaping at his handiwork for minutes. Yellow. White. Red. The colors perfect against the blue of the chair.

How he wanted to stay and watch.

But, more work needed doing.

He exited the lounge and returned down the hall. The door to the closet was closed, his other bucket-partner still waiting, hiding inside. Benito yanked at the door, slipped in, and seized the bucket and mop, then reentered the corridor and wheeled his prize to the center.

The hall now resembled a busy bus station, people milling everywhere, confused, lost and panicked. The sounds of distress, people shouting, and the alarm layered upon each other creating a surreal, slow-motion image.

Two nurses ran up and down, shouting and banging on doors. The throng grew by the second, the terror rising like a temperature gauge on its way to overload. Pajama-clad residents shuffled down toward the exits, assisted by each other or a nurse or orderly. Several used canes; Mrs. Best moved achingly slow in her Zimmer frame.

Then the overhead water sprinklers exploded.

More screaming erupted as though the downpour of water had accelerated the scene. For Benito, the alarm volume grew in his head until it was all he could hear. Like a sword through his ears, it entered and speared his brain. He wanted to put his hands to his head; the agony more than he could bear. He couldn't. He wasn't finished yet. The voice had said, was still saying, *Straight and true. Straight and true.*

"Yes, I will," he replied, in his mind. And, somehow felt he was heard.

The water from the sprinklers made the polished-smooth floor wet and treacherous for uncertain, aged feet. One resident slipped and fell in his haste. Then another. Both were helped up, but one of the old men now leaned against a wall crying like a baby. Something was broken, judging by his contortioned face.

Benito watched, unmoved by their plight. They were part of a great plan, worthy of their sacrifice. Nobody noticed him. His five years of work here made him invisible. He pushed at the bucket, using the mop as a handle, and patiently waited as two octogenarians, Eli Kahn and Bill Baster, hobbled past him, arms entwined, moving faster than he'd ever seen them move before. He pushed the bucket in front of them. They stopped, puzzled, their mouths quivering, as they looked at him.

"Fire, Benito. Can't you hear the alarm?"

An idea occurred to Benito, an idea that would work perfectly. He reached into the bucket, where he'd placed a container of methylated spirits on top of the cloths and paper. The contents slopped inside as he raised it up. Unscrewing the lid, he smiled back at the men.

They even smiled back.

He shook the bottle's contents at their feet like it was ketchup. The liquid splashed their worn slippers and the bottoms of their striped pajamas. The beautiful, pungent smell came again. Even the sprinkling water couldn't douse its perfume.

"What the hell are you—? Benito!" cried Eli Kahn, but he didn't finish his sentence. Suddenly he knew the question's answer. Out of his shirt pocket, Benito pulled the silver Zippo he knew would be there. *Where did he get the lighter? He didn't smoke.*

One small flick of his fingers and a flame flared. He threw the glowing, lighter into the air; it sailed in a fine arc to land at their feet. Instantly, flames pawed at the men's legs as they screamed and clawed at themselves with more energy than men half their age.

Bill Baster ran screaming down the hall, flames crawling up his legs, the fire too well fueled to be doused by mere sprinkles of water. He didn't get far, falling to the ground, rolling about, while those around him stood back, afraid of the fire catching them.

Someone came running from behind. Catherine, the night manager, ran past Benito, to the other man, Eli, a blanket in her hand.

"Get down. Get down, Eli," she shouted as she hurled the blanket over him, pushing him to the floor, beating at the flames attempting to escape. His screams had taken on the tone of steel against steel, high and painful, even against the backdrop of the alarm.

Smoke, billowing up the passage, filled the hall. Dark and gray, it traveled; consuming those it touched as though seeking victims to smother.

Benito turned away from Catherine and Eli, and Bill who now lay still on the floor, the fire eating away at his body, now turning a mottled black and red. Benito walked back to the closet, unhurried as though he was simply carrying out another chore. He pulled open the door and slipped inside to the relative calm within.

Inside it was dry. No sprinklers; perhaps an oversight considering the nature of fluids stored in the room. The enclosure felt magical filled with the bright, almost fluorescent colors of the cleaning fluids. The matches in his pocket itched at him again, speaking to him. He drew them from his jacket's inside pocket. Still dry enough, protected as they were by the lining. *Last one. Very last one.*

He spied several oil containers on a shelf to his right. Polishing oil. Turpentine. Something blue, labeled with a skull and crossbones. They would do very well. He pulled the beautiful things from the shelf. The caustic odor rose around him, as he spilled them onto the floor, splashed them against the walls. The cloying smell, strong enough to momentarily cloak the smell of smoke seeping beneath the door.

In a corner, he spied more bags of cleaning cloths. Benito emptied them onto the floor, swirling them through the oil with his foot. The smell, so intoxicating, he wanted to swim in it, to die in it.

He held the match above the soaked material, taking in the moment.

A sudden banging on the door interrupted.

"Benito, what's going on in there? There's a fire! For Pete's sake get out."

It was the night manager, Catherine.

The door flew open. Smoke whirled into the room with the force of the displacement of air. Catherine stood in the doorway, startled. Her gaze traveled over the room, over him, to his oil-soaked pants.

"Shit, Benito. You? What're you doing?"

He reached for her, pulling her inside. The fifty-something woman, probably too surprised to react, screamed as she slipped and fell to the floor at his feet, her body resting on his mound of rags.

"Benito, please ... whatever you've done. Please, we've got to get out. Please—"

When he smiled, she screamed: "Why? Why?"

He knew why, but couldn't say. Destiny had arrived. Catherine would have a ringside seat.

The match tingled maddeningly, wonderfully. The time had come. Catherine groped at his legs, pleading with him, attempting to raise herself. Benito didn't look away from the match, he now held in his hand, the match that seemed to spark even before it was struck. He anticipated the tiny swish of the head against the matchbox's roughened side. Musical, delightful.

He wanted to smile, to say, "It's alright. We're witnesses to fate," but he couldn't speak. He did try, but nothing came, the words trapped inside his head, just as Catherine was trapped inside this room with him and destiny. All he heard was the voice. *Straight and true. Straight and true.* In the end, she'd understand. His actions would speak louder than words.

Benito Tavell struck the match.

CHAPTER 10

O'GRADY, TRIP, AND ALLEN, THE audio-visual tech, had stared at the video screen for more than an hour. Something about the man on screen looked familiar to O'Grady. The second he'd appeared in the recovered security footage, the hairs on the back of O'Grady's neck stood up like the hackles of an annoyed dog.

"I feel like I know this guy, Trip. You recognize him?"

Trip leaned into the screen, studying the grainy black and white image. He stood back and slowly shook his head.

"No, can't say I do. He just looks like your everyday garden-variety psycho."

"There's something about him. His face. Or the way he moves, maybe. He keeps angling his head, twisting his neck. See there?" O'Grady pointed to the screen. "Like a nervous twitch. I don't know, maybe I interviewed him once."

O'Grady sighed a long, tired sigh, rubbing at his eyes with a fingertip. "Maybe, I'm just imagining it. I'm kinda beat."

"Maybe it'll come to you later."

"What do you think we're looking at here, anyway?"

"Beats me," said Trip. "It's like the guy's a robot. I've never seen a vic act quite that way."

"See, look there." O'Grady motioned to the corner of the screen.

He addressed Allen. "Roll that back? What's he doing there?"

On screen, the man they now knew as Benito Tavell had stopped in the middle of a corridor while people moved in a wild panic around him. Tavell stood, rooted to the ground, gazing around like a tourist admiring scenery. It was one heck of a *Twilight Zone* episode, considering the fatalities.

"What kind of crazy person just stands there, even if they're *insane* enough to have set fire to the place," said Trip, rubbing the back of his head, his habitual response to stress or tiredness. After three years, side-by-side, O'Grady knew his partner's quirks like he knew his own.

As O'Grady watched the scenes captured on video, O'Grady wondered at the misfortune that saw them catching two mass murders in a single week. Some kind of freaking bad lottery ticket, right there. This Benito Tavell and his gruesome little play was a piece of work. Images like this never left you. They faded, but always remained, waiting to float back unexpectedly. Eventually there were too many; they were like a steaming garbage pile begun to ferment.

If Tavell had been arrested, right now a shitload of bodies would be assigned to this. Instead, it was just them and a couple of wet-behind-the-ears boys. If the killer were still out there, a taskforce would have been assembled to hunt him down. The D.A. would brief them on what they could and couldn't do, and the pressure from the food chain above would be immense. But this case, like the Café Amaretto killings, was open and shut. Both killers had died in the process. A good thing.

The downside was he and Trip were left with cleanup duty: a mountain of paperwork and liaising with the necessary departments handling media and enquiries. They'd brief the sergeant, once they had all the facts. No doubt, then, all the white collar number crunchers and analysts would have a field day with their long-winded reports on how the police force could develop freaking mental telepathy so something like this wouldn't happen again.

Luckily, they had plenty of the Kenworth Home's security footage from the dozen-plus cameras installed through the hallways and common rooms. Their security was good. They just hadn't planned on one of their own employees turning *Firestarter*. The other piece of luck was the Cloud. The footage had been fed online for security. Otherwise, this evidence would have been destroyed with the majority of the building.

Ten people died in the inferno, including one of the managers. Six more lay critical in hospital, two with little hope of survival. It was one of the worst fires in the city, especially heartbreaking for the population because these were defenseless elderly folk.

They'd already interviewed some of Tavell's friends and his family. He lived with his parents—no wife or children. The parents hadn't seen him since that morning, when he'd left to run errands before starting his shift. When he didn't come home from his afternoon-evening shift, they hadn't worried. It wasn't out of the ordinary for him. He had many friends and, according to everyone, was well liked.

The main witnesses were fellow workers at the nursing home, who'd briefly seen him before the fire. They'd made nothing of him coming back to work, even though his shift had ended two hours earlier.

"I thought he was working overtime or got called back in," a shocked middle-aged female nurse told them, between sobs.

One of his co-workers and several residents, who remembered seeing Tavell during the evacuation, described his behavior as strange. As *too* calm.

Another co-worker saw him before the fire took hold. She said: "He was carrying a wastebasket filled with paper up a hall. I thought he was emptying it. It was odd—him emptying the trash—the cleaners do that normally. If only I'd thought about it, maybe he could've been stopped." She, also, began to cry, requiring some consoling.

They didn't realize it was Tavell, at first, before they had the footage. It took less than a day, though, to isolate him as a suspect. The security footage confirmed it. Benito Tavell purposely set the fire and then succumbed to it, a victim of his own handiwork.

O'Grady paused that thought.

He was hardly a victim. He was a cold-blooded killer; his movements calculated, disturbing. That was, except for the piece of the video they were staring at now. Fourteen seconds of Tavell standing amid the chaos.

Fourteen seconds, where he stopped being a robot and appeared to suddenly understand what he was doing and what was happening around him. He seemed to have awoken not from a nightmare, but *into* one. For maybe five of the fourteen seconds, his face was the face of a terrified man.

On the screen, the dark-skinned twenty-nine-year-old—well on his way to overweight—looked down at his hands as though surprised he possessed fingers. He turned his gaze slowly then to look around the hallway.

"What's he doing?" said Trip under his breath, the first time they watched this scene. "Lost. He looks lost, doesn't he?"

"Yes," agreed O'Grady, "Every movement before this looks determined. Calculated. Like everything's planned. Then it's as if he changed drivers mid-race. Then back again to zombie land.

Trip rubbed at the back of his head as though something had stuck there. "Is it drugs, do you think?"

"He sure isn't behaving like any wacked-out addict I've ever seen. Nobody we've interviewed has mentioned drugs. Nothing, except he was the perfect employee and a *good guy*. If he was using, someone would've noticed or it'd show in his work."

Trip shook his head and sighed. "Then what sets someone off in the middle of the night to do this? Blows your mind, really."

O'Grady leaned back in his chair and rubbed a hand back and forth across his mouth. "I don't want to say this, because it makes me sound as crazy as him. But this guy's behavior has similar hallmarks to our café killer Benson."

Allen, who'd remained silent the entire time, piped up. "I've seen my share of this kind of footage—goes with the job—but this one, it's playing on me, too."

Trip patted Allen on the shoulder. "Just be glad you're only seeing it in black and white and on a screen, man."

The three men returned to the horror film starring Benito Tavell. Slowly the killer pushed a mop-bucket up the hall. The action appeared so innocent. Four minutes and forty seconds later, he returned to the janitor's closet.

"Shit, he's merciless," said Trip as Tavell pulled the night manager inside the closet. Then close on a minute later it was like a bomb exploded. The door flew outward, slamming against the wall across the hall. A fireball burst from the room and traveled up the hallway, engulfing two stragglers with ferocity. The film ended abruptly, the screen turning to black, as the blast reached the camera.

Nobody spoke. Words didn't come easy after seeing something like that. Allen hit a few keys and the screen returned to the original opening frame of an empty hallway.

Finally, Trip spoke. "Wow, that sure is one hell of a horror show."

O'Grady blew out the breath he hadn't even realized he'd held in. "That it is. That … it … is."

Allen turned to them. "Do you want to watch again?"

"Not now," said O'Grady. "We need to check in with the coroner. Later this afternoon a preliminary arson squad report should be ready we need to look over. The second story partially collapsed, so the place looks like a warzone."

"You know," said Trip, "I honestly don't get this guy. Why would he be so obvious? It's not your usual arson m.o."

O'Grady stood back from the screen. He agreed. He'd never seen anything like it and hoped he never would again. What O'Grady actually needed was to get away and mull everything over. What he knew; what he needed to know; and why he couldn't help thinking a connection between this crime and the Café Amaretto killings existed. The only thing certain: that for the second time in one week, people had died at the hands of a madman in a city that usually didn't breed madness.

Questions would be asked: How could two mass killings occur? Could they have been prevented? It was human nature to ask *why*. Another even more frightening question: What if there was no reason? What if Tavell and Benson were normal everyday people just like everyone they'd interviewed had attested? What then?

Were they dealing with serial mass killings or terrorists? Or just something in the air? Bad luck, maybe? Could these have been created by circumstances they were yet to discover? The last question, truly the most frightening when, after all these years, O'Grady thought he'd seen everything evil. Was this a *new* evil?

CHAPTER 11

KENDALL FELT SICK TO HER stomach. Initially, she'd thought the fire was an accident, but already early news coverage had speculated it was another mass killing. How could anyone kill innocent, elderly people? It was just too horrible.

What made her so upset now was the predicament suddenly facing her.

That darn article she'd written on the Café Amaretto killings, had, in the minds of news editors, made her some kind of expert in mass killings. Her, of all people! If it didn't make her feel sick every time she thought about it, she would find it amusing.

After she'd interviewed Beverley, the survivor from Café Amaretto, a management attorney had weaseled his way in. All other news agencies were forced to pay a sizeable figure to speak to Beverley, except for Kendall. Beverley had taken a real liking to her and had been happy to speak to her again, feeless. Turned out, Beverley's vantage point had been the best to literally see everything, making her a valuable witness. She'd become the face of the surviving victims.

Her tear-streaked appearance, complete with running mascara, was center stage on two morning shows—one of them syndicated—and several evening current affairs programs. Only yesterday, she'd seen a *Sixty Minutes* commercial with Beverley seated on the very lounge that just over a week ago Kendall had sat sipping coffee. In print media, Kendall's articles had become the main source material for other media outlets.

The article fee was financially welcome. The big thing: it had put her in demand, too and given her a *name*. The downside: the appalling violence still sickened her. The last thing she really needed was to interview the relatives of these poor old people who'd burned to death. Kendall couldn't imagine a worse way to die.

It crossed her mind she should call her therapist. Four years ago, she'd left his offices, uncertain whether she could go forward without the weekly sessions. He'd given her tools to deal with her fears. She was always afraid, though, that one day they simply wouldn't work.

"It happened a long time ago," Dr. Shepherd had repeated to her that last day. "Your past can only hurt you if you allow it into your present and your future."

"I know," she'd said, thinking it sounded perfectly simple. It would be, if she could control her dreams. When she thought about the night her mother died, she still shuddered. Once the memories flooded into her mind, it didn't matter how many times she told herself she was safe, that they couldn't hurt her. Somehow, she still found herself gasping for breath.

Dr. Shepherd had told her witnessing violence at a young age could rewire your brain permanently. He and Kendall had worked hard to remove the wiring. She would never believe she could ever comfortably listen to other people's descriptions of terror touching their lives. She identified too much with them. She knew exactly how it felt to *know* you were going to die, *know* it in your blood, and then survive.

With all this, she would be tested, had already been tested, and she couldn't allow her mind to fully travel back to that night. Right now, she needed to find her way around hearing the details of these killings. Listening to Beverley had caused the sleepless nights to start all over again. She needed to use Dr. Shepherd's tools.

As long as she focused on writing the story, pretended it was just a fictional story, she was okay. Later, the words and images conjured would haunt her. Follow her into her dreams. Then it was *her* facing a man with an axe or a gun or a knife or trapped in a burning building. *Her* waking up screaming.

Kendall thought, after another sleepless night, she might be better digging around a little into the past of the killer Benito Tavell. Having already completed her Internet and social media searches, she had become increasingly frustrated. Tavell didn't have much of an electronic footprint and his family wasn't talking to the media.

A friend of the Tavell family had made a formal announcement on their behalf. With people already labeling the fire a terrorist attack, they chose not to discuss their son now or in the near future. The friend read from a statement simply expressing the family's sorrow at the innocent deaths and proclaiming the idea as ridiculous that their son was associated with terrorism.

Unfortunately, the media camped out on their doorstep weren't going to allow them that time. Kendall had driven past their home in the hope she would have the same luck she'd had with Beverley, but the street was so overrun with vans and journalists, she could barely squeeze by.

While consuming the breaking news reports, what struck her were the witness descriptions of the event. How methodical Tavell had been in setting fire to different rooms, leaving little chance of the fire being extinguished quickly. The characterization of Tavell by his friends was odd—his quiet and well-mannered demeanor and dedication to the residents of the home.

Why revolved in her head, and she wasn't certain she wanted the answer. Frustratingly, she still needed this commission. A sneaking thought, too— maybe these events crossed her path to help her *overcome* her past. Whether she wanted to or not, she would need to find a way into this story.

An idea suddenly sprang to mind. Quickly she began to type on the keyboard. What she discovered shocked her. In fact, she couldn't believe her eyes.

CHAPTER 12

YOU23 SCANNED THE SYSTEM. HE'D noticed a small discrepancy during the last mission. It hadn't affected the outcome, but he wanted to understand what had happened. That was his nature.

He rolled back the video and bookmarked it for Boss17. The mission had gone well. He was impressed by how well Boss17's plans had come to fruition. When Boss17 had first explained the steps they would take to create this amazing future, You23 was skeptical. It seemed like something out of a science fiction film. But Boss17 had done it, all right, just as he'd promised.

This made You23 even more determined to perform at his best. If Boss17 could do this, then maybe his vision for the world, for You23's own future, could really happen. That was really something to ponder.

You23 had worked on this coding for six months. Once he'd discovered the baseline, the rest had slowly come together. They were still in uncharted territory, but that was the fun of it. He was curious when they would reveal their purpose to the world. That was the plan, wasn't it? Two missions completed without a hitch. Now they had something exciting to share.

Boss17 had told him yesterday, when he'd asked the question of when: "Everything needs to be perfect. We must be sure they understand the message."

Boss17 gave him this opportunity when no one else had cared, so if

Boss17 wanted to wait, then who was he to argue. If not for Boss17, he'd still be alone, ignored, still on the street, and treated like a criminal. His great crime being what? That he was different.

Boss17 had told him, repeatedly, he was a genius. Those words of praise made him want to try harder. Nobody had ever told him he was good at anything. Nobody had ever treated him with such respect and kindness. You23 often wondered if it was good luck or something else like fate that brought them together. His skill and Boss17's vision seemed so perfectly matched.

The voices had gone, too. Like a miracle, somehow, Boss17 made them go away. Now all he remembered of before was the darkness in the cave of his mind, filled with what felt like a virus eating at his thoughts.

This new drug of Boss17's had not only removed the voices, it had allowed You23's true voice to shine through. He was a new man at the ripe age of twenty-two. And he was beginning to enjoy this game. Even the nickname bestowed upon him —You23— felt right. *Yes,* right was the word.

Initially, it had seemed strange and awkward, especially the time he'd forgotten his name and signed a report with his *real* name. The only time he'd seen Boss17 angry was then. His face had turned red.

"Anonymity is the key. Don't you understand? That was *just* stupid." He'd grasped You23's shoulders and looked deep into his eyes, like he saw inside his soul. Then he seemed to catch himself, and calm down. He'd whispered, "This is an important mission. We must stay straight and true if we're to change the world. Straight and true."

After raising his voice and slamming the table moments before, Boss17's sudden composure and quiet manner seemed a little frightening.

Eventually, You23 realized, it was his fault entirely that he'd angered Boss17. He needed to be more careful. He couldn't blame him for becoming annoyed, when he'd clearly broken the rules. He was stupid. Sometimes his brain didn't work properly. Anonymity was important. He knew that. Had it drummed into him from day one. His name was You23. His old name, gone.

Sometimes before he fell asleep, he heard the words, *straight and true,* repeat in his head like they were on a broken loop. The words made him feel complete; they filled the space where the voices once lived.

You23 turned back to his screen. He'd spent the past fourteen hours staring at it, looking for another candidate. It wasn't easy to find the right one. He was determined, though. He needed to please Boss17.

First, their records needed to be in the system. Then they had to live within proximity of their base. He loved that term, too—base—it made this sound like an online game. The problem, usually, came down to the geographic. Boss17 was particular. He'd found plenty elsewhere, but once they'd begun, there was *to be no compromise*. Another Boss17 catch phrase: *there is to be no compromise*. He liked those words, too.

He swigged a Coke direct from the bottle—his fourth today—as he watched and waited. The program worm, a clever unseen digital spy, continued to burrow through the medical databases, searching through tens of thousands of records.

Boss17 had told him to sit there until he found something. Why suddenly an urgent deadline, he hadn't had the courage to ask. Seeing Boss17 annoyed once was enough. It wasn't so much he was afraid, it was disappointing his benefactor he cared about more than anything.

He was grateful, too, to be on *this* side of the program. He'd realized early on, he would be a perfect candidate. He had all the criteria they needed. Whether Boss17 knew this, he couldn't tell.

So if Boss17 told him to stay here until he found a candidate, then that's what he would do. If it took three days, he would sit here for three days.

A *ping* erupted from the computer, startling him from his thoughts. You23 reached out and grabbed the edge of the desk, then pulled his chair in. He leaned into the screen and began to read. It took him a minute to take in the full report. He smiled. Boss17 would be pleased.

They had another candidate. A woman. She filled all the criteria, including the ever vital geographic. A thrill ran through him as he anticipated sharing the news with Boss17. He'd found her quicker than the other two.

Yes, Boss17 *would* be pleased. She was perfect.

CHAPTER 13

FOR THE UMPTEENTH TIME, KENDALL told herself she should drop this article. But she had an angle. If she pulled it off, the story might be good enough for a chance at national, if not global, syndication, meaning long-term residual payments.

She still had bills to pay, and no way she'd admit that to her brother Marcus that after all these years freelancing she still couldn't make ends meet. Sometimes as she stared at her bills, her brother's voice would enter her head. *Why don't you get a proper job? At a magazine or a newspaper or one of those big Internet website companies.*

He was right, too. She *should* get a permanent, on-staff job somewhere, but the idea of freelancing had always appealed. This was just a hump period, the industry in flux with online content taking over and all the magazine closures. That was all. She just had to juggle her finances and ride this little wave she'd managed to climb aboard. Her foot was in the door. She simply needed to keep it there long enough to make an impression on a few of the larger magazine's editors.

Her Google search had turned up something interesting. In 2012, a news outlet created a website documenting the past twenty years of mass killings across the country. The site had a built-in search facility using several criteria: type of weapon used; numbers killed; and the murderers' relationship to the victims. The results could be shown as a list or a geographical map. The two most recent mass murder sites in their city,

Café Amaretto and the Kenworth Home, were already loaded into the database.

That wasn't the surprise for Kendall. Goose bumps rose on her arms about something else. The latest two mass killing weren't the only two events in the Danbridge city area.

In 1995, a massacre had also occurred here. With this information, and the location, she Googled the twentieth century crime. Of course, the two most recent massacres featured prominently on the first few pages. Buried way back on the third page at the very bottom, though, was another entry. This article was about a mass killing that had occurred just on the city limits. Kendall supposed that *might* explain why nobody had put it together with these two. Or it could be the crime was just too long ago. Most likely it was because, technically, it wasn't a mass killing.

Only three people had died on the scene. She'd learned from the website a mass killing was only considered a mass killing after four deaths. In the case of the 1995 killing, one of the victims died months later after slipping into a coma following the event. He became the fourth victim. Probably by then, his death wasn't as newsworthy.

Twenty years ago, Lyall Wright drove through a fast food drive-thru and, apparently, was kept waiting longer than he thought reasonable. He entered the restaurant and when the manager asked him to leave, something snapped in him. He pulled out a gun and killed, indiscriminately, a server behind the counter and the manager. Turning on the customers, he seriously injured three and killed another employee, before killing himself. Two teenage workers died, along with the twenty-eight-year-old manager, then months later the customer who'd been in a coma.

The same two photos of grieving families accompanied the articles Kendall read. Particularly poignant was the portrait of one victim's family. The boy was the sixteen-year-old only child of a widower. Imagine losing your only child and being left with nothing.

Kendall's thoughts turned to that night, when she also lost so much. She shook the thought away and continued to read through the heartbreaking interviews with survivors and family members of the victims.

This could definitely be a unique angle, *if* she could bring herself to explore it. A prickle crawled up her spine, not only because again she would face her demons, but this raised a seriously frightening question: How could three mass murders occur in one city?

She imagined she could pitch several articles, all with slightly varied slants for different media outlets. This one story could end up providing her with a good buffer against the current lack of work.

Could she do it?

If you want to eat, Kendall, you'll do it.

She simply had no choice in the matter. The nightmares would come, that she knew. She would just have to find a way to deal with them.

CHAPTER 14

THE INTERVIEWS WITH THE RELATIVES of those killed in the 1995 murders turned out to be nothing like Kendall's interview with Beverley Sanderson.

With twenty years having passed, the people involved, especially the parents of the three murdered employees, had adjusted somewhat to a life without their loved ones. Although, Kendall noted a pale, washed-out feel to them, as though some of their life energy had leaked away over the years. They talked of the day they'd lost so much as though it were yesterday, as if they'd just kissed their loved one goodbye, unknowingly, for the last time.

The odd thing was they all told Kendall how relieved they felt talking about it again. It had been years since anybody had wanted to listen again. The world had moved on. They had not.

The thought her own grief might remain with her for decades was a sobering thought. She'd really believed one day she would wake up and it would have slipped into her past, that she could face the future without darkness in her heart.

The *Falling Down* Murders—named for the scene in the early nineties Michael Douglas film of that name, where Douglas's character pulls out a semi-automatic in a fast food restaurant—had caused one divorce, one heart attack, and turned innocent people's lives into nightmares. The widow, who had lost her daughter Jennifer, told Kendall how the light in her life was extinguished that day. Jennifer had the misfortune to be cleaning the table nearest the counter.

"An engineer, that's what she intended to be." A solitary tear rolled down Jennifer's mother's cheek. "It was only a part-time job to help us with her tuition fees. Such a good girl."

John, who was there alone, simply eating his lunch—had just started a new job. He didn't die instantly, but two days later, his wife turned off his life-support.

Charlie McKinley was the employee who served Lyall Wright at the drive-thru window. He was the employee who'd forgotten he'd directed Wright to wait in the parking lot while his order was filled. An easy mistake that cost four lives. Five, if you counted the killer.

Kendall had managed to locate a witness quoted in the old news article. She was no Beverley, possessing no joy at being the center of attention. Now in her sixties, the woman talked of taking her family to the restaurant as a treat. Her kids, now grown, loved the burgers. Two decades later, neither of them would eat in a Burger Boys' restaurant. Kendall could identify with that. Avoiding reminders was normal.

The woman openly wept as she talked of the sheer fear when Wright brandished a gun and began firing; her first thoughts, to put herself between him and her children. She talked of the vividness of the red of the blood, the feelings of knowing she would die, that her children would die, and that she had no way to prevent it.

This time Kendall did remember to ask each person she interviewed the question she'd forgotten to ask Beverley: *"How did you live with what happened that day? How did you come to terms with it?"*

The most impressive answer came from Charlie McKinley's father, Doug. He shared that after the years it took for the shock and depression to wear away—he called it "the erosion of heartbreak"—he'd gone on to do his own research on the event. Doug told her he wanted to try to understand how it could happen. As part of the healing process, he felt a need to discover what had lived inside Wright's brain to cause him to snap and inflict such violence. His hypothesis was fascinating.

According to McKinley, Wright had been on medication, an early version of Prozac. This drug fell into a group labeled as SSRIs—selective serotonin reuptake inhibitor—an umbrella term for drugs most commonly used as anti-depressants.

He spoke animatedly about his research. "I saw a link between SSRIs and mass murderers. So I spent more than a decade after Charlie died trying to motivate the government to look more closely into the idea these drugs could be the cause of some of these random killings."

A statistical analyst before his retirement, his research sounded thorough and somewhat convincing to Kendall. Still, he'd taken quite a leap. She wasn't surprised to learn he'd gotten little acceptance of his theory.

"Take it." The gray-haired, bear-of-a-man pushed the file across the table toward her. "Please, look through it. It's important. Maybe there's a story in there for you. I couldn't get anyone to listen, but maybe now with these latest…"

Doug McKinley's voice trailed off; his mind had wandered away. A pained look came into his eyes, replacing the enthusiasm glowing there only a moment before. Kendall could imagine the tender memories these latest events had dredged up for the poor man, whose drawn, weathered face spoke to years of anguish. She didn't need to ask how he survived such a great loss, his enthusiasm for his research, his obvious salvation.

"I lost my wife Gloria to cancer three years before. She was only forty-two. Charlie came along the year after we married. Gloria couldn't have any more children. So Charlie was our world, my world after Gloria." He smiled at clearly pleasant memories.

Then his brows knitted as dark lines formed across his forehead.

"That man took my son. And I'd already lost Gloria. Statistically, that's a lot of bad luck. Too much death. It took years to fight my way back, to not feel bitter that this *thing* had happened to me. I wished every day that I'd died instead. You can't imagine. The doctors actually put me on similar drugs to Wright. Anti-depressants. The answer to everything."

A wad of sadness stuck in Kendall's throat. This was the reason she avoided these types of interviews. She *could* imagine. She knew exactly how it felt to lose someone, the incredible pain, the days that felt longer than a year. The nights, the very dark nights, where you felt as though you could crawl up the walls, pains in your chest so deep it felt like a stabbing knife.

She wanted to say that to him; she even thought to apologize for reminding him of something he probably wanted to forget. Kendall didn't, though; she had a job to do. As she listened to his voice cracking with emotion, she knew this was going to make for a great story. She hated herself for thinking it, and calmed herself by repeating: *a girl's gotta eat.* Thinking about the story and not thinking about emotions his words created helped.

The introduction for the article formed in her mind:

Twenty years later, still visibly shaken, Doug McKinley faces each day with trepidation. He had lived in a world of numbers, but when your number is up...

No, no she'd have to reword that, but something like that. A play on numbers fitted. Doug McKinley continued, drawing her attention back. She'd work on the words later.

"I lost myself in my work and, yes, you can do that with figures. For a time, they filled my mind and blocked out the pain. The numbers and the drugs worked. As the years wore on, I came to see that, statistically speaking, I should count my blessings for having had those two in my life. Gloria and Charlie. I decided to live the rest of my life in their honor. So every day I wake up and say to them, 'I live for you today.' No matter how hard some days and nights are, I work hard to keep my promise."

For the second time since she'd met Doug McKinley, Kendall felt tears at the corners of her eyes. She reached up and dabbed at the side of her face with the back of a knuckle.

"That's beautiful and very brave, Mr. McKinley."

He smiled at Kendall, a trembling smile that told every moment of those twenty years of heartache. Then he gathered himself, his pale blue eyes igniting with fire, as he tapped the manila folder sitting on the table between them. His SSRI research notes.

"These. You think you can use them? I sent them to the newspapers, many newspapers, but they did nothing. They just wanted the gory details of Charlie's death and how I felt about that. As if that isn't the stupidest question to ask. How did they think I felt?"

He leaned forward and lowered his voice as though the walls were bugged.

"That's what sells newspapers, you know. Answers to stupid questions and death and violence. Those pharmaceutical companies, well, they advertise in those papers, don't they? They're not going to run negative stories about their customers, are they? Even if people are dying because of these drugs."

Kendall nodded to assure him she was on his side, even though she'd been about to ask one of those stupid questions: *How do you feel all these years later?*

"Of course, I'll read them. I'm a freelance journalist. I don't technically work for a newspaper. In this case, I do have a specific brief. I'm sorry, but I have to pretty much stick to it."

McKinley frowned, and Kendall quickly added, "But if there's something I can fashion into a story *and* I can find someone wanting to publish, then, *absolutely*, I'll write an article."

Even as she spoke the words, Kendall knew it wasn't going to happen. She couldn't afford to write stories on spec—unless she was desperate. If she put time into an article, even research, she needed to know a paycheck waited at the end. *This* story he was asking her to write would take a lot of research and probably pay no better than a health article on the latest diet she *could* sell.

Kendall felt compelled to share her secret with Doug as a consolation.

"Don't tell anyone, I take anti-depressants myself. I had no idea of the dangers of my little pick-me-ups."

"They're very dangerous. You definitely need to read this."

Doug McKinley picked up the folder and handed it to her. It seemed to be his way of saying the interview was over. She had enough details anyway. Charlie's death and this interview would probably only feature in a paragraph or two. If that.

Kendall gathered her bag and notebook and took the folder from his outstretched hand. She stood there a moment, holding the bulky dossier to her chest as though it was extremely valuable. She didn't want Doug McKinley to have the slightest inkling she probably wouldn't read it. It wasn't just time but her emotions she needed to protect.

"I know you'll do the right thing." He patted her arm. His touch felt firm as though he were attempting to press his fervor through her skin.

"I'll try Mr. McKinley."

"Call me, Doug. *Please.* You get in touch if you need anything else, won't you? I'm always here. These latest murders, they're terrible." He looked down and shook his head.

"Maybe if they look into this old case and view it with these new ones, something good might come of it. Yes, maybe something positive."

"Yes, yes, of course. It's an ill wind, isn't it?" Kendall offered, immediately wishing she hadn't. It seemed too flippant a thing to say. Doug, seeming so thrilled she held his folder, didn't seem to notice.

Doug McKinley walked her to the door and thanked her again almost too profusely. She barely noticed. Kendall was already thinking she would change the article's opening sentence:

Twenty years later, still visibly shaken, Doug McKinley faces each day with trepidation. He also lives in a world alone, looking for answers that will probably never add up.

Yes, that would be a good opening. She could include a sentence on his research. If she tailored it so there was some ambiguity in his facts—make it sound less fanatical—then it might get past the outlet's lawyers and keep the newspaper's advertisers happy. Nobody offended meant more chance of it running in full and, for Kendall, return contracts.

This article had turned into a strange journey. As much as she welcomed the work, she was hankering to get back to her lollypop no-brainer articles. Even this meeting had brought her too close to her own sad memories. Doug McKinley may have found his way around grief, but she still felt on shaky ground.

Since this had all started, everything felt a little out of control. Kendall wondered where the story would take her next. She hoped back to the tried and true.

She heard the door close behind her as she walked toward her car. Words slipped through her mind. Words for the article. Words for the dark feelings stirring inside her. Words to describe how she felt, forced to address her past so unexpectedly. *Ironic* sprung to mind.

If *she* were asked to describe her feelings by some journalist asking *that* "stupid" question—*How does it feel?*—she would answer with one word.

"Dangerous."

CHAPTER 15

KATE WILKER HAD SAT AT the family gathering, listening to this crap for almost twenty minutes. In fact, she felt she'd listened to crap for most of her twelve-year marriage to *Idiot Boy* Randall.

That's how she thought of him these days. Not Randall, the man she'd married when she was young and reckless, but Idiot Boy who was now her torturer-by-stupidity.

Young-and-reckless and desperate-to-escape-your-parents is not a good basis for marriage. How long had it taken her to realize she'd made a catastrophic mistake? Oh, about twelve months. What did she do? Silly, little twenty-two-year old she was. Did she go back to her parents? Did she do what a couple of sensible friends had done? Get a divorce?

No. no. Nooo. Kate, being stubborn Kate, refused to admit defeat. She knew her parents would rub it in, as they always did when she screwed up. So she decided if they made a couple of babies it would give her something to do. Then it'd all turn into a wonderful fairytale and they'd live happily ever after.

So, along came Joseph, then Samantha, and because Idiot Boy decided he liked having children (Who wouldn't when you don't have to do any of the work involved?) he convinced her one more kid would seal the deal.

Well, it didn't.

In fact, it made everything three times as bad. Ten times as bad. One hundred times as bad. No scale was large enough to measure it, to weigh the depths of her disenchantment with her lot in marriage.

Post-natal depression. That's what they'd called her feelings. *Discovering reality* she called them. The doctors had told her it might take years for the feelings to subside, for the hormones to settle back to normal.

The tablets they'd given her did take the edge off, but they also made her feel sluggish and she couldn't sleep, which made her depressed, as well. So, they upped the quantities. It was like a merry-go-round with no way to get off.

How many of these tedious family birthday parties had she endured?

Let's see, she thought, as she sat at the dining table, enveloped in over-loud chatter with kids climbing over adults as if being a parent meant you were some kind of swing set.

This gathering was to celebrate one of *his* brother's kid's birthdays. She thought the kid was turning six. She couldn't really remember, there were so many of them. She added up *his* family members, including nephews and nieces, his parents and their own kids. Twenty birthdays. Then she calculated the math of the twelve years they'd been married, times the birthdays. Two hundred of these she'd endured so far, and that didn't include Christmas, Thanksgiving, and Easter.

She thought forward to when the next generation grew up and married. There would be even more birthdays to attend. Kate was growing suicidal just thinking about it.

Her sister-in-law, Annette, sat to her right at the *adult's* table; they were seated like airline cattle-class around a dining area meant to accommodate five fewer people. The kids, seated at a separate table, happily shouted at each other and wrestled with napkins. No doubt, as usual, they were creating a god-awful mess.

In the middle of the table, amid the coffee cups, lay a spread of cookies and cake. Kate had already eaten more than she should just to fill the time. Her head throbbed with sugar overload. And something else she couldn't quite put her finger on.

"So the kids have grown," said her sister-in-law, Annette.

Of course they've grown. That's their job. They grow.

She was tempted to speak her thoughts, instead of her reply: "Yes, where does the time go?"

The conversations she endured at these things! Ever since she'd left the shopping mall an hour ago, after having coffee with her friend Wendy, she'd felt a building buzz in her head. She'd put it down to the thought of sitting here with *them*.

The weather, *buzz-buzz*.

The kids and their activities at school, *buzz-buzz*.

The baseball score, *buzz-buzz*.

That was all Kate heard. Just a crap-load of words and a wall of noise growing ever louder until it became an itch inside her brain she couldn't scratch.

Buzz-buzz. Blah-blah.

She'd taken an extra Prozac this morning as fortification against the relatives and her husband, who grew even more intolerable around his family. She wondered if this buzzing noise was some kind of adverse side effect from taking too many pills. The doctor had upped her dosage a few months back when she'd admitted to feeling overwhelmed.

Lately, she'd gotten to thinking what the doctor really needed to prescribe was for her to get away from Idiot Boy. Then she wouldn't need the drugs anymore. She could get high on life.

She felt a twang in her head like something had burst. Instantly the buzz grew into a brain-numbing pain akin to someone digging around in her head with a needle.

Kate scanned the table, staring at her in-laws merrily chatting, sipping and eating, eating and sipping. She felt increasingly distanced from them as though she were inside a bubble travelling backward, an alien observing strange earth creatures.

One of the children ran past and bumped her elbow just as she raised her coffee cup to her lips. Coffee sloshed into her lap. When she looked down, light brown spots colored her cream skirt.

Stupidly-inane-Annette immediately grabbed a glass of water from the table, plunged in her napkin, and dabbed the cloth over the brown marks as though she was killing a bug. Then she grabbed the edge of Kate's skirt and examined her handiwork.

"It's okay." Kate desperately wanted her sister-in-law to just let go of her skirt.

"No, I don't mind, really. Let's see if I can get it out. It might stain permanently otherwise."

She called to Kate's other sister-in-law, My-kids-are-better-than-yours, and said, "Do you have any soda water, Helen? Kate's spilled some coffee on herself."

She spilled coffee on herself! Right, it couldn't conceivably be one of their precious little darlings, could it? Kate glowered at Annette, who was far too busy dabbing and pulling at Kate's skirt to notice. Her sister-in-law's actions made her headache worse. She needed to make her stop.

Kate slowly lowered her palm over Annette's hand and clasped it tight. She leaned in, until only inches separated her lips from her sister-in-law's ear, and whispered through gritted teeth, "Annette, it's *okay*. Would you please take your hands off me? *Please.*"

Annette's assured expression faltered. Her hands, so busy seconds before, retreated to rest in her lap like little, scavenging crabs scurrying back under shelter.

"I was only trying to help. Are you all right, Kate? You look tired."

Kate stared at her. She would have answered, but white noise now filled her mind, and she couldn't find the words. Then it came to her. She didn't need the words because none of this mattered.

Kate stood, ignoring Annette's continued questioning about her wellbeing, and walked around the table and out of the room. In the hall outside, three of her nephews rumbled past her, jostling each other. One bumped her again as he went by.

"Sorry, Aunty Kate."

You will be.

She felt a smile spread across her lips. This was a feeling she liked.

She moved to the front door, pulling it open. The moment she stepped into the sunlight, she was hit by a powerful feeling of crossing an imaginary threshold. Behind, inside the house, the noise of *them* traveled to her. The chatter over nothing. The laughter at unfunny quips. The faux arguments on politics, which went nowhere. With each footstep down the short set of stairs and along the pathway to the drive, her mind began to clear. The gnawing buzz faded, leaving behind a beautiful golden peace.

Today was the day she would step off the treadmill. Today was the day she would make a stand. One thing she'd learned over these wasted years of marriage, it was that actions speak louder than words. Kate was about to get loud.

CHAPTER 16

IDIOT BOY'S GREATEST FEAR WAS being car-jacked. Thanks to this, a gun was always stowed in the glove compartment. Twice a year he'd take Kate to a practice range to "brush up on her skills."

Kate climbed into the passenger seat, then unlocked and opened the compartment. It was her job to keep the compartment key safe while he drove, because he figured a car-jacker would go for him first. Somehow, she would access the gun and save the day. Or night.

The revolver sat nestled in a soft cloth bag, innocuous and innocent. You could mistake it for nothing more than a pouch for storing coupons and spare change.

Pulling the weapon from its concealment, she wrapped her hand around the barrel. It felt surprisingly good and moral in her palm. The buzzing had returned, and she felt odd like her body didn't belong to her anymore. Kate pulled down the visor, flipping open the cover of the fixed mirror to stare at a woman she didn't recognize. This person sported gray roots, several weeks overdue for a color; a sallow face, creased as though she'd just awoken from a bad sleep; and blank eyes, underlined by dark semi-circles. This poor creature was a lost ghost. How had this happened? When did she become this woman?

She pushed up the visor, thinking what to do next.

"A necessary evil," said the voice in her head. She knew this voice. Liked this voice. Wanted to please this voice. Whose voice it was she didn't know.

Now she thought about it, she didn't care. The voice was right. This felt like a necessary evil. In fact, evil was the wrong word. *Life changing*, more accurate.

The words, *straight and true*, circled in her mind.

Her hand folded over the gun. Instantly, it felt like an extension of her body. She pushed on the car door; it squealed as though excited, as if the door were screaming, *yes!* The sound, tenfold louder than when she'd entered the car; the world, suddenly amplified. Kate touched a hand to her ear, now aching as though infected.

Half way up the path, she heard them inside—still laughing, still drinking their coffee, still prattling about inconsequential minutia (she could insert manure for minutia—*manuritia*—and it would be more apt).

The aqua-green door loomed. Standing before it, she experienced a momentary feeling of being a shrunken Alice in Wonderland after swallowing the *drink me* potion. Then the awareness of the gun in her hand grew her back bigger than her normal size, like Alice with the *eat me* cookie.

Kate watched as her hand reached out toward the barrier—that's how she thought of the door, as a barrier to her mission. Her shoulder pushed into it as though her body was possessed of its own mind, she merely a passenger.

The barrier swung open. Inside the voices from the dining room flew at her like marauding demons. The sound assaulted not just her ears but her entire body. Her index finger tingled as she nestled it into the trigger, as though it were the most natural thing in the world: to bring a gun to a family gathering.

Three steps forward to the right would take her to the living room. Through there, she could enter via the rear of the dining room. Kate paused, thinking it through. *No, not that way first.* Her mission required more of her than randomly shooting at these people. There were criteria.

Four. She must take four.

So Kate turned left into the hall, toward the bedrooms and a bathroom. From one of the bedrooms came the sound of giggling and children's voices. Seven more steps and she stood outside Helen and her husband's bedroom. The door stood ajar. With her shoulder, she nudged it open wider. Empty. Perfectly tidy like a just cleaned hotel room.

The click of the latch, as she pulled the door closed sounded freakishly loud, whirring like a buzz saw, echoing inside her head. She pushed the side of the gun barrel to her temple. The coolness felt good against her aching skull.

Damn, the noise. It burned.

Turning slowly, she moved to the closed door of the next room. She listened. Her nephews and nieces were behind that door. From the voices, it was nine-year-old Isabelle, along with Adriana, ten, and Kelten.

Kelten! Helen's twelve-year-old son. They had another boy, too. Oscane.

Really? Oscane?

Her neck burned with a dull throb. The only thing seeming to help was stretching. She elongated the muscles as far as she could to the left until her ear almost touched her shoulder. Then back as far again to the right. Something cold and small crawled through her spine. Her entire body shivered.

She leaned forward and pushed open the door, careful to keep the gun at her side so the children wouldn't be alerted. After all, it wasn't their fault. Only a twist of fate found them born into this family to be here on this day.

The door opened to reveal her two nieces and nephew avidly viewing something on an iPad. Kelten sat between the two girls. They all giggled at a YouTube video playing at full volume. Didn't her sister-in-law know pedophiles lurked on sites advertised there? The two girls looked up, eyes wide and innocent. Kelten continued to stare at the screen.

"Aunty Kate," said Adriana, "come look at this video. Sooo funny. There's a dog. And the man won't give it bacon, and the dog has a human voice. It's really good. Come see."

Yes, that would work. Their minds occupied, unaware.

Kate walked over to stand behind the three.

"Make it go back, to the beginning, Kelten," said Adriana, "so Aunty Kate can see."

"It's really, really funny," added Isabelle, pleading in her voice, as though her aunt's silence meant Kate might leave before viewing the all-important video.

Kelten began the video again, and the three children's heads bowed collectively to stare at the screen.

The voice in Kate's head exploded, the volume turned up to screaming-jet decibels. Relentless waves of compelling words crashed inside her mind. *You will. You will. You will.*

She understood what she had to do as though it was something she'd known all her life, as if it were the most important thing she would ever *do* in her life.

Slowly Kate lifted the gun and moved the barrel to rest just an inch behind Kelten's head. She noticed a cute, little wave in his tousled, brown hair; the way it curled at the nape of his neck like a question mark.

What came next would be just a simple movement—the pulling of the trigger.

Then Adriana saw the gun.

"What are you doing, Aunty Kate? Is that a toy gun?"

Kate didn't answer, and the child must have suddenly grasped this was no toy. This was no game.

Adriana shouted, "No, Aunty Kate. No. Please, nooo. Please. Please."

Kelten suddenly swung about to look at his aunt. His eyes widened as he faced the gun, inches away. Instantly his hands shot upward to cover his head. He cowered for a moment, then must have thought better of it, scooting on his bottom away to the other side of the room, his stare never leaving the gun.

Isabelle had turned, as well. Unalarmed, missing that it wasn't a game, she said: "Aunty Kate? Can I have a turn? I want to be the baddy next."

Kate eyed the little girl, so sweet, so innocent. Everything froze. The veil of gray lifted from Kate's eyes, her thoughts suddenly wild: *What am I doing? Good God, what am I thinking of doing? Run away, children, while you can.* She wanted to address little Isabelle: *You don't want to be this baddy, baby. I can't stop, now I've started. Now I have the gun.*

Her neck pulsed with a pressure ready to explode. If a gauge were in there, the needle now neared the danger zone. She wanted to put down the gun. She wanted to not hurt the children.

Then the moment of lucidity passed, and all Kate felt was the ache in her neck. It made her want to tear at her skin, excise the muscle or tendon or whatever it was twisting away inside.

Adriana rose to her feet.

"Please, p-p-leeesse, don't hurt us … Aunty Kate." Her cheeks were wet with tears. Snot ran from her nose and dripped from her chin. Her shoulders heaved as she spoke, each word a convulsion of her small body.

The voice was insistent.

Don't hesitate. Move. Straight and true. Mooove!

She felt merely carried along, like a silent hand pushed at her. Fulfill the mission. Please the voice. That was all she wanted in the world.

Kate's eyes narrowed as she held out the gun and aimed at the nearest child, Isabelle.

"Sorry," she wished to say, because she felt she should. Her voice wasn't there, and she knew what needed to be done.

Her finger nuzzled into the trigger, the muscles tensing against the metal. She began to pull.

Another voice entered the room. A shout from the door, "Oh, my, God. What are you—?"

Kate wheeled to face Idiot Boy's brother, Bill. She'd always wondered if she'd met and married Bill instead, would everything have turned out fine. Now he was simply an obstacle to the mission.

Bill wavered at the door taking in the scene. All three children cowering before Kate, with the gun pointed at Isabelle. Bill didn't seem to think; he charged at Kate. But too late. His hesitation, his downfall, for it gave her time to swing the gun, aim, and fire.

The bullet struck his upper body to the right. A surprisingly small groan escaped his lips. As though he'd hit an invisible wall, he stopped and looked down at his chest. His right hand moved to the wound. When he pulled it away and held it up, his fingers were coated in thick blood. He stared for a moment, then looked back at Kate, his eyes saying so many things.

I can't believe this.

I'm scared.

I misjudged you.

In fact, Kate was certain he knew they'd misjudged her. That was definitely in his eyes. They'd all misjudged her. Soon everyone would learn that.

Everything next happened in seconds. As though she'd fired a starter gun, to begin a chaotic race for the door. The children screamed as they ran like it was fright night. Adriana led them out, followed by Isabelle, the two disappearing into the hall. Kelten stopped at his father, bawling and pulling at his arms to follow them.

"Dad? Daaad. Come—." Bill looked down at the boy, pushing him behind his body.

"Run," his father implored. A last glance at his dad and the boy was gone.

Bill turned to escape, but his injury slowed him. Kate felt a smile touch her lips. She'd used the few seconds to take better aim. The gun now leveled at his head.

The side of his skull appeared to explode even before she'd pulled the trigger. Bill crumpled to the ground as though he were a balloon character, all the air escaped from his legs.

Dead as dead.

One down, three to go.

Through the walls, a clamor of chaos erupted from the dining room. Chairs falling, screams, frightened voices, and the sound of running feet. Kate needed to be quick. She stepped over Bill's body, pausing to look down at her handiwork. When she looked up again, Stupidly-inane, Annette filled the doorway, her mouth round and open. For the first time in a long time, the woman had nothing to say.

It took only one shot to stop those lips from ever moving again. One moment she was there, hand stuffed into her mouth, eyes wider than a cake plate; the next she was on the floor with her husband, face-first in the carpet.

How many bullets had she used?

Two for Bill. One for Annette. Three.

They'd be waiting for her, she guessed. She reached inside her pocket, feeling around for the bullets. She needed to hurry. She *needed* two more. Needed a point to be made. A message to send.

Kate reloaded the extra bullets as she moved past the bodies. Enough bullets to finish the mission. Annette stared up at the ceiling, her eyes empty, her mouth open as though there was one last dumb thing she wanted to say. Bill lay on his side, buckled over, blood still pulsing from the gaping black hole in his head.

Kate swung through the door into the hall. And there he was at the far end. Idiot Boy, himself. Next to him, Ellen, her other sister-in-law. This one she actually liked—Adriana was *her* kid. She'd rather take others more deserving, but she needed the four. From the noises of movement from the rest of the house, she knew her targets were escaping, that time and her advantage were evaporating by the second.

Just as the man who stood before her had taught her, Kate clasped the gun in both hands, put her weight a little forward, and took careful aim. "A gun isn't for playing with," he'd told her.

No, it wasn't. And she wasn't playing.

Both Ellen and Idiot Boy inhaled a sharp breath. Ellen raised her hands in the air, and in a surprisingly calm voice said, "Kate, what's happening? Are Bill and Annette okay? Can we talk about this?"

Then *he* spoke, angry and impatient. As always.

"What the fuck are you thinking, Kate? Shit. What the hell?"

She *would* have liked to explain her thinking, but she couldn't find her voice. All she had was the message. *A wrong to be righted.* She couldn't remember the wrong just now, but something told her it was all that mattered.

The throb in her neck was at her again. Someone playing guitar with the tendons. She twisted her head and stretched the muscles, but the pain was stubborn as shit. *Forget that now. Work to be done. Four to be taken.*

Kate leveled the gun.

Ellen began to cry; she must have realized her mistake. Kate only needed two more, and there they were. Get this done now and she could get painkillers for this fucking insidious thing stabbing at her neck. Then, she'd sleep for a day or however long, until the buzz and the ache disappeared. Her mind wandered away to the car. *Had she brought some tablets with her?*

"Kate, can you hear me?"

It was Ellen again, her hands still in the air like this was a robbery. She'd gathered herself. Kate had looked away, not concentrating, thinking about the pain. Now she turned her head and looked straight at Ellen.

"Kate, I think something's wrong with you. Whatever it is, we can work it out. Okay?" Ellen's head nodded vigorously as she said, "okay."

Then *he* must have seen where Ellen was heading, because Idiot Boy's demeanor immediately changed. "Honey, the kids. They're scared. You don't want to frighten them, do you?"

Kate couldn't speak, but she thought to blink him a reply. How to blink *I don't give a shit?*

Ellen took a step forward, her arms outstretched. "Kate, please,"

The trigger felt small against Kate's finger as though she'd grown to the size of the Hulk. All the years of frustration bottled inside surged through her into that finger, resting lightly against the trigger. She pulled back like it was a ring-top can. It was that easy.

Ellen fell backward, landing with a thud. The force of the bullet's impact threw her off her feet.

"Nooo," she cried, her body writhing for a moment, then motionless. Whimpering sounds came from her, but she didn't move.

Kate now trained the gun on *him*, as he bent to Ellen, then looked back up at her. It was in his eyes that he saw she wasn't done. He moved quicker than Kate had anticipated, throwing his body to the left toward the living room door.

Straight and true, hit her mind.

She hoped he understood this was his payday. All those years of unhappiness; all those pills she wouldn't have needed; all those good things she might have done. She couldn't say it in words, but the bullet would deliver her message. The world would be changed, and she would be heard.

He should be proud of her aim. The way she pulled the trigger, no hesitancy in the movement. He'd taught her well.

He'd almost made it through the door. Almost escaped. Not quite quick enough, he lay slumped like a sack of potatoes amid a nice pool of blood for someone to clean. He clutched franticly at his neck, making gasping, gurgling sounds. She'd thought she'd missed, the bullet gone wide, but the thing had gone clear through his neck. By quantity of blood, she'd hit an artery. He wasn't dead yet, but soon.

As much as she would have liked, Kate couldn't wait and watch for his end. She needed to move.

The thought pumped through her mind and her body. *Keep moving. Straight and true.*

Kate had the four, but she would keep going, just to be sure.

It takes many to change the world.

Ellen had begun to move. While focused on ending her marriage, Kate hadn't noticed her sister-in-law dragging herself away. A sweep of crimson followed her along the honey-colored wood floor. Ellen moaned as Kate came upon her. One arm stretched out before her, pulled her forward, before reaching out again.

Even as Kate stood over her, Ellen continued, her head bobbing up and down as she cried in deep, body-shaking sobs. Without raising her head or looking up, she pleaded. "Please. No. Please."

Kate *had* liked Ellen. She would have liked to let her go, let her crawl away, to escape, but that wasn't part of the plan. *Take four.* She needed Ellen. She was a message needing to be sent.

Kate crouched down, stroked her sister-in-law's hair and placed the gun to her bobbing head. Ellen tried to speak, but she was sobbing so much, it came out as a jumble of vowels. "Eee. Aaa. I, I, aa—"

Kate couldn't understand. Anyway, listening to *them* wasn't part of the plan. It was *their* turn to listen to her.

Kate turned her head away as she pulled the trigger. Flesh and skull fragments still splattered her face and her clothes; the blood hot on her skin. A spray of gore had hit her eyes, stinging them closed. When she opened them again, Ellen's body lay slumped in another expanding pool of red that circled her head like a spilled tin of paint.

A blanket of quiet followed as though the bullet had not only silenced Ellen but also extinguished all energy and air from the house. The sudden peace, a reminder soon those who would stop her would come.

The police will come. Until then, keep moving.

From behind her came the sound of a door unlatching. Then, crying. She turned, her arms outstretched, the gun, solid and warm in her hands. Her twelve-year-old daughter Samantha stood outside the bathroom. A few feet away, in the bedroom across the hall, her uncle and aunt lay in merging pools of blood.

Kate looked at her, memories swimming into her mind. She loved this child, her first born. Twelve years ago, she was the symbol of all things good, of a happy future that never came.

Samantha's gaze traveled across to the open bedroom door and the bloody scene inside. Her hands flew to her mouth. A scream escaped her lips. Slowly she looked back at Kate, then her stare moved to the gun.

"Mo-om? Mo-oo-om? I don't understand."

Samantha's words grew distant as though her daughter were being pulled away. The memories and feelings she had for this girl, also, traveled away. When she looked at her, really looked, she felt nothing, no connection.

"Mo—."

Kate pulled the trigger, because that's what she knew she must do. That was the action required to get the message through.

She missed.

Samantha, young and agile, bolted the split-second before, sprinting forward and throwing Kate off balance. Before Kate could gather herself, her daughter sidestepped into the kitchen and disappeared from view, her ponytail flying behind her.

She needed to find the girl, but time pressed in on her. She felt *them* coming: the police, the others, people who would stop her. *You must take four.* Five, though, would be even better than four. *As many as she could.*

Kate moved quickly after Samantha into the kitchen, ready to do what was asked of her. But the room was empty. The sudden sound of the slamming back door alerted her to her mistake. Why didn't she get hold of the key somehow and lock it before she'd begun.

Chairs lay askew from the table, pushed haphazardly away from the table, one upended on the floor. Stacked next to the sink, a party load of dirty plates and coffee cups. Along the bench sat left over cake and cookies, and a plastic grocery bag filled with torn gift wrap. A spilled milk container rested on the floor in front of the open fridge door.

A rustling paper sound came from the pantry. *Samantha?* She'd imagined her gone, escaped.

Stepping over the milk puddle, Kate reached for the slatted pantry door, tugging it open to reveal a small, narrow room with cans, produce, and food stacked neatly on shelves.

The noisemaker crouched at the end on the floor, amid bags of rice and potatoes. The dog, some kind of weird half-poodle, half-labrador, looked up at her, his eyes glowing in the darkened space. She couldn't remember its name. She didn't like dogs. Or cats. Or people, come to think of it.

Suddenly the name came through as though gears had shifted in her brain. *Crispin!* His name was Crispin. Crispin bared his teeth and expelled a *Hound of Hades* growl just as she pulled the trigger. A single yelp, and the dog fell sideways to the floor.

As she stared at the animal, the pain in Kate's neck and head eased a little. The fever-pitch ache had dwindled to a level just above pulsing. Kate sighed in relief. Maybe the pain was going. Maybe this was her reward.

She exited back to the kitchen to the realization it was now just her and the silence. Instinctively it came to her: nobody remained. She was alone in the house. She *could* rest. Kate had her four and her divorce—twelve years in the making.

Now she needed to—.

What was it she needed to do? If she'd done what was necessary, if she'd sent the message, then the voice said...

... you wait.

What for, she didn't know, but wait she would.

Kate moved through the dining area into the living room, where something caught her attention. She stopped before the window facing the street, pulled back the lace curtain and peered outside. Something about the colors—blue and red, blinking in rhythm—called to her like in a dream.

Two police cars, their lights flashing, had parked in the driveway. Another oddly had stopped in the middle of the road. She hadn't heard them arrive. Then again, she'd been busy. *Focused.* It was only now after she'd taken her four, while she waited, that she could relax.

Movement up the street caught her eye. Samantha stood twenty feet down the road, a blanket over her shoulders. A woman, beside her, a woman Kate didn't know hugged her. Several police squatted behind open car doors. Waiting, just like her.

A voice spoke to her. Not the voice in her head, but another voice outside, calling her name.

"Kate Wilker, please put down your gun and come out with your hands up."

She looked through the curtains at the man leaning halfway into his car. In his fist he clutched a small microphone. His mouth, a single line barely moving as he spoke.

"We don't want any more people hurt."

Her hand went to her neck, kneading the skin, her fingers digging, pushing into the muscles. Yes, the pain had calmed right down. Her head almost felt normal again.

She brought the gun up to the window. The barrel, gray with a dark, polished sheen, glinted in the sunlight. The weapon suddenly felt heavy as though the light particles had added to its mass.

Above the window, a dreamcatcher hung from a hook. Samantha had a smaller version of these Indian things; her daughter's, also, hung in her window. This one, a cobweb of string, crystals and glass, shed glorious, colored sparkles and lines in all directions like a multi-dimensional rainbow.

Her daughter once told her she'd learned in class these flimsy ornaments, pretty as they were, filtered out bad dreams. Only good thoughts could enter a room under their mystical watch. Kate wondered if it were true.

Another thought crossed her mind: *I love my children. I'll miss my children.*

Her eyes followed the lines as they danced about the room. As she tracked them, she noticed the wrapping paper and abandoned gifts lying on the floor and the chairs: a Lego set, a ball, a pack of balloons, a loom weaver, console games, a doll and more.

She tried to understand what they meant, tried to remember why she would miss her children. Sudden silence closed in on her. She remembered on their visits, this house was never silent, their family get-togethers *always* loud, *always* boisterous.

All she heard now: the sound of her heart beating so loud it was as though it had left her body and floated next to her ear. Her foggy mind as though feathers had nestled into the crevices and dampened her feelings, muting her personality.

The last thing she remembered clearly was her sister-in-law, Annette, talking *at* her, as per usual. Then her mind was blank like it had shut down or she'd blacked out.

Until now.

Until right now, as she stood at this window. Near the dreamcatcher … the dreamcatcher, like her daughter's … her daughter, who was outside in the street … with the police … who were there for Kate … because of something … something she'd done. She didn't know how she knew that, she just knew and, she knew she was awakening from a nightmare that she didn't want to remember. Because something had gone wrong, something had gone terribly wrong. That's *why* she was alone.

Where was everybody?

Why would they leave without telling her? Did she go to the bathroom, the bedroom, somewhere? Was she unwell? Did she fall asleep? She remembered something about the bedroom, something *terrible* about the bedroom. While she was gone, in the bathroom, the bedroom, what did they do? They all ran outside?

Something *was* wrong.

She turned from the presents scattered about the room to stare out the window again. With each breath leaving her mouth, she found herself gasping, as though there were holes in her lungs where the air leaked out before it could feed her body.

This must be what drowning feels like.

Outside, two more police cars joined the fray, one now on the lawn, one in the driveway, all angled toward the home. Behind the open car doors, police brandished guns, and those guns were aimed at the house. A big black van moved slowly past to park down the street. The words on the side: Metro Police S.W.A.T.

What?

Kate's heart flew into her mouth. Something was happening in here, inside this house, and they'd left her behind. *How could they?* Her knees felt weak as a barrage of thoughts smacked into her mind:

Was she trapped?

Could she die?

How could her husband leave her?

Randall? He could be a fool; she'd nicknamed him Idiot Boy, for his forgetfulness. Would he really leave her behind, even if he were panicked?

Unless … *unless,* the children were in danger! If anything happened, he'd prioritize the children. She would, too.

That's what he'd done. He'd been busy saving the children, and he'd forgotten her. She found her breath again. At least the children were safe.

Suddenly, Kate became aware of a weight in her right hand, warm and heavy. She looked down, to see she held the gun from the car. *What?*

No, wait. This was good. Thank God, at least she could protect herself.

From outside, an amplified voice drew her attention from the gun.

"Kate, it's okay. We need you to come out."

Kate ignored the voice. Now she'd seen the gun in her hand, the one from the glove compartment, the one for emergencies, she needed to understand what was happening to her. What *was* the emergency? She raised the weapon to her face for a closer look.

Yes, it was their gun. Why *did* she have it?

A red dot appeared, dancing on the gun, shivering along the dark gray metal.

Now, how did that happen?

Had she pressed a switch and turned on a light inside the thing? Did it even have a light switch? She couldn't remember. It mustn't be her gun, then. It must be a toy, one of the kids', a very good replica.

Her gaze followed the dot as it ran down the front of her shirt. That's when she saw the blood-red fluid clinging to her clothes like pieces of dark berry cake mix.

What is that? Sauce? Wait, blood?

The crash of shattering glass barely registered in her mind. It sounded distant and charming like the tinkling of twirling ice in a cocktail glass.

Then everything was gone, disappeared into a blackness so thick she couldn't breathe. The tinkling sound—the ache in her neck—the shimmering red dot—the colors of the dreamcatcher, dancing about the room—all disappeared in a flash of white, just before the black.

Kate was falling, falling, faster and faster, into a pit of night that felt oddly warm and comforting. Two thoughts fluttered into her mind before she gave herself over to the pillowy softness: *The dreamcatcher worked; it's made everything warm and good—I hope my dreams* will *be good.*

Then finally, before her mind flickered out: *Thank God, the gun's not real. Real guns kill.*

CHAPTER 17

I T TOOK KENDALL A WEEK before she found the time to look over the research given to her by Doug McKinley.

Since then, her interesting encounters had filled her time. Some good. Some bad. The hospitality of the families of the Kenworth Home victims was astonishing. While some wouldn't see her, many welcomed the opportunity to talk about their lost loved ones. After each interview, she found herself drained and worn from the inside out. For a few nights, she struggled to sleep, the words of the families echoing in her mind. *Devastated. Shattered. Barely coping.* No shortage of adjectives to describe the fallout of the death of a loved one.

She'd submitted her story on the fire yesterday, including a couple of prime quotes from Doug McKinley.

"Every day I wake up and I say to them, I live for you today."

That was a Facebook meme if she ever saw one. She saw the picture in her mind accompanying the words: a cat lying on its side or curled up in a chair staring at the camera. *I live for you today.*

She giggled at the thought—then immediately felt guilty. What happened to that poor man's son was heartbreaking. She needed to find a better way to cope with this assignment than making jokes.

She needed more for her story in order to stand out from the pack of articles. She'd even contacted one of the investigating detectives. That encounter fell into the not-so-good basket.

Marianne Best, *Scoops Magazine's* editor—Scoops being one of the biggest magazines in the country—had contacted her directly and given her the idea.

In the media business, Marianne Best was known as Beastie Best. She was one of the worst editors. Beastie wanted everything *last* month. Most editors wanted articles *yesterday*, but *Beastie* actually signed off every email and phone call with that phrase. "By the way, I need this *last* month."

She meant it, too. If an article wasn't turned in by her ridiculously short deadlines, it ran a risk of cancellation with barely an apology. The only reason Kendall or any other freelancer worked for her was that *Scoops* paid considerably more than other magazines and enjoyed national distribution.

This story had wide appeal: international interest. Lucky for Kendall, Beastie needed her insight from the original articles on Beverley and the Amaretto Café murders. So, for a change, her grandstanding was minimal, which must have been hard for Beastie. Now, with this second mass murder spotlighting their city, she treated Kendall like a long-lost sister.

Who would have thought Kendall would hold initial exclusive with the only witness to see everything that night in Café Amaretto? *Thank you, Beverley.*

Kendall had herself been interviewed on two morning news shows and one syndicated evening broadcast.

Thanks to those five minutes of fame, she'd managed to swing access to a few of the relatives of the fire victims. Beastie, though, was pressing her for more than their statements, none of which *were* particularly exclusive. She wanted another Beverley story, another eyewitness.

"What I want, Kendall," she'd said, "Is something new, a theory or insight from the investigating detectives. Yes, get me that."

She'd said it as though Kendall possessed a magic key to open any door or a pass to speak to anyone she chose. It wasn't just accessing these witnesses that troubled her. These were doors Kendall was uncertain she wanted to enter. She wasn't sure how much strength she still possessed to keep listening to these tragic stories.

Money. She hated that it influenced her, controlled her, but the opportunity was just too good to ignore. She'd decided that for this one and only story, she would play hard-nosed investigative journalist, even though she was the furthest from that type of person you could find. It showed, too.

Her inexperience meant when she'd tracked down one of the detectives handling the Kenworth Home fire, a Lance O'Grady, the contact turned out badly embarrassing. Thinking about it now, she still cringed.

"I hear there's a theory the two cases are connected," she'd said, even though she hadn't heard anything of the sort. She'd just thought they *seemed* connected, and it was worth a shot.

Detective O'Grady worked out quickly she wasn't telling the truth, when he asked for her source and she froze. He didn't mince his words just before he hung up: "If you ever pull this little number again, pretend to be anything but the fucking bottom-feeder you are, then I'll personally ensure you are charged with perverting the course of justice."

When she'd reported to Beastie the investigating officers were a "no go," that hadn't worked out well, either.

Her frustration level grew hourly. She needed to find a way to get the story she needed or who knows how that might impact her work. Beastie knew a lot of other editors. One word from her Kendall was unreliable and the work could dry up for good. She'd promised Beastie a story and she had to deliver one. So for the past two days, she'd wracked her brain on how she could locate a contact inside the police squad handling the cases.

The attitude of this Lance O'Grady had rankled. She hadn't really done anything quite worthy of his anger. *And* she wasn't a bottom feeder, either. She was about to apologize and tell him that when he hung up on her.

Maybe she'd do a little bottom feeding investigation of Detective Lance O'Grady.

She Googled his name and found articles mentioning him as an investigating officer on several cases. Seemed over the past five years, he'd handled quite a few major crimes. She found him on LinkedIn, too. Nothing, though, on Facebook, Instagram, Twitter, or any other social media site. That made sense. When you worked in crime you probably needed to keep a low profile.

Kendall enlarged the picture of O'Grady attached to his LinkedIn account. He looked nothing like she'd imagined. He wasn't a dried up, worn down cop, with every year and every case etched in creases on his face. No, he actually had a warm, gentle look to him, trustworthy and familiar, the kind of face more suited to a pediatrician or a counselor. It was the thick, wavy, black hair and deep brown eyes; they reminded her of someone she felt she knew well. She chuckled, when she suddenly realized who it was. He had quite the actor *"Mark Ruffalo look"* going on, casual, but sexy. Basically, he was a good-looking asshole.

As interesting as it was to research Detective O'Grady, this wouldn't pay her bills. She closed her browser window. The time to capitalize on this story was ticking away. A week in the media industry was a *long* time, and Kendall couldn't be sure if she was riding the crest of a wave or about to be dumped and left high and dry.

Then a silly idea entered her head. She brushed it away, but it flew right back. *She* knew what Detective O'Grady looked like, but *he* didn't know what she looked like. Maybe, just maybe, if she had the courage, she could *accidentally* run into him, start a conversation about something, and maybe charm him.

It couldn't possibly go worse than the phone call. Even if it did, surely he couldn't arrest her for being a *bottom feeder?* She laughed out loud at the idea. *Her?* Some amoral, hard-nosed journalist? Kendall, with the softest nose in the business. That *was* funny.

For want of a better plan, was she seriously considering a bump-into-the-detective-and-see-how-it-goes plan? Maybe it wasn't such a bad idea. First, though, she'd sleep on it. Hopefully overnight she'd come up with something better. Surely she could *think* like a bottom feeder just for a few days.

CHAPTER 18

KENDALL DIDN'T SLEEP WELL. THE witness interviews had invaded her dreams with rolling images of that night, ten years ago. In the shadows of this nightmare, though, instead of her mother sitting beside her in the car, it was Lance O'Grady.

He turned to her and said, "It'll be okay. They're just bottom feeders, and I'll protect you."

Her dream—nightmare—felt so real, yet she had an overwhelming feeling he was wrong. Somehow she knew he shouldn't be there. She wanted to warn him, draw her gaze away, to look beyond his smiling face, through the car window. They were coming. In her dreams, they were *always* coming.

Kendall began to reply, to tell him nothing would ever be okay again, when suddenly he was gone. Now her mother sat there. She smiled at Kendall as though this was just another night, even as a flood of tears streamed down her cheeks. Kendall felt her heart break as her mother looked deep into her eyes and said: "Please don't hurt my daughter."

Kendall reached for her mother, hugging her in an attempt to comfort her. She whispered in her ear, "I've found Detective O'Grady. We're safe now."

She laid her head on her mother's shoulder and luxuriated in the feeling of closeness, soaking up the smell of roses and frangipani—the way her mother always smelled.

The moment dissolved, and Kendall knew instantly something was wrong. Her skin suddenly felt itchy and sore. She pulled back quickly to stare at her mother. It wasn't her mother anymore. Some kind of half-dead thing leered at her. Maggots and small, black beetles climbed in and out of its eye sockets and nose, a mass of white and brown pulsing horrors. The thing's mouth opened and closed as if laughing at her, but there came no sound.

She screamed, forcing herself awake. The last thing she remembered from the dream was shouting, "Detective O'Grady, please save us."

Kendall lay awake for hours after, her pillow uncomfortably wet with sweat. Lying there, she made herself a promise. This was the end of it. The very last story she would write on any kind of death. No more suicide or accident stories and definitely no more murders.

She needed to face facts. She would never ever get over that night and the tragedy of her mother's death. The best she could hope for was in the coming years the emotions would fade. This assignment had churned up everything all over again. Her decision was made—she would finish this last story and that was positively, absolutely it!

Several hours later when she hadn't managed to fall back asleep, she arose early and readied herself for the day, the dark mood of the nightmare hanging over her. She had a plan. It wasn't good, and she wasn't sure if she could carry it out. How *real* investigative journalists tracked down people, she didn't know.

So without any better ideas, she found herself waiting outside the modern glass and gray-steel Central Police Offices for O'Grady to come out. It wasn't a grand master plan. In fact, she felt kind of silly, but maybe she would get lucky. Surely, she reasoned, detectives came and went often in the process of investigating crimes.

Kendall had waited across the road from the building, sitting at a conveniently positioned bus stop for nearly two hours. Now at eleven-thirty, Kendall seriously considered giving up. She'd even begun to compose the email to Beastie Best explaining the story was a no-go. When she saw *him* come out of the building, it was like winning a prize.

She recognized Lance O'Grady instantly. It was the hair. In real life, it was even thicker than in photos. The detective could definitely pass for a taller version of Mark Ruffalo.

Kendall was surprised to feel a warm flush spread across her face as she watched him walk confidently from the building, talking earnestly with another man. The memory of him in the car in her dream and the way he looked at her felt so intimate. Somehow, it had translated into a feeling of connection with him. It was a ridiculous thought—a connection to a man who'd threatened to arrest her—but there it was, and she couldn't shake it.

He wore the scowl she'd imagined he'd have after he'd hung up on her. The memory of the anger in his voice was enough to remind her the man in her dreams was imaginary.

Straighten up your mind, Kendall Jennings.

The bald-shaven man walking beside him, smiled and gestured and seemed to be doing most of the talking. Kendall put him at around mid-thirties. Unlike O'Grady's oddly gentle-looking façade, he looked like a real detective. She guessed he could be O'Grady's partner.

"Please. Please. Please. Don't get into a car," whispered Kendall under her breath, as she followed them, walking along the opposite side of the street. She hadn't considered what would happen after they'd left the building, so had left her car parked a block away, the nearest space she could find.

The two detectives continued for several blocks, the bald man still talking, with O'Grady simply nodding. Her gaze never left the pair, which caused her to collide with several people as she followed. Each time she apologized, then quickly double-checked if the men were still in sight. They were, and Kendall began to feel at least some luck was going her way.

After four blocks, the detectives turned down a small side street. Kendall was forced to wait for a break in the traffic before crossing. Here's where she could lose them. Finally, she rushed across the street, dodging between the two lanes of stopped traffic. Several drivers honked their annoyance at her.

She entered the smaller street, jogging, but immediately realized luck *was* still with her. Even though they'd disappeared from sight, she *hadn't* lost them. The street had only three businesses: a flower shop, a tailors, and a small café. Kendall's only knowledge of police behavior came from television shows, but she guessed the café must be their destination.

She stood outside the eatery, doubts nibbling at her plan, which wasn't really a plan at all, but more an exercise in wishful thinking. What would she actually do should she run in to O'Grady? This wasn't a movie. She wasn't Jennifer Aniston or some other confident, sexy character, who could strike up a casual conversation with two strange men, and instantly have them divulge their secrets. Especially, if those men were cops. Even if she could somehow connect with them, how would she steer the conversation around to the murders? How long before Lance O'Grady realized who she was? Confrontation was not her strong suit.

She stood outside the café; chatting patrons passed her by to enter, as every elapsed moment caused her to lose more of her nerve. This was *really* a stupid idea. She actually began to turn away, when she realized one of the exiting patrons was holding the door open for her. Before she had time to think of *all* the reasons she should leave, and not walk through that door, she'd entered and was inside the bustling room.

The café possessed a cozy, early 19th century vibe, with bright imitation chandeliers hanging majestically from the ceiling, while mock gas-lamps dotted the wood-paneled walls. Framed black and white pictures of unsmiling, stern-looking men and women from early last century hung in a jumbled layout.

Kendall felt as though she'd stepped back in time, and she hoped some of the courtesies of the era might find their way into a certain patron. The room possessed a real energy with the place full and bustling, and the buzz of happy diners and clinking china and cutlery. In turn, Kendall felt uplifted. Maybe she *could* pull this off, if the opportunity arose.

As she followed the slender passage between the tightly packed tables to the elevated counter, she reconnoitered the room searching for the two detectives. She was relieved to spy them deep in discussion at a table by the window. By the time she'd reached the glass counter and surveyed the delicious looking cakes and filled rolls and wraps, Kendall realized she was hungry and in desperate need of a coffee.

As she placed her order—buttered banana bread and a mug of coffee—with a woman who clearly wished her shift had ended two hours ago, Kendall was *again* rethinking her plan.

"For here or to go?" said the waitress, scribbling the order on a form.

What should she do? She still had no plan, whatsoever. After O'Grady's reaction to her call, the thought of just walking up to the men and introducing herself as a journalist covering the massacre stories seemed too daunting. Thirty feet away sat a possible story that might not only pay her rent, but look extremely impressive on her resume. The distance seemed more like thirty miles as she calculated how to *bump* into them.

"Hi, I'm a writer. Can I pick your brain about the local murders?"

"Hi, I'm Kendall and you look a lot like Mark Ruffalo. You know the actor who plays The Hulk?"

"Hi, I had a dream about you last night, and I wanted to see if in real life you are ..."

She could make a joke about it, but any line she came up with sounded just as ridiculous as these. *Oh, for Pete's sake, this was plain crazy.*

Suddenly Kendall had lost her appetite, not just for the food, but also for everything that lay ahead if she pursued this path. Dampness seeped beneath her armpits, and it occurred to her she might even be sick—or the stress of this was making her sick. A dull, thick feeling had grown in her throat as if she'd swallowed a cup of sand.

"You want that to eat here?" the waitress repeated, sterner this time.

Kendall found herself replying, "I'll have it here, thank you." Her decision was made. Then she spent the following minutes panicking as she waited for her coffee to be made, and the banana bread to be placed on a tray.

Kendall picked up the tray, turned from the counter and looked for an empty table. Again, luck liked her. Next to the two detectives, was one of the few vacant tables. She would actually pass right by them to reach it. The closely packed tables made maneuvering, while balancing the tray, difficult. Kendall was also mindful she didn't want to attract the detectives' attention until she'd worked out what to say or do. She hoped being this close to O'Grady would provide some inspiration.

Concentrating on just getting to the table was probably why Kendall didn't notice her bag slip from her shoulder. She'd almost made it to her table, too, when the bag's strap snagged on an occupied chair pushed back a little. The caught strap unceremoniously yanked her backward, throwing her off balance. Even though she managed to keep hold of the tray, the plate with the banana bread began to slide. When she attempted to stop it by leveling her tray, the coffee cup flew sideways, loudly crashing to the floor. On its way down, half its contents spilled over her shirt and pants. In her surprise, Kendall then flicked the tray. The banana bread and its plate coasted upward like a lobbed baseball.

Everything happened in slow motion. When no sound was heard of the cake and plate hitting the ground, Kendall looked anxiously to see where they'd landed. When she saw, her heart stopped beating for a second. *What were the odds?*

Lance O'Grady stared up at Kendall, smiling, her plate in his lap and the banana bread lying in front of him on the table, buttered side down. She was acutely aware as she stared into eyes the deepest brown she'd ever seen, that she'd garnered the entire café's attention. Her face instantly bloomed the color of embarrassment. She was suddenly boiling in her skin as though she'd stepped inside a sauna.

Kendall instantly bent to the floor and began to pick up the pieces of the broken cup. This did two things: it broke their eye contact, which had felt uncomfortably *good*, and it gave her time to gather herself.

Oh, my God. What a mess!

Then O'Grady was beside her, reaching for the remaining pieces of the cup. She glanced over at him, self-conscious at his proximity. His head was down. All she saw was thick, wavy black hair, so close she could reach over and touch it. Her first instinct was to stand up and move away, which she did. This only made things worse. The sudden movement made her dizzy. Taking a woozy step back. She found herself clinging to the edge of the detectives' table, waiting for the giddiness to subside.

O'Grady followed her up and firmly gripped her arm.

"Ma'am, are you okay?" His voice was warm and concerned, nothing like how he'd sounded on the phone.

As the faint feeling passed, Kendall surveyed her clothes, still avoiding his gaze. Her shirt was covered in coffee, with the rest of the brown liquid splattered at her feet. Finally, she couldn't avoid it any longer. Her heart was jumping, as she raised her head to look at him again.

"Oh, my God, I'm so embarrassed. Did I spill coffee on you?"

O'Grady actually laughed. She wasn't expecting that, the encounter taking on the same surreal sensation as her dream. In her imagination, Kendall heard him say, *I will save you,* before she came to her senses. This same man had called her a *fucking bottom feeder.* She needed to get a grip.

He looked down at his shirt, and then gave her a smile so far from someone who'd call a woman a *fucking bottom feeder,* she almost laughed.

"No, its fine. I've had worse spilled on me."

He indicated toward their table with a nod of his head and said, "It seems your bread likes our table better."

Kendall looked down at the tabletop. She couldn't even easily scoop up the bread. It had fallen butter side down—*of course*—and lay in front of the other detective. He also stared at her, looking amused.

Kendall brought her hand to her mouth. "Oh, no, I'm really sorry."

She really *was* sorry, too, for more reasons than the detectives knew. She didn't have this in mind when she'd come up with the *bump*-into-O'Grady plan. Now she'd had a minute to gather her wits, she realized it couldn't be more perfect.

Kendall felt the warm and sticky feeling of the coffee soaked through the material of her shirt to her skin. As much as she wanted to get away from here, from him, and get out of her now-uncomfortable clammy shirt, she couldn't look a gift horse in the mouth, even if its name was Fate. The café patrons had returned to their own conversations, the show now over, and she was starting to feel more confident she might just have some success with this encounter.

A waitress appeared beside them clutching a cloth and a dustpan. She started on finishing the cleanup job Kendall and O'Grady had begun.

Kendall stepped aside and gave a little embarrassed laugh, with a sprinkle of flirt thrown in. She reached down and picked up the banana bread slice, holding it by a corner.

"Let me just clear that bread up for you. I'll take this as a warning to avoid coffee and all things sweet for the day."

When both detectives smiled at her comment, she was instantly filled with bravado. *Too much bravado.* Suddenly she began talking, saying the first thing that entered her head.

"You're that policeman, aren't you? From those terrible murders?"

The words tumbled out, sounding so unnatural to her. The way she'd phrased it, too, made it sound like *he* was the killer.

"Sorry, I mean the investigating detective. Not that *you* committed the murders. I didn't mean … I saw your picture in the paper."

Kendall was uncertain if she had actually seen his picture. His name had been there, but she'd actually found his picture on LinkedIn. Hopefully, he didn't check the papers looking for articles on himself.

Why was he creasing his brow and squinting at her like that?

She had this terrible feeling he was thinking: Is this that crazy journalist who called me yesterday? *Had he recognized her voice?*

Blood loudly rushed through her ears; she experienced it like a pulse in her head. Her stomach felt as though it were filled with solid chunks of banana bread, even though she hadn't yet taken a bite.

O'Grady stared at her, the smile on his lips now fading.

The other detective answered. "Yes, that's him, the famous Detective O'Grady. I'm also working that case. Trip Lindsay. We're not supposed to share information with the general population."

Trip was still smiling at her.

Thank God! But why was O'Grady not smiling?

Trip continued. "But since we currently share custody of your bread, I guess that makes us friends."

He winked at her, and Kendall immediately knew she liked him. Not romantically—he wasn't her type—but she saw he might be more amenable to talking with her than O'Grady.

When O'Grady spoke, his voice still sounded warm and friendly.

That was good. She'd just misread him. Relief swept through her body. When she thought about it later, Kendall realized that's what caused her to lose concentration, and losing concentration ruined everything.

She suddenly morphed into a silly teenager, throwing caution to the wind. Turning back toward O'Grady, Kendall held out her hand, and, for no good reason, said, "Hi, I'm Kendall Jennings, and I spoke to you yesterday. The writer."

Even as the words left her mouth, she thought: *What have I done?*

A second, and the warmth slid from his face and the sparkle left his eyes.

O'Grady slowly tilted his head to the side and examined her face for what seemed like minutes, but was only seconds.

"I'm sorry, what did we speak about?"

I'm okay. He must get so many calls.

She began to breathe again. The pounding of her heart became a patter. And the churning feeling in her stomach eased.

Then her heart sank as his eyes transformed from a look of confusion to something else as recognition traveled across his face, and his body suddenly tensed.

"Ah, now, I remember. Yes, you wanted details on the Kenworth fire. We don't give out particulars, ma'am. *Especially to journalists.* I think I made myself pretty clear yesterday."

"I… Yes, sorry. I'm really, *really,* very sorry."

She was blathering as though English was her second language.

Now the other detective stopped smiling, his eyebrows raised. Kendall began to panic, thinking maybe she *could* be arrested for making stupid phone calls to the police.

O'Grady addressed her, barely opening his mouth, his lips a tight straight line. "What did you say your name was?"

"Kendall. Kendall Jennings."

With hope, she moved her still outstretched hand further toward him. Now he'd met her in person, he might reconsider his perception of her as a bottom feeder.

O'Grady glanced at her hand, studied it for a moment, and then returned his poker-faced stare to her eyes. Kendall felt a flush rise on her face, but she tried to meet his stare without revealing her anxiety. And fear.

"Miss Jennings, do you honestly think that because you run into us here and *pretend* to *spill* your food, I'm going to become your buddy and *spill* everything to you. This isn't a *Die Hard* movie. Real people died. They certainly wouldn't want details of an investigation, vital information or not, splashed across newspaper pages. You might want to sell newspapers, well, *we save lives.*"

He spat the last few words at her as though they left a sour taste in his mouth.

Kendall stood with her mouth half-open, as she struggled to think what to say. She felt herself shrinking under both men's glares. The bald partner hadn't said anything yet, but she braced herself for a berating from him, too. Foolishly, she hadn't planned an escape route if anything went wrong.

Stupid, stupid, Kendall.

She was a freaking *health and lifestyle* writer, period. In fact, she was a health and lifestyle writer so far out of her depth, she was now considering turning on her heels and running for the door.

In an attempt to save what little face she still possessed, Kendall swallowed a chunk of pride and demurely addressed O'Grady, from whom palpable waves of displeasure were surging toward her.

"Detective O'Grady, I sincerely apologize. I was trying to do my job. My editor assigned me the story, you see. In fact, I don't do these stories. I'm so sorry. And I'm sorry my food landed on your table, and I've spilled my coffee and interrupted you. I was born a klutz or I grew into one, or I don't really know, I'm just clumsy. Believe me, it wasn't intentional. At any given time, you can find three or four bruises somewhere on my body."

Kendall realized what she'd just said and quickly added, "Not that I mean you would check my body. I didn't mean you should body search me."

He raised his eyebrows and Kendall corrected herself. "No, I don't mean you normally body search people. Generally, I was talking, generally."

Oh, my sweet goodness, she was making this so much worse.

"You know what I mean. Don't you?" she stammered, before gathering her thoughts enough to stop moving her mouth and shut up.

Trip's face showed amusement. He was enjoying this. His smile gave her a little hope that this situation might be redeemable. So she addressed Trip.

"I wouldn't normally do a story like this. I can't handle violence. Even the thought of violence upsets me, but I've hardly won any of the jobs I've pitched recently, and look, I'm really very sorry."

Kendall paused to catch her breath. Suddenly she felt close to tears. She swallowed several times and that seemed to send the tears back from wherever they'd swelled. *Thank God.* The last thing she needed was to let this O'Grady know he was getting to her.

When she looked back to O'Grady, he was still stony-faced. She should have followed her first instinct and run from the café.

Kendall was hoping O'Grady would be the one to reply, who would realize she wasn't a threat, hadn't meant any harm, would say that now he understood. It was Trip, who, instead of addressing Kendall, spoke to O'Grady. Kendall had already started to think of him as *good cop* to O'Grady's *bad cop*. Good cop, he certainly proved to be.

"O'Grady, you hard ass. She's just trying to do her job."

Trip then spoke to Kendall, his face open and friendly, ignoring the dark look O'Grady now gave him.

"Sorry, Kendall, but we can't talk to you about particulars. It's an active case. If we did, we'd get our balls beaten by our sergeant. But maybe, we could—" He paused and looked back to the still frowning O'Grady, then swung his gaze back to Kendall. "—listen to a few questions. *If* we can answer them or part of them, we will. If we can't, you'll just have to live with that."

113

O'Grady glared at Trip, as though he couldn't believe what he was hearing. He shook his head, even as Trip continued to talk, seemingly uncaring of his partner's annoyance.

"You've got to admire her guts to follow us in here, O'Grady. I like a woman with chutzpah."

And there it was. Now Kendall understood. The way he was smiling, the wink he'd just given her. Her *guts* weren't exactly what he admired.

Trip looked her straight in the eye, and said, "That's what you did, wasn't it?"

Perspiration dotted Kendall's upper lip; the back of her neck felt clammy. *What should she do?* Play along with him or take advantage of her reprieve and get out of there?

"Yes, I guess. Yes, I did follow you. And I *am* sorry. I won't bother you again. Sorry. Really."

Kendall turned away from both men, her heart crumpling. She felt useless. Useless and embarrassed. She wasn't just a fish out of water, she was a school of fish in the wrong class, out of water. Tears stung her eyes. All she wanted to do was get home, eat a big tub of ice cream, and let the tears come.

Then she felt a hand on her arm.

"Wait."

She turned to find herself facing the now standing, six-foot tall, *Good Cop.* Trip was mid-thirties, with a wide nose and a wider mouth. A glint in his eyes and still the smile on his face warmed her a little.

"Where are you going, Kendall? I *was* serious. You *can* ask me a couple of questions. Let's start again. I'm Trip."

He held out his hand, which Kendall took and shook. He held her palm a little longer than seemed normal. Yes, she *had* been right. He did like her.

"I'll help if I can. Maybe in the future, you might be able to help us. Who knows? Maybe—"

O'Grady interrupted, speaking directly to Trip as though Kendall didn't exist. "This is *not* a good idea. You don't tell them anything. You *know* what could happen."

Trip raised a hand to his forehead in a *I don't care what you think* salute.

O'Grady stared at Trip for a moment, his mouth clenched, eyes squinting. "Right, I've given you my opinion. Ignore me, and it's on you. But I'm not staying."

Without acknowledging Kendall, O'Grady turned and headed away. Trip and Kendall watched him weave his way to the door. Even the way he walks looked angry. She continued to follow him until he yanked open the door and was gone.

Now Kendall and Trip were alone, she didn't know where to look or what to say. She mumbled "sorry," again, wondering if he would now be angry, too, since she seemed to have caused an argument between the partners. Trip continued to smile, though. He wasn't her type, but as bad as the encounter had been, this was an unexpected advantage. If she didn't seize this opportunity and work it, somehow, she would never forgive herself.

Trip smiled a big toothy grin. "Please sit. Do you want me to grab you another coffee?"

"I should be buying *you* a coffee." She returned his smile as sweetly as she could.

"No, no," he said, pulling out a chair for her. "It's a rule I never break. Always buy a pretty girl a coffee on a Saturday. Look at that, today is Saturday, and I haven't filled my quota. So help me out, let me get you another coffee."

His gaze flicked to the piece of banana bread still sitting upended on the table. "We've already got the food."

Kendall smiled. This was turning out better than she could imagine. Trip did seem like a nice guy. Just maybe she'd end up with something for her article and keep Beastie at bay.

Trip left to order the coffee, giving her time to gather her thoughts. Lance O'Grady had unsettled her, even though, thanks to her dream, she still couldn't shake the odd feeling of intimacy. It felt as though they'd just had a lover's spat even though neither of them knew the other.

Trip interrupted her thoughts as he placed a cup of steaming coffee before her.

"Right, here's the deal. For every question you ask, I get to ask you a question. I'm not promising I can answer everything. Maybe there's a few things I can share without getting anyone into trouble."

The first question she now wanted answered surprised her. It had nothing to do with the mass killings.

"How long have you and O'Grady been partners?"

"That's easy. Three years. He's not a bad guy. That thing today with you, that's something else. Don't take it personally."

"Okay, second question then. What's the something else?"

"I think you'd better ask him. My turn. How long have you been a journalist?"

Kendall had begun her reply of "I'm not a journalist, I'm a freela—" when the door to the café opened with a heavy whoosh. O'Grady practically flew into the room. Kendall, facing the door, saw him before Trip, and the look on his face caused her to gasp. He was changed from the angry man who'd left five minutes before, his face serious and drawn as though he'd just witnessed something terrible.

He was across the room and at their table before Kendall had time to motion to Trip his partner had returned. When O'Grady arrived beside them, Trip must have presumed he'd reconsidered, had come back to apologize. He casually threw his arm over the back of his chair and smiled a greeting at his partner.

Ignoring Kendall—yet again—O'Grady leaned into Trip's ear and whispered. Suddenly Trip's smiling face mirrored O'Grady's serious demeanor. Kendall overheard a few snatches of words, but all she made out was: "Again. Bad. Famine?" *No, wait, was that family?*

Trip nodded, as O'Grady spoke, until O'Grady finally stood back, and Trip said, "Yep, okay. Give me a minute."

O'Grady glanced at Kendall as though whatever had happened had been her fault, then turned and headed for the door. Trip pulled out his wallet to leave a tip. While he did, he addressed her, but his thoughts were clearly wherever O'Grady was headed.

"I can't stay. Sorry."

"What's happened? Bad news?"

"*Very* bad news."

Trip gathered his phone from the table and stood.

"Since it'll be all over the news in the next hour, I'll give you a heads-up. It's happened again."

"What's happened?" She didn't understand what he meant.

"Another mass killing."

A shiver ran through Kendally's body, her mind immediately puzzling. *How could there be another mass murder so soon?* Impossible. Mass killings were random and rare, that much she knew from her research. *Where? How?* More pressing, why?

Trip pocketed his phone, pulled out his wallet and retrieved a small, plain business card. He placed it before her on the table. The tone in his voice, the tight pursing of his lips, and the intensity in his eyes told her their flirtatious moment was done. His mind was back in work mode.

"Oh, my God, no. What's happened?"

"Don't know. A family is all we know so far. If I knew more, sorry, I couldn't tell you anyway. You understand, right? Take my card. Call me, and..."

He paused, rocking his head slightly from side to side as though he were trying to make a decision. "I didn't tell you this, either, but, if you drive past three sixty-three Bentley Street West, you might see something worth writing about. Now, I'm gone. I'm sorry. I hope to see you again. *Soon.*"

Trip turned and hurried toward the door. Kendall picked up his card, clutching it in her hand as she gathered her bag—the bag she'd cursed fifteen minutes ago but which had truly been her ally—and hurried to follow him.

Outside, in the bracing autumn air, Kendall squinted in the bright sunlight after the darkened interior. How different she felt from when she'd stood outside, less than an hour ago, thinking everything was lost. Now she was excited, her body pumped with adrenaline.

This might be good for her, not just professionally but personally.

Finally, she might overcome her fears that lightning could strike twice in her life, that violence would find her again. People always say confront your fears. This story was forcing her to do just that.

As the door closed behind her, she realized she'd forgotten the banana bread. She'd recovered the bread while Trip was getting her coffee and had placed it back on the plate.

You win some; you lose some, she thought. Today, crazy as it had already been, felt like it was the beginning of a win.

CHAPTER 19

INSIDE 363 BENTLEY STREET WEST it looked like a war zone. After making his way from the bodies at the front entrance to the bodies in the bedroom to the dead dog in the pantry, O'Grady decided he'd already seen too much death in the past two weeks. It took all his strength not to walk back out the door and heave.

After forty-five minutes of checking the bodies and perusing the scene, the horror of it finally overwhelmed him. Cops were presented as tough and all-about-the-job in films and books, but the reality was they were just people who saw more misery than the average Joe. O'Grady couldn't fight the urge to just get out and breathe air that didn't reek of blood and shit and death. Trip could manage alone for a few minutes.

Despite the churning in his gut, O'Grady maintained a calm exterior as he walked outside and away from the commotion inside and out on the front lawn. He strode past the white-suited CSIs and their vans, the police cars, and the media who mobbed him as he left, asking—no, make that shouting—for details. Always they wanted details, when all people needed to know was innocent people had died. *Wasn't that enough?*

He walked, his mind filled with the visions of bodies, here and at the other two massacre scenes. He walked until he couldn't hear the noise of the reporters and police attending the scene anymore and couldn't taste death on his tongue. He walked, thinking life was shit and life was precarious. He'd seen death before; that came with the job. These past two weeks, though, and then this: a mother slaughtering her relatives and husband practically in view of her own kids, it was … well, he didn't know what it was.

What was wrong in their city suddenly for this to happen? In fact, what the hell was actually happening? He needed a drink or a cigarette; something to stop his hands from shaking, when his hands didn't normally shake. O'Grady had given up smoking in his twenties, but right about now, the idea of one of those cancer sticks taking the edge off sounded good. On his way out from the crime scene, he'd bummed a cigarette and some matches from one of the officers.

He had choices. He could ask to be taken off the case. He'd already investigated two of the mass killings, and who would blame him for wanting a break? That though, would land him in counseling. Once on your record, that black mark was there for good, a psychic hole into which the powers remained ever nervous you might fall at some future date.

O'Grady stared at the cigarette before placing it in his mouth and lighting. He dragged deeply, coughed, and then determinedly dragged again, feeling the chemicals in the smoke instantly fire in his brain. A calm flowed through him as he gathered his thoughts.

He looked around his surroundings, noting the middle-class brick homes, set on perfectly manicured lawns complete with palm trees and hedges that would take constant care. Madness rarely visited communities like this, where neighbors shared backyard barbecues on summer Sunday afternoons, where kids rode their bikes in the streets until dinnertime, and where family worries centered around kids passing exams or how to cover the tuition. Nobody expected his or her family to become target practice on a Saturday afternoon.

Kate Wilker didn't even remotely fit a killer profile. His preliminarily interviews at the scene told a different story to the results of her actions inside the house. So far, everyone who knew her was vehement in her defense.

Kate's a perfectly normal mom who loved her children and family.
Kate's the very last person to be violent.

Kate wouldn't do this. It must be a mistake.

Somehow, though—and it was his job to work out *how*—this normal, non-violent, loving mom suddenly transformed into a killer and shot four innocent people and a dog dead. Just like Toby Benson. Just like Benito Tavell. Kate Wilker had suddenly morphed from good person into a killer.

O'Grady drew deeply on the cigarette, breathing in and out slowly, the tension in his shoulders easing, the wild kicking in his stomach fading. Holding out the glowing white stick, he stared at it. He needed to get hold of his emotions.

He dropped the half-smoked cigarette onto the pavement and rubbed it out with his sole. The smoke left a bitter taste in his mouth, and he instantly regretted breaching the promise he'd made to give up the stinking things.

From behind, he heard the sound of footsteps. Thinking it was Trip come to find him, he turned, smiling. When he saw who it was, the smile faded instantly from his face.

It was her, the journalist, Kendall Jennings. *What the hell was she doing here?* The last person he would appreciate sneaking up on him during a moment of vulnerability. For the second time that day, his anger flared. She was just about all he *didn't* need right now. They were all the same, journalists. Half the time they got things completely wrong, and the other half they purposely made things up. *Their* truth was usually a long way from the *real* truth.

Interacting with this woman, piled on top of these crimes, annoyed the heck out of him. She was a liar, a manipulator, and what really needled him: Trip seemed a little sweet on her. That wouldn't ever end well.

He turned on her before she could utter a word, "What the hell are *you* doing here?"

She looked taken aback. *What had she expected? A kiss and a hug.* She clearly couldn't take a hint. Add dopey to the list.

"I'm sorry. I saw you leave that house, and I wanted to apologize. You know, for what happened at the café. We got off on the wrong foot."

O'Grady shook his head. *Self-involved. There's another trait.* Fumes of indulgence wafted from her.

He would admit—if you stuck bamboo shards under his fingernails—she was attractive. Her pale-blue eyes—he'd never seen eyes that color—struck him the first moment he'd looked into them at the café. Trip's interest in her was understandable—unprofessional, but understandable. As she shook her head during her apology, he hated himself for noticing the way her golden-brown hair bounced on her shoulders. So when he spoke, he tried to ensure his tone was as unfriendly and mocking as he could manage.

"You know, here's a little fact. The world doesn't revolve around you, so no need to apologize. The minute I left the café, I'd forgotten you. Actually, I'd like to thank you."

Her blue eyes widened, puzzled.

"Yeah, I do appreciate you following me while I'm working and reminding me how much I don't like journalists."

Her smile instantly wilted. Her eyes narrowed and darkened, changing from their light blue to dark gray.

Good, she'd gotten the message. *Now slink away, writer girl, and never cross my path again.* If Trip wanted to encourage her, good luck to him. It would take more than a pretty smile to change his mind.

"Now, if you don't mind, could you please go back to whatever rock you live under and let me do my job. I won't forget your name, either, Miss Jennings. If I see you again—

She didn't let him finish. Instead of retreating, she surprised him by squaring her shoulders and facing him full on, her eyes boring into his.

"You know, you're just rude. I haven't done anything that warrants your disrespect to this degree. For a start, I'm not a journalist. I'm a freelance writer. There's a difference. Okay?"

O'Grady was about to reply based on her behavior, he couldn't tell, but as he opened his mouth, she put her hand up to indicate she hadn't finished.

"Look, I'm just trying to pay my bills. I don't even want to do this story. Somehow, I ended up interviewing that witness from Café Amaretto.

Then Beastie wanted another story. Really, I'm just doing what I'm told. Your being an asshole won't stop me. I *have* to do this."

O'Grady felt an unintentional smirk lift one side of his mouth. *She was pretty when she was angry.* Fire touched her eyes, her skin reddened and flushed, only accentuated the gold in her hair. It rankled him he was looking at her as anything but another parasitic scum. Nobody who did her type of job was a decent person. No one.

"If you only knew the dangers in what you do, you wouldn't hang your hat on *I'm just doing my job.* Innocent people die because *you're* just doing your job. Innocent people like my brother."

Shit, what did he just say?

He didn't want a snoopy journalist knowing about his personal life, about his brother Jack. The past two weeks of no sleep and stress made him clumsy.

Her brow furrowed; the anger on her face faded. Even as her lips parted, he saw the next question on them: *What about your brother?*

O'Grady did the only thing he could do to avoid the question. He shook his head and took off at a pace, back toward the crime scene, back where he should have stayed. *Damn,* he wished he still had that cigarette. Anger bubbled in his gut as thoughts of Jack filled his head. Damn, damn, *damn* her, bringing it all back now, when he didn't need it, when he needed to concentrate on doing what he did best. His job.

He walked faster and harder, his footfalls sounding loud on the empty street, the vista of a normal neighborhood fading away to *that* night and *that* phone call.

He heard his brother's voice. *"I'm not sure how much more of this I can take."*

His voice had been empty and hollow down the phone line that night. If O'Grady could have replied across time, he would have said: "Neither do I, big brother. Neither do I."

CHAPTER 20

JACK WAS ONLY TWENTY-SIX AT the time, and Lance, twenty-four. So close in age they'd shared most of their childhood adventures. They had very different personalities, so the usual sibling arguments and rivalries were there, but they'd matured into friends. Jack was cavalier, fun loving, with a quick wit, while Lance quieter, the thinker of the two, who knew exactly what he wanted to do with his life. Inspired by the cop shows he loved to watch, he wanted to join the police force and become a detective.

Jack spent his later teenage years and early twenties searching for *his calling*—as their mother labeled it. Straight after high school, he'd traveled to Europe, fallen in love with dozens of girls, and tried his hand at any work not requiring study. Despite his world travels, he remained too naïve and trusting.

Jack had returned from a three-month trip around Asia, and in order to save for his next adventure—always a next adventure—he took a job as a general laborer at the construction site of a twenty-story apartment building. Jack's job that day was to secure a concrete slab with chains so it could be lifted into place by a crane. Maneuvering slabs and building material was an action completed on hundreds of sites across the country every day.

On an ordinary day that should have ended as an ordinary day, one end of the slab came free from the chain without warning, swinging the flat block into the building's metal frame. The impact dislodged the other end of the slab from the chain's hold. Forty feet it fell, too sudden for anyone below to react. Two workers died, including the poor guy on the walkie-talkie guiding the crane operator. A workplace investigation ruled Jack had failed to properly secure the chains. Knowing he'd caused two deaths landed enough guilt on Jack to crush him. What he didn't need to compound that guilt was some lousy journalist stirring up a story on workplace accidents and digging into Jack's life.

When finding muck is your goal, you'll find it, all right. The slaphappy investigation turned up that Jack had visited a bar the night before. An unknown source was quoted—as if that made it credible—that Jack's breath smelled of alcohol the morning of the accident.

Poor Jack, tried, convicted, and condemned in the media, was declared a reckless drunk, a killer, and every bullshit name you could call someone. In the public eye, Jack suddenly bore the sole responsibility for what was *just* an accident. He was treated like a murderer. The headlines called it "a triable crime."

Jack admitted to being at the bar. To Lance and his family he explained, *"I swear I left early. I thought I was coming down with something, the flu I thought. The only thing on my breath was the smell of menthol cough-lozenges."* His brother tried to tell his side of the story, but none of it made the news. They already had their story, and they were sticking to it.

Poor system kills man on worksite

Drunk laborer found to blame

The fatal drink that killed two men

Broadcast news journalists hounded him, chasing him in the street. *"How do you feel about causing the death of your workmates?" "How do you live with yourself?"* Vans sat outside their family home for three days, until they all felt like prisoners, trapped and set upon if they even walked out their front door.

Jack was never charged, the allegations, investigated by police but found untrue. It was just a dumb accident, plain and simple. Jack found no relief after he was cleared of responsibility. He still wore the guilt like a neck clamp, the notoriety from the headlines already burrowed deep into his brother's fragile soul. Lance's carefree, grab-life-by-the-balls brother was now a shadow, broken, and lost.

Jack slipped into a deep depression, left his job, even though management did support him through the entire thing. *He couldn't face the risks,* he said. *What if he killed someone else?* The prescribed anti-depressants didn't help. The doctors said they would, but they were wrong. The dosage wasn't right. Jack sank further and further into himself like he was made of tinfoil, easily crushed.

Despite the passage of fourteen years, the night of the phone call was always fresh in his mind. He could still see the time on the wall clock. Eleven-ten. He'd checked that clock as they'd talked, calculating if he went over to his brother's and talked it out, whether he'd still catch enough sleep to avoid feeling shattered the next day. There and back with an hour or so of talking, would probably see him climbing into bed after two a.m. He had an early seven a.m. meeting. Yeah, he'd be shattered.

"I can't take it anymore."

"You can, Jack. We'll get through this."

Lance's heart hurt for his brother, but Jack needed to pull himself out of it. Lance had begun to think Jack was almost enjoying the attention.

"No. *They'll* never let me get through this. Every time there's any kind of accident at a worksite, *they* bring it up, again. This morning, did you see the headlines? Two pedestrians died when a partially-constructed brick wall collapsed. *And there it was.* My name. The accident. *Again.* It's been nearly a year, for Christ's sake. I will *always* be the drunken guy who killed someone."

A tremor shook Jack's last words. Lance knew his brother was close to tears. Hell, *he* was close to tears, but if he ran over there every time his brother broke down, would that really help Jack?

"Jack, you know it *will* blow over. I know it's tough, but, brother, you've got to hang in there. *We* know the truth. You're a good man." Lance couldn't help himself: "Look, do you need me to come over? I can be there in thirty minutes."

Dead space filled the line, an empty silent divide hanging between them. All the conversations about the accident they'd had, Lance trying to encourage his brother, Jack nodding but not really listening, his mind somewhere else, mired in guilt, Lance knew it would be another one of *those* conversations. He knew that. But however many talks it took, that's the number he would have. One day Jack would get better. Lance hoped with all his heart, that day was coming soon.

"Jack. Jack. Are you still there?"

Long, long seconds ticked by. Just when Lance had begun to think Jack had hung up, his brother answered. Several quick, deep breaths echoed down the line, then his brother caught himself. When he spoke, he sounded a little more solid.

"Nah, it's okay. Really, it's okay. I just get overwhelmed."

Lance jumped in, "I want to come over. You know I don't sleep until late. I don't mind." Then quietly, "Please, buddy, I'm worried."

"No, no, I'm fine. Really. I don't want to be a drag. You've got work tomorrow. I'll just go to bed. Really, I'm good. It was good to hear your voice. I love you, little brother."

Jack *had* sounded more positive, and he *had* sounded as though he'd wrangled his emotions. A minute later their call ended but only after Lance had made Jack agree they'd catch up the next night for a meal.

The next day when Lance tried to call Jack to organize dinner, he couldn't get hold of him. Worried, he went to Jack's apartment. He found him there, hanging from his bedroom door, his belt around his neck. Lance would never get over finding his brother like that. The guilt had burrowed so deep in his psyche, it still hadn't left him, still pounded him on occasion, to the point where he would be physically sick. *What if?* was a dangerous, soul-draining game.

As angry as he was with himself, Lance was even more incensed with the newspapers, the journalists, all those who had harassed his brother. If they'd just left Jack alone instead of using him to sell newspapers, he felt for sure

Jack might have pulled through. He'd been tried, convicted, and sentenced to death by professional newsmongers.

The ache from missing his brother was always there, and this damn journalist, freelance writer, or whatever she called herself, had churned everything back up. O'Grady realized his fists were clenched so tight his knuckles throbbed. He cursed under his breath; he didn't need these feelings clouding his judgment.

His fury exploded like an over-inflated balloon. O'Grady turned suddenly, striding back to the Jennings woman. She wasn't far behind him, having the audacity to follow him back to the house. He came to a halt in front of the startled woman, standing over her, his intimidating height dwarfing her five-foot-six, slim frame.

O'Grady kept his voice calm. He wouldn't give her the pleasure of knowing how much she'd upset him.

"When you say it's *just* a *job*, keep in mind that for the people you're using to *do* your *job*, this is *their* life, *their* nightmare. And you're just adding to the horror."

Kendall Jennings eyes were wide—even more incredibly blue—and surprised. She clutched her bag tightly and looked afraid. He felt pleased he'd unsettled her. Some of her own medicine, back.

"There are dead people back in that house. They have friends and relatives who'll need to come to terms with this, live with it for the rest of their lives. Children whose parents are gone. Brothers and sisters who've lost a family member in the worst possible way. So saying it's *just* a job sounds just as bullshit as a texting driver killing a kid and saying it's *just* an accident."

Kendall Jennings' eyes glistened. Good, she was getting the message. O'Grady bet she wondered now what kind of Pandora's box she'd opened. *Well, that's what you get when you play with people's lives.*

He jabbed a warning finger at her.

"Take some responsibility for your actions for once in your life. Grow a soul, while you're at it."

He turned away from her once again and headed back down the street to return the two blocks to the crime scene. The feeling of winning stayed with him for one block, then he chided himself for rest of the way for allowing her to rile him up.

By the time he reached the house and waded through the hive- activity of crime scene investigation, he'd cooled right down, even feeling a little remorse. Jack's death wasn't her fault. She'd just pressed the wrong buttons at the wrong time.

The instant he passed the two bodies inside the entrance his brain refocused on the job. Kendall Jennings disappeared from his thoughts. The only thing on his mind: *Who does a thing like this?*

He wasn't a criminal profiler, but this already seemed wrong. If this was a murder investigation and they were interviewing Kate Wilker, they wouldn't make her for this crime. Women didn't tend to go crazy with a gun. They might shoot an abusive spouse or kill out of jealousy, but mass murder just wasn't the norm. This was like a film where the scriptwriter had mixed up the characters.

Add to this anomaly the fact this was the third mass killing in twelve days in their jurisdiction and it all seemed way too bizarre and coincidental. Was there something in the water? Was there some kind of copycat activity going on here? Would he wake up tomorrow to discover this was all in his imagination, the guilt after all these years having eaten into his mind?

O'Grady felt his world tilt at an uncomfortable, slippery angle. What he *did* know was Kendall Jennings had stirred up memories he didn't want stirred. That pissed him off, big time. Add that to a feeling in his gut that something *was* wrong with all these killings, that they were connected, even if that made no sense. Suddenly he felt afraid.

Until he established what it all meant, maybe nobody should feel safe. When ordinary people, without provocation, suddenly start killing that wasn't merely a mystery to be solved, it was a nightmare beyond comprehension.

CHAPTER 21

ONE WEEK AFTER THE DEATHS on Bentley Street West, the headlines had already moved on to the new government budget and what it would mean to families. Boss17 shuffled the pages of the newspaper, the sound of the rustling paper overloud in his ears. The mass killing now relegated to page six. Even then, it was nothing more than a picture of the surviving children and an unflattering photograph of the killer Kate Wilker. The funerals were to be held in two days. No doubt there would be a mass turn-out of friends and relatives to bid farewell, along with curious onlookers come to gape at the sorrow.

He knew what would happen after that. *Absolutely nothing.* The killings would diminish to small mentions when something similar occurred in the future. His other two pieces of handiwork had disappeared from the news quickly, too. That surprised and dismayed him. He'd incorrectly calculated a cluster of mass killings would be seen as a pattern, causing serious questions to be asked. He'd imagined calls for an inquiry.

Such a shame. Such a terrible, wasteful shame.

He pondered his mistake. He'd clearly misjudged the police, the media and the general population. *Didn't anyone care? Didn't anyone have questions?* Maybe the police *had* put it together, and they weren't talking to the media. That *might* be a reasonable scenario.

All last night only one thought plagued him: he might not have done enough, that he needed more. It was a decision he hadn't imagined facing.

He should have factored in society's preparedness to readily accept mass-deaths. If he tried again, surely at some point, the police *must* realize something wasn't right, that these killings were an anomalous cluster.

"Hmm," he said, as he folded the paper in half and placed it carefully, thoughtfully, on the table. He picked up his cup of tea and took a sip. "Maybe I'm being too subtle."

CHAPTER 22

KENDALL'S MOOD HAD GROWN WORSE. Every time she thought about that detective, she felt a tug inside. He was a jerk, but he was also a good-looking jerk. She had a feeling below the tough, I-don't-play-well-with-fools persona, a softer man existed, a man who'd been buried by something and needed love to pull him out.

Seriously Kendall, you need to give up reading Nicholas Sparks' romance novels.

Yes, she did, because she'd even caught herself looking for a reason to contact him, find a way to smooth things over. Like the last time went *so* well.

She couldn't totally understand his anger or why he blamed her for the entire media's behavior. Maybe if they could just talk he'd see she wasn't like other journalists. *That Nicholas Sparks perfectly outrageous plot had crept in again.* In real life, people getting off to a bad start rarely ended up together. At least as far as she knew.

Kendall tapped away on her laptop while staring at the wall behind, hardly an inspirational view, but she found sometimes looking at nothing cleared her mind and helped her think. She looked at what she'd written. The cursor blinked accusingly at her.

Yes, she hadn't achieved much on this story so far. After writing a few more words, she backspaced until everything she'd just written disappeared, leaving her with an empty screen again.

She had to write something about the aftermath of the murders—labeled "The Mommy Killings" by one of the big presses—and she couldn't find the words. She'd organized two interviews with neighbors living in Bentley Street West, but now struggled with remaining objective with something that tore at her heart.

This morning she'd met with Trip over coffee. She was surprised he'd agreed to meet her so soon after the latest murders. After seeing him, she realized why. His personal questions about her and her life outnumbered her interview questions. She hadn't made a point of discouraging him, but she also hadn't led him on. The way he asked the questions reminded her of a puppy bounding about in all directions, eager and excited.

Most of what he revealed about the three mass killings wasn't anything she didn't already know. She knew he had more details, and she needed more time to get him to open up.

How wily had she become? She almost didn't know herself. At some point, she would need to gracefully exit from his advances, but she only needed to think of her bills and Beastie Best's constant email demands to keep her pushing forward.

Kendall caught herself wishing it were Lance O'Grady who wanted to meet with her. Not Trip. Nicholas Sparks was off the reading list for good if that's what it did to her emotions. *Focus Kendall,* she told herself for the umpteenth time. She redeployed her mind to the blank screen and the story that was *not* writing itself.

Seven Days Later. What they lived through.

This wasn't her headline; it was another of Beastie's headlines. The woman loved to fling these titles at writers, which sometimes made difficult stories even tougher because they confined a story's angle. This was absolutely the very last article she'd write on these murders. She'd told herself that several times already but today was it. Another nightmare last night was the last straw. Emotionally, she was burned out.

Kendall had done her homework. She'd managed to interview a teen relative of the "The Mommy Killings" the day before, even though *Sixty Minutes* hovered nearby with their checkbooks. Beverley still treated her like a long lost niece. She'd spent several hours again with her and another witness from the Amaretto Café murders, so she had material.

Today, though, the words wouldn't flow. Her mind kept drifting back to the night random violence visited her own world. The question, could she have changed what happened, was never far from her thoughts.

Survivor's guilt was a powerful emotion. Kendall could easily insert her own first-hand experience into this article. She would never do that, though, because she didn't want to dig in to those still-raw feelings. Nightmares were bad enough.

The fear suffered by those in the Bentley Street West house, Amaretto Café, and in the Kenworth Home facility wasn't unimaginable for her. As she'd written those words—*inconceivable terror*—the blinking cursor became her heartbeat.

For her, the terror *was* imaginable. Face your own mortality. Stared in death's eye. These were clichés, yet they didn't come close to how you felt when something random and violent came at you. In fact, you feel nothing at all—at first. First, you don't understand what's happening. You initially think somehow you've fallen into a television show and soon the director will call "cut," and you'll go home and talk about this crazy experience like it's a ride at a theme park.

Later, of course, you feel as though your insides have ripped apart. Even days later adrenaline still explodes through your veins at the slightest sound.

"It's shock," her therapist explained. Your mind goes into autopilot as a way of clearing out anything unnecessary in order to survive.

After the shock fades, the guilt fills the space left behind. Remorse winds around every memory associated with the event and strangles you.

Thoughts of that night tortured Kendall. If she hadn't drunk so much that night and been unable to drive her own car home. Instead of calling her mom, she could have so easily accepted a friend's offer of a lift. If her mom had driven a different way or if the lights at the intersection had been green instead of red, all these minute differences could have changed everything. In penance, she'd never touched a drop of alcohol again. Not even in cooking.

She saw the intersection in her mind, the yellow traffic light changing to red, felt the car slowing, the rain beating on the windshield, the way everything looked blurred through the side window, her mother humming the tune on the radio even though it was one a.m.

Kendall pushed the thoughts from her mind, but her stupid Nicholas Sparks-influenced mind turned to O'Grady again. Without thinking, she Googled him, this time she checked back through older links.

Success.

Fifth page, near the bottom, was something she'd missed in her earlier search. Clicking open the page, she began to read.

He'd had a brother.

"Oh no," she said to the screen as she read the article about the accident and subsequent suicide. "That explains a lot."

Now she completely understood and felt for him. In fact, it made *her* feel a little better. It wasn't personal. In his mind, she was part of a collective who'd hounded his brother.

Kendall never gave much thought to what happened after she finished interviews. Even though she didn't normally write about sensational events, what did happen to the subjects after she left? Did she harm them in any way? She didn't mean to. Often people's stories touched her, but they were, in the end for her, a story that paid bills.

Suddenly she saw herself through O'Grady's eyes and felt ashamed.

The cursor drummed a beat in her mind. *You-suck-up-people's-misery-and-spit-it-out-for-money.*

Her fingers went to the keys and she actually typed it.

You suck up other people's misery and disaster and spit it out for cash.

She stared at the words. Yes, there lay the truth, ugly and careless, in black and white. She hadn't even given poor Doug McKinley much more of a thought.

His words bounced into her head. *"Please look through my research. If it receives publicity maybe we could make a change."*

Preoccupied with Beastie's deadlines, she hadn't even bothered to look at the folder yet. She'd only taken it to keep him happy in case she needed him later. She'd told herself one day, when she had a spare ten minutes, she'd give it a glance.

She saw his face, desperate, sad, and hopeful as she took the folder. Maybe he sat there each night wondering if she had read it yet, counting on her, imagining Kendall had more pull than she actually did, that she was some kind of investigative journalist. Maybe he even thought she could get a story on it published in a big newspaper like the *New York Times* and bring the world's attention to his cause.

Doug McKinley was still inside the story of his son's death, and he would stay trapped inside there for the rest of his life, unless ...

Kendall looked across her desk, across the mess of newspaper clippings, bills, the collection of empty coffee cups, the stacks of books she was supposed to review for a measly twenty bucks apiece, and a half-empty box of chocolates (she told herself chocolate improved her writing). Now where had she put his folder?

Still seated, she rolled her chair over to the two-drawer filing cabinet at the side of her desk and pulled out the drawer with such vigor the side of it clipped her leg.

"Ouch."

Is that what I get for my trouble? Could be a sign this was a bad idea, a squandering of her time.

She peered inside the bottom drawer, expecting to find the file where she threw most get-to-it later things. Nothing there, except a jumble of old files and a packet of candies she'd forgotten. Rifling in the candy packet, she pulled out a sugar treat, popped it in her mouth, and chewed, while she returned to scanning her desk.

Nope, it wasn't there and, right now, she didn't have time to look further. She'd look later. If it were difficult to find that would be the Universe pushing her in a different direction. She vaguely remembered advice to that effect from a tarot card reader she'd interviewed. Chris Lamben, if she remembered correctly. He'd flirted and hit on her twice during the interview.

Kendall looked back at the screen. The cursor flashed as though it was sending a message. Boy, she hated that cursor right now. She had nothing to offer it, no words to fill the page. She gathered up the three empty coffee cups from her desk and walked toward the kitchen. A pile of dirty dishes awaited her. If she went into the laundry there would be a pile of clothes waiting, too. Everything had been put on hold for these stories. For her own sanity, she really needed to get off the merry-go-round.

A bunch of queries and pitches to her usual editors was probably what she needed to do. Ideas fired in her brain instantly. *What bananas can do for you? Mid-life crisis, real or imagined.* Myriad banal headlines were there for the plucking, all of them doing nothing for anyone except filling a quarter page of a magazine or website. And that used to be enough for her.

So why couldn't she do it? Why couldn't she just do the washing, clean the apartment, then get on the computer and compose the emails, which would remind editors she was still available and ready to work?

She didn't like the answer.

Even though the nightmares tore at her, the recounting of the killings making her sick to her stomach, she realized something about herself. She relished her byline in the papers. A thrill flared in the pit of her stomach when she thought about people talking about her articles on their way to work or around their dinner tables. As much as she'd told herself repeatedly she was giving this up, the time had not yet arrived.

Fate must have had a point to prove. She suddenly remembered where she'd put Doug McKinley's file—in a box in the spare room, where she put everything that was *really-get-to-it-much-later.* Later for this box usually being a once a year tidy-up and throw out.

Kendall set the coffee cups down on the sink, where they joined the rest of the mess, walked into the spare room, and found the box. The file lay on top, overflowing with pages and looking larger than she'd remembered. A thumb drive would have been nice, but Doug McKinley was probably not of the modern age.

Kendall pulled out the folder and opened the cover. Inside, to her surprise, was a handwritten letter addressed to her. She hadn't realized he'd been so prepared for her visit. How did he know she would even take the folder? Smiling at the determination of the man, she walked back into the living room, made herself comfortable on her sofa, and began to read.

The more she read, the more she wished she'd read it sooner. What it contained was totally unexpected. No, rephrase that—shocking.

CHAPTER 23

Dear Miss Jennings,

Thank you for taking the time to look through my research.

I've spent a great deal of money and effort collecting this information, but nobody will listen to me. I'm hoping if you help me gain publicity for my findings, maybe these senseless killings can be stopped.

The killers are not who they seem to be.

My son didn't need to die. If the corruption that caused his death had been exposed earlier, he might still be alive. In fact, I believe he would be alive today.

It's been twenty years since then, and you will discover there are many people to blame for what is happening now.

If you need my help with anything, please feel free to contact me.

Yours very sincerely,
Doug McKinley

Kendall read the letter twice. What did he mean by *many people to blame for the killings*? Surely, this was nothing more than a man grieving for his son, looking for reasons to explain madness, when no reason existed?

Turning the letter over and placing it face down, Kendall checked the wall clock—a Felix the Cat clock she'd bought to remind her to never watch time-wasting cat videos on YouTube. The folder contained a great deal of information, and it would take some time to get through. Doug McKinley had done his research, and even the first few pages held startling revelations, if there were any truth to them.

After she'd read a dozen pages and looked over the accompanying graphs, she began to understand why McKinley was passionate in his beliefs. What Kendall couldn't understand was why this hadn't become general knowledge, even as an urban myth. There certainly was a story amid all the supposition.

First, though, she needed to complete some research, and she needed to speak to someone in particular, even though he probably wouldn't want to speak to her.

CHAPTER 24

WHEN O'GRADY SAW THE IRRITATING journalist standing at the front desk, he did a double take. *What the hell was she thinking?* Last time he'd seen her, had he not made himself perfectly clear.

He admired her determination, but either she was brainless—and she didn't seem to be—or ignorant. Since she was a journalist, he voted the latter.

He had mixed feelings: resentment, curiosity and something else he didn't care to admit—she filled her jeans and pale-blue t-shirt very nicely. The minute the last thought entered his head, he experienced another emotion: annoyance. Right now, he didn't care to think like that about any woman, especially her.

Clearly, he needed to up the ante. He headed toward her, running multiple lines in his head, all of which should piss her off enough to send her packing and assure she left him alone.

As he drew closer, she moved toward the elevators and stood looking up at the floor indicator. In her hands she held a large folder and over her shoulder was slung a big green slouch bag. He hated to admit the casual look suited her.

He came up behind her and waited. She hadn't noticed him yet. She was so close he could reach out and brush his hand across her hair. He noticed again the way the strands curled on her shoulder and bounced as she looked up from the folder checking the elevator's floor location.

He used his deepest, harshest voice. "I thought I'd made myself pretty clear last time."

She swung about to look up at him, and the color of her incredible blue eyes struck him again. He had to bite down on his lip to stop himself from smiling instead of frowning.

"Oh, it's you." As if she wasn't obviously on her way to his squad's floor to find him. "Clear about what?"

"Clear that I won't give you an interview or any information about these murders. So you can just crawl away and write about something else. Or make up lies, like you people normally do."

She fixed her stare on him, and he was surprised at the confident way she met his own glare. He hadn't expected that after their last meeting and he didn't expect her answer.

"You know what? I really appreciate your *wise* advice. But I hope you won't mind if I *don't* take it."

She turned back to face the elevator door, leaving O'Grady looking at her back and noticeably squared shoulders.

"Seriously, there's no interview here. So scoot along why don't you, back to your lair."

Still facing away from him: "I'm not here to interview you." Then after a pause, "You really are very self-important, aren't you?"

Then he understood.

"Ah-hh, right. *Trip* has agreed to talk to you. Shows you where your morals are, doesn't it."

She whipped around to face him.

"My morals are in the exact right place, thank you. You wouldn't have a clue."

The sound of an elevator bell interrupted them. They both looked away toward the three elevators. Above the furthest car, glowed a red arrow.

Ignoring his comment, Kendall Jennings began to walk toward the opening doors until suddenly she stopped and glanced back at him. Their eyes met for just a moment too long. It was he who now felt uncomfortable.

She smiled. "Now, if you'll excuse me, I have someone to see who has better manners than you. And may I give *you* a piece of free advice?"

O'Grady raised an eyebrow. She really did have spunk. Even as he feigned disinterest, he actually found her quite amusing. In other circumstances, he might have called her *cute*.

"Work on a decent attitude, Detective O'Grady. Not everyone is out to do the wrong thing. You must live in a horrible world if you think *everybody* is so selfish. People might surprise you if you gave them half a chance."

The lift doors opened wide. Kendall Jennings moved quickly inside, gave him one last shake of her head, then the doors closed and she was gone.

O'Grady shook his head, too, as he turned and walked toward the front door. He'd been on his way back to his desk, but if she were going up to see Trip, then he would make himself scarce. If Trip had an interest in her, then more fool him. She *was* feisty; more so than he ever imagined. Possibly another trick of her trade—concealing her true personality to get what she wanted.

Anyway, it gave him freedom to finish up the last few interviews in order to finalize the file on the Mommy Murders. Images of the crime scene flashed in his mind. Sudden emotions flamed in him. This Kendall Jennings was selling a story on these deaths. If she'd seen what he'd seen— the red splattered walls, the thick pools of blood and the shattered bodies— maybe she wouldn't be so enthusiastically seeking details.

Out in the brisk air as he walked to his car, O'Grady felt himself begin to sweat. He loosened his tie. Why *was* he so annoyed at this woman? It was more than her being a nosy journalist. Maybe it was because Trip hadn't told him he was meeting with her. Or that she had the audacity to turn up at a crime scene. How had she known about the event, anyway?

Of course. Trip.

That did it. He decided he'd work through these interviews on his own. When he got back, he and his partner would have a serious talk. Trip was playing a dangerous game.

CHAPTER 25

WENDY THOMPSON SAT ACROSS FROM O'Grady, bouncing a baby on her lap. She leaned down and kissed the child's ruddy cheek before looking back at him. Her eyes were red and her face drawn.

"Kate and I've been friends for four years. Her daughter and my Ellen went to school together. It's a tragedy. A real tragedy. Those kids ... I've seen her with those kids at school, on play dates, in the supermarket. I can't imagine what's going to happen now. Do you think they'll be alright?"

O'Grady nodded. "The extended family seems close-knit. There's support there."

He looked down at his pad, at the few questions he'd noted to ask. They'd already interviewed this woman, but he had a few more questions. In fact, he wasn't exactly sure what he was after. It was just a common comment he'd noted made by witnesses from both the Kenworth Home's facility and the Café Amaretto crimes that nagged at him. Really, he was fishing in murky waters.

"Mrs. Thompson, you mentioned you saw Kate the morning of the event?"

"Yes, I saw her. She was with me on Saturday, maybe an hour before she went and kil—"

Wendy stopped, dabbing a tissue at the corners of her eyes as she bent again to kiss the top of her baby's head.

"I can't understand it. How could this happen? Kate wouldn't hurt a fly. She loved those kids. They seemed happy, Randall and her."

More tears welled in her eyes. She reached up with the back of her hand to wipe them away. The baby gurgled happily on her lap.

It was the same story with every one of the mass murderers. Every witness who knew the killers—Benson, Tavell, and now Kate Wilker—had said the same thing: they were all decent human beings who didn't have a violent bone in their body. Descriptions of cold-blooded killers usually didn't include words like kind, thoughtful, happy, or wonderful. More likely the words would be moody, angry, loner, irrational. Not one person had attributed a single motive or warning sign.

The other thing they had in common bothering O'Grady was one anomaly in the reports. It could be nothing. Probably *was* nothing. He hadn't even mentioned it to Trip, because, well, it was slim at best. It was odd. Each killer was out in public only an hour before beginning his or her spree. Benson was at a club. Tavell was eating at a diner. Kate Wilker was shopping with this friend, Wendy Thompson. Being out enjoying yourself just before you violently took lives seemed extraordinary behavior.

There were also witness reports from Benson and Tavell's outings noting a stranger had approached both men. A club doorman remembered a man approaching Benson in the street outside. He'd noticed them because he'd thought Benson was about to be mugged. Instead, though, the man pulled out a piece of paper and held it out to Benson. The doorman had, momentarily, returned to dealing with the club's parade of patrons. When he looked back, he noticed them farther down the street, walking together.

Less than an hour later, Benson would take seven lives. What was on the piece of paper, the identity of the stranger, and even if the meeting was relevant, remained a mystery.

In the case of Tavell, they had security footage taken by newly installed cameras outside the diner and along most of the surrounding street. He'd left the diner just after ten p.m. and walked half a block before a man wearing a dark jacket and a scarf wound about his neck approached him.

The man walked with an uncertain gait initially. He seemed irritated. Then O'Grady decided he only thought that because of the way the man kept scratching at himself as he approached Tavell.

With Benson, they worked with just one fixed camera outside the club, so the footage wasn't great. Blurry and over-dark, like a lot of this type of video.

O'Grady hadn't pursued either of the encounters because there was little to go on. Separately, too, they just didn't appear to be anything more than random events. Yet, if they *were* random, why both times did the unidentified man pull out a piece of paper and hold it out to Benson and Tavell? Was it the same man or a freak fluke?

Kate Wilker messed up the whole *connection* theory. As far as O'Grady could ascertain, she was out shopping prior to the killings. He'd checked the mall's video footage, and found no stranger intercepting her. All O'Grady had was an itch at the back of his neck and a throb in his gut, but he'd learned to trust that itch and that throb.

Sitting across from Wendy Thompson, O'Grady hoped she would answer his question in the affirmative. Then he would know he was onto something, even if he didn't know the *something*.

He leaned forward.

"Mrs. Thompson, there's one thing I neglected to ask last time we spoke."

"Yes?" Her sad eyes studied him as she held her baby so tight O'Grady feared she might squeeze the life out of her.

"When you were out shopping, did anyone approach you? A man, perhaps?"

His question caught her off guard. She'd probably expected him to ask her more about Kate's demeanor or her history. Had she been angry with her husband or mentioned she wanted out of her marriage? All questions she'd already answered in the negative.

Her gaze flicked down and to the side as she pulled one hand away from her baby, ran her fingers through her long hair, and pushed it behind her ears. She was revisiting her memories of that morning.

"Hmm. That's an interesting question."

She puzzled for a few more seconds, before looking back at him, her brow furrowed.

"Do you think Kate actually planned this with someone? I can't imagine that. I've thought about this ... it's all I've thought about since that day. That I was the last person she was with, before ... I can't sleep anymore, you know. Just a few hours. Then I wake up crying. I feel guilty and sad and I can't stop thinking about those kids. I'm trying not to think back to that day. I know Kate did a terrible thing, but I feel so sorry for her, too. Then I feel guilty for feeling sorry."

She kissed the baby's head, yet again, leaving her chin resting on the child's crown. Tears rolled down her cheeks.

O'Grady vehemently shook his head. He should have phrased the question better. "No, no, we don't think she acted with anyone. It's something else we're following up. I'm sorry to upset you, but can you remember anything? Or anyone?"

Wendy sighed as she wiped the fresh tears from her cheek.

"No, nobody spoke to us. We had a coffee. Kate needed to buy a birthday gift for her niece. The poor little thing, orphaned. Her parents—"

Wendy lowered her head for a moment, gathering herself. When she looked up again, she seemed more together. She'd stopped crying.

"We went into a gift shop and bought her niece a card. She was turning twelve. Kate found one with gold numbers on the front. You know, 'Happy Birthday 12-year-old!' Then Kate still couldn't decide on a present for her and it was getting late. I suggested a Pandora charm or a bracelet if she didn't have a bracelet. Kate got excited then, because her niece *did* have a Pandora. She loved the idea that a charm would remind her of her aunt, and—"

Wendy fixed O'Grady with a steely, adamant stare.

"Do you see how crazy this is? She bought the girl a *damn* charm. You tell me how she then takes a gun and kills the same girl's parents and the others. Tell me!" Her eyes burned with frustration, confusion, as though her friend had been wrongfully accused of murder and she a witness pleading her innocence in a trial. "You tell me, Detective O'Grady, how that works?"

What *could* he tell her? He didn't know himself.

"I don't know. Look, sometimes there's no answer. People just snap."

"Well, I don't know how she snapped. Kate wasn't like that. Something terrible must have happened to make her do what she did. Maybe she was afraid for her life or something. I guess in your job you always look for the worst in people."

"Actually, no, I'm *always* looking for the truth. Good or bad."

Now they were off track—if he'd ever been on track with his hunch. He wished he could explain the practicalities of his job: that sometimes he never did find the truth. Sometimes it wasn't there to be found. People just did crazy things. Human beings needed reasons, but misfiring brains don't always leave explanations. He'd learned to live with that in his job, otherwise he couldn't keep doing it.

O'Grady looked down and read from his notes. "So in the original interview you mentioned you accompanied Mrs. Wilker to an ATM. A few minutes after she'd taken some cash, you parted. Right?"

O'Grady looked back up as she flipped the baby around to face her and held the chubby bundle up to stare into her face. The little girl gurgled happily, then rested her head on her mother's shoulder. Wendy rubbed and patted the baby's back as though to burp her.

"Yes, that's about it." She suddenly stopped patting her daughter's back. "Don't these shopping malls have security cameras? Can't you check those?"

"Yes, they do."

Of course he'd looked over all the mall footage, but it simply confirmed what Wendy had already told him. The two women wandered the mall for close to ninety minutes, stopped for coffee, visited the ATM, and then parted. Nobody approached Kate Wilker inside the mall. Even though he'd found nothing, he couldn't quash a niggling worm of doubt he'd missed something.

"The footage showed nothing."

"I'm telling you, we walked to the parking lot together. Nobody came near us there, either." O'Grady already knew that, too, because he'd checked the parking lot footage yesterday when the connection theory had occurred to him.

"I went to my car. She went to hers. We drove out together. In fact, I was behind her, right up until the lights at the end of the street exiting the mall. I waved to her as I drove by. That was it."

O'Grady settled back into the sofa, suddenly realizing he'd moved so far forward he was now perched on the edge of the chair. He'd hoped, more than he wanted to admit, there'd be some shadowy stranger approaching Kate Wilker, complete with the mysterious piece of paper. Then all the crimes would fit perfectly into a scenario for which he *still* had no answer.

His mind drifted around the idea of synchronicity, meaningful coincidences, and then alighted on Kendall Jennings. He wondered what she and Trip might be discussing at this very moment. It irked him she'd even entered his head. She'd become a distraction his mind kept homing in on, and he couldn't understand why.

He hadn't even realized he'd lost focus, when Wendy Thompson's voice interrupted his thoughts.

"Detective O'Grady, when I waved goodbye to Kate at those lights, she was just Kate. What did I miss?"

"Nothing. Sometimes, people just snap."

As he spoke, O'Grady made a note on his pad: *Check traffic cam footage outside mall.* Folding his notepad back into his pocket, he began to stand.

People just snap wasn't entirely true. He had no better answer, because that's exactly what seemed to have happened. He still had nothing. This had been a waste of time.

CHAPTER 26

BOSS17 FLICKED THROUGH THE magazines scattered on the table. He'd scanned the Internet all morning, just as he'd done for hours in the preceding week.

Stories of all the killings were heavily featured after the last mass murders perpetrated by Kate Wilker. Background snippets on all the killers and their history were included together. Everyone now looked for answers as to why they'd suddenly become killers. Just as he'd hoped.

The gun lobby and the anti-gun lobby were at it again, throwing statistics at each other. The president spoke out against gun laws and the need for change; something he'd never done before. Some groups even called for more research into violence in society and the relationship to increased violence and video games.

Boss17 found that laughable, as if there were a formula within humanity to be mined and then manipulated. *Good luck there.* Man was just genetically programed to enjoy killing or he would have died a few million years ago and some other beast would now rule the planet. You can't blame evolution. It was a beautiful thing, if its results didn't come after you.

No mention of the correlation between the drugs taken by the killers and their actions had appeared. So far, everyone seemed to have missed the point.

His plan was so beautiful, too. They never saw it coming, so they couldn't prepare. His little seeds, as he called them, his wind-up toys, were messing with the minds of the experts and the police and their precious statistics. They still hadn't figured it out, but they needed to up their game and start getting close.

He opened another magazine and flicked through it. Plenty of nothing articles. *Voyeurs Inc.,* he called these rags. Tidbits for the blood thirsty, discussion points for mealtimes, in the comfort of their safe worlds. Worlds, no longer safe.

The door opened behind him. You23 entered and nodded in his direction, before sitting at his computer and immediately commencing to tap keyboard.

Boss17 was happy to see his protégé had understood the urgency required in finding more subjects. He wouldn't call it looking for a needle in a haystack, but the required criteria were still somewhat limiting.

He'd hoped the woman would be the last, but it wasn't looking that way. With the news coverage not hitting upon the requisite issues, he'd decided they *must* initiate another mission. Plant another seed.

Boss17 stood and walked over to stand behind the young man, who was currently scratching his scraggy, oil-steeped hair like he had an infestation of nits. He didn't think the kid had nits, but his hygiene left much to be desired. He did, though, look a whole lot better than when Boss17 had first found him as a filthy, angry, lost young man living in a halfway house.

You23 was a genius, but he was incapable of functioning in the world. Boss17 had done his research. He knew he couldn't embark on this plan alone. He needed someone with this boy's skills. Not that You23's skills were unique. His other attributes made him valuable. He needed someone with the naivety of this boy, someone who would believe in the world he'd created. To appeal to the kid, he'd turned it into a game, of sorts. The names, the subterfuge, and the drugs the boy required to stay focused and on track, turned him into a pliable co-conspirator who didn't really understand what he was doing. The boy passionately believed Boss17 cared about him and was his friend. Nobody else had shown him any sort of care, so that part was easy.

Ironically, drugs proved to be Boss17's greatest allies. They brought him

You23 and a facility to harness his abilities, and they brought him the solution to his problem. Now he could right a wrong and deliver justice with bittersweet irony. He hoped they would listen. So far, he'd gotten nowhere; the police, the profilers, all the experts who weren't looking or didn't care enough to pay attention, had failed.

Years in the planning, the time had now arrived. Like a starving man whose meal was held at arm's length for too long, his stomach gnawed with the need for it to be done.

And it *was* getting done. *He* was getting it done, because all those years ago the same so-called experts, who'd failed then, were failing now.

He reached out and placed his hand on the boy's tousled brown hair, unwashed and thick with knots. Gently he patted his unlikely ally's head. The boy ignored his touch and continued to stare at the screen.

"Anything?"

He'd given You23 an earlier directive. The kid wouldn't stop until he was finished. That was how it worked with people with his type of mind.

The screen flickered with photo after photo as You23's program rapidly searched the online files using the particular search words it was given. Instagram made everything so easy. He could have used Twitter or Facebook to hunt them down, but he'd discovered, well, You23 had discovered, that Instagram users' hash-tagged more thoroughly and explicitly.

Once dispatched, the program searched for #depression #sad #lonely #depressed #depressiontime, and any variations of these. Then the clever boy had written a program that accessed the password-locked Instagram accounts and revealed the account owner's details.

In its first pass, the software located accounts mentioning any negative emotion more than once. It then ranked them based on the frequency they posted those mentions. This threw up thousands of likely candidates. These numbers were then pruned by a geographic search until they found a likely seed living within the city area. After that, qualifying a subject became a manual process of checking for regular posts, which provided their whereabouts. He'd particularly looked for men. They were harder to find, because they didn't tend to share as much online as women.

Not everyone posted the minutiae of their lives. Many though invested enormous time, sharing life's mundanities down to where they ate breakfast or shopped, seemingly more obsessed with living in the public eye than the Kardashians.

"This is me driving over a bridge."

"Me at The Aviary kicking back with my pals."

"Here I am alone in a park."

"Look at my new car, my new shoes ... new bike ... new, whatever."

The look-at-me-world now worked for Boss17. He possessed a doorway, to them, and their need to share was all he required.

Suddenly, the program stopped shuffling through images. A face appeared on the screen. You23 leaned forward, studying the information below the picture. Then he brought his fingertip to a fraction of an inch above the screen and pointed.

"I think ... Yes, I think this one is good."

You23 continued to scroll through the layers of collated information, muttering. He always struggled to read silently. From what Boss17 could see, it looked as though he was right. Hundreds of pictures layered across the screen, all highlighted with time stamps. The program would now check back through several months of the account's photos, noting the time stamps and if any location reoccurred regularly. It sought a pattern. The success of their operation relied upon pinpointing where a subject would be at a certain time.

This one did indeed fit the bill. Consistent posting, seemingly happy, but peppered in between his comments were mentions of something else. Something dark. Maybe the FBI and the police didn't see it, but it was there for anyone, who cared to look, to see.

A ping sounded from the computer. Boss17 leaned into the screen and studied the picture of a young man in his early twenties, with sandy colored, short hair, and a wide, winning smile. A clean-cut professional.

"He seems a fit." You23 nodded toward the screen. "See here, he talks about feeling 'a kind of lonesome pills can't smooth.' This *Fix Coffee Shop* seems to be a regular stop. Time stamps put him there at pretty much the same hour several times a week."

Boss17 gazed at a selfie of a smiling young man holding a coffee cup toward his phone camera.

Boss patted the boy's shoulder.

"I think you're right. Well done. Create a report on him for me to look over. Then we'll make a final decision."

You23 turned back to the screen, his hands flying across the keyboard.

Boss17 knew this one might not work. They sometimes looked good initially, and then some small thing ruled them out. They'd been lucky to find the three they had. He'd actually thought three was all he would need. He'd been wrong. The world lacked imagination.

An idea suddenly occurred to him. Why didn't they do something bold? Why not use someone who was already in the public eye? It might be riskier than their previous subjects, but things weren't going to plan anyway. He needed to shake it up.

As he ran the idea through his mind, the excitement built in his core. It even had a certain poetic justice. He smiled at the thought.

He turned back to You23, and gripped his shoulder. The boy almost purred beneath his touch.

"Change of plans. Check this name as well. I'll spell it for you."

Yes, this could be the one.

CHAPTER 27

THE MORE KENDALL READ THROUGH McKinley's research, the more intrigued she became. The man was thorough, that was for sure, and his theory compelling. He'd even inspired her to do some research of her own.

The death of his son was a sad twist of fate. Now she understood his fighting for some reason to the randomness. There'd even been a book written on the mass killing in which his son died. What surprised her were the news outlets neglecting to mention this first mass killing in relation to these recent murders. Even with Danbridge's population of one million, surely the odds of this many mass killings occurring here was statistically enormous.

The two nights it took her to read the book had reignited the nightmares that had only just started to dissipate. Written from the perspective of the killer, it had an authenticity that filled Kendall with a sense of claustrophobia and impending doom. She wanted to use some of the details in an article she'd begun to formulate around Doug McKinley's report. Despite not totally buying his hypothesis, she could still sell the article and help him at the same time. Then it was a win-win.

Kendall decided to reread through a few of the chapters of the book again, this time paying attention for hooks and small quotable lines she could use. She'd then contact the author seeking permission to use partial pulls from her work. Emotionally difficult as the research was, she felt a little thrill. If she wrote this right, it might turn out to be one hell of a story.

Kendall snuggled down in bed, pillows propped behind her, her laptop, note pad and several pencils beside her. She drew in several deep breaths and exhaled slowly to calm her thumping heart. She'd learned that relaxation trick from her therapist.

Looking up to the ceiling, she whispered, "Mom, look how much I've grown since—."

She opened the book and began to read.

CHAPTER 28

1995

THROUGH THE SLATS OF THE dusty window's partitioned blinds, light swam into Lyall Wright's eyes. It reached into his brain, winding its way into places already soft and wounded, making him cry out in pain. He couldn't find the voice to call for help. Instead, he ground his teeth and clenched his jaw until the muscles in his face ached from the effort to stifle the scream.

Hunger suddenly gnawed at him, ravenous, eat-your-own-arm hunger. He'd held off going out for as long as he could, unsure if he could handle the people out there, the voices, the stares, the way they said, "thank you" and "please," as though the world was a perfect, rosy place.

Lyall's world had fallen apart. He couldn't remember when it hadn't felt as though the walls of life were crumbling about him, raining down, and crushing him with their weight. His own personal tower of Babel with nobody speaking his language.

Every day his body grew wearier, as though it, too, were giving up on him, just like his mind. As he physically weakened, the urges grew stronger, pushing at his sanity, asking of him the impossible and the terrible. He shrank from them, but they pursued him in the deepness of the night.

He'd tried to practice Dr. Willis's advice. He tried to think positively; to take his medication; call a helpline when he became overwhelmed; and seek out friends and family.

He'd done all that. Yes, he'd done *all that*. He'd pulled on every lifeline, one rope at a time, only to discover they weren't connected to anything solid, anything that would pull him out of this nightmare. As each one failed, he tumbled deeper, even as he looked upward, praying to a God whom he knew had abandoned him.

He was only twenty-six. *A wonderful life lay ahead of him.* His family and psychiatrist's words, and even the various voices on the other end of the telephone lifeline had repeated them ad nauseam.

"What is wonderful?" he'd ask. He had so little experience of it, spending much of his adult life doing battle with this dark, horrible thing inside his mind that insisted on living life its way.

He thought of it as evil oil that had entered his mind around age seventeen, taking him on some terrible trip without the pleasure of mind-altering drugs.

Lyall *had* tried.

He'd tried for his family. He'd tried for his mom. He'd tried for his wife. For Karina, he'd tried *so* hard, because she hadn't deserved him, hadn't deserved the absolute shit he'd put her through. She was a good woman, harsh with their son sometimes, but he figured that came down to him; she was raising the kid on her own. She'd left him two years ago and he'd tried to win her back, see his boy. Then she'd moved twice, changed her number, and it was over. He didn't want to ruin their lives, so he didn't look for them. Set them free.

Then he'd met Helen, who seemed to understand. She'd stuck by him through the therapy, the doctor's visits, the manipulation of his drug dosage for the depression and the episodes when the drugs didn't work. Her support helped. For a while. For a while, he was almost happy, could almost reach the golden lifeboat within himself and sail off toward the happy horizon to join the life he saw thriving around him. The life he just couldn't seem to touch.

In the end, Helen left, too. Took her own lifeboat and saved herself from the darkness he exhaled every day.

Lyall couldn't keep going. Yet, he couldn't stop. The courage he needed to do the right thing eluded him. He'd almost managed it once, a bottle of scotch and three beers his fortification to take the last step. He'd passed out before he could wrangle the rope; a two-day hangover was all he managed for the effort. Like everything else in his life, the attempt wounded him, but didn't kill him.

What doesn't kill you, hurts you.

Tonight, the darkness crept up on him. He'd swallowed down a double dosage of pills. Prozac helped, taking the edge off, making his brain feel less like some alien was in there running the show. This past week, he'd needed extra doses to fight the insomnia and fight back the insects crawling beneath his skin.

When he'd finally gained the strength to go out to get food, look what happened. The Burger Boys drive-thru was so fucking slow, he thought he'd die waiting. Five cars, shunting toxic fumes back at him, were queued ahead.

"Fuck this." Lyall slammed his hand against the steering wheel. Why hadn't his stupid body decided it was hungry earlier, before the mealtime rush?

The dashboard clock read seven twenty-four. He wasn't in a hurry to be anywhere. If his stomach weren't filled with savage piranhas nipping at its walls, he wouldn't care if he sat there all night.

The pills were to blame; insatiable hunger a side effect, but he needed those shitty chemicals to maintain *his* version of sane. They weren't the lesser of two evils. It was *all* evil.

Today, he'd planned badly, skipping lunch at work, too down to leave his desk. Finding no food in the house when he arrived home, he'd spent too long debating whether to leave the house again. Attending his part-time nowhere job took all his strength. Now here he was, starving and waiting in this fucking line of cars fantasizing about eating a soggy, bullshit, carry-out meal.

Two cars ahead moved through the order area. He hated those ordering speakers. He could never understand the metal android voice and *it* could never understand him.

"Two down. Three to go," he muttered, rocking himself in the seat. The fumes from the three cars ahead were killing him. *Really killing him.* He was in a gas chamber. He reached over and shoved the side air vents closed, just as another car took off. The interior still reeked of exhaust fumes. He coughed. Hunger pangs combined with the noxious fumes. Nausea punched him in the guts, but he held it back.

Another car drove off. Its yellow indicator flashing as it waited to turn onto the road; the flashing matched the pulse in his head.

Food. He needed food. He could almost taste the burger, feel it slide down his neck, and meet his clawing gut.

Lyall checked the clock again. He'd glanced at it four times in the past few minutes. Seven thirty-one. Another minute, surely that's all it would be.

More long minutes throbbed by. Something was wrong up ahead. The last car hadn't moved in what seemed like hours. Fucking hours that were killing him. If he didn't eat soon, he would start eating his own hand.

Lyall leaned forward in his seat to stare ahead through the dirty windshield, trying to see what was happening, what could be causing the delay. Heads moved and bobbed in the car, which stood only ten feet between him and sating his hunger. It looked like a woman in the driver's seat and a couple of kids in the back. She leaned out the window, talking into the speaker, for what seemed like far too long to be making an order. He rolled down the window, listening, but all he heard were snatches of the metallic voice, too distant and disembodied to understand.

Was it saying: Move on? Collect your order at the next window?

Please, let it be saying, "move on."

Nothing happened. No movement.

This wasn't fast food; this was fry-your-fucking-brains-waiting food.

Seven thirty-one.

Seven thirty-two.

Seven thirty-three.

Wild panic and all kinds of pain sparked in his brain like a firework display. Colors, explosions, the whole shebang. He needed to eat. HE

NEEDED TO EAT!

This woman … this woman with these kids bouncing in the back— yeah, they were jumping up and down like it was Christmas—was in his way. Who lets their kids do that in a car, while the poor fuck behind starves to death?

He'd been doing the right thing, waiting for his turn that, in his life experience, rarely came. When was it his turn for love, his turn for happiness, his turn to get out from under the fucking hunger killing him right now.

Lyall's palm smashed down on the horn, as though it were an enemy to be beaten into submission. He held it down—his palm now throbbing from the blow—to make his point.

HOOONNNNK! HOOONNNNK!

In the path of his headlights' glow, he caught a glimpse of her blonde hair and a hand movement. The image burned into his eyes like the aftermath of a camera flash. A single raised finger, standing erect from a fist. A message to him.

"Fuck you," he screamed. "Fuck you!"

She was the one holding *him* up. Holding up all the others waiting behind. And *she* had the fucking attitude to give *him* the bird? The world was wrong on this Friday night. So very truly wrong.

He should get out of the car, abandon this shit, and show her what happens to women with attitude. If he did, though, it might cause a scene, stop the line, and slow the food. His gnawing stomach put paid to that.

Finally, at seven thirty-four, the bitch's car inched away toward the collection window. Fucking great for her. She scored no punishment for using more time than she had a right, to order a fucking, simple meal.

When Lyall arrived at the speaker box that usually made English sound like a foreign language, he studied the board of food images. Fat and sugar delivery systems. *Exactly* what he needed.

The metallic voice addressed him: "Can … take… yo… orda, ple.se."

He wouldn't be *that* bitch, selfish and inconsiderate. He already knew what he wanted. He'd had long enough to think about it, that's for sure.

"Yeah, give me the Great Southern Burger meal." For the splurge, he craved the chill and sugar rush of a slushie. It'd been on his mind the entire drive here. "And can I have a Coke slushie, too?"

"Sorry, masheeen's brok'n."

Nearly every fucking time Lyall wanted one, their machine was broken. Fuck their machine. Why advertise it? *Why?*

Dr. Willis's voice entered his head. *Calm. Calm. It's just a slushie. Just a slushie.*

"Another time." He spoke aloud, soothed himself, using all the tactics embedded in his brain from his bi-weekly sessions with the doctor.

They did help calm him sometimes. *Sometimes.* The problem, lately: he felt someone else talking back. Another voice, not his. This voice wasn't on his side. It didn't like the interference. It didn't like the calm. It just wanted to be angry. Sometimes it wanted him to lose control.

This time: no voice. He felt in control. He just needed to keep talking to himself, reminding that a broken machine and no slushie were okay. *Yes, he could deal with this.*

Lyall's voice when he replied was even-toned and composed. See, he *was* in control.

"Okay, then. Just give me a chocolate Great Shake."

"Wha..t? Can you repee—, ple..se."

He answered a little louder this time, as though that might compensate for the fucked up wiring or whatever shit was wrong with the thing. "I *SAID*, give me a chocolate Great Shake."

Nothing. No sound, not even the crackling of static. How hard could it be? It was a burger and a shake, for fuck's sake. And his stomach was killing him, churning with the smells drifting from the building's multiple cooking vents.

"Okay. So that's a Great Southern Burger meal and a strawberry Gr..t Shake. That'll be seven, twenty-nine. Dri.. thr.., p..ease."

It was a simple request. They couldn't even get that right. He felt a tremor of something dark flare inside.

"No, I said, a *CHOCOLATE* Great Shake. CHOCOLATE.

ChoooCaaLaate. Okay?"

Silence.

He wondered if in shouting he'd offended the operator. *Too bad. They got it wrong, not him.*

"Hello? Did you hear me?"

Another beat of silence, then: "Yes, sir. Sor…y, w…'re out … choc—ate."

"How can you fucking be out of chocolate? HOW? Forget it. I'll just take the meal."

Silence answered.

"Okay. That w… be five, sev…ty …ght. Drive through."

A loud squawk ended the conversation.

Lyall wanted to yell at that box. In fact, he wanted to get out of the car and beat the crap out of the thing. He imagined everyone waiting behind him cheering.

Lyall, calm down. It's done now. Get your food and go home. You don't want to lose your cool over a little thing like this, do you? Well, you don't. Trust me. You don't want to let that fucking bear out of the cage.

Dr. Willis's soothing voice sounded less convincing than before. The other dark voice had arrived. He heard it in there prodding at him like a frustrated parent, churning, churning.

Lyall drove his car slowly around the corner of the building to the pick-up window. Ahead it lay, glowing like a yellow beacon in the darkness. His stomach juices sizzled at the sight as he anticipated shoving food down his throat; beating back the savage dog, hunger.

Arriving at the window, his chest tightened. Empty. Unlike the lame-ass commercials, no friendly human waited to greet him. Only a closed window welcomed him. That was it. The empty gateway to his food.

Lyall wanted to get out of the car, slam his fist on the window and shout, "My fucking stomach is eating itself. Give me my food!"

Calm. Stay calm, Lyall.

"Yes, Dr. Willis. I'm working on that, sir. These fuckers, though, sure aren't helping much." This time he'd spoken out loud, his hands gripping the wheel as he stared at the glowing window, willing someone to appear.

He rubbed his hand across his stomach—which in the past year had turned to paunch. The clock taunted him in a singsong voice. *It's seven forty-three and you're still not fed. Ha ha. You're still not fed.*

He'd been trying to get food—supposedly *fast* food—for over fifteen fucking minutes. Fury devoured his hunger, rolling through his stomach, flowing into his blood as though he'd bitten down on a hate pill.

Lyall reached for the door handle to open the door, go bang on the window, and point out they were useless fuckers, when a laughing long-faced teenage boy materialized at the window. The boy continued to laugh, looking over his shoulder, as he slid back the clear panel.

"That'll be five seventy-eight, please."

The young server stood at the window, acne flaring on his face as though red mold colonies had taken up residence. The kid didn't even have the decency to lean out the window to take his money. Lyall had to unbuckle his belt and stretch half way out of his car to hand the kid the money. A hot, worm of anger slithered inside his head. *Didn't they train these little shits in customer courtesy anymore?*

Without thanking him, the server took his money and said, "There'll be a wait of approximately five minutes. Sorry, we've been slammed."

Acne Boy added the glimpse of a smile.

He wasn't *really* sorry. *No, he wasn't.*

Then he pointed just off to the side, to a dimly lit area of the lot. "Park over there. We'll get your food out to you when it's done. If you prefer, park in general parking, come inside and wait near the counter. Here's your receipt."

Lyall gritted his teeth. *Calm, Lyall, calm.*

"If I wanted to get out of my car, go inside and get my food, I wouldn't have lined up for fifteen minutes in your drive-thru, would I?"

The kid's face reddened. His spots seemed to melt together in an ugly, crusty, inflamed mask, perfectly matching how Lyall felt inside.

"I said we're sorry, sir. We're short-staffed."

The boy shrugged, palms held face-up as though he was Jesus floating above his flock.

Lyall wanted to reply: "Fuck your staff problem." Instead as he hung on to the doctor's voice, he said, "Okay, but you'd better get my meal to me in the five minutes or I'll—"

The kid turned and walked away from the window. He hadn't even waited for Lyall's full reply, leaving him sitting there like some kind of idiot, one-upped by a pimple-faced kid.

Lyall eased the car toward the waiting bay. There was another car there: the woman who'd given him the finger and her bouncy children. The three brats still leaped around as though the seats were trampolines, the mother screaming at them, uncaring he was watching. Even with the window closed, he heard her.

He thought of his own son, Jamie, out there somewhere with Karina. Gone. For good. Maybe *he* was the lucky one. Maybe his son was bouncing around with Karina yelling at him. Even so, he wished he were there to yell at his own son. Why did she get to do that and not him? *No, that was wrong.* He didn't want to yell at Jamie. He wanted to play with his son, be there for him.

Something exploded in his head. Something wild. The fury, the despair, the unfairness of this life flooded through his mind and his heart.

Calm. Calm. You can do this Lyall. You can—.

No-thank-you Dr. Willis, I won't remain calm.

The clock read seven forty-five, the numbers blurred through a red haze. *Where did that color come from?*

He should be home at this moment, watching TV, having eaten his fill, having salved his hunger. Why was he here, sitting in the dark, watching this woman scream at her brats, with Mr. Future-acne-scars mocking him as if he, Lyall Wright, were a cosmic joke?

Rage exploded like the carnival game where the metal puck shoots up to' hit the bell after you swing a hammer. It fucking hit his bell like a rocket launched.

Ding. Ding. Ding. You win the prize. Finally.

Fuck Dr. Willis and his calm, calm, calm.

Lyall leaned down to reach for the lever beneath the seat to flip the trunk latch. He stepped out of the car and moved to the trunk, a yawning and dark hollow calling to him.

It was wrapped in a towel, nestled snugly at the back, long, black, and powerful, waiting for him.

Ding. Ding. Ding. You win the prize.

The hunger was gone. He no longer cared about Dr. Willis, Jamie, Karina, or any fucking thing. He'd had enough of the world and its poor service. He'd deliver a complaint to the Burger Boys' chain. It mightn't be official, but one thing for sure they'd be getting the message loud and clear.

CHAPTER 29

WHEN THE CUSTOMER FIRST ENTERED the dining area and stood at the back of the line, Charlie didn't notice him at first.

They'd been slammed tonight. Everybody living within a ten-block radius must have decided Friday night was eat-out night. He felt bad every time he repeated: "Sorry, the wait will be a few minutes."

They weren't even close to keeping up. Clumps of people had grouped a few feet to the side of the counter, while others sat at the one nearest vacant table—not that there were many of them—staring hopefully at the counter staff every time an order was stacked on a tray.

This was what you got when three people call in sick claiming flu thirty minutes before their shift. You got chaos times ten and grumpy customers times twenty. Charlie flipped back and forth between the counter and the drive thru, seemingly getting nowhere fast. As soon as he served five customers, another five replaced them.

Tomorrow he'd talk to his dad about quitting this job. It sucked. He didn't need complete strangers spamming him with their frustrations. The guy he'd just served at the window seemed ready to explode. *Screw this for a joke.* These days he had too many assignments and too much homework. He was falling as far behind with his schoolwork as they were tonight with the orders.

His manager had told him to prioritize the drive thru orders. "Lines of cars looks bad for the business," he'd said.

He'd followed the manager's orders, but Charlie couldn't do much. It was down to the cooks. Three cars were now in the waiting bays. That woman with the kids who couldn't make up her mind hadn't helped matters, either. Minimum wage wasn't enough to deal with this crap.

When he did spot the asshole from the drive thru, he recognized him immediately. He'd been kind of creepy; something about his eyes said *Freaksville.* Charlie had actually slammed the window closed, even though the guy was still talking. He wasn't paid to serve weirdoes.

Freaksville moved from the back of the restaurant to stand in the area between the tables and the counter, blending in with the other customers awaiting orders. Maybe he'd come in to change his order. He didn't move toward the counter, though. Instead he stopped near the window staring at the menu above the counter, rocking from one foot to the other.

Even though Charlie was busy loading an order on to a tray, he kept glancing toward Freaksville. Something about him was off center. *Way off.* Maybe he wanted to put in a complaint to the store manager. Charlie started thinking back, wondering if he'd served him properly. He *had* been a bit short. He'd actually pretended he couldn't hear him properly on the drive thru speaker. Possibly he could say Charlie was rude. Well, what was he supposed to do on such a busy night? They couldn't blame him, surely? Blame the shitheads who didn't turn up for their shift.

Charlie pushed the completed tray toward a customer, and checked Freaksville again. He felt certain the guy had simply forgotten something on his order. That had to be it.

His gaze traveled from Freaksville's face down his body. He looked like a hobo; his dirty, holed t-shirt hung limply over tattered jeans. His thick, ragged hair could use a wash, too. Maybe not a hobo, but he had an I-don't-give-a-shit air. Why did Charlie have to get *him* as a customer?

Charlie had missed spotting the rifle the first time he'd looked. The gun must have been held behind his back. He had no time to tell anyone. He didn't even have time to say "gun." Charlie watched, speechless, as Freaksville raised the weapon to stomach-height and scanned it around the room.

This can't be real. I'm supposed to do something now. What, freaking, WHAT?

Every staff member was trained on hold-up procedures, but he couldn't think of a single thing to do. *Except, run away.* Was *run away* a procedure?

Adrenaline deluged his body. With that, he suddenly remembered. Instructions flooded into his mind: Give them the money. Don't offer resistance. Don't make sudden movements. Alert someone in authority.

Where the shit was the manager?

There's a gunman in the store. The manager should deal with gunmen.

Oh, shit, what was he supposed to do?

Suddenly, someone in a group of waiting people took any decision out of Charlie's hands when a woman screamed. Like some kind of mental transference, everyone in the gunman's immediate vicinity realized the reason for the scream. As if a mini-bomb had erupted between Freaksville and the other customers, immediately a wide circle of space appeared around him.

A cacophony of scraping chairs and murmurs erupted. Frightened voices filled the restaurant, as word spread instantly around the room. A hundred plus eyes turned toward Freaksville and his gun. At the far side of the dining room a baby began to cry. A child's voice called out, "Mommy, that man has a gun." Then the sound of a woman shushing the child.

If Charlie's heart beat any faster, it would crack his ribs.

Alert someone in authority banged in his head.

He didn't know if he could do it. He didn't know if he could move. While he could see Freaksville, he felt a modicum of safety. If he turned away… *shit, was he actually going to die?*

Freaksville continued to scan the room, the rifle held a little higher. Charlie couldn't see if his finger was on the trigger. He, also, didn't want the guy to notice him. Freaksville might remember it was him. It might piss him off. He didn't want to piss him off or stand out in the crowd.

Slowly he turned just his head to look over his shoulder toward the kitchen. Through tight barely-moving lips, he half-whispered, "Cody.

Codeee!"

Cody, the manager, should be in the kitchen keeping the cooks on pace. He didn't answer. Charlie turned back to face ahead.

What was he supposed to do? A panic button was situated at the end of the bench, but he was too far away. *No sudden movements.*

Without being told, the restaurant patrons had suddenly stopped talking. Even the crying sounds were muffled. Several coughs came from a nearby table, piercing the silence like a gunshot.

Shit, don't think gunshot. Not like a gunshot. Like a cough. Like a cough. This was all going to be nothing. No gunshots.

Freaksville wanted money for drugs, for food, or for whatever a freak would need. He'd get the money and go.

Not like a gunshot. There would be no gunshots.

Charlie had done nothing wrong today, except come to work. This wasn't supposed to happen. Not to him. Not to anyone who'd just wanted a fast food fix.

Just get on with it, Freaksville, so we can all go home.

His hand shook like it was minus-thirty inside. He moved the out-of-control appendage slowly to grasp the edge of his register, to still the tremors. It didn't work.

Why hadn't the freak spoken? He just stood there, all zombie stare, panning the gun like it was a camera and he didn't know what to film.

Shit, where was Cody?

He risked a half-body turn to the kitchen and snatched a glimpse of Cody standing over the fry station, directing more fries to be loaded into each basket.

Charlie whispered as loud as he dared. "Phsst. Cody, you need to be here." To him, it sounded so freaking loud, he might as well have shouted.

Cody looked up. Must have seen the look on Charlie's face. He moved quicker than Charlie had ever seen him move. In a second, he'd skidded to a stop at the counter. Charlie nodded toward Freaksville, who'd now raised the rifle to chest height and held it stiffly out from his body. He moved the weapon up and down as though beating the air with it. The gunman muttered under his breath, but the words were indistinct.

Why wasn't he speaking, demanding money, taking hostages, doing something, for shit's sake?

Cody held up his arms, even though the gunman hadn't said "hands up."

His boss's voice sounded surprisingly calm. "Okay, man, no need for the gun. You can have everything in the tills. No problems. Okay?"

Cody kept one hand in the air; with the other, he slowly reached down and hit a register button. The manager was a real hardass. He barely smiled on the best of days. Charlie flicked a glance toward Cody. He was, also, pretty kickass. He hadn't even raised a sweat. Charlie felt as though he was *drowning* in sweat. His underarms were wet and sticky, and he desperately wanted to reach up and wipe the wetness dripping down his face.

No sudden movements, stopped him.

The cash drawer slid out, the sound cutting the air like a rocket launch. The drawer protruded between Charlie and Cody like a cubicle divider.

"See, man, it's all yours. Probably a few grand in all of them. Can I move to the next one, please, sir?"

Cody took a few hesitant steps around Charlie, and then moved along the counter.

Freaksville's gaze flipped to the next register, but still he didn't speak. He just followed the manager with the gun, as he traveled to the next register, where Cody gingerly pushed a button to slide out the drawer.

Everything was surreal, so quiet, so civilized. No one moved a chair. No one tried to escape. Probably no one believed anything would happen, that they'd just have a scary story to tell their friends.

That's what Charlie thought: *This was one to tell the gang, if he didn't die. Of course, he wouldn't die. That didn't happen to kids like him.*

Random sobs erupted around the room. Many quickly stifled by hands over mouths. Charlie wanted to cry, too, but he didn't dare, didn't want to draw attention to himself. Cody was in the spotlight now. He could stay there.

A small child's voice called out from somewhere out in the restaurant.

He wished he were out there, instead of here, facing a gunman who looked like a zombie, who looked like a guy who didn't care anymore.

The mother of the child tried to shush the little girl, but the child kept repeating the same questions: "What's he doing, Mommy? Why has the man got a gun? When can we eat?"

Her mother's voice replied, tense, strained to breaking: "We'll eat in a minute. Shhhhh."

Freaksville moved the gun toward the voice, then circled the weapon around the room as if to say *I am serious. Shuddup.*

Two female teenagers sitting at a booth, all black hair and blunt-cut bobs, screamed and cowered, hands over their heads as the barrel of the gun momentarily pointed at them. Nearest the counter, a man in his forties, in an open-necked business shirt and dark gray pants, moved a few steps back. He angled sideways to face the gunman, stretching his arms wide, so his body was now between the imminent danger and a woman and young sandy-haired boy. Nodding to them, he indicated they needed to move behind, that he would be their human shield. The boy snuggled into his back, pressing his face into the folds of his shirt. A sob escaped the child, overly loud in the eerie quiet. A few patrons had climbed under the tables. On any other day a disgusting idea, to scrabble on the floor of a fast food joint. Today, it was instinctive.

Freaksville returned his attention to the counter, his eyes distant as though his mind had traveled somewhere else, like he was listening to a song only he could hear.

Taking Cody's lead, thinking the sooner this crazy got his money, the sooner this would be over, Charlie moved to the last register, his shaking hand hitting the *open* button. The sound of the drawer sliding out like a dozen drawers sliding open at once.

The gunman's gaze followed Charlie's every move. Sweat rolled down the guy's face as though his pores were discharging his crazy in little, wet drops.

Then Freaksville spoke.

Charlie jumped. Cody, too. Charlie's heart burst in his chest. He'd been so focused on the registers, on getting the money out and handing it to their captor, he'd been on autopilot.

Freaksville pointed the gun directly at Charlie.

"You. You're the one who served me. Aren't you? I say *serve* loosely, because I *still haven't got my food!*"

Charlie didn't move, didn't dare speak. He wasn't sure what to say, or if he even had the ability to answer. His jaw felt locked. His breath, trapped in his lungs. His hands shook, vibrating like an earth tremor had hit.

"I asked you a simple question. I was hungry, you know. In fact, I bet there's a *lot* of hungry people here. Now ... Was. It. You?"

He again tracked the gun around the restaurant. Every pair of eyes inside the room followed the gun's movement. When its aim passed by them, they nodded in agreement, as though the gunman was their leader.

"Hey, man." Cody, his hands back in the air, the cash register he stood behind, abandoned, his voice now an octave higher than normal, sounded less confident. "We're really sorry if your experience here has disappointed. We can work this out. Take the money, and we'll be good, okay?"

Freaksville swung the gun back toward Cody, narrowing his eyes, beginning to take aim.

"You're the manager, right?"

Cody slowly nodded.

"No, sorry, we won't be good."

He fired the gun. Charlie's eardrums rang with the sound, loud and shocking. His heart exploded into a gallop. Screaming erupted in the room. It was strangely muted and low, as though he heard it through a glass wall. Then more shots followed in rapid succession.

Bang. Bang. Bang.

Charlie threw himself below the counter. He was going to die. He *was* going to die. *How could this happen to him? How?*

Cody was there on the floor face down beside him. Charlie took in the blood, pooling around the manager. Three big dark patches had appeared on the back of his shirt. He wasn't moving.

Holy shit, is he dead?

Charlie *had* to get out. He *had* to get home. To his dad. It was just him and his dad since his mom's passing. He couldn't leave his dad alone. They were a team. He had to get back to him. This was just a shitty part-time job. *Who dies doing something like this? Really, who?*

"Cody?" He whispered into his boss's ear. His heart thumped louder than his words. "Cody, you got to get up."

Then more gunfire. Sounding closer, nearer him.

Shit! Was he coming toward the counter? Holy shit.

He looked at his manager; for all he knew he was dead. He couldn't help Cody. He had to save himself. Charlie had blood on his hands and blood on his shirt. It was sticky and warm and he was going to be sick. He wasn't a hero. He was sixteen and terrified. He started to cry.

The sound of thunder from the back of the kitchen startled him.

Shit, what the hell?

It was crashing kitchen trays. He'd swung his head to the noise in time to see the fry cook, Ben, running for the door.

That was it. Charlie didn't stop to carefully make a life and death calculation. He just moved, pulling his body up, ready to run, ready to get out, get away, get home to his dad. He couldn't take it anymore. His mind felt filled with thick, cloying fluff. He couldn't think anymore, could barely control his limbs.

Ben got away. Why couldn't he?

He'd only reached a crouch, when the warm metal of the gun barrel touched the back of his neck. A jolt of electricity entered his skin. Instantly his bladder let go; the rush of urine warm down his leg. It dripped onto the floor, drip, drip, but he didn't care. *He just wanted to get home.*

"You know, all I wanted was a meal. I tried to be calm. Dr. Willis won't be happy. If it wasn't for you …"

Charlie hunched his shoulders. In his mind, he saw a ten-ton weight flying through the sky, aimed at him, bearing down, him trapped waiting for it to descend. He felt his life slipping away, the weight of his choices wrenched from him, the regret of never seeing his dad again. Still half-crouched, he raised his hands to either side of his face, and then clasped them behind his head.

"Plee-aase. Please … don't."

The words stuck in his throat like tough meat. A hundred miles away, he heard gasps from the dining room. No sound from Freaksville. All he saw looking down—he didn't dare look up—were the white floor tiles, splattered with blood and a growing pool of red. Cody's blood.

Shit, Cody's blood. Don't let that be the last thing I see. Please, God, please.

The gunman's voice remained calm, as though he were simply ordering a meal, not standing over a person with life—and fear—coursing through his veins.

"Consider this an official customer complaint."

Charlie didn't hear the gun explode. He thought he would. He thought there'd be some warning. No, the last thing Charlie heard was the voice of that child, the words so clear as though whispered in his ear.

"Mommy, I want to go home."

"Me, too," Charlie mouthed. "Me, too."

CHAPTER 30

"**Y**OU NEED TO COME BACK to the precinct."

That was the total of the message Trip left. O'Grady had planned to go straight home from his interview with Wendy Thompson. He'd barely slept since this had all started. *Was it only three weeks ago?* The last time he'd eaten a decent meal was probably even longer.

He'd been so certain Kate Wilker's friend would confirm his "stranger theory," he felt somewhat disheartened to discover he'd been wrong. It was a random idea, he knew. That's why he hadn't floated it with Trip.

Nothing but remote circumstantial evidence linked these killings. He needed to face facts. The killings weren't terrorism, nor were they the product of a gang or any kind of collaboration. Danbridge City was just having a very, very bad run of crazy. Still, as he wearily headed back to the precinct, he couldn't shake the feeling he was missing something important.

Trip hadn't answered his call back, and O'Grady wondered if this had something to do with that journalist. Had Trip revealed too much to her and now needed his backup? It wouldn't be the first time. His mind wandered to the Jennings woman. He surprised himself to find he smiled as he thought about their last interaction.

My morals are in the exact right place.

She'd said it with such conviction, he wondered if she was one of the few journalists who did follow a decent code of conduct. Why did he care, anyway? After the sensation of these killings had died she would move on to something else and he'd never see her again. He corrected himself: *Never have to deal with her again!*

His mind was all over the place. Lack of sleep and too much caffeine and sugar. Once Trip explained what was *so* important, his next meeting was with his pillow. Tomorrow he'd arrive early and start working on the paperwork so they could finalize the reports on the mass killings. O'Grady just wanted to get back to normal, where killers looked like killers and some kind of reason for the violence emerged. Even if it were a crazy reason, he'd take it.

By the time he entered the squad room, his mind was back under control. Trip was alone, hunched over, and reading something on his desk.

O'Grady headed across the room to stand beside his partner. "I tried to call you. What's the big urgency?"

Trip looked up and swung his chair around to face O'Grady. He pushed the large manila folder he'd just been reading toward his partner.

"This."

He tapped the top of the folder. It was thick with a clutter of papers.

O'Grady tapped the dossier. "This is what, exactly?"

"I'm not sure, but it's very interesting. And weird."

"Weird? Weird comes with the job. What makes this *standout* weird?"

Trip leaned back in his chair. O'Grady sat in another chair, positioned at the side of the desk.

"Take a look," Trip said, pushing at the folder.

O'Grady opened the folder and flicked through the papers inside. It contained word-dense pages and sheets of what looked like research notes interspersed with complex-looking graphs. It certainly didn't look like anything he'd understand in a hurry, or something he felt like reading when his eyes felt like they'd been rolled in sand.

"What am I looking at? Help me here. I flunked science."

"It's a study on SSRIs and research dating back to 1987."

O'Grady twitched the side of his mouth, as though to say, *I should care, why?* "And that would be some new Russian country, right?"

"Nope, they'd be anti-depressants. S.S.R.I. stands for Selective

Seratonin Reuptake Inhibitor. A class of drugs which includes Prozac, for instance. Basically, the thing hypothesizes that with the growing uptake of these drugs, there's been an increase in mass killings."

O'Grady held up a page containing a brightly colored graph. He couldn't, at a glance, completely understand what all the bars and numbers meant, but a few things *did* stand out to him.

"Hmm," O'Grady said, "I didn't realize these drugs have only been around since early nineties. Seems *everyone's* been on anti-depressants forever."

Trip pulled out a post-it-note-marked page and placed it between them.

"See here. Someone has gone to a great deal of trouble to create a map of every mass killing since 1989. They've been meticulous, too. Even cataloging mass killings incorrectly categorized by the FBI. In most cases, so the report claims, the killer was prescribed one of these SSRIs."

"I don't get it, though. Aren't these drugs supposed to *stop you* from being violent? From *being* suicidal?"

Trip shrugged his shoulder. "You'd think."

His partner pulled back the file and rifled through it. "What's even more interesting is violence is a *known* side effect. According to this—." He pulled out another piece of paper and passed it to O'Grady. "since the drugs went on sale in 1987, the increase has been amazing. Look at this chart, here."

O'Grady studied the graph on the paper. If the figures and graph were correct, there did seem to be a case to be made these drugs did play a role in some of these documented killings. On the other hand, figures could be made to say anything you wanted. The report's author probably had a political agenda. Maybe he was with the gun lobby. *Guns don't kill. People do.* Yeah, that's always been a good one.

"Check this." Trip handed him another sheet. "Here's the conclusion of a study done by internationally renowned scientists."

A paragraph was highlighted in green highlighter.

"These data provide new evidence that acts of violence toward others are an unpromoted, but real and serious, adverse drug effect of a small group of SSRI."

O'Grady shuffled through a few more pages, glancing over them as he went. Jesus, the documents were thorough. The killings were even segmented into the number of victims, the area, and the type of murder—knife, gun, asphyxiation, or other—and whether or not the victims were family or strangers.

"Okay. This is fascinating, but what good does it do us?"

Trip's face lit up as though he was a kid on his first fishing trip having just snagged a wriggling fish on the line.

"I already checked our perps in these three cases. Every one of them was prescribed one of these drugs. I've been on the phone all morning. Just had the last one confirmed. Every one of our killers was taking a SSRI."

Trip grew somber and thoughtful.

"I think there's something to it."

O'Grady exhaled a long breath. Even if there were something to this, his brain, his very tired brain, was having trouble processing it all.

"I hear what you're saying. But I don't get how it could really fit our cases. Even if they were taking the drug, isn't that something for the FDA to investigate? They're the ones who approved these things. Surely they need to investigate."

"I know. I know. It seems like that, right? What if this person, who wrote the report, worked out something else with these drugs? You know the FDA, or any of these bullshit departments that are supposed to check on these things, they don't always get it right."

O'Grady opened his mouth, ready to say, "But it's still not our problem," when Trip silenced him, raising his hands as though he were about to speak at a podium.

"Okay, just stay with me here. The report-writing person is really vested in this. I mean look at the work."

Trip pulled the folder back, turned it to face himself, and then whipped more post-it-noted pages from within. The folder was now a brightly colored patchwork of notes, with green, blue, yellow tags everywhere. He pulled out a few more pages and shoved them toward O'Grady.

"Look here and here, at the research on all these different drugs. This guy, who takes all this time to create this, seems to know a hell of a lot about what is going on with these crimes. Maybe—"

"Wait, a second," interrupted O'Grady. "You keep saying, *this guy. Who* is this guy? *Where* did you get this file anyway?"

"Ah-ah-ah, let me finish, before I tell you. Okay, so he's an expert now on these drugs. He has an agenda, too. So I figure, maybe, he's got something to do with our mass-killings."

O'Grady furrowed his brows. "You figure that, how?"

"Maybe he's a chemist or something like that, and he's worked out a way to convince these people to do what they did. It could be a cult or terrorists, or something we don't even know. Who knows, right? Why else would these killings happen now, here, in this short space of time?"

"I agree, it's a weird coincidence, but that's quite a stretch to call them terrorist attacks. We've found no evidence to connect the three crimes. No demands. No threats. Nobody has claimed them. So I think that rules out terrorists. What would they hope to gain anyway?"

Trip pursed his lips and sighed.

"Yep, you're right." He stopped and scratched his forehead. "I hadn't actually worked through that, yet. It just kind of made a weird sense. Nothing else makes sense, so I thought, let's get weird.

"If we're dealing in science fiction, then I'd be with you. I just can't get my head around the *how*. Then you've got to emphatically answer the *why*, too."

O'Grady picked up the pages Trip had foisted toward him and dropped them back on the top of the folder. Trip's theory read like something out of an FX Channel series. O'Grady enjoyed conspiracy theories as much as the next guy, but he really needed to get some sleep. If his partner was taking this as seriously as he seemed to be, then Trip probably needed to get some sleep, too.

"Now, who's this guy? Something tells me, by your reticence to share that detail, I won't like it. Where'd you get this from, anyway?"

"You're right. You won't like it."

"Yeah? Try me."

Trip held up his hand in a *don't-shoot-me* fashion. "Kendall Jennings, the writer—she gave it to me this morning."

O'Grady immediately felt something ignite inside him. He knew she was trouble! Now she'd gotten into Trip's ear and filled his head with hocus pocus speculation.

It annoyed him that because of her he was here listening to this and looking at this file, when he had other more important things on his agenda, like sleeping and real detective work. For all he knew, this was made up. His first instinct—that this was a document to further someone's agenda—looked even more right now. Trip was easily wound around a pretty woman's finger. Kendall Jennings was playing him.

Trip jumped in and continued.

"Kendall called me last night."

Overly familiar already.

"She'd already spent several days studying the file. I've only read some of it. She's convinced there's some validity to the link between these SSRIs and mass killings. Maybe the drug companies had something to do with the killings? Maybe one of the victims was a whistle-blower? The rest of the victims, a cover up?"

O'Grady laughed. "I think that's a plot from a Jack Reacher novel—mass killings as a cover-up. I wouldn't give any credence to what a journalist thinks."

"Look, I know you don't like her."

"It's not her, in particular. It's any of them. If she was a fifty-year-old chain-smoking, overweight journalist, I doubt *you* would like her, either."

Trip smirked. "Low blow, man, but you might be right. There's something about her. I know you like things buttoned up and straight, but—"

Trip stopped and pushed the folder back to O'Grady. "Take the file. Read it. Then tell me you don't think there's more going on here. I know it sounds crazy, but what's been happening is crazy, anyway."

O'Grady picked up the file, shaking his head. "Okay, okay. I'll give it an hour. You haven't answered my other question. Who *is* the author? Who's this expert on mass killings?"

"Slight problem there. Kendall won't tell me. *Yet.* Says she's protecting her source. Told me to get back to her, once *we've* done some investigation. And, ah, she has some conditions, too, if we want the name."

O'Grady raised a quizzical brow.

"Conditions?"

"She has to come along to any meetings with *the guy.*"

Annoyance lodged in O'Grady's throat. Miss *my-morals-are-in-the-exact-right-place* Jennings!

"That's just perfect. We've got an outrageous theory about insane people, who turn crazy, while taking a drug to stop craziness. We can't interview anyone, because the one person—who given half a chance will take this department down in a hail of accusations—has us chasing down conspiracy theories instead of doing our jobs. *And* she wants to come to our interviews. That will go down *so well* with the boss."

"I hear you, but what if it's even half true?"

"How could it even be half-true?"

The massacres couldn't be connected. Yet, since the Kate Wilker killings, it had occurred to O'Grady the three crimes *were* connected. The lack of evidence had caused him to dismiss his instincts, but what if he followed those instincts and approached this study seriously, regardless of who had brought it to their attention?

If the theory was correct, what did that mean? Millions of people took anti-depressant drugs, these SSRIs. Could it be the drugs *were* randomly activating murderers? If so, then why now, and why Danbridge City? If SSRI's turned people into killers, then surely mass murders would be suddenly occurring all over the country.

O'Grady picked up the folder and walked back to his desk. If there was some veracity to this, Kendall Jennings had vital information. That gave her power. He didn't like that. The question mark floating over her head, since her first dubious phone call, was dangling high and bright. Was she trouble with a capital *T*, or was she a fortuitous messenger setting them on the right track? Or was she involved, somehow, and possibly dangerous, playing a game with them? These were questions requiring some thought. If he believed this drug theory. *Which he didn't.*

First, he needed to examine this file, even though his eyes were telling him what he actually needed was sleep. O'Grady opened the folder and began to read. Nearly three hours and three strong, black coffees later, he still had no answers to the question marks above the journalist. Although, one thing he did know for sure.

Kendall Jennings and he needed to talk.

Immediately.

CHAPTER 31

KENDALL SAT AT HER FAVORITE table, situated on the sidewalk outside the small, bustling café bar two doors down from her apartment. She found the noise and atmosphere of the place sometimes helped inspire her. She enjoyed writing amid the type of people who might read her work. Besides, the owner knew what she wanted without asking—cappuccino and chocolate muffin.

She tapped away at her laptop, attempting to craft an article. Her thoughts hadn't left Doug McKinley. Since reading his file, she'd thought about nothing else. It didn't make sense to her at first. How could a drug turn a normal person into a killer?

So far, she'd investigated six massacres in which the perpetrator had not lived. Most died during the event, either by their own hand or by the police. Kendall had contacted the nearest relatives of the killers. Most were very willing to talk over the phone, with only two insisting they would only speak with her in person. One woman, whose son was shot dead by the police in a siege, refused to discuss anything, telling Kendall, before abruptly hanging up, she just wanted to put it behind her and never hear her son's name mentioned again.

Kendall had also found some detailed corroborating studies validating McKinley's research, some of it highly disconcerting. A study on the army's use of anti-depressants, Prozac, Zoloft, and Paxil correlated with an increase in soldier suicides. As recently as 2009, a massacre had occurred at Fort Hill military base in Texas. Illinoisan Raymond Pedroza, a 28-year-old corporal, killed fourteen people and injured eighteen. Here, the report suggested, was a perfect example of a cover-up.

On the day after the killings, in answering a journalist's follow-up question, commander Lieutenant General Andrew Miller reported the military doctors had prescribed Pedroza with the anti-depressant Zoloft (an SSRI) in treating him for depression. Other reports, subsequently published, only listed him as taking Ambien to help him sleep.

It wasn't the only case, although it was the most famous in the military. Where the perpetrator had been using an SSRI, it was minimalized in all the reports. Twenty percent of army soldiers took some form of anti-depressant. From this subterfuge, it seemed the army knew a correlation between SSRI use and escalating violence in those prescribed the drugs was real.

To Kendall, this seemed a disaster. Was the army feeding these soldiers the drug to increase their violent tendencies? Or was it just fictional speculation?

Even more puzzling was the lack of coverage on the violent side effects in general. Drug companies, psychologists who prescribed the drugs, the FDA, must have all known something wasn't right. Yet they seemed to have ignored it. Where were the journalists, the hounds that covered these types of story? There seemed a band of white noise surrounding any direct link between SSRIs and mass killings. How could it be that two and two together hadn't added up to "something's very wrong?"

This story seemed big. No, make that *huge*. Much bigger than her ability to write or research it. She'd never done work for the type of magazine or newspaper section editor who handled this type of content. Kendall didn't write articles with the potential to change the world. Hers, at best, merely changed shopping or eating habits.

She couldn't do it justice. She needed help. Doug McKinley deserved better than her. Kendall had decided, when she'd finished reading the report, the best thing to do was get the information into the hands of someone who could do something with it.

Fortunately, Trip *had* shown interest in reading the contents of Doug McKinley's report. She suspected it wasn't just about the revelations, that the detective was also using it as a way to stay connected with her. She'd take the help, however it came, and worry about how to extricate herself later.

Kendall held something magical in her hand. Something frightening and dangerous, too. Could this research really have discovered a way to minimize massacres or maybe predict them? At the very least, it opened the door to take an in-depth look at the drugs' side effects.

Her first thought after leaving the file with Trip was to contact Doug McKinley and let him know she'd given his work to the police. She'd decided, though, to tell him in person. She wanted to assure him, at least, she took him seriously.

Kendall sipped her cappuccino, the sugar and caffeine, sweet and energizing. She'd hardly slept the past few days, what with reading through the hundreds of pages of information in the folder, and then following up with her own research.

Kendall felt as though a countdown clock hung over her, ominously ticking down. To what, she didn't know. The more she read, and the more she dug deeper into the files, the faster it seemed to tick. Maybe it was the look in Doug McKinley's eyes when he'd handed her the folder, as though he were handing a baby over to her care. Maybe it was the misery detailed in the files. Or maybe it was her inability to shake the thought that with three mass killings in their city in such confined time, there might be a fourth.

This morning, Kendall had received an urgent commission for a large health and beauty website: *How to create luscious, movie star lips without plastic surgery.* As much as she wanted to continue her pursuit of the SSRI story, this commission was urgent, and the site always paid within seven days.

Kendall stared at the three lines she'd written, trying to force her muse into a more productive space. Not so long ago, this had been easy terrain. Now the topic seemed like mulch, like something you pack around the base of a plant to keep it moist, something containing a lot of shit.

She'd changed in these past three weeks, her only goal before was paying her rent. She'd never set out to change the world or write a Pulitzer Prize-winning article when she took that first commission and happened upon Beverley Sanderson. She'd just needed the money.

Be reliable. Be no trouble. Get the house-style right. That was Kendall Jennings, freelance writer. Now she cared about the impact her stories had on people and on the world. She'd lost the desire to write this piece and was about to stand and take a walk to encourage inspiration when her phone alerted her she had a message.

It wasn't a message, though, but a reminder the rent was due.

She logged into her bank account and stared at the balance. Her car payment had just been automatically withdrawn. So, too, a payment for the MacBook Air she'd bought on credit, telling herself it would increase her productivity.

The three-digit figure stared boldly back at her as though it were proud of its impact on her mood. She felt ashamed that, as much as she wanted to believe in morals and changing the world, the reality of life came down to that number and the fact it was so small. That number controlled her life.

She logged out of her account, put down her phone, and began to type. Somewhere out there she hoped lived someone whose life would be changed by luscious lips, because luscious lip tips were all she had for the world. Luscious lips paid bills.

She began to type:

If you've ever wanted Angelina Jolie's lips, you might be surprised how easy they are to attain. Celebrity beautician to the stars, Amber Wakley, shares her secrets—

It was enough to cause depression. After digesting Doug McKinley's report and even after her own research, she still couldn't face living each day without her own pick-me-up pills. Occasionally, she needed a little help with the day.

Kendall wished she could close her file and work on sharing Doug

McKinley's revelations, but they would need to wait. He'd waited years to get his message out into the world; a few more days surely wouldn't matter.

She breathed deeply and continued to type.

The right color lipstick, as well as enhancing your look, can even change your mood. Don't stay down, get some color in your life ...

CHAPTER 32

DOUG McKINLEY WATCHED THE GIRL from across the street. He'd been patient. He'd waited a very long time and what had it gained him? Patience was a price afforded only to the young.

He'd worked at this for so long, he'd almost forgotten what it was he really wanted to happen. Had he wanted justice? Had he wanted to stop the inevitable? Had he wanted to assuage his guilt over the past? After everything, all the sacrifice, the waters had become muddied. With each new headline piercing his skin like a rusty needle, he'd begun to wear each death on his soul as a symbol of failure.

Here, after all his work, was his best chance of forcing them to listen. He'd done everything right. After discovering the drug, creating his plan, he'd chosen his seeds carefully.

Sometimes he wondered at his strength in taking action. While most people dreamed and wished, and paid lip service to a cause, he actually had the courage to move forward.

The police, the media, anyone watching, had all they needed to solve the puzzle and save countless lives. When they hadn't, he surmised it was the money. *The drug money*, as he thought of it. Even though they were legal drugs, they still spread misery and disaster, as if they were heroin or crystal meth.

If it wasn't money causing the authorities to ignore the obvious, then it was the population's desensitization to violence. Murders, now so frequent, rarely made the front page, only remaining headlines for a day or so even if they did. Terrorists, with their beheadings and random urban attacks, now filled the dark imagination of the populace and installed themselves as the modern-day boogeymen. A whole generation took it as normal to be frisked and forced to remove their shoes at an airport gate, to be treated like they were the enemy for simply taking a holiday.

What everyone ignored was a neighbor, a work colleague, a teenager, a parent, or relative could be incubating a time bomb in the form of a chemical reaction to a commonly used drug. Maybe their ignorance stemmed from the perpetrators rarely surviving to face the legal system. Defense lawyers might have put it together, deducing eventually their clients *were* innocent, that it was the drugs that should stand accused, the pharmaceutical giants lining their coffers with blood money, the guilty parties.

Maybe the government did know, but the drugs served a greater purpose in keeping young soldiers fighting. What a perfect scenario, no? Scarred souls, returning from horrors no man should see, needing respite, were instead stuffed full of these anti-depressants and simply sent back. When they were no longer of use, the poor boys were left, addicted to the chemicals, their violence switch resting on standby.

Since Kendall Jennings had found him, the idea luck had intervened inhabited his thoughts. She seemed perfect. Her naive enthusiasm was the polar opposite to the other journalists he'd approached. He'd hoped she would take up the cause and run with his story. He'd prayed for it, in fact.

He'd checked the papers every day. Her articles on the killings ran for over a week. Then nothing. She hadn't been in contact with him again, no doubt having moved on to something else, like every other journalist he'd met had done.

She wasn't the first. He'd sent his research to so many, but he'd barely caught a nibble. Some small articles, amounting to sweet nothing, were all he'd managed. One writer, who'd won some kind of award, who could have helped him so much, wrote a malicious story painting him as some kind of obsessed, depressed survivor. Then a keen documentary filmmaker, who couldn't get funding, came and went. A senator made some noise in the capitol—before his enthusiasm disappeared behind a deal on a medical insurance bill.

A few years ago, a friend's son built him a simple website. Ever since, he'd posted his research up there. The Internet was the great leveler, the boy had told him. One person could do so much, if their message caught on and it went viral. He just didn't know how to *go viral*. He was old school from a time when viral was something you caught that put you in bed.

Then the hate emails came. *Anti-depressants save lives,* they wrote. *What did he have against the mentally ill? Ordinary people needed these drugs just to get through the day. Who was he to judge and cast aspersions?*

He wrote responses trying to explain. Fuel on the fire, they just escalated to nastier vitriol. The irony being, he, more than most, understood depression and sorrow and living days that felt longer than a year.

After writing to every drug company selling these killer-makers, he received replies which, ultimately, were variations on: *"Our studies do not suggest your conclusions are valid."* Or *"All side-effects are listed on accompanying instructions."*

He'd read every label. Not one was stamped with: "May create murderous tendencies."

There seemed an impenetrable wall around the truth, and no matter how much he threw, he couldn't dislodge a single brick. Innocent people would continue to die because he had failed to find a way to share the truth.

Innocent people like his son.

Charlie would be thirty-six this year. Every time Doug stood over his son's grave, his heart still bled. He cried as he stared at the stone memorial that shouldn't exist. Charlie should still be alive, enjoying his life. Doug might have even been a grandparent by now. Between the tears, he always made Charlie a promise. He hadn't died in vain and, as his father, he swore to find a way to stop this poison in their midst.

Doug tried hard; he tried everything. But he couldn't keep his promise. The massacres kept on happening. Every two weeks, somebody, somewhere, went crazy and took four or more people with them. He'd almost given up, except, one day he found a way. Initially it seemed inconceivable.

Once he understood he would need to take lives himself, he'd cried. He didn't think he'd have the strength to do it. In the end, he consoled himself with the idea innocent people would die anyway. This way, at least, they weren't dying in vain. The drug companies justified their drugs' use by stating the good done outweighed the side effects. Ironically, this became his motto.

Three massacre clusters in one city were all he thought necessary to incite an investigation. He'd imagined the police and government agencies stretching their thin red strings across a board, suddenly seeing all roads led to SSRI drugs.

Three had not been the number.

Every time he thought about his failure, his stomach churned. He would need to act again.

He had other problems, too.

The drug, key to his plan, was almost gone. He'd only reckoned on needing three doses. Luckily, his frugality had saved enough for one more dose. This was his very last chance to send his message. This time he couldn't fail. Failing meant Charlie died for nothing. He wouldn't have that.

The more he thought about it, the more he trusted his change of plan. It seemed perfect. This time it *would* work. Even though You23 had found a candidate, this would put the odds even more in his favor.

Kendall Jennings hadn't done her job anyway. *She* should have delivered his message through a story. Now she would deliver it in person.

He continued to watch the writer as she sat sipping coffee, life bustling about her. Had she swallowed her little pill pick-me-ups with her coffee? Little pick-me-ups, she'd called them, when she'd innocently shared her secret; she, also, one of the millions using anti-depressants.

"Don't tell anyone, I had no idea of the dangers," she'd said. Now she would see first hand, how dangerous.

He hoped, no, he *believed*, shortly the headlines would display those same words—danger and anti-depressants. All he needed was to stay straight and true for a short time longer. In reality, he had zero choice. Doug McKinley wasn't just out of the drug he needed. He was also out of time.

CHAPTER 33

O'GRADY FELT UNEASY AS TRIP and he traveled in the elevator toward the third floor, to Kendall Jennings' apartment. Trip seemed overly excited to be seeing her again. All O'Grady wanted was to get this done and get back to the real job. Trip wanted to be here and, sometimes, you indulged a partner.

O'Grady planned to ensure this wouldn't be the casual visit Trip might imagine. He intended to ascertain file author's name from her without messing around. Then if Trip wanted to play Romeo, he would leave them to it. He hoped this Jennings woman showed her true colors sooner, rather than later, so Trip would see what he saw. She could then go graze in another paddock.

He'd read a chunk of the file, but he wasn't convinced. It read like *worked data*, statistics with an ulterior motive. Departmental analysis systems worked in a similar fashion. Solving cases was one part skill and knowledge, one part luck, and one part criminal stupidity. Those in management still liked to make up these screwed-up statistics to tell them how cases *should* run. Departmental stats came down to a stick or a carrot and matching numbers with some hypothetical super cop.

At Kendall Jennings' door, they stood in silence, side by side. O'Grady contemplated the odd coincidence this apartment block was so near to the original mass killing at Café Amaretto. Then again, everything was odd about these cases.

Trip knocked on the door and, without turning to his partner, said, "You know you don't have to be here, O'Grady. I can handle this. It's not a formal interview."

"Oh yeah, wouldn't that be cozy. I think one of us here needs to have his mind on the job."

He felt Trip look over at him. O'Grady continued to stare ahead.

"I could take offense, if I didn't already know the asshole side of you."

"Oh, yeah, *I'm* an asshole, when I'm covering your butt with this writer. You shouldn't be meeting with her. She's playing you. If you accidentally say something, and she uses it—" With his finger, he made the motion of a knife slicing across his neck. "—then it's desk duty for you. So, think of me as 'Lance the babysitter.'"

Babysitting was the right description. This whole detour would probably go nowhere, even with the file author's name, but O'Grady liked his T's crossed and his I's dotted where he could see them.

The door opened just as O'Grady was about to remind Trip anything he said could and would be held against him by this journalist. Kendall Jennings stood at the threshold, her hair slightly wet and still tangled from a recent shower.

In the bright sunlight streaming through a window from the living area behind, natural light-brown streaks glinted like bands of gold through her damp hair. Either she was feigning disinterest at their visit or she really didn't care how she looked. O'Grady acknowledged to himself that, honestly, *she* was an attractive woman.

She smiled at Trip first, and then simply nodded toward him, before standing back and inviting them inside. She kept her body half-turned from O'Grady and avoided meeting his eyes.

"Sorry I kept you waiting. I was just in the shower."

Kendall settled herself into a red, plastic designer chair, which looked extremely uncomfortable. She motioned them to sit opposite on a sofa.

"No problem." Trip unbuttoned his jacket. "We were early, anyway."

"Do you want something to drink?" She made to get up, glancing at O'Grady when she asked, but immediately averting her gaze when their eyes met.

Trip gestured for her to stay seated. "No, we're good."

O'Grady became acutely aware how uncomfortable he felt sitting in this proximity to her. The skin on his arms tingled. A strange, curling feeling vibrated in his stomach. He really needed to cut this as short as possible.

Of course, Trip began with small talk. They'd be here forever if he let that continue.

O'Grady cleared his throat, trying to send Trip a signal: *stick to the job.*

Kendall Jennings suddenly looked over at him. Her blue eyes fixed upon him through dark eyelashes. He locked eyes with her, refusing to allow her the gratification of feeling she had some control over the meeting. He was trained to stare down criminals in interviews. Making people squirm was his forte. To his surprise, the space between them felt awkward as though the air had thickened. It was a peculiar feeling, which he didn't like.

She smiled.

Wow, she had the audacity to smile at him.

"How are you, Detective O'Grady?"

He intensified his stare. *She* would need to look away first. Let her feel uncomfortable. Let him be the intruder into her life.

He kept his tone business-like. Cold. "Fine."

She conceded the challenge, and turned her gaze to Trip as though O'Grady was no longer in the room. He'd seen something in her eyes, felt something in her eyes. He couldn't understand the feeling. What he should have felt from her was frustration, annoyance, even anger. There was something else, though.

Embarrassment?

No, but an emotion. A current of something intangible. He'd felt something, too, something sparking and strange. That wasn't supposed to happen. He was supposed to be in control.

"So what do you think of the file. Amazing, right?" She was sitting on the edge of the red chair and beaming at Trip. *Over-beaming*, if there was such a thing.

Trip leaned forward to answer, but before he could, O'Grady gathered himself enough to interrupt. He needed to put a stop to the fawning and niceties. He tried to sound as official and brusque as possible.

"Miss Jennings, we don't tend to deal in *amazing* stuff. We deal in evidence. To be frank, whether a certain medication makes a person suicidal or homicidal falls outside the range of police jurisdiction."

Kendall Jennings' lips tightened. Her eyes immediately darkened, the blue turning an unusual near-violet color. As she leaned back in her chair, pulling her arms about herself protectively, she looked annoyed.

Just in case she was left with any doubt, he added. "I'm sure you understand this is police business into which you've interjected yourself. We're meeting with you today simply as a courtesy."

He was about to add: *and this isn't a game; you've one minute to give us the file author's name*, but Trip spoke.

"Please, ignore my partner. We appreciate you bringing this information to us." O'Grady felt Trip's eyes on him. "I recognize you didn't have to share this."

O'Grady sighed. Now they were playing a doubles match.

Trip tipped his head toward O'Grady. "What my partner is *trying* to say is while it *is* compelling information, it's not of much use in this case. Maybe it's something for a civil pharmaceutical case."

O'Grady studied her face. Maybe this wasn't a bad strategy. Good cop, bad cop might get this thing done quickly. Kendall Jennings was avoided looking at him, her focus now entirely on Trip.

Through the open window, a slight breeze caught wisps of her hair; the tiny strands floating about her face glowed in the light. She gently pushed the errant pieces back behind her ear.

For one moment—a moment that would keep him sleepless for the next few nights—he imagined the feel of pushing back those strands of hair while cupping her chin in his other hand. The thought caught him unaware. Immediately a pulse of anger shot through him. Stress had to be the cause, stress, a lack of sleep, too many bodies, and too much death. He was on an emotional rollercoaster.

He needed to get this done, get out, and leave her to Trip. No matter how careful he and Trip were with regards to this file, they might still be damned in some distribution-hungry newspaper. He saw the headlines in his mind: *Police ignore strong leads. Police follow crazy theory.* The minute they'd stepped foot in this apartment, they *were* on shaky, dangerous ground.

When he spoke, O'Grady couldn't hold back his frustration.

"No, actually, what *his* partner is trying to say is we can still arrest you for obstruction. We want the name of the author of the files. Now."

Kendall Jennings turned from smiling at Trip and fixed him with a surprisingly calm stare. She almost looked amused. O'Grady had imagined she would bite at his words. At least, that's what he'd hoped. He wanted to get this moving, wanted her to understand this wasn't a game. Most of all, he just wanted to get away from her and this odd, unsettling attraction he felt.

"Seriously, Detective O'Grady? Really? You think I'm an idiot? I'm trying to *help* not obstruct you. What would I actually have to gain?"

Trip chimed in: "We understand that. Don't we, O'Grady?"

O'Grady ignored Trip and continued to stare at Kendall. "I think it's what *Miss Jennings* understands that's important here."

Kendall's chest rose and relaxed as she took several deep breaths. Fingers, which had been resting, intertwined in her lap, began to tap. A small crease appeared in her brow.

Maybe now she was getting the picture.

He continued: "Here's the reason we want the name. You could be in danger. This person may be involved."

When she didn't respond, O'Grady added, "Maybe you're involved."

Trip motioned to O'Grady. "O'Grady, that's not really the best—"

Before he'd finished, Kendall turned her body to face O'Grady full on.

"Let's get this straight, here and now. *I am not the enemy!* You've got some kind of problem with me. I get that. I don't think it's me you dislike so much; I think it's something else, something to do with you. Give me a break. I'm not giving you my source's name, unless I know, for sure, you won't harass him. Like you're harassing me! He's suffered enough. He's done a better job of finding out all this information than the police, the FBI, the CIA, and the FDA combined."

He hadn't actually thought she was involved. He just wanted to prod her a little. See what gave. She was naively innocent, he'd realized. Nothing quite like a beautiful, angry woman, though.

"You know, Miss Jennings, if you aren't involved, protecting your *source* isn't helping your cause."

"Hang on. Hang on." Trip motioned with his hands to take it down a notch. "Kendall, we appreciate your help. Really, we do."

Kendall turned away from O'Grady giving him more than a cold shoulder. *Frozen shoulder, perhaps?*

"It certainly doesn't show. I've done nothing to warrant being treated like a criminal. I'm a writer. That's it."

"No. No, I understand."

Trip glanced toward O'Grady. Suddenly, O'Grady felt outnumbered.

His partner rose, motioning to O'Grady to meet him outside the door. "I think my partner and I need to have a quick chat. Would you just excuse us for a second?"

Kendall stopped him by raising her hand.

"Don't worry. If you need to talk, I'll leave. I need to check my emails, anyway. I'm waiting on something."

Trip remained half-standing, while O'Grady made no motion to move, to show her not even the courtesy of standing as she left the room. Instead, he glared at the corner of the ceiling across from him.

Only after they were alone did Trip reseat himself and address O'Grady. "Man, what are you doing? She's totally fine. Why play full-on angry cop?"

"Maybe you should tell me what *you're* doing. That report is flimsy at best. You're pussyfooting around like she's the mayor's niece. Maybe you and I are here for different reasons."

Trip opened his mouth to reply, then paused. He looked like a schoolboy who was discovered passing a secret note in class. He really liked this woman. It was in his eyes, a pleading desperation. A thought ran through O'Grady's mind, which he instantly hated: *I don't blame him.*

O'Grady's demeanor softened. "Why don't you just ask her out, man?"

Trip stared at him, his brows knitting together, then relaxing, then knitting together again. The tension between the two of them dissipated.

Trip shook his head and sighed. "Yeah, you think I haven't? Buddy, feel free to threaten to arrest a girl I really like. That's a huge help. Not to mention, she is *not* giving us the name if you don't chill."

Maybe Trip was right. Maybe her sins were imagined and related to his past and not the present circumstance. Trip was looking at him, expectantly.

"Okay. Okay. It's cool. But right now, can we just get the name, get out of here, tick the mad drug theory box as explored, and close these cases? *Please.* Whatever you want to do with your high school crush after that, you can do. I don't need to sit across from you and endure your big, soppy eyes."

"Roger. Now we're both on the same page."

Now Trip looked as though he'd gotten an *A* for his note instead of detention.

"When it comes to the author of those files, I'm going to agree to keep her in the loop when we interview them. Keep her happy. Then, maybe, who knows."

"It's your funeral when it comes to women. Stick to staying on track, and I'm good."

"Look, I still think there's something to that file. Aren't *you* curious as to why we haven't heard more about this drug link to mass killings?"

"I'm curious, but I'm tired more, and I'm not trying to get into anyone's pants, so I'm not sharing your enthusiasm. Like I said, I'm with you. Can that just be enough?" O'Grady pointed a finger at Trip. "You owe me one, though. *Love-struck* looks ugly on you."

Kendall reentered the room. She also seemed to have wrangled her emotions, carrying an air of confidence similar to the demeanor she had when O'Grady intercepted her at the precinct.

"Right, have you decided if you're going to arrest me? Probably a story in that I can sell."

O'Grady concealed a smile.

Trip chuckled. "No, you're safe. Too much paperwork. However, regarding your source, we do need to speak with him."

"I've decided I'll give you his details, but there's a proviso. This is my story, my source, and I can assure you this person has nothing to do with these crimes. And I don't want him harassed. So like I told you Trip, I'm coming with you."

O'Grady jumped in. "We can't agree to that. We don't do ride-alongs. This isn't *Cops.*"

"He's right," agreed Trip, "but—"

He stopped mid-sentence, seeming to consider her proposal. A flicker of a smile caught his lips.

"What we have no control over though is an acquaintance of this person being there when we arrive."

Kendall tipped her head to the side, clearly pondering Trip's proposition.

"Hmm. That sounds … workable. Okay, I agree to those terms."

O'Grady shook his head. This was definitely not a good idea. No matter his protests, this was obviously going to happen. He, though, didn't want any part of this excursion. Any fallout was on Trip. Trip, who now looked happier than O'Grady had seen him in weeks.

"When can we head over there?" asked Trip

Kendall smiled the smile of a woman who'd gotten her way. Trip still smiled like a fool. All O'Grady could think was: *This could become a huge mistake that'll wipe those smiles from both their faces.*

Even as he thought it, he sincerely hoped he was wrong. It would be he who'd clean up the pieces, and at this point, he didn't have the energy.

CHAPTER 34

"**I** DON'T UNDERSTAND, BOSS17."

You23 shrugged his shoulders. His gaze flicked everywhere except back at Doug. The boy couldn't look him in the eye. Within seconds, the piece of paper he held in his hand had been screwed into several little, crumpled balls.

"The seed was perfect. Why are you switching out now? We've spent days on this one. Did I screw up?"

Doug McKinley shook his head. The boy was agitated. That wasn't good.

"No, no, you did a good job, but we must be careful. Other factors are in play now. Time is a problem, and the drug—"

He stopped mid-sentence. You23 didn't need to know about that. Doug noted the kid had started to look even more disheveled. His greasy hair stuck to his face as though glued, and fine red veins colored the yellow-tinged whites of his eyes. Even the skin on his arms looked scaly-dry. He'd started scratching at himself lately like a dog with fleas. Possibly all side effects of long-term use of the drugs Doug had administered to him.

You23 tilted his head and began mindlessly scraping at his forearms. Doug knew he was attempting to work through the new information. He'd noticed the boy did not handle change well. It didn't matter. This was almost over.

The kid was a wind-up toy he pointed in the direction he needed him to go. A toy that enjoyed the chase and the product of his work—chaos—but had no true appreciation of the greater picture. He did what he was told for his own reasons. You23 also knew if it wasn't for Doug, he'd still be on the streets or at that disgusting, filthy rat-infested halfway house where he'd found him a year ago.

When their mission concluded, he would no longer be able to supply the drugs keeping him productive. His supply of those was also running low. The boy would end up back on the streets at breakneck speed. He should feel guilty—he'd been a good kid—but Doug wouldn't allow himself to feel guilt. Guilt was a luxury for those who couldn't stay on the straight and true path. He could. And *he* would.

He'd already endured enough guilt in his life. Quite possibly, he'd run out of space to carry any more. There was plenty of guilt over Charlie's death—him being the one who'd suggested his son get the job at Burger Boys to teach him the value of money. In the end, he was the one who'd learned the lesson. Money made the world go round and against that life had little value. Now it was his turn to serve the lessons.

Pure accident had him stumble upon his research's beginnings, while investigating the side effects of Prozac. His doctor prescribed the anti-depressant for him to help with the melancholy after Charlie. When he came across the medical journal reports, the correlation between SSRIs and violence, it was curiosity that saw him follow the trail, begin to read more widely, and then head passionately in search of the truth. Research gave him a lifeline to pull himself back into meaningful life.

Once he understood the drugs' dangers, he was incredulous. Years went by with nobody paying any attention to his warnings, until he found the most ingenious solution to make them listen. When he'd first discovered the drug—he thought of it now as a miracle substance—he couldn't believe it actually existed.

Incredibly, a YouTube video delivered his prize. From then on, he became convinced Fate had tapped him on the shoulder. Something extraordinary could be accomplished. The minute he watched the video he understood the potential.

The Ten Craziest Drugs you never Knew Existed.

The minute he'd viewed the six-minute video, he immediately replayed it. Then again.

Could it be true?

He Googled it. As far-fetched as it sounded, this drug, if it were true, possessed amazing powers. Any person ingesting it could fall under the suggestive power of another, the effect, almost instant and easily delivered. You simply blew the powder into the victim's face or dropped it into drink or food.

Seratolamine, a close relative of scopolamine, was nicknamed Zombie Breath by the Colombian locals of the only region in the world where it grew. The drug was odorless, tasteless and undetectable. *A miracle.* Derived from a flower grown on a tree found in a small area in the South American country, it was more dangerous than cocaine or heroin.

After watching a documentary on the drug, Doug suddenly felt more energized than he'd felt in years. He had an idea. In the film, a local man stated matter-of-factly, "I could give someone a gun, tell him or her to go kill a person of my choice, and they'll have no choice. They *will* do it. They won't remember it or me. They become the perfect zombie accomplice."

That one line three years ago was enough to find Doug McKinley on a plane to Columbia. After another four days of searching for the right people to access the drug, he struck gold. During his travels, he heard incredible and frightening stories of the drug's power. Bank accounts emptied by their owners and handed willingly over to thieves; a woman who'd helped men ransack her own apartment; a young man who'd aided robbers in carrying his own belongings from his apartment, assuring his doorman he was happy for the thieves to take his property.

Later, victims claimed complete ignorance of their complicity. In cases where they did remember, they spoke of being aware of their actions, but said it had felt right to them, even though they were acting completely out of character.

Days of nervous enquiries finally brought him to Carlo, whose brother knew someone who dealt in the drug. The drug dealer—nothing like he'd imagined—was a friendly twenty-something young man, who looked more like a surf bum. He was friendly and enthusiastic, even taking Doug into a small forest area to show him one of the trees from which the seratolamine was derived.

The devil trumpet tree, with its beautiful pink trumpet-shaped flowers hanging upside down, bloom to the ground, was stunning. The flowers so tempting and delicate, exotic in appearance, belied its danger. The seeds and leaves were so rich in this most powerful hallucinatory drug, local legend warned if you should fall asleep beneath the tree, you might never wake up.

The rare drug was expensive and dangerous, but the reward far outweighed the risk. Doug had a plan. First, he would test Fate's willingness to partner with him. It was a game. He told himself if he was stopped at the border then he would take it as a sign this was wrong. If he made it through customs with the powder hidden only inside his toiletry case, this then would be his green light.

Fate acquiesced. He wasn't stopped.

He'd seen You23 on a current affairs program. The segment headline, *The Genius Homeless*. The show highlighted musical geniuses, poetry masters, an elderly man with the deepest, richest voice, equal to any national announcer. All were destitute, living on the streets.

Twenty-two-year-old Andy Waites, born to a troubled family was a mathematical and program coding prodigy until the teenage onset of schizophrenia robbed him of his future. A year after winning a scholarship to a prestigious university, he was eating at soup kitchens, living by dumpsters, one of the lost.

Fate smiled again, nodding her further approval. Andy Waites possessed the skill-set he needed to move forward. He even lived in Doug's own city. *What were the odds?* Doug set about volunteering at the same soup kitchen where Andy was interviewed.

Andy could run the spreadsheets and write programs he needed. He had no connections anymore—his family abandoning him when he became ill—nobody with whom he could share Doug's activities or plans. Even if Andy did open his mouth, nobody would believe a schizophrenic claiming to work on a project to change the world, with names of those involved You23 and Boss17, sounding like something out of science fiction.

Doug had spent years researching drugs. So he'd also learned of other pharmaceuticals, expensive and experimental, which could possibly stabilize and even reverse some of the damage schizophrenia caused in the brain. With enough money, you could get your hands on these. They took a big chunk of his savings. He needed Andy stable, so the cost was worthwhile.

The names You23 and Boss17 were part of the game. Andy invented them, after Doug told him a tale of important secret government work and how vital they were to the future of the world. Doug conjured a story of aliens hidden among them, these aliens needing to be activated. Only aliens knew where their fellow aliens hid. It was like a videogame to Andy. He wasn't an accessory to the killing of human beings, but saving the world from invasion. The two of them were unsung heroes.

Ironically, it was almost true. These SSRI drugs *were* invaders of sanity and thieves of lives.

Irony is a snake, twisting through good fortune. And bad. In Fate's final endorsement, she delivered Doug's exact needs. Suddenly in life's chessboard, his opponent's King was in check. His Queen had come into play, Kendall Jennings the final move.

Doug patted Andy's shoulder—he'd come to think of him as his flawed version of Charlie, as his own son. He'd fought the guilt for a while now, of leaving the boy to fend on his own, but he couldn't ignore Andy's contribution. As he neared the end of his plan, he'd thought long and hard what would happen to Andy after this was done.

The kindest gift would be to spare him a return to his previous life. He'd saved enough Zombie's Breath to take care of the boy, the powder so concentrated that a gram was enough to kill fifteen people. He'd saved a fifth of a gram to be certain. Andy wouldn't know. Doug would place it in his Cola. The kid drank the stuff like water.

He waited patiently for Doug to explain why he'd changed their target. Andy's right eye twitched as it did when he needed a booster of *his medicine.*

Doug kept his voice gentle. "Remember that girl who visited a few weeks ago? She's a defecting alien wanting to help. She's against her fellow aliens invading Earth. This is better, you'll see."

Andy's eyes glassed over, thinking. Then he smiled and nodded enthusiastically.

"The pretty one?"

"Yes, the one I checked personally for you and you commented she was so pretty you couldn't believe she was human. I used your program while you slept. You'd been working so hard, I didn't want to bother you."

Andy's program was amazingly quick and accurate, but Doug didn't need it for this. He already knew enough about Kendall Jennings. Still he used Andy's program to hunt back through Kendall's accounts to their origin.

Nothing disappeared from the Internet. Closing an account only removed the owner's access. The account remained beneath the Internet, searchable with the right program. How easy it was to track people using their social media posts. If they weren't *checking in* their exact location on Facebook or other sites, they uploaded photos unaware of the detailed metadata contained within the pixels.

Nobody realizes each digital photo includes EXIF data an acronym for Exchangeable Image File. Information freely available about someone and their activities was all stored there: shutter speed, exposure compensation, even if a flash was used, myriad of information. A snapshot of digital wonder, it also carried something else invaluable, the date and time the image was taken and the GPS coordinates.

Since people were creatures of habit, Andy could easily match the times and places visited by the candidate. Delivering the drug was merely a matter of waiting outside a restaurant, club, or anywhere and seeking fake directions.

When Andy held out the drug-impregnated map to the unsuspecting candidate innocently requesting directions, it took only a flick of the paper to deliver the Zombie's Breath.

The compliancy of their candidates was astonishing. They became docile, disciplined children.

Follow me. Walk this way. Get into the van. Sit here. Tell me what makes you angry? What is unfair? What will make the unfairness better? Will you kill them? Yes, you'll kill them. Then we can change the world. Fulfill your destiny. Right a wrong.

The first candidate, Toby Benson, initially presented a challenge. He didn't seem to hold a grudge against anyone. Then Benson mentioned a café where he'd suffered food poisoning that put him in the hospital for two days. He'd missed an important meeting, subsequently an account was lost, and a promotion stalled. He'd never returned to Café Amaretto until *Doug McKinley* sent him back.

Doug only needed to plant the seed in his mind: those in the kitchen needed to be stopped before ruining more lives. They needed to die. The other two, Benito Tavell and Kate Wilker were variations on this. Benito, with his low pay and late night shifts they wouldn't allow him to change, felt used. Kate Wilker lived in a troubled and unhappy marriage. Always, something.

Now, here they were, set for the final battle. He couldn't lose this one. It had to work. One dose left for the next candidate. One dose for Andy. Soon, very soon, he'd be with Charlie again. He hoped Charlie would be proud.

Andy's mouth dropped open as he ruminated on Doug's words. Doug the preacher and Andy his faithful flock member. The boy still seemed lost.

"I'll tell you why this girl fits better. She's a journalist. What happens when one of the police is killed in the line of duty? They go all out to catch the killer."

Andy nodded, enthusiastically.

"Same for Journalists. Something happens to one of them, it's like attacking their home ground. They'll swarm, investigate, and discover the invasion. The world will suddenly know and join our fight against the aliens. You'll be famous, too, when word gets out. Society should have taken better care of you—of all special people like you. The world needs to know the things you've done. This one is the last one, You23. This one will save the world."

Andy's head bounced vigorously. The boy would die never knowing his real achievement. He'd deceived a trusting soul. Doug fought against the sadness in his heart, consoling himself the story carried some truth—SSRIs *did* turn people into a type of alien.

"You're good to me, Boss17. You care about me and protecting the world. You care about the journalist, even though she's an alien, don't you?"

He ruffled the boy's hair.

"Yes, I do care. We'll help her be free, just like the others."

Andy's face lifted, a huge yellow-toothed smile easing the dark circles beneath his eyes.

Maybe he should clean Andy up before the end came, so in death he looked as though someone loved him, someone cared.

"Do you want me to track her accounts? I can have the movements ready for you by Wednesday."

Doug shook his head, placing a firm hand on Andy's arm.

"No, it's fine. I already know where she'll be. Remember, she's on our side. You understand what needs doing next, right?"

Andy's head bobbed again. His tongue flicked out, licking his lips like a lizard.

"Do you have a target position in mind, Boss17, or do you want me to find one?"

"Oh, no, that's fine, I know exactly where I'm sending her, too. It's all worked out perfectly."

Andy swayed in his chair. "I'm so excited."

"So am I, my boy. So am I. We're almost done. Almost there."

Doug McKinley had stayed straight and true. And he was almost there.

CHAPTER 35

Kendall felt proud. She'd stayed in control of her emotions in the presence of the high-and-mighty Lance O'Grady. Why did he harbor such animosity toward her? Yet why couldn't she stop her heart pointlessly spinning like a crazy top when near him?

Kendall waited on a call from a *Vanity Fair* editor. *Vanity Fair* was the big time, the real big time. She'd made some headway on a story on Doug McKinley's SSRI precipitating violence theory. *Vanity Fair* was interested after she used a contact to get to the commissioning editor.

She should be happy, but every time she thought of O'Grady, she suddenly wasn't so on top of the world. Where was her head, no, wait, her heart going with such a pointless emotional exercise? For the umpteenth time, she told herself: *get it together, Kendall.*

But she *couldn't* get it together. Couldn't stop thinking about the way he'd looked at her as they sat only feet apart. She'd detected—maybe imagined—something in his eyes, something more than animosity or disgust. She'd even caught him glancing at her, not in the way he'd looked in her dream, but glancing with something else besides hostility.

Kendall checked the clock on her computer. *Where was this editor?* It was thirty minutes past when he'd said he'd call, and she was getting herself more worked up. She just wanted to know what was up and what wasn't. If she could get stuck into the story, then she wouldn't have time to think about O'Grady.

Ten minutes later, still no story. Without thinking, she'd absently tapped O'Grady's name into Google.

Lance O'Grady police detective

Then, as an afterthought, she typed

Angry. Crime.

523,000 links appeared.

The third heading down caught her attention:

Detective speaks out on brother's death

Kendall clicked on the link to a newspaper page.

"They drove him to suicide," claims brother.

The date was ten years ago. Everything suddenly added up. Kendall read through O'Grady's interview, and realized, by the way he spoke of losing his brother, that Lance O'Grady was not the tough, unemotional man she knew. At least, he wasn't then.

By the time she'd finished the article, it crystalized for her that it wasn't personal, it was her occupation. He couldn't differentiate between her and those journalists who'd hounded his brother. She wondered if she might find a way to show him she was different. Maybe it might help him heal. Not that she was the expert in handling grief. Although, she'd found the more she'd written about the massacres, the more she felt somehow released from her own tragedy. Maybe when this was all over, she'd find a way to speak to him. Now wasn't the right time. No doubt, he'd think it was further subterfuge.

Her thoughts turned to O'Grady's partner, Trip. Around her, he was like a puppy chasing a ball. At some point, she must take away the ball. Maybe after they'd visited Doug McKinley's this morning, she'd explain to him while she was flattered, she wasn't interested.

She decided to call Doug McKinley yesterday, give him warning she was coming, that she had some news—the Vanity Fair article. He'd sounded excited, but insisted they wait until today, that he had some preparations to make. She hadn't told him about Trip yet, either. She wanted the *Vanity Fair* commission and the police's renewed interest to be a surprise.

She looked at the time on the toolbar of her computer: nine forty-four a.m. In fifteen minutes, she needed to leave for Doug McKinley's house, and still the editor hadn't called. She had this terrible feeling that today, which had dawned with promise, was sliding downhill toward disappointment.

She had a small health piece needing filing before close of business today, so she decided to get on with that. She'd only written fifty or so words when she pushed back from her desk.

O'Grady was in her mind again, and it was driving her nuts. He wasn't some lost animal needing saving, he was an angry, obstinate man who somehow, because of a stupid dream, meant something to her.

Okay, change of plans.

Visit Doug McKinley. Tell Trip she wasn't interested. Contact Lance O'Grady and insist they meet. After that?

Let fate decide.

CHAPTER 36

O'GRADY GLANCED UP AT THE wall clock. Thick red hands and a dark black circle surrounding the face, it was an ugly relic of the seventies. That was about how he felt right now, as though he'd sat here since bell-bottoms and long hair were the rage.

Every time he glanced at the clock, another thirty minutes had silently ticked away. It was already ten-thirteen, and he'd been here since six this morning. He'd wanted to do this on his own with no one around to query his line of thought and cause him to second-guess himself. The small video room was empty when he'd arrived.

Several coffees later, the fingers on his right hand throbbed from hitting the rewind and play buttons dozens of times. His eyes stung like they'd taken an acid bath after staring at the blurred black and white images for so long. He'd printed several stills, thinking perhaps on paper the image of the mysterious paper man might be clearer. It hadn't helped.

He hadn't shared his thoughts with Trip. Let him pursue his ghosts with Kendall Jennings and O'Grady would chase down his own. These cases had left him unsettled and uneasy. He'd missed something. He knew it like he knew his brother would still be alive if it weren't for parasitic journalists like Kendall Jennings. Although when her face came into his mind, she didn't really fit in the same box. She didn't have that harsh, rough feel about her.

He couldn't think about her now. She was with Trip, he was here, and staying focused was the order of the day. Let Trip and the girl visit Doug McKinley and waste their time. McKinley was a bereaved father on a wild goose chase attempting to make sense of his son's death. When they found him on the DMV database, turned out the guy was almost seventy. In his experience, there weren't many near-septuagenarians involved in major crimes.

O'Grady raised his cup to his mouth, anticipating the hit of caffeine. The precinct's coffee was harsh, but it was all that stood between him and exhaustion.

Nothing came with the swig. The cup was already empty.

He sighed. Ten more minutes of checking footage and he'd call it quits. He figured the three cups of caffeine coursing through his veins would last him about that long.

What had he missed? Something was there in the captured film footage of Tavell and Benson prior to their crimes. An alarm pinged in his head like a broken doorbell. Damned if he didn't feel the answer was there plain as day, he just unable to see it.

His remembered his first partner's words. They always came to him.

Hickok was a hardass, O'Grady a fresh-faced detective, if there was such a thing. They never did get along, but he'd taught O'Grady one thing. Co-incidences were rarely random.

"If there's one thing you respect, it's coincidences. They never are and never will be just coincidences. They're shining neon signs, and you gotta read the signs."

The neon lights shone bright over this video. Common sense told him these mass killings couldn't be connected, yet this stranger who briefly interacted with Tavell and Benson had to be the same man. Something happened in those moments when he stood with the killers. But what?

A thread dangled before him, long and glistening like a spider's web in the sunshine. No matter how many times his mind swiped at it, it remained there annoyingly close, teasing him.

He'd run the man's image through Viisage, their facial recognition software. That threw back 263 possible matches. It wasn't as accurate as they'd hoped; a real hit and miss system, nothing like the moviemakers would have you believe.

Staring at the screen, though, wasn't getting him anything except tired, stinging eyeballs. He yawned and ran both hands through his thick hair, then buried his face into his palms. He'd call it quits for the moment and grab some breakfast, before it became more appropriate to do lunch.

O'Grady stood, the noise of the scraping chair, loud in the small room. He reached for his jacket, draped over the back of the chair. As he leaned in to shut down the computer, the niggle hit him again.

What would one more Viisage search hurt? Maybe while he'd sat there something new had come in. His fingers hovered over the keyboard, paused. Kate Wilker's face flashed into his mind. She was part of the trio of mass killers. But no stranger had approached her. Could his gut instinct be wrong? Maybe, sometimes, coincidences were just coincidences.

He pulled his notepad from his pocket. He'd made a note to check on something to do with her while interviewing her friend Wendy Thompson. Flicking back through the pages, he found the comment.

Check traffic cam footage outside mall.

He'd requested the footage, but he hadn't checked whether it had arrived. These days it was a simple process to access requested files from government departments. Once actioned, they'd simply be placed in a designated secured cloud file. This sped things up when several agencies were involved in a case. O'Grady opened the Wilker case file and scanned down the titled video files.

It was there.

08.21.15. Danbridge_Fair_Carson_Street CCTV Time_11.06.04—11.07.25 angle_camera 31.

Allen was meticulous with his metadata.

O'Grady clicked on the file and settled back. Allen had done a good job editing down to what they needed. Within five seconds, Kate Wilker's Toyota sedan appeared on the screen leaving the mall. At the end of the street, just as her friend Wendy had said, the car came to a stop at a red traffic light.

The car was stationery at the lights for only a few moments, when a windshield washer suddenly moved from the intersection to begin madly scrubbing at the front shield of Kate Wilker's car. Then he came to her window, looking for money—just like they all do. The lights changed, and the car moved off, turning left into busy North Taylor Road. O'Grady watched two more traffic cam files, which had captured her movements, but there seemed nothing suspicious. No stranger holding a piece of paper had stopped her.

O'Grady, sick of staring at the screen looking for God knows what, felt drained. His concentration wasn't helped by his mind bouncing back to Kendall Jennings. He'd begun to wish he'd gone with Trip and her. If nothing else, he could have babysat Trip, and ensured he follow protocol—least that's what he told himself.

Too much death, too little rest, and too many people telling him to put these cases to rest had fried his perspective. Kendall Jennings had gotten under his skin, even invaded his sleep. He had a vague memory of the journalist last night in his dreams. Upon waking, all he recalled was an enormous spider's web, she trapped within it, while the monster creature lumbered slowly toward her, its murderous intent clear. Hard as he frantically climbed over the sticky twines, he knew he would reach her too late. That as much as he wanted to save Kendall Jennings, he would fail.

Yep, he certainly needed a break!

CHAPTER 37

I T SURPRISED KENDALL TO SEE Trip alone when he arrived to
pick her up. He was acting as though this was a date and not an
interview. He'd called her thirty minutes prior, suggesting he swing by
and grab her.

As she climbed into his large sedan, she'd asked, "Wasn't I supposed to
happen to be there? Won't you *burn in hell* for consorting with a
journalist?"

A smile had flickered on his lips. "Don't mind O'Grady. His bark is
worse than his bite. Unless you're a criminal, then both are equally savage.
Anyway, I thought it gives us a chance to talk on the way over." He'd
thrown an even wider smile at her.

Kendall didn't want to get to know him better. Everything had become
too complicated, way too quickly. This massacre story, Trip, and the way
her heart tightened just a little when she thought of O'Grady. All she
wanted was to get this meeting over and move on to solid ground, wherever
that might be.

Trip had spent the fifteen-minute drive chatting and cajoling her life
details from her. Kendall had been polite, but she didn't want to be drawn
into banal conversation when they were about to meet with a man with
such a noble focus.

She knew Doug would be sitting there, excited and anxious she was
returning. The more Trip spoke, the more she'd recognized he didn't care

about Doug's report. Every time she'd tried to steer the conversation around to Doug, the SSRIs, and what angle the police might take on his research, he'd redirected the chat back to her personal life.

Now she worried that, because of her, Doug would experience more disappointment. For the rest of the drive, she'd tried to keep her responses monosyllabic. It was like playing tennis with words. By the time they'd arrived at Doug McKinley's doorstep, she'd felt they were at forty-all, with no one gaining an advantage.

Doug greeted them at the door with a warm, kindly-uncle smile.

"How are you, Doug?" she said, as she entered his home, which today had an air of darkness reflective of her own dark feeling of what was to come. The curtains were drawn, the only illumination coming from dimmed lights fixed to the wall and a table-lamp in the corner of the living room.

His "I'm good" seemed to belie the truth. Kendall almost didn't recognize Doug McKinley. In the week or so since she'd seem him, he'd aged twenty years. His red-rimmed eyes, sunken cheeks, and the wheezing, whistling sound escaping his lips with each breath were signs of an ill man. His hunched shoulders and stooped body spoke of a human being in pain.

Yet the man could barely contain his enthusiasm for the visit, his eyes bright and sparkling. Kendall's guilt welled up inside. Breaking the heart of this poor, sick man—because that's surely what he seemed to be—was the last thing she wanted. He reminded her so much of her own father the weeks before he passed, a broken man after her mother's death. Kendall's heart felt thick and swollen in her chest.

Doug must have seen her studying him. He straightened his body, then grabbed her hand with a firm grip, leading her deeper inside the living room. He didn't even give her time to introduce Trip, who'd followed them in, close behind.

"This is Detective Trip Lindsay." Kendall nodded over her shoulder.

"Good to meet you, Mr. McKinley."

Doug ignored Trip, continuing to hold Kendall's hand and draw her to a chair. Again, she was reminded of her father, and of his gentle touch as she'd mourned her mother.

Doug only let go of her hand when they parted to sit across from each other, she on the couch next to Trip, and Doug on a worn leather recliner. He appeared slight and hunched in the chair's oversized encompassing arms.

"How have you been, Mr. McKinley?"

He smiled warmly. "Oh, … tired."

A hand ran through the wisps of growth on the top of his head, flattening the threads of fine hair to his scalp. "I know I don't look the best, but now you're here I'm feeling energized."

Doug looked across to Trip, who patiently waited, as Kendall had demanded of him, for his cue to gently begin with his questions.

"And this lovely girl has finally gotten a detective involved. Thank you Detective. Finally, the police are taking my research seriously. This means a great deal to me."

"No problem, Mr. McKinley. Your research is interesting and Miss Jennings, persuasive."

"Oh, I know." Doug gazed at Kendall as he spoke. "I think she'll become even more persuasive in the very near future."

Doug slowly looked over to a half-poster-sized photograph of a teenage boy, hung prominently on the wall—one of those stiff portraits the discount photographers churn out by the dozen every day.

"My son appreciates what you're about to do."

His voice drifted off as though he were thinking about something else, a distant memory. Then, he looked back to Kendall, and, in almost a whisper, said, "As do I."

A shiver ran through Kendall. It wasn't *what* he said, it was *how* he looked at her as if he … pitied her? His eyes had suddenly changed, too, as though a heavy barrier came down. Then it was gone. He was again, an old, sad man.

"My condolences on your son, Mr. McKinley. I remember the event from back when I was a new cadet in the P.D. Terrible thing. Just like these current events."

Doug leaned back in his chair, the recliner creaking with the movement. Then, as if a thought had suddenly occurred and fired up his nerves, his eyes were instantly alert and wide.

"If they'd paid attention to my research lives could have been saved. I couldn't save my son, but I tried to save others."

Trip's face remained impassive. He'd slipped into tough, detective mode.

"I know you believe these drugs had something to do with all this, but I'm not sure these things are as predictable as you think. Saying it was a drug that set off these people sounds more like wishful thinking than reality. I'm sure we'd all like a neat answer to insanity."

Doug's face emptied of warmth as though he was a child whose favorite toy was just taken away.

"But did you read the report thoroughly? Surely you can have no doubt?"

Kendall wondered at Doug's frailty. If he became too upset, she worried he might collapse right there in front of them. She jumped into the conversation.

"Mr. McKinley, I read the report from beginning to end. I certainly see why it seems SSRIs are literally controlling these people. I even read the book about your son's death. I *really* get it. Honestly, if it were my child, I'd want answers, too."

Doug looked down as though mulling the words.

Kendall turned her head to Trip and nudged him with her elbow, signaling for him to back off, let this poor man believe whatever he chose to believe.

Trip winked at her, as though to say, *"I've got this."*

The detective jumped in. "I read most of it, too. It's an interesting theory. You've done a good research job. Whether I believe it or not, it's not something we can follow up."

Doug's eyes narrowed.

"So why are you here? If you think I'm just some old crackpot who can't get over his son's death, why are you bothering?"

Kendall noticed the tremble in Doug's hands as they rested on his knees. His right hand moved to rub forcefully up and down his thigh as though he were attempting to wipe away a stain from his pants.

Kendall felt sick. He'd suffered so much and *she* was adding to that suffering.

"Mr. McKinley, please, you don't know what can come from any of this. The detective only has a few questions, things he needed clarified that didn't sit right."

She turned again to Trip and stared pointedly. "That's what he told me, anyway." Then back to Doug: "I promise I'll write this story one day. In fact soon I might have some news." She wished she could tell him about *Vanity Fair*, but by the time she'd left, she still hadn't heard.

"What was unclear in it?" Doug McKinley sounded affronted. "I did this for a living once. Figure analysis and systems. Million-dollar decisions were made based on my advice. So what exactly doesn't *sit right?*"

Doug's face reddened. Kendall had hoped that once Trip met Doug, he'd see he couldn't be involved in killing anyone.

Doug's rheumy eyes swelled with emotion as he began to speak.

"I'm telling you, if you look at even a couple of the charts, you'll see my analysis is sound. Those damn, filthy drugs are causing people to kill. If this were a disease, we'd be fundraising to cure it. The drug companies or the government are hiding the statistics. Maybe even the media. One percent of all murders are mass killings. Why isn't that statistic plastered across the top of newspapers, instead of what some actress does on her holiday?"

Doug stopped, sucking in deep gulps of air, his wheeze even more pronounced.

"Tell me that," he spat, spittle flying from his mouth.

Trip held up a cavalier hand, traffic cop style. "Mr. McKinley, for what it's worth, I'm with you. I think these bastards are getting away with murder—sorry, that didn't come out right. But, like I said, it isn't a police matter."

McKinley's hand slowed from its frantic rubbing of his knee and thigh, gradually coming to a stop. Kendall could almost feel Doug's thoughts flying at her. *Why did you bring him here? Why did you pretend you would help me?*

Trip reached inside his jacket and pulled out a pen and a pocket-sized spiral notebook. He flipped the cover of the notebook over and shuffled through the pages. The air in the room had turned thick and heavy as though the detective were about to read out a court verdict. Trip seemed unaware of the change in mood.

"A few questions, Mr. McKinley. If you could answer these, then maybe I can pass your report on to an agency once we've closed off these current cases. Okay?"

Doug looked over at Kendall, a pleading look in his eyes, as though he was looking to her to save him. What a terrible mistake for her to give his file to the police. What was she thinking? *Probably about Lance O'Grady.* How stupid.

She studied Doug as he waited for Trip. His graying skin, his hands, shuddering with small tremors, his cracked and dry lips... Was he dying? That certainly would explain the urgency in his voice. He wanted to see something happen with his report before he died. He looked worn out, no, worn down. Maybe he saw this visit as his last chance.

Kendall's impulse was to reach out and hug him. Instead, she said, "Mr. McKinley, I really want to help you. It just might take some time. Detective Lindsay wants to help, too. He's just not explaining himself well."

Doug's face softened. He bowed his head, shaking it slowly as he did, and drew in several rattily breaths.

"Sorry, yes, of course. I shouldn't be so rude. Excuse an old man's tantrums. I get worked up when I talk about my research. It's become an obsession."

Kendall wanted to assure Doug. She was worried about him. "Mr. McKinley, upsetting you was the last thing *I* wanted. Your research is amazing."

When Trip spoke next, she wanted to hit him. His voice was all business. *Was he even listening to her?*

"Mr. McKinley, in your report, which I noticed also included these recent murders, you've listed a few observations we find concerning. Questions to which we need honest answers."

Where was Trip going with this?

He'd told her he had some belief in the research. If Trip upset Doug McKinley again, when he was so frail, then she would intervene. Doug McKinley was *her* contact and should be treated with respect.

Trip's gaze flicked from his pad to Doug McKinley's face as he spoke. Neither man smiled at all now.

"For instance, you've noted all three of the recent perpetrators of the massacres were taking an anti-depressant."

"Yes, they were." Doug's eyes lit up, his voice gaining energy. "Isn't that interesting?"

"How did you know that, Mr. McKinley? That they were taking anti-depressants? This information wasn't in the news reports. In fact, we only discovered Benito Tavell was prescribed Prozac through reading *your* report. Checking with his doctor, we found, surprisingly, you were right. We didn't find the medication at his home because he kept it in his locker at work."

Trip paused, his stare fixed on Doug. "So, how *did* you know about the medication?"

Doug McKinley seemed not to hear Trip's question. He started chewing on his lips, pulling at them with his bottom teeth until several dry cracks began to bleed. He must have tasted blood in his mouth, because he moved his hand to his face and wiped his palm across his mouth. His fingers came away stained red. His eyebrows knitted together as he examined the blood, rubbing his thumb across his wet fingertips.

"Oh, I'm bleeding. Sorry, please excuse me a moment."

He leaned under the coffee table, pulled out a small blue tissue box, and placed it on the arm of the chair. He pulled out a tissue and dabbed at his mouth.

"Sorry, now what were you saying? Oh, yes, how did I know these people were medicated? Well, I'm not exactly sure. I wonder was it in the newspapers?"

He looked at Kendall. "Perhaps you told me, Miss Jennings, do you think?"

Kendall shrugged, but was certain she hadn't told him. She hadn't known herself. It hadn't occurred to her, either, he shouldn't have known about the three killers' medication.

Kendall turned to Trip. "Maybe it *was* in a news article?"

"No, I went back through them. Not a mention anywhere. Either you've guessed at it to make your studies look more compelling or you know something we don't."

Kendall watched Doug carefully, looking for signs of distress again. He continued to slowly dab at his still bleeding lip.

"Really, I don't know detective. I'm an old man. Maybe it *was* a guess based on probabilities. I'm sure you can't read *everything* printed in the news. How could *I* possibly know information before the police? Maybe *you* just weren't doing your job."

"Except, Mr. McKinley, you were spot on in your research, even listing the brand of drugs."

A small, gentle smile touched Doug's lips. "Did I? That *is* interesting, isn't it?"

"Yes, I think maybe you do know more than you're telling us."

Doug looked up to stare at his son's photo again. Once more, his mind seemed to have left the room. The tremors in his hands were back. He held his palms forcibly to his knees, perhaps to minimize the shaking.

"I think, Detective, if you don't believe me, then arrest me."

As though Trip was no longer in the room, Doug looked to Kendall and smiled the sweetest of smiles. Once again, he was the image of a kindly uncle.

"I really appreciate you coming here. You're the first journalist in recent times to pay much attention to my story."

Kendall half-smiled and nodded, uncertain why he seemed so happy and calm when Trip had literally accused him of lying.

"Well, Mr. McKinley, it's an interesting idea."

As quickly as his mood had turned upbeat, it now fell away to something else darker, like a light had gone out on his emotions.

"It's not an idea. They're facts. Why can't people see that? I've never understood."

His head snapped back from the photo to address Trip.

"I think, Detective Lindsay, you've come here under false pretenses. You've come asking ridiculous questions and wasting my time. You're not here to help me stop what's happening at all, are you?"

Kendall didn't know where to look. Doug McKinley's lip, which *had* stopped bleeding, had started seeping red again. Her annoyance with Trip was growing.

Trip waved his hands as though to say *calm down.*

"Mr. McKinley, like I said, we're merely trying to tie up loose ends. They're simple questions."

Doug McKinley suddenly stood, almost toppling over in his haste. His hand reached out to steady himself on the arm of his chair. He righted himself, then shuffled around the coffee table and headed toward the door. At the doorway, he stopped and looked back at them.

"I can now appreciate *you*, Detective, are like the rest of them. Blind or part of the cover-up. I don't have to answer your questions. In fact, I think you'd better leave. I'm not feeling well."

He rubbed at his chest, as though to indicate he had a problem with his heart.

Trip stood. "Mr. McKinley, I apologize, but you *will* have to talk to us at some point. I'll come back tomorrow with my partner when you're feeling better."

Trip motioned to Kendall they should leave. Kendall was flabbergasted. This hadn't gone the way she'd expected at all. Trip's ambush shocked her.

She picked up her bag and threw it over her shoulder. But instead of following Trip, who now stood at the doorway waiting to leave, she approached Doug.

Placing her hand gently on his forearm, she said, "Mr. McKinley ... Doug, I'm so sorry. We didn't want to upset you. This is a misunderstanding." She glanced over at Trip, and gently squeezed Doug's arm. "Trust me, I *do* want to help you."

Doug looked into Kendall's eyes. Suddenly she had the sense of a switch flicked inside his head, as though he'd made a decision, wrenched back emotional control. His mood changed instantly. Before her was, again, the sweet and eager old man she'd first met.

"You're a good girl, aren't you? You will help me, won't you?"

Before she could answer, Doug called to Trip. "Detective, could I possibly chat privately with Miss Jennings? I have a few more notes. For her story."

Kendall turned to look at Trip now standing in the hall next to the front door. She felt Doug's hand on her upper arm, surprisingly steady and strong.

"Is that all right with you, Miss Jennings? It'll only take a few minutes. I have them in the kitchen all ready."

Kendall looked at Trip with a sinking feeling. She could almost predict like a fortuneteller that she would do even more damage to this man by raising his hopes when she had little control over what might come of any article she might write. It was too late, though.

"Do you mind, Detective?" she asked with a smiling grimace hidden from Doug, but one that told Trip she was an unwilling participant.

Trip reached into his hip pocket and pulled out a wallet from which he retrieved a card. He placed the card on the side table beside the door.

"My card, Mr. McKinley. I *will* be in touch tomorrow. You'll be seeing me again." Then to Kendall: "I'll be waiting in the car. Take your time. I have some calls to make."

Kendall watched Trip exit. Even before he'd closed the door, Doug McKinley had grabbed her hand and led her from the living room. Once again, his firm grip gave a different impression to his appearance. Maybe he wasn't as ill as she'd first thought.

"Come this way, Miss Jennings. You are a lovely girl. *Really.* And you'll be a big help to me. I don't think even *you* realize how much."

"If I can help you, I will."

"Yes, you will."

A fly being led into a spider's parlor, was how she felt. Kendall smiled at such a silly thought.

CHAPTER 38

"N O PROBLEM," SAID KENDALL, FEELING even more uncomfortable in the face of Doug McKinley's enthusiasm. These stories she'd found herself writing had taken her to places she did not enjoy. She didn't like hurting people, and she didn't like disappointing people. She felt sure she would end up doing both to Doug McKinley.

As soon as she left here, she intended to make some life changes. First, she'd stop wavering over the direction of her work and find a way to ensure she had regular paying jobs. A friend of hers was doing well writing content for a large website. She could do that. Secondly, she would get as far away from anything involving crimes and death. That included Detectives O'Grady and Trip Lindsay.

Whatever Doug McKinley wanted to show her, she would find some other writer to take up the story. If it turned out he'd gotten it right, then let that writer enjoy the career boost. Kendall didn't want that anyway. She wanted her old life back, where the things she wrote, or didn't write, hurt nobody. She might not change the world, but, then, she wouldn't damage it either.

As they entered the tidy green-themed kitchen, Kendall spied the dark-blue manila folder sitting on the melamine table, pushed up against the wall. On the folder, handwritten in big black marker-pen letters, was her name.

Doug shuffled his way to the stove and switched on the burner below a kettle.

"Tea or coffee?"

She hesitated. Trip was waiting outside. After everything, though, the least she could do was give the man ten minutes.

"I'll take a coffee, thank you, but I think it'll have to be quick. I don't want to keep the detective waiting long."

She put her hand on the top of the folder. With his back to her, Doug pulled two cups from a cupboard above the kitchen sideboard. "Now, don't you open that folder until I'm there. I want to walk you through it."

Kendall instantly withdrew her hand from the folder.

Seating herself into one of the two chairs at the table, she swiveled herself around, so that her arm hung over the back of the chair and she could watch Doug. She wanted to give him her full attention. Make him happy, even if it was only for the next few minutes.

"I'm sorry the police seem to have missed the point of your research, Mr. McKinley. *I* admire your tenacity."

Doug shrugged his shoulders, then turned toward her and smiled before returning to the coffee cups. He dropped a spoonful of instant coffee into each.

Opening the fridge next to the bench, he said, "Milk? Sugar?"

"Black, thank you. One sugar."

"Charlie took his coffee black. We used to sit and drink it together. Unusual for a kid his age. Usually they're out with their friends. I think because my wife passed when he was so young, he felt he should be there for me. We were a team."

Doug McKinley still hadn't looked at Kendall. Moments before, his spirits seemed lifted at having her attention. Now, joy slid from his voice, which had become a monotone drawl.

As he talked, he moved back to the fridge to return the milk he'd used for his own drink. Even more slowly—if that were even possible—he moved back to a cupboard above the sink from which he retrieved a sugar bowl.

Kendall turned her attention to her iPhone and began to type a message to Trip … *Be about ten minutes.* After blindsiding her like that and bullying Doug, he was lucky she didn't keep him waiting an hour. He might have a job to do, but he wasn't dealing with a hardened criminal. Doug was a sick, old man. And *her* contact, after all.

Just as Kendall hit send on her message, the shriek of a whistle announced the kettle had boiled. While she was at it, she decided to check her Facebook account.

She heard the sound of water being poured into the cups, then tired footsteps as Doug made his way to the table. Looking up from her phone, she smiled at him, just as he gently placed a cup on the table before her.

"There you go. Black and hot."

"Thank you."

Kendall picked up the cup and sipped at the dark liquid. It was boiling. She wished she'd asked him to add a drop of cold water so she could finish it quickly.

Doug McKinley lowered himself into the chair across from her. Something had changed about him that she couldn't quite figure. He still smiled, but there was flatness in his eyes when she looked into them. It unsettled her. If she hadn't known him as a sweet, old man, she might have made an excuse and left right then.

Instead, she waited for him to speak. He continued to look at her, watching, as she took another sip of the coffee. Doug didn't appear to be in any hurry, so Kendall took control.

"Okay, Mr. McKinley, what else do you have for me? I only have a few minutes, remember? Detective Lindsay's outside."

"Of course. Of course. I'm sorry. I don't mean to delay you. I know you've more important things than having coffee with an old man."

He moved his hand toward the folder and pushed it across to her. Kendall reached for it and was about to open the cover, when he reached over and placed his palm on top of hers.

"I just want to say one thing before you look inside."

Was that a tear in the corner of his eye?

The folder's new contents must cover issues dear to him—something more about his son, possibly. In a way, she was grateful babies weren't on her near-horizon. She thought about her mother and now understood why she did what she did that night.

"I'm all ears." Her voice was warm. "And if you want me to stay, if it will take longer than a few minutes, I can tell the detective to go and I'll catch a cab.

"No, no. This won't take a minute. I just need to say I'm sorry. If I could have found any other way, I would. You're the kind of girl I would have liked Charlie to marry."

That hit Kendall in the heart. She thought if he kept this up, she'd become a sobbing mess.

She placed her other hand over his.

"Mr. McKinley—Doug, whatever is in here, I promise I will help you in any way I can. I think you're very brave. You've done more than most people. Some things are just inexplicable. And unfair."

"Yes, unfair, but necessary."

He dragged in a deep breath, exhaling slowly, before pulling his hand away. The glistening in his eye had become a single tear streaking down his cheek. Kendall couldn't look at him or she'd start crying herself. She bowed her head to the folder and opened it.

What she saw was unexpected. She stared at the page for long seconds, wondering if she was missing something.

The page was blank.

She reached inside and slid the top sheet partially downward to look at the page below. It was the same. Blank.

Doug must have seen her confusion.

"You must look more closely," he said, "and turn that page over. It's a few pages in. Then you'll understand."

She did as he asked, dipping her head lower as she flipped over the top page as instructed. The reverse side revealed printed words. The printing, though, was minuscule, barely readable, forcing her to lean her face right down, so her nose almost touched the page.

A fine mist of talcum powder like particles erupted into the air. As she peered at the writing on the page, the particles disappeared. Had she imagined them?

The two microscopic words printed there were bizarre.

I'm sorry

I'm sorry?

What did that mean?

She looked up at Doug. The tear was gone. His dark eyes were locked upon her, making her feel like … feel like, like … prey.

"I'm sorry? I don't under-saannnd—"

The words sounded slow and distant like she spoke within a vacuum. Then her voice disappeared. Her mind felt as though it were being absorbed, stripped away from her. The surroundings of the room, everything, took on a phosphorous green and silver hue.

The shapes in the kitchen, the fridge, the coffee cups, the table, the sugar bowl on the bench, even Doug McKinley seemed to phase in and out. Distorted. Then clear. Gray and white. Then dark. Her head felt ready to burst. A pounding roared in her ears, as though her heart shunted blood at a gallon a second. Small flexing shadows of red and pink floated before her eyes.

Just as suddenly, the pressure began to fade. An instant relief flowed through her as an odd silken calm engulfed her mind, a tsunami of peace.

When she looked over toward Doug, all she saw was his face, swimming in a peaceful, blue fog, reaching out to her. When the vapor's wisps touched her, they felt cool and wonderful.

Where was she?

A voice spoke to her. Not a normal voice, a sound that surrounded her, as though she were transported inside a gigantic speaker box. The words were stretched and distorted, playing at slower than normal speed, forcing her to concentrate to understand their meaning. She closed her eyes, and listened. Those words held a sense of importance. Great importance.

232

"Ken-dalll. Kennn…dal."

Her name. Was that her name?

"Yes," she heard herself reply even though she hadn't thought to answer.

"I haave a mishun foor you, Ken—dal. Do you underrr-stand?"

"Yeess."

The voice grew clearer. Relief embraced her. She really wanted the words to remain inside her head, to understand their meaning. Her life depended on those words. They were her life raft on this strange ocean, the voice, her way home. The voice became everything to her. *Everything.* It was the voice of her father, her mother, her favorite teacher, her first love. Whatever words the voice spoke belonged to her.

"You know Kendall. You're a very, very good girl. You'll help them understand."

"Yes. I want to help you."

Every word felt clear, entering her brain like water poured into a long glass. "Tell me, Kendall, what made you the angriest you can remember? What wrong in the world must be righted?"

Kendall's mind went in search of the feeling.

Of course, the answer was simple.

Her mother. That night. The terrible men at the car's window. Looking in, at her, at her mother.

The thought, amplified by the voice, made the image raw and overwhelming. She felt nauseous as though someone had punched her in the stomach.

"Mom! They killed my mother."

"Who killed her?"

She heard the question distantly, sweeping down from the heavens.

Was this God talking to her?

"Those men at the window. We're stopped at the lights. They want the car. *Get out. Get out. GET THE FUCK OUT!* They're screaming. My mom … she's saying *NO!* Protecting me. *Don't get out! Kendall. Kendall. It's okay. Okay. We'll be okay. Okay* … The door. They've got the door open."

Kendall felt her breath catch in her throat. She saw her mother struggle with the man as he attempted to pull her from the car.

"*Kendall, run.* Then … blood. *On me.* Everywhere. Blood dripping from the window. Blood. So much—"

The feelings she'd hidden, avoided, all these years came flooding back with the fury of a wild winter storm.

"My fault. I couldn't drive. Drank too much. Mom told me, call. Anytime, she'd come. Get me. *Too much blood.*"

The storm of emotion swirling inside, elevated her above the scene. Now she had a bird's eye view of the inside of the car. Her mother's body slumped in the driver's seat beside her. The two men, men she could never identify, never brought to justice, running away down the darkened street. A sound came, so filled with pain she wanted to tear her head from her body. A scream. *Kendall's own scream.*

"Mom. MOM! Nooo—"

The words entered and then whirled inside like a pop song stuck in your head: *I hate them. I hate them. I hate them. I hate me.*

"They killed my mom. My fault. I called her."

Hot, burning tears ran down her cheeks. Her heart shattered. The voice must be God come to take her to her mom.

"Terrible, Kendall. So unfair. But we can fix it. We can stop them from killing again. I've found them for you. This time you *can* stop them, so they never hurt anyone again."

Happiness flooded into the darkened places the memories had exposed, relief following close behind.

She could avenge her mother. She *wanted* to avenge her mother, wanted to save others. Kendall's tears slowly stopped. A smile spread across her face.

"Good, girl, Kendall. Now listen carefully. This is important, the most important moment of your life. You must promise not to stop until it's done. To follow straight and true. Do you understand?"

The words filled Kendall's world.

"I understand, yes. Straight and true."

CHAPTER 39

THE RADIO ANNOUNCER SEEMED FAR too chirpy for O'Grady. When he'd awoken early this morning, he'd thought he was better off working, looking over the video footage. Nothing had come of it, except he now felt even more tired after staring at a video screen for so long.

Trip was still with Kendall Jennings exploring the notion this McKinley had a source within the coroner's office. They both believed his knowledge of the drugs prescribed to the killers was either a good guess or somebody had loose lips. In any case, they needed to satisfy themselves how he'd gotten the information. Cross your T's and dot your I's was O'Grady's mantra.

O'Grady had decided to take a break. After hours, he'd gotten nowhere with the video, so he thought to head home and get some rest. He could then revisit the CCTV footage with fresh eyes. The last time he'd enjoyed more than three hours sleep was … heck, it was so long ago, he couldn't remember.

He switched off the radio, preferring to listen to the engine than Mr. Happy's irritating banter. Every single traffic light seemed against him. A higher authority was against him getting home. The idea of using the siren had even crossed his mind.

A few miles from the precinct, stopped at his fifth or sixth red light, was when a dreadlocked kid with a torn t-shirt, shorts, and flip-flops, jumped out in front of his car. He carried a water bucket and a squeegee and, after delivering a big smile toward O'Grady, began to clean his windshield.

O'Grady sighed. *What next,* he thought, as he absently stared out his side window, trying to put mental distance between himself and the teenager. The kid went at it as if performing high-quality detailing.

Normally, he didn't pay them. Sometimes he told them who he was and warned them off. It was an annoying practice at best, and dangerous at worst. The windshield, in fact, the car hadn't been washed since … actually, he couldn't remember that either.

O'Grady rifled through the center console looking for change. Amid the fuel vouchers and candy wrappers, he found a few quarters. The lights would change any second, and Dreadlocks, having just finished, had moved toward his driver's side window.

Pressing the automatic window button, O'Grady waited nonchalantly, while the window lowered.

"Hey, man." O'Grady, dropped the coins into Dreadlocks open hand.

"Thank you, sir." Dreadlocks nodded and pushed the change into his pocket. "Have a great day."

Then Dreadlocks was gone, repositioning himself at the intersection ready for the next red light. He had a cocky swagger to his walk and O'Grady pondered what the windshield cleaner would think if he knew he'd just illegally scrubbed away at a police car.

As O'Grady pressed the button to send the window up again, his gut tensed. *His walk.* Wendy Thompson's words struck him. "When I waved goodbye to Kate at those lights, she was just Kate. What did I miss?"

The windshield cleaner walking toward Kate Wilker's car in the CCTV film flashed into his mind. The way he walked, the hunch of his shoulders as he stood at the driver's window, the way he scratched at his arm, O'Grady had noticed them, their familiarity. But he'd dismissed the interaction as anything important. The guy was less than fifteen seconds at the window. That couldn't be enough time to relay a message or whatever had occurred between the mysterious stranger and Tavell and Benson?

He'd watched the videos of the killers prior to their actions so many times he saw them in his mind's eye as though they were playing on a screen. He checked the *walk*. Most of all he thought back to the way Kate Wilker's windshield washer scratched his arm like something crawled under his skin.

He thought back to Tavell's and Benson's stranger. Did he scratch at his body as well? Such a small, common action, he'd paid little attention. The videos weren't great, that didn't help. *Damn*, he was trained to notice unique body movements, and he'd missed it.

The nagging thoughts, the coincidences, the strands on the web, so distant and unreachable, wrapped around him in that second. It'd been right there before him. This *could* be the connection.

These seemingly random events were *something*. What kind of something and how they fit together, he needed to work out. But first, he needed to check the videos again, side by side, to confirm what he suspected—that they were dealing with the same guy making contact.

O'Grady swung the car around, brakes squealing, and headed back to the precinct, his mind ticking over the possibilities.

Why would the perps be so open, meeting in public so near to the eventual crime scene? A new type of terrorist activity, he bet.

No, that didn't fit. If the FBI suspected these were terror attacks and not random massacres, they would be involved? Hell, if it were terrorists, Homeland Security would be on their doorstep quicker than you could say, "suicide bomber." There'd been no demands, no claims of responsibility, so cross out terrorism.

What if it were some kind of suicide or murder club?

No, problems there, too. The killers didn't fit any criminal profile he'd seen. He mentally drew a line through the theory. No matter what area he prodded, it didn't make sense. If it turned out to be an alien invasion, he wouldn't be surprised.

By the time he was seated back in the video room and had begun to revisit the Kate Wilker CCTV footage along with Benson & Tavell's encounters, O'Grady had come full circle. Was it just his weary mind grasping at straws?

He glanced at the clock. *Ten-forty-eight*. He needed his partner back here. Extra eyes sometimes made all the difference. He dialed Trip's number, but the call went to voicemail. Could he still be interviewing McKinley? Surely he was done by now. More likely, he was with Kendall Jennings somewhere else? Annoyance played with him.

It should have been a simple, quick interview. O'Grady had checked McKinley's history the night before. Clean. A few parking tickets was all. The access to the drug usage of the killers had played on him. He'd pointed it out to Trip, who'd simply said, "I'll ask the question."

It was another anomaly with this case—itchy strangers, psychic retirees, and killers with erroneous profiles. How did the coincidental anomalies tie together? If they tied together.

As he cued the video, his old partner's voice banged in his head. *They never are and never will be just coincidences. They're shining neon signs.*

They might be neon signs, but he just wasn't getting the message.

CHAPTER 40

O'GRADY CONCENTRATED ON THE SCREEN, trolling through the dozens of multiplex videos they'd commandeered, looking for a man who resembled the windshield cleaner inside the mall. He still wasn't certain if he was anything more than what he appeared to be. Completely focused on the task, O'Grady didn't even notice Allen enter the room, until he heard the voice from behind.

"Good morning and good news."

O'Grady jumped, and swung his chair around to face the video tech.

"It better be good news. I just lost five years."

Allen seated himself in the chair next to O'Grady.

"Those films from the Tavell and Benson cases came back. I had them enhanced."

"I thought you said the images were as good as we'd get?"

"Correct, they *were* as good as *we* could get. I like a challenge. The minute they installed this equipment, it was outdated. A buddy who's genius with this stuff created this wicked app. It compensates for poor light, reimaging unrecognizable areas using awesome algorithms. His program's not commercial yet, but it's magic on a chip. When it finally hits the App Store, he could be one rich dude."

"I've been here too long checking through the Kate Wilker footage. And I've got nada. I got a hunch, that's it."

Allen slid a thumb drive into a computer slot and began hitting keys. A still from the Benito Tavell video from the time he left the café, before he went back to the Kenworth Home facility, came up on the screen. A second later the image came to life. The recording was miraculously improved, clearer and brighter. Remarkable, actually.

"I've already viewed them at my bud's. You're correct in thinking something isn't right. It isn't."

Allen squared his body to the screen.

"See Hoody here approach Tavell? Two things can be seen now which were blurry before. See there?" He pointed to the screen. "Tavell bends his head down to look at the paper—which, from this detail we now see is a map."

O'Grady moved closer to the screen. Allen pressed a key, and the video ran backward a few seconds. He pressed another key to run it forward, this time at a tenth of the speed.

"Hmm. I think you're right."

What was also visible was that just as Tavell leaned down to look at the map, Hoody flicked the paper gently. The video now so sharp even the flex in the paper he held was visible.

"Then," Allen went on, "note how Hoody leans back at the exact same moment. There *is* something happening with the paper. Whatever it is, Hoody doesn't want to inhale or get it on himself. If that's a map and he really was asking for directions, why would he lean back from Tavell at the very moment he should be looking down to follow directions?"

The same question now played in O'Grady's mind.

"Now, here's the really freaky thing. Check this out."

Allen zoomed in on the map clutched awkwardly by Hoody, his hands askew on each side of the paper. The way Allen tapped at the keyboard, O'Grady got the idea he could do this in his sleep.

The video moved on.

"What is that? That's definitely not right. The stuff coming off the paper, right into Tavell's face, that is some weird shit."

Allen was right. It was *definitely* weird. A faint white mist rose from the paper, like fine ash dust. Without the magnification, it was easy to miss, especially if you weren't looking.

"Yeah, what is it?" O'Grady frowned. "Play it again a few times."

Allen complied, belting a few keys. This time he placed the few seconds of footage on a slow loop. They both watched as the white substance floated up repeatedly.

"Tavell definitely inhaled the stuff. Some kind of poison, maybe? Or a drug?"

A drug. The idea settled in his mind. He rolled it around, pushing at it.

What did it mean, though? How did it all fit? He'd actually been thinking a completely different scenario. He'd thought, somehow, the three killers knew this contact, that Hoody had met with each one and given them instructions. He hadn't considered they'd been drugged and Hoody was actually a legitimate stranger, the map a ruse to administer some kind of drug.

What kind of drug had this effect?

Every witness reported the killers as methodical and in control. Not a drugged person's standard behavior. A frightening thought: was this a new synthesized drug?

The video stalled on the screen.

"And there ends the enhanced footage. Not much more footage, anyway."

O'Grady sighed. "Still can't see Hoody's face."

"Too dark to get a good look at the guy's face. Reasonably low crime area, not much call for security."

To find this map clue, but still have little information to identify the stranger was frustrating.

Allen attacked the keys again with swift, deft keystrokes.

"Ah, but don't despair, my friend. Nightclubs are different. With the Café Amaretto killer, we have a bag of luck. He was coming out of a bar smack bang in the middle of the entertainment district, corner of North Park Street and Harter Road. Voila!"

Clear, focused images appeared on the screen. In this video, the stranger next to Benson was partially turned away from the camera, making it impossible to see his face. This guy was dressed differently. Still he wore something to conceal his face—a baseball cap. It might be Hoody. Identification wise, this video was as much help as Tavell's. A probably, but nothing definite.

"Same guy, do you think?"

Allen grimaced, his head wobbling like a bobble head as he considered the question.

"I don't know. Now the footage is clean, maybe. But look at this—"

He hit a few more keys. The still enlarged. Benson's head and the piece of paper filled the majority of the screen. The video began to play, and O'Grady held his breath.

"Come on powder mist," he whispered. If it happened his instinct was right. That's all he needed to open up this investigation. Proof.

Benson's head bent to the paper. Yep, there it was. Clearly another map. For the beat of long seconds, nothing happened. Then, a flick of the paper. Minute particles erupted into the air. Benson's head suddenly moved back as if in surprise. He'd seen something, too.

"Wow," exclaimed O'Grady. "What a brilliant cover. Someone lost. A simple, innocent map."

Allen slowed the video even more, moving the footage a frame every second. The club entrance's multi-hued flashing lights behind the men turned their faces into colored, mottled shadows, but the surprise on Benson's face was still discernable.

The stranger reacted in the same way as seen on the Tavell video. He stood back just before flicking the map, protecting himself from the powder fallout. Benson's face, after his initial reaction of surprise, relaxed into an unalarmed, casual look. Then, just as Tavell had done, he walked off with the man as though they were buddies making their way home from the club. At the end of the street, they exited the camera's range.

"Damn," said O'Grady. "Tell me you picked them up elsewhere."

"Since you asked so nicely, I will tell you. *I picked them up elsewhere.* Remember, I said this district was loaded with cameras. I pretty much have most of their movements for several blocks. I've joined the various camera feeds into one continuous footage."

"Show me."

Allen sped up the video to four times normal speed. The images of the men waddled up the sidewalk, rocking side to side like penguins. Phil slowed the video again.

"They walked four blocks, then stopped here in the recessed entrance of a women's clothing store."

Outside the closed store, Baseball Cap and Benson stood in the shadows. Baseball Cap reached into his pocket and retrieved something. A phone or an iPod, with ear buds attached. This was why he'd felt uncertain about his *stranger* theory and had paid little attention to checking through these other videos. From the start, the way they interacted these two seemed to behave innocently enough.

Baseball Cap handed the device to Benson, and then moved so the two were side-by-side. He motioned to Benson to place the buds into his ears. He pressed the screen of the device and waited. Benson stood still, appearing to listen intently to whatever played into his ears.

"Can you zoom in on Benson's face?"

"Yep, I can."

With three clicks, the well-groomed face of a man in his mid-to-late-twenties filled the screen. At this resolution, it was somewhat pixelated. Benson looked like a billboard model on a giant Jumbotron screen. Even so, his eyes appeared empty and emotionless, his face flat and unmoving, like he was in a trance. His mouth, though, moved, like he was talking to himself.

"He's joined the zombies. Freaky. What *was* that stuff?" asked Allen, as though commenting on a TV show.

"I don't know," said O'Grady. "A drug this powerful, reacting that quickly, should really knock you out. Benson seems to be in control of his body. No staggering, no signs of intoxication. What's the time stamp on this?"

"Ten-twelve."

"So this guy introduces some kind of drug to Benson, plays him this audio, and, bang, less than thirty minutes later he's performing the lead role in *American Psycho*. Then the same guy—I'm pretty sure it's the same guy—approaches Tavell in the same way, in the same time period prior to the crime. Somehow, this drug gives this guy control over these people. If you told me about this, I would have said you were crazy."

Allen nodded, continuing to study the screen. He paused the video, tapped a key, decreasing the magnification. Again, a long shot of the two men filled the screen. Benson continued to listen to whatever was on the device, but Baseball Cap drew his attention.

That was the moment O'Grady knew his hunch had been right.

Baseball Cap scratched madly at his arm, like a dog scratching at fleas.

O'Grady thought back to the dreadlocked windshield cleaner, the image of him with his squeegee scrubbing, O'Grady lowering his window to pay him. He imagined Kate Wilker at her window, turning toward the cleaner, unsuspecting. A normal occurrence, no reason to feel endangered.

Kate Wilker's windshield cleaner, Hoody and Baseball Cap were the same man.

They never are and never will be just coincidences.

No they certainly weren't.

All the killers encountered this guy and his powder drug.

One puzzle piece now fit in place. What did they have? A plot from an *X-Files* episode. Where to search next?

"What's on that audio? That's what I want to know," said O'Grady.

"Shame we're not flies on the wall," said Allen.

Suddenly, an idea struck O'Grady. "We need a toxicologist. While we're at it, a lip reader, too. I need to know what he's saying, and I don't have days for a requisitions to come through. This guy could strike again."

Allen turned to O'Grady, a wide grin on his face.

"The lip reader I can't do, but a toxicologist, that's easy."

"You know someone?"

"Yep, so do you. Name's Google."

Allen shuffled his chair across to a computer to his left.

"Let's try these phrases." He typed words into the open search engine.

Drug. Zombie. Instant.

The first two results related to the television show *Walking Dead*. The next couple picked up *Zombie Hunger*, and why a new drug called "bath salts" could damage your brain (as if that wasn't obvious anyway). After scanning two pages, still nothing matching the behavior. O'Grady was thinking he'd be better off heading to the club to interview the doorman. Perhaps he might know Baseball Cap/Hoody.

"Try *drug, instant, dangerous*," offered O'Grady.

The second last entry on the first page was the winner. Within seconds of clicking through, O'Grady knew he'd found the answer.

10 Crazy Drugs You Don't Know (And Don't Want To)

#9 on the list was:

Seratolamine —The Drug Criminals Blow Into Your Face

"Bingo," said Allen. "Good old Google, your corner toxicologist."

"Let me look." O'Grady shuffled the video technician aside, so he could sit directly in front of the screen.

Taking over the keyboard, albeit with a lot less dexterity, O'Grady read the short paragraph. He then copied and pasted *seratolamine* into the search engine. The top result came back from Wikipedia. He clicked through and quickly skimmed over the scientific description of the drug, its history, etcetera. It's common name Zombie's Breath seemed apt.

A sudden chill ran through him.

O'Grady needed to talk to Trip. If he was right, these people *weren't* killers. Their friends and families were correct in their descriptions. They were just as much victims as those they killed.

Zombie's Breath! How the hell did he not know about this stuff?

"Great work." He squeezed Allen's shoulder. "I've got to go. Do me a favor, paperwork the lip reader. I'll call the boss and get a rush on it. If this drug is here in our city, we're in real trouble."

Drug.

His stomach quivered. Doug McKinley's report tabled a relationship between drugs and violence. That man seemed to know too much about drugs.

There are no coincidences.

He saw those four words scrolling across a big, red neon sign hung before his eyes. As he rushed back to his desk, he ran the concept through, looking for parts of the scenario that might not fit. He wanted to be wrong. By the time he'd reached his desk he was convinced of a link between McKinley's report and these killings. He'd remembered something else nestled amid the hundreds of pages of research.

He'd seen that name seratolamine before. He only skimmed. Some of the drug names, though, had stuck. He'd checked to see if any of them were the same as the ones his brother had been prescribed for the depression. The link between suicide and anti-depressants was personal for him. It had even crossed his mind, if he'd known this information before, his brother might still be alive. The idea had so involved him he hadn't paid careful enough attention to McKinley's other assertions that these drugs created mass killers. Seratolamine, though, had vaguely registered.

He rushed toward his desk. Where was the file? He couldn't remember what he'd done with it after he'd finished. Maybe Trip had taken it?

He looked over his desktop then shuffled through his overflowing tray, lifting yesterday's newspaper. No, not there. He pulled out the hanging file drawer beneath and flicked through the files. It wasn't there either.

Without the file, he couldn't confirm his thoughts.

What *was* he thinking?

That this old man with his long-dead son had accessed this seratolamine, masterminding these mass killings like an evil comic book anti-hero? Was he really thinking this, based on a word he *thought* was in a report?

He couldn't find the file. He smashed his hand against the desk. *Damn.* Trip must have it. He needed to try Trip again. He checked his watch. Ten forty-nine.

It hit him then.

Trip was with Kendall Jennings. And they were with Doug McKinley.

Chapter 41

KENDALL HEARD THE VOICE INSIDE her head. Deliciously warm, reminding her of her father's voice when she was a child. She trusted the voice, the sound of comfort and safety and love. It swelled in her head like an incoming tide washing over her, until it was only the voice and her and the words. All that mattered was the voice.

"Sorry," the voice said.

She wanted to reply, assure them it was okay. The voice needed to make no apologies.

"Straight and true," it said.

Those familiar words resonated with her.

Straight and true.

She'd give her life for those words.

A face swam into her vision. A sweet old man. She knew him, his name, though, remained elusive as though the connections to the memory had fallen away like unstable Wi-Fi.

What mattered wasn't his name. What mattered were his words swirling inside her head. Words like a drug, bringing contentment.

Something heavy was in her hand. Kendall looked down. Her movements felt slow like her body was moving through water.

A gun. Smooth, beautiful, and filled with promise. What promise, she didn't know, didn't care.

Normally a gun would terrify her, after her mother, the violence that stole her away. Now she felt kinship with this gun; it was a good and precious thing. The gun would save her. Bring back her mother. Bring back the life she enjoyed before that night.

The voice grew insistent, talking to her of the gun and a plan and her role in the *greater* destiny. She nodded, so the man and the voice would understand. Yes, she would follow. Remain straight and true.

"If you do this thing, you will enjoy your reward."

She knew the reward would be her mother, back again, alive and loving.

Her first task lay outside. *He* stood in her way. *He* would prevent her from helping her mother.

"You must stop him, before he stops you. Be quick, straight and true."

Yes, she said, inside her head, her mouth moving, miming the answer. She couldn't find her voice.

"You must be close."

I must be close.

Kendall walked to the front door. As though in a dream, her hand reached out and turned the knob. The metal felt like cool stone to her warm touch. A good feeling.

Straight and true, remember.

The voice swam into the very depths of her being.

The door swung inward, and suddenly everything changed. The sunlight streamed into her, each ray a sharp needle piercing her eyes. It burned with a pain that tore into her mind. She wanted to stop, cover her face, go back to the cool of the house.

She couldn't stop.

Her feet moved forward, outside her control.

Under her breath, she mouthed: *Yes, I will. Yes, I will. Yes, I will.*

Kendall saw *him* as soon as she'd stepped down the stoop. He was bald and tall, leaning casually against the side of a car parked in the driveway. At first, he didn't notice her, preoccupied with his phone. The sound of the door closing alerted him. He looked up. A smile flew toward her.

"Ready to go?" he said. "Tell me what happened once we get going."

She knew him, but his name wouldn't form in her mind. His name didn't matter; he was simply the man who would stop her. She clutched the gun tightly, behind her back.

Close. She needed to be close.

A few more yards.

Nearly there.

With each step, strength infused her body with steel. The thoughts and her next actions spun in her mind, sounding like a hundred airplane propellers whirring at once.

His phone rang, the sound cutting through the whine in her mind. He held out his cell phone, checking the number, then swiped his finger across the screen.

He smiled at her as he answered as though he wanted this to happen. She tried to smile back so he wouldn't be alarmed, wouldn't understand until it was too late, but her face felt stiff and awkward.

"Hold on a sec," he said into the phone. He looked up at her, his eyes wide and concerned. "Everything okay, Kendall?"

Finally, she'd found the facial muscles. A smile appeared on her face.

Walk up and smile.

Follow the voice exactly. To save her mother.

A few more yards, she'd be close enough. One foot after the other. No hesitation.

The mission beat in her head, her love for her mother, in her heart. The gun, a golden throbbing pulse in her palm.

The man returned to his call, his gaze still on her face.

"Let me call you back, O'Grady. Something's up."

She saw his thumb disconnect the call.

"Kendall, are you okay? You look sick ... something wrong? What did he say?"

She was inches from him, so close, she felt his breath upon her forehead. She looked into his eyes, her gaze meeting his. Confusion met her stare.

"Kendall, I don't under—"

The gun was there between them, the beautiful, cool gun. She tilted it upward, felt the pulse shoot through the finger resting gently against the trigger.

He saw the gun a split-second before her finger twitched. His eyes suddenly widened.

"No," hung on his lips and was then expelled into the air between them. She heard the word as a distant sound, echoing from another place. Then, a ringing in her ears, and the world became a silent movie.

His face exploded in a brilliant flash. Blood and bone fragments and speckles of gray erupted as though his head were a melon smashed with a hammer. The moist droplets felt warm on her skin. Everything so silent within the empty vacuum, made it seem like a slow motion film. He fell with a graceful movement captured in glorious Technicolor.

The man who would stop her, now lay at her feet, a bloody mess where his head had once been. Kendall felt at peace, even as blood pooled around his head. Thin red rivulets meandered their way down the gentle incline of the concrete drive, as though seeking an escape to the road.

She stared at the body, blinking away blood spatters in her eyes. The needle pain in her head returned. A blinding torment erupted inside, swallowing her mind.

Kendall elongated her neck, stretching at the hurt. It helped a little, encouraging the sharp tendrils of ache to dull down to tolerable. Uncommanded, a hand reached up to wipe away a strand of hair, fallen across her face. When she looked down, thick, warm blood clung to the fingers. As her hand slid across her shirt, a smeared arc of red appeared.

The gun grew heavy. She wanted to put it down, but something told her she mustn't, couldn't. Not yet. She held up the gun to stare at it, trying to remember what came next.

Then the voice came and she remembered.

The garage farther up the drive. There, an old man, beckoning her. A running car, gray puffs of smoke fuming from its exhaust. She hoped he'd seen what she'd done. Hoped he was pleased.

He smiled at her. "Remember what I told you?"

Yes, she mouthed. *Straight and true.*

"You're a good girl."

Inside her, a child's delight.

As the old man pulled a coat about her, she smiled at his touch.

"There, you've gotten some blood on your clothes. Let's cover it up."

He dabbed at her face with a cloth he pulled from his pocket.

Was there blood on her face, too? She appreciated his kindness.

"Ah, that's better, you look like you again, my dear. All ready to go? Soon, my good girl, all will be made right with your help. Soon."

CHAPTER 42

O'GRADY CALLED TRIP REPEATEDLY AS he drove toward Doug McKinley's address. He'd also sent several texts, concern growing, an expanding knot in his stomach. Trip had picked up, but then he'd cut O'Grady off. Before the line went dead, he'd heard Trip say: "Kendall, are you okay?"

What had happened? Trip's tone sounded off. Something was wrong. His foot was heavy on the accelerator as he dodged around cars and ran red lights. Instinct warned against using his siren. If there was somebody dangerous at McKinley's, such as Hoody, he didn't want to warn them.

O'Grady's phone rang. He slowed, relieved, thinking it must be Trip. He hit the Bluetooth button on his steering wheel.

"Trip, where've you been?"

It wasn't Trip. It was his sergeant, McCarthy.

"O'Grady, where are you?"

"Heading to meet with Trip."

"Would that be at the same address you left with the desk clerk? Park Way Road, Belmont?"

"Yeah. Trip headed there earlier, finalizing a few loose ends on these massacres. Why?"

Suddenly a thousand tiny needles pierced his gut. Something felt wrong.

"Shots fired in that street, number thirty-five. You'll be first responder to the scene."

"At thirty-five? That's where he is, and … Kendall Jennings."

"Who's Kendall Jenn—"

O'Grady hit the end button. Please let it be Trip doing the shooting.

Seconds later, he turned into the street. Thirty-five was four houses along. He saw the body in the driveway immediately.

"Shit. Trip!"

His heart beat in his chest like it meant to hurt him. All the oxygen evacuated instantly from his lungs.

Thirty yards away, he slammed his foot to the accelerator because he knew.

He knew.

At the house, he threw the wheel a hard left, the car's tires screeching as he bounced over the curb to reach a standstill on the front lawn. O'Grady wanted to leap from the car, race the remaining few yards to Trip, but his training and experience kicked in. He couldn't help Trip or anyone if he got himself shot. From where he sat, that's what it looked had happened. Trip had been shot.

He grabbed the radio mic from the dash and called dispatch. They needed backup. More than that, medical assistance. Minutes might count. Seconds. As he spoke, he scanned the neatly kept garden, looking carefully for any telltale movement of the gunman. He checked the windows of the house for signs of a figure or the barrel of a gun poking through the dark drapes.

Nothing.

O'Grady drew his gun, holding it to his chest, as he climbed over to the passenger side, continuing to search the surroundings. Uppermost in his mind was that Trip and Kendall might have found themselves in the center of another mass killing. He needed to get to Trip without being added to a body count.

Carefully, he eased open the passenger door, holding it like a shield against the open expanse of the lawn. Several of McKinley's neighbors stood at their windows staring out. He motioned them to move away, to take cover. Curiosity not only killed cats.

O'Grady allowed another half minute to pass. Still no movement. He couldn't wait any longer. He would need to risk leaving the car or risk being too late to help Trip or the Jennings woman, wherever she might be.

Climbing out, O'Grady stayed low, moving along the side of the car, his gun held at shoulder height. Raising his head above the car's hood, he looked over toward Trip. He was only ten feet away. So much blood there. Too much blood. If he wasn't dead, he would be soon if O'Grady didn't hurry.

Sweat ran down his face. He wiped it away with the back of his hand, and drew a long, deep breath. He could hear his heart thumping loudly inside his ears. One more long breath, and he launched around the car and ran toward Trip, his legs pumping like pistons.

Even before he reached him, the realization hit him. He fell to the concrete drive beside his partner. Trip's remaining eye was open, staring unseeing toward the house. Half his face was gone. All that was left was a jagged crater-like hole instead of an eye. Thick blood splatters ran like spilled paint down the side of Trip's car. He'd been shot at close range.

Trip was a good cop with good reflexes. O'Grady's instinct: *he knew his killer.*

He bent over Trip, his core aching. He wanted to touch him, but he didn't. Trip was now part of a crime scene. He leaned in and whispered into his friend's ear, "Trip, what happened, man? *What happened?*"

The time to mourn would come later. A killer roamed out there, and he needed to find them. O'Grady scanned the area again. He figured, by the still-pooling blood, he'd missed the killer by mere minutes. Minutes, the difference between life and death.

Guilt rushed over him. If he'd only joined the two of them this morning, maybe he could have done something. Maybe Trip would still be alive. If he hadn't been so annoyed with the Jennings woman, he *would* have been here. She'd infuriated him, and it was more than her being a journalist. She'd gotten under his skin. Not because she was a journalist. No, because she'd awakened something in him. He hadn't wanted to care about *anyone* again.

Sudden panic filled him. He looked around the garden, to the house, and then to the street. Now, he had just one question. Where *was* Kendall Jennings?

CHAPTER 43

EVERYTHING WAS COMING TO FRUITION as planned. In fact, even better than planned. Kendall was wildly receptive to the drug.

Now the police couldn't ignore him or his research. Certainly, they couldn't put the detective's death down to a random crime. Eventually, they would put it together, discover Kendall Jennings was taking anti-depressants and that all four mass killers were using some form of them. These drugs created violent killers out of peaceful good people, that's what they'd discover.

He'd allowed himself a moment of regret as the detective fell and Kendall walked back toward him. Then he pushed the emotion aside, replacing it with thoughts of his son's death and of his duty to make his sacrifice count. This plan was proof of his love. Doug reminded himself that in years to come, without his intervention many more would die.

In the passenger seat, Kendall sat quietly. In less than ten minutes, they'd reach their destination, his plan's final act. He felt a sense of pride swell in his chest. He'd stayed straight and true over the long, difficult years.

His stomach fluttered at what lay ahead. He was certain, yet afraid to fail. There would be no confession. Nobody would know what he'd accomplished, his sacrificial act. Someone else would receive the credit: a forensic doctor, the police, maybe a news reporter. Someone, just not him.

He glanced over at Kendall, the sweet girl. If there were any other way, he would have tried. She was too perfect, though. The girl's identity, linked intrinsically with the massacres, would become part of the story, her name tomorrow's news headline.

Kendall quietly stared ahead through the windshield, small earphone pods in her ears. Zombie's Breath was amazing. She experienced everything, but felt nothing emotionally, as if she watched a film of her life with no concern for the storyline. Doug felt comforted. He didn't want her to suffer.

The recorded instructions were on a repeating loop, so by the time they arrived she would have heard them at least four times, hopefully more. His preference would be more, but his biggest adversary was time. This, the final mission, was also the toughest with the least preparation. In doing this, he'd given up some of his control.

The detective Kendall had killed had been on his phone. It couldn't be helped, but potentially that could mean they had only a short head start. He only hoped by the time they found his body it would take them a little longer to go inside. He needed the police there at the final act, so he'd left them a message on one of the computers. Calling them from the destination to alert them, might give him away. Better if it was organic, everything leading from one step to the next. They would believe it was Andy, poor, innocent, damaged SSRI-taking Andy and Kendall Jennings.

With the previous candidates, he'd had more time to complete the programming. Andy was instructed to give them fifteen minutes minimum to listen to the recording. Seven or eight repetitions of the instructions was what he knew worked.

Andy was his first subject. Doug hated wasting the drug, but he needed to be sure. He'd had Andy walk to various destinations and buy food he knew he hated to eat: salads and sushi. McKinley followed behind, a stopwatch in his pocket, measuring not only the effects, but also how long before they diminished.

He needed his subjects strong, held close in his control, until the police arrived in time to end it. The killers couldn't survive. This was a one-way trip.

After experimentation, he'd discovered six reiterations over twenty minutes delivered a strong control, as though his hand were resting on shoulders, his voice inside their heads, guiding them to success. He hoped Kendall's programming took, so she'd play the game to the finale.

Doug's hands shook as he pulled the wheel and maneuvered the car into a spot in the parking lot. Reaching for the ignition, his hand could barely grasp the keys; his fingers had a mind of their own. He glanced at Kendall, who displayed opposite emotions; she, calm, peaceful even, her lips silently reciting the words feeding into her mind.

Eleven forty-five read the dashboard clock. He'd figured the lunchtime rush would create the greatest casualties, send the loudest message: *Nobody* was safe. Cafés, private facilities, citizens' own homes, and now family restaurants like this, dotted across the country. The furor of the aftermath would surely force the government to do something. The people would demand it. When you can't trust your neighbor, your friend, your co-worker, or your parent to stay sane, then society is lost.

His hand snaked across to pat Kendall's arm. "Thank you."

She ignored him and continued to listen to the track. He'd felt compelled to say it, anyway.

"You may not understand this now, but in a few minutes, *your* life will have meaning. This will be your gift."

Through McKinley's plan, Charlie's life had become a grand contribution to the world, his passing the spark to begin all this. Today, he would bestow the same gift to those souls who would die. It didn't make him happy. But righting great wrongs took courage, and Doug McKinley understood his only course was straight and true.

CHAPTER 44

THE DOOR TO DOUG MCKINLEY'S house was unlocked. The shrill scream of sirens from a few streets hurried O'Grady. He was inside the living room when he heard the slamming of car doors outside. He only had a minute or so in here on his own.

Another siren sounded distantly—the ambulance for Trip. Wretched sorrow gripped him as he imagined what lay ahead: speaking to Trip's parents, the funeral, the enquiry, staring at his partner's empty chair until he was replaced. Even though he was irreplaceable.

O'Grady couldn't think about that now. He needed to find Kendall Jennings. That's what mattered. He shrugged an imaginary coat over his emotions. His feelings about Trip would be dealt with later.

He scanned the living room, his gun held before him, his senses on high alert. The room was empty. Gun still at the ready, he circled the space, then exited to move back into the entrance hall. Opposite him was a closed door.

O'Grady stood to the side of the door, his back flat against the wall, as he reached out to grip the handle. He pushed it down slowly. If Trip was here, they'd nod to each other, both knowing what the other would do next: he to move in first, Trip to follow back up.

The door opened with a haunted-house groan. For some reason, he'd imagined it would be locked, protecting a secret room. This house felt full of secrets, hidden behind its normal façade, just as the killers were hidden beneath their normality.

He edged his head around the door, but couldn't see anything. The room was oddly dark for late morning. Four small, red lights on the opposite side of the room blinked *hello* to him. Reaching his hand inside, he fumbled for the light switch and flicked it down. Fluorescent light flooded the room.

A custom-made, over-long office desk ran along one whole side of the room, upon which four computers sat in an even-spaced row. Their standby lights were what he'd seen. It looked like rocket-launch central. Two high-backed office chairs sat empty and abandoned. Heavy blackout curtains completely covering the windows were the reason for darkness. They'd been taped to the walls so to block any stray ray of sunlight.

The room was a mess: empty chip packets, candy wrappers, and dirty paper plates lay in untidy piles on the floor, a strange juxtaposition to the computer desk, meticulously tidy as though it were a holy alter.

A convertible sofa bed was pushed against the corner of two walls. It was a mess, too, covered with a pile of blankets and pillows, as though someone had dumped a bag of washing there.

O'Grady walked over to one of the computers and patted the space bar. The screen sprung to life. A Twitter feed instantly began feeding, line after line of tweets scrolling and changing every few seconds. He'd never understood this social media site. Staring at it now, it looked like perpetual, fast-moving ads.

Stepping to the next screen, he tapped its keyboard. This one had some kind of code scrolling against the black of the screen like the Twitter feed. This wasn't Twitter, though, but jumbled letters and numbers. Programming code, maybe? He was no expert.

The next in line had the largest monitor, double the size of the others. When he tapped this one to life, he was expecting more scrolling of some kind of program. Surprisingly, a paused shoot 'em up game appeared on the screen.

The fourth computer displayed a Google map.

He didn't understand the use for the computers considering McKinley wasn't exactly the demographic for this much investment. He turned from them and scanned the room again. Something about the sofa bed caught his eye. The dumped clothes and clump of bedcovers concealed something.

"What the—?"

Once he recognized what he was looking at, his heart stopped.

A hand poked through the clump of bedcovers.

Kendall. God, Kendall.

O'Grady rushed across the room to the sofa bed, then tore at the clothes, barely breathing, throwing the apparel and bedcovers to the floor. Only when the body was revealed, did he breathe again. Relief rushed through him even as a shot of adrenaline coursed through his blood.

It wasn't Kendall.

A young man, maybe even a teenager, with matted dark hair, pale and sick looking, his skin almost translucent, lay curled on his side. His head rested on clasped hands, as though he were peacefully sleeping.

He wasn't sleeping. Drying white foam bubbled around his mouth, and his eyes stared back at O'Grady as though to say, *you arrived too late.*

O'Grady reached down, placing his fingers on the boy's neck. A lock of curly, matted hair fell back off his face. There would be no pulse.

Was this Hoody? The height and build looked right.

From the hallway, came the sound of police entering. He called to them: "In here."

He walked back to the bank of computers, to the screen with the Google map. He stared at the entry for the map. It had to mean something. The neon sign flashed in his mind again. *What?*

It took him a minute, but suddenly he understood. It made sense: this kid, the massacres, and Doug McKinley's report. If he was right, then more were about to die.

And Kendall Jennings was in terrible danger.

CHAPTER 45

THE VOICES WERE CLEAR. KENDALL had this mission to complete before everything could be perfect, the world made safe. Then she would see her mother again. She sensed the old man by her side, there to help; he, too, part of the plan.

The Burger Boys outlet was like most fast food outlets, situated on a busy main road. Cars whooshed past as she stood at the entrance, making the world feel as though it were flying by at an incredible pace, as though her life was set to fast forward.

Something about this place caught and wouldn't let go of her mind.

Death. Charlie. Something from long ago. Many deaths. And Charlie ... the name Charlie, important.

While the old man went inside, she would wait.

Wait at the entrance door ...

Yes, she would.

A family hustled past her, pushing through the door, causing her to step back. A little boy, about four, looked up at her. "Hi, I'm getting a kid's meal. I want the toy."

Kendall stared at him. She would have answered, but no words arrived in her head except for the voice.

For the count of sixty.

The seconds counted down as though a timer ticked inside.

Twenty-eight ...

A group of teenagers went by, ignoring her, talking animatedly as they pushed through the door. The smells of burgers and fries encircled her.

Ten...

A couple entered. A group of office workers departed.

Three ... two ... one ...

She felt her legs move beneath her, sluggish and restrained, her muscles and joints feeling rusty and worn. Kendall pushed against the resistance and felt energy flow into her limbs, which gave way to her command.

The woman with two children had stopped inside the doorway and now blocked her way. She turned to Kendall: "Sorry, kids, you know? I've told them to say *Excuse me,* but they always forget."

Then, to the little blonde girl: "Ainslie, you can't shove in front of people."

Kendall looked beyond them, ignoring the mother.

The cooking oil and fried onion smell surrounded her, the aroma so strong she imagined tendrils winding through the air. The bustling sounds of the crowded interior battered her senses. Her olfactory and ocular pathways seemed rewired, boosted to super strength. Every input felt like razor-sharp claws slicing through her brain. Kendall winced at the pain.

She stood inside the entrance, trying to control the pain, filing it away, pushing at it to recede, so she could keep moving forward, carrying out the mission.

Tables and three lines stretching from the counter, each four to five deep segmented the room, crowded with lunchtime patrons. She'd never been here before—she didn't like burgers—but, she *did* have a vivid memory of this exact same room. A picture flashed into her mind.

Bodies. Terror. Death.

Something *had* happened here. Whatever it was, however, she knew it didn't matter. Good would visit here now, and Kendall would deliver that good. Heal what had come before. Save her mother. Save everyone.

Keep moving.

The voice, insistent, demanding.

Walk to the right. Near the window.

She turned to the large window with its view to the parking lot. Nobody noticed her. Nobody spoke to her as she gently moved between the waiting patrons. Snatches of conversation filtered into her consciousness.

Two middle-age men in long-sleeved white shirts and ties talking in line: "*He's a lame-ass, and I cover for him. If not for my mortgage, I would—*"

A t-shirted teenager carrying a skateboard spoke into his phone: "*There in a sec. Just grabbing some fries.*"

A child on her mother's hip demanded a soda, even though her mother kept repeating *no*.

Two denim-clad girls discussed a night out. "*and a hangover from hell.*"

Saturated with life, conversation, and inconsequential moments, this place exuded normal. Normal, that would soon become extraordinary and the beginning of change.

Kendall knew she should care about these people, care that some of them would give their lives. But the voice, repeating in her mind, made too much sense. Its promise nullifying those thoughts, so they became small smudges in her consciousness.

Behind the counter, servers dodged back and forth taking orders, fulfilling them, and then quickly moving to another customer. Everyone so occupied, nobody recognized her for who she was. The messenger. The savior.

Now standing at the window, she was close to the kitchen. The smells of burgers, fries, and oil overwhelmed her senses. Her stomach rolled. Kendall willed the nausea to calm.

Straight and true, she mouthed. Just the mere thought of those words gave relief as the soundtrack in her head played on.

Wait until you see the old man. You know him as Doug McKinley.

The gun was heavy in her jacket pocket. She itched to pull it out, complete this mission, be with her mother again.

Wait for Doug McKinley to stand at the counter.

Kendall searched for him, scanning the moving bodies and nodding heads of customers. She spied him, third from the front in the middle line. He stood casually, staring up at the large menu board. In his hand he held an iPhone turned toward her.

We need a record.

A woman passed near Doug McKinley from the line nearest Kendall, pushing a baby in a stroller while balancing a loaded tray. A toddler followed at her side. The old man politely stood back to allow them passage.

He didn't acknowledge Kendall. Both had roles to play. Both understood what needed to be done.

A customer received his meal and backed away from the counter, excusing himself as he moved through the lines to search for a table.

Only two people now stood between Doug McKinley and the counter.

Warmth traveled through Kendall's core, endorphins released at the thought of how close she was to completing her mission and seeing her mother. The next step, exhilarating, almost upon her.

As he places his order—

The instructions fell into her head like a roulette ball falling into a slot. She nodded her understanding, even though acknowledgement wasn't required. It simply felt the right thing to do.

Kendall rubbed her hand across the back of her shoulders, squeezing the muscles with her thumb and fingers. In response, the throb eased slightly. She straightened her neck and squared her shoulders. Only minutes to go. A thought flittered into her mind and Kendall felt a flicker of a smile.

Now it begins.

CHAPTER 46

O'GRADY DIDN'T CALL IN HIS suspicions. He didn't call for backup. Even if he had, he had no intention of waiting for the backup. He'd ignored protocol for two good reasons. All he had was a hunch of a crime in progress at the Burger Boys restaurant. His main reason, though, was if he even intimated a potential siege was happening, the panic button would irrevocably be pressed. Within ten minutes, the place would swarm with squad cars and a S.W.A.T. team. In fact, they'd probably beat him there.

If Kendall Jennings were involved against her will, then the situation could easily spiral out of control, transforming into an even greater disaster. Already his partner was dead. He didn't need the tally of people-he-knew-who-died-today to grow.

At the final intersection, he didn't let a red light slow him, carefully weaving around a car crossing on green.

"Sorry, buddy." He nodded an apology toward the other driver who signaled his disapproval.

The ticking clock in his head felt heartless. It watched and taunted with the sound of irrevocable fate working against him. He kept calculating the time.

Five or six minutes before he found Trip after the report of the gunshot.

Three minutes to enter the house.

Four minutes in the computer room.

Two minutes to get out past the incoming police and take off.

Maybe fourteen minutes start on him. At current speed and traffic lights he ignored, he'd probably gained a couple of minutes.

So ten minutes? Twelve minutes lead?

Was that enough time before they did whatever they were planning? If it hadn't happened already.

He saw the Burger Boys' sign just ahead. A hand holding a burger on high as though the meal were an Olympic medal. He swerved into the Burger Boys' driveway, tires angrily complaining. He might need the seconds he would save from the action.

He swung in to the drive-thru lane, the same drive-thru where an enraged killer twenty-three years before had begun this chain of events, echoing down into this decade, into *his* life, and every other life destroyed in these past three weeks.

If Kendall and McKinley *were* inside, then he wasn't going in via the front door. The staff's side entrance was his best bet. He could scout for Kendall and it might give him time to attempt to defuse any situation he might find. Leaving his car in the driveway would also block any other civilians from entering and be caught in a dangerous situation.

He knew his ass would be kicked for everything he'd done today, or more correctly, hadn't done, but he'd gladly take that risk. He trusted his instincts like he'd been trained to do. His instincts were now his partner. Uppermost in his mind: find Kendall Jennings and ensure her safety.

Ahead, two cars idled in the drive-thru. He parked at the entrance, jumped out and ran down the drive. As he passed each car, he paused to flash his badge through the drivers' window and instructed them to drive on. He didn't have time to explain anything else, other than they needed to leave for their own safety. They received the message loud and clear. Both cars immediately took off at a pace.

At the service window, a young girl with curly, blonde hair tucked under a dark-blue baseball cap sporting the intertwining Bs of the Burger Boys logo, greeted him.

He showed her his badge; her face instantly registered surprise.

"What?" Her customer service training kicked in. Shaking her head, like she'd made a foolish mistake, she corrected herself. "Can I ... can I help you?"

"I need to get inside. I don't want to come through the front door. Don't be alarmed, but there could be a—."

He paused, not wanting to panic her. How to make her understand the gravity of the situation? "We've received a report. You've been ... that you've been targeted for a robbery. I'm here as a preventative measure."

She squinted at him, then her eyes grew wide. Nothing else registered on her face for a second. Then both hands flew upward to cover her nose and mouth. Her next words came out muffled.

"Uh, maah God. A robbery! Here? No way. Guns? Do they have guns?"

O'Grady indicated with his hands to remain calm.

"Guns, no, well, I *hope* they don't have guns. What's your name?"

"Carmen."

"Right, Carmen, what you need to do now is let me in. Okay? Can you go to the delivery door and unlock it?"

She nodded slowly; her stare never leaving his face as if she looked away the world would end.

The problem, though, she wasn't *actually* moving. He needed her to move. Fourteen minutes kept ticking in his head like a broken clock hand, stuck. They had fourteen minutes lead. Standing here was costing him time, time that might count, time that might save lives.

"Carmen ..."

"Yes?"

"Can you do it now? I need to get in quickly. And, Carmen..."

"Yes?"

"Be very quiet."

She wrapped her arms about herself as though she were suddenly chilled. Still she didn't move.

"Carmen?"

Suddenly her batteries kicked alive. Her arms dropped back to her sides. Then in a hurried, whispered voice: "Oh. Yes, yes, sorry. It's around the other side. I'll be there in ten seconds. Hey, should I tell the manager?"

"No, first let me in. Don't tell anyone. If the robbers are already there, we don't want to start a panic, do we? Stay calm. Go to the door. And Carmen …"

"Yes?"

"Act normal. You *can* do this, Carmen. I'm going around now. I *will* see you at the door. Okay?"

She nodded again, but didn't move. She was good at nodding. Carmen was panicked. He needed to jolt her into action. He pulled out his gun and held it so she could see.

"Now, Carmen. Now!"

"Ah, yes. Okay!" Short, sharp shakes of her head punctuated each word.

Carmen spun on her heel, turned from the window, and disappeared. O'Grady bolted back past another three cars in the drive-thru that had since lined up behind his. The drivers gave him a look varying from curiosity to annoyance. For all they knew, he'd blocked their access to a meal. Until he flashed his badge and shouted, "Move along. It's not safe."

It took him twenty seconds to sprint around the building and find the side door. As he ran, he kept the gun close to his chest, concealed but ready. If McKinley or whoever he had drugged was anywhere in sight, he didn't want him alerted someone was there to stop him.

O'Grady rounded the corner in time to catch sight of the door swing open. He raised his gun. Just in case. But it was Carmen who stepped outside. She stood at the entrance, holding the door open, her face whiter than the burger buns they served.

He lowered his gun and came to a stop next to her. His hand went to her shoulder and squeezed. "Thanks, Carmen. You've done well."

She gave him a limp smile. Tears glistened in her eyes.

He moved by her and entered the building. Carmen continued to stand there, holding the door, looking uncertain what to do next.

O'Grady turned back. "Carmen, get away. Get to the other side of the road."

She gave the nod to which O'Grady was becoming accustomed. Then she abruptly spun and took off. The door swung slowly closed. O'Grady turned and focused himself, his attention now on what lay inside.

Directly to his left was a storage room. To his right, the side facing the restaurant dining area, a white tiled wall jutted out five feet, presumably to conceal the arrival of deliveries. Now it possibly hid him from the eyes of a killer. He moved to the edge of the wall to peer around.

O'Grady gripped his gun tighter, but held it down near his hip, mindful of the havoc it would create should he be spotted.

The workers, just kids, really, four … five … six … of them he counted, were uniformly dressed in blue and white, along with the same baseball cap worn by Carmen. Nobody had noticed him, all too busy filling orders.

He waited, wondering if he was making a complete ass of himself. He'd broken every rule in the book. If he was wrong, he could always blame his behavior on the shock of finding Trip. Probably wouldn't get him far, except into suspension and a psych eval.

He watched the kitchen activity, weighing his next move. Maybe he should just let whatever might happen, if anything, play out. Play it defensively. He thought of Kendall and his heart stirred; then his brother, who was dead because O'Grady ignored his intuition.

Into his mind came the words: *There are no coincidences.*

No, he wasn't wrong. Something *was* going to happen. This restaurant was the scene of the killings that had taken Doug McKinley's boy. That could be no accident.

Doug McKinley, once a victim, was now a killer. Finally, he had to be stopped.

CHAPTER 47

ENDALL WAITED. SHE COULDN'T MOVE until given the signal. Only then would she play her role. Since she'd walked through the door, the restaurant had grown more crowded. With now no spare tables, the noise had grown exponentially as hungry customers accumulated near the front counter, waiting to be served or have their order fulfilled. All three lines ran from the counter almost to the door.

The old man, the good man, the man she knew as Doug McKinley, was now third in line from the counter. Before him a teenager, wearing a headset, bobbed his head in time to unheard music. Next in line, the mother from the door with the two young children bent down to them as they pointed up at the board and made their requests.

Kendall felt heat travel through her body, as though she'd stepped into a luxuriously warm bath. Her heart slowed. The pain at the back of her neck, like shards of glass digging into her skin, eased. Calm enveloped her.

If they only knew, these people surrounding her, they would be grateful to be here, to help make the change, to help send the message. She couldn't change the world with her articles, but she could do this one thing and make her life truly worth something. For the rest of her life, she would live in the warmth of that knowledge.

The mother with the children had now placed their order and waited. She gripped the children's hands, but the toddler boy squirmed and complained as they waited for the young employee to fill their tray.

Looking frustrated, she picked up the boy and placed him on her hip, where he continued to object to the restraint. He wanted the plastic bonus toy on the tray, and screaming his complaint. "I want it. I want it. Give to me."

The sound pierced her skull. Kendall reached up with both hands to cover her her ears against the excruciating noise. She closed her eyes and imagined the warmth taking her away, taking the *pain* away.

Like magic, the sound suddenly stopped. When she opened her eyes, the family was making its way to a table. The boy, now clutching the toy, looked over his mother's shoulder to stare at Kendall. He gave her a wave.

As if he knew.

Now the teenager with ear buds was all that separated Doug McKinley from the counter, and Kendall from her destiny. As he moved up to be served, the young man pulled out his ear buds, which now hung about his neck like a futuristic chain.

Doug shuffled forward, looked over and nodded at her. The five yards between them disappeared, as though they were both spinning inside a vortex, the DNA of their shared future intermingled. She would never be able to thank him. The best she could offer was a nod, in that gesture was her gratitude. Doug McKinley slowly closed his eyes, and then opened them again in reply.

He knew. Like she knew.

Soon.

CHAPTER 48

FROM O'GRADY'S VANTAGE POINT, HE could see most of the kitchen, with a partial view of the dining area. He'd counted five cooks working madly to fill orders. The restaurant dining room was jam-packed. Even worse was the number of children out there. If he couldn't stop this—whatever *this* was—it would be a nightmare. Newspaper images of the Mason Preschool massacre spun in his mind.

No, no, he wouldn't allow that to happen.

On the other side of the counter across from him, a redheaded teenager pulled up a steaming hot basket of fries from the deep fryer. He looked up and his and O'Grady's eyes met. The kid's face registered surprise. He dropped the basket back into the boiling oil, causing small droplets of oil to splash out from the metal tub.

"Hey," he directed at O'Grady. "What are—?"

O'Grady held up his badge while at the same time holding his index finger to his lips.

The boy's eyes widened. His mouth fell open. Luckily, he was quicker than Carmen and nodded that he understood. The black hairnet holding his mass of red hair jiggled on his head. O'Grady beckoned the boy, and he glanced to either side at his co-workers, as if to be sure O'Grady was actually talking to him. Letting go of the fryer basket's handle, he moved quickly around the silver counter toward O'Grady.

The other workers continued cooking, ignorant to O'Grady's presence.

For the moment, he wanted to keep it that way. If McKinley *was* in the restaurant, he didn't want to alert him. He hoped if Kendall were with him, she wouldn't accidentally give him away.

"What's happening?" the boy whispered as he reached O'Grady to stand alongside the wall.

"What's your name?"

"Kevin. Why?"

"Kevin, where's the manager?"

"In his office in back. Is he in trouble?"

"No, get him, please? Tell him it's urgent. Then I want you to calmly approach your co-workers and ask them to move outside. One by one. The one by one is important. Okay?"

"But why?" A tremor entered his voice.

"Kevin, can you just do this for me, please? I don't have time to explain. Carmen's already outside. When you exit the door, move away from the building. Go across the street. Find Carmen. Okay? Got it?"

Kevin nodded he understood.

"So, now, go get the manager. And Kevin—"

"Yes, sir."

"Hurry."

Kevin took off toward the back of the kitchen. O'Grady figured thirty seconds to get the manager here. Another minute to alert the rest of the kitchen crew.

Ninety seconds. He hoped he still had those ninety seconds.

CHAPTER 49

OUG McKINLEY DREW IN A deep breath, held it for a count of three, and then exhaled. The boy with the headphones in front of him had just given his order to the young, bored girl at the counter. No doubt, she'd already served a hundred people that day. This day, supposed to be just another day, another normal lunch rush she needed to survive to earn her weekly paycheck.

It had been the same for Charlie; just another shift to make minimum wage. He died earning pennies. This young girl probably didn't deserve to die or, if she survived, live with what the next few minutes would hold. A niggle of remorse entered his thoughts. She, just another Charlie, really.

He could walk away. Being here, felt entirely different, staring into the faces of those who would be sacrificed. Until this moment, his only contact with the deaths, the headlines in the newspaper.

He wasn't a cold-blooded killer, he was a civilized man who'd tried everything to save those who would become victims of what he believed was a conspiracy of drug companies and corruption at the highest level. In the end, this was all he had left. He'd come too far, stepped over that line in the sand. Too many had given their lives—Andy, the other subjects, and their victims.

The road ended here for him, too. He welcomed the future, the peace he would find. He wanted to see Charlie again. No more aching inside. No more guilt. No more fighting.

Should he fail, he died doing everything he could, sacrificing all that he had. Everything was in place. Only minutes remained. In those minutes, he would pray. Pray that finally his message would be heard.

CHAPTER 50

O'GRADY TOOK ONLY THIRTY SECONDS to explain to the manager what he believed was about to happen. Another twenty seconds and the manager was on board.

Gary—who looked as though he'd eaten too much of his own product—listened attentively. Without asking a single question, he moved as though his life depended on it. It did. Along with many other lives.

What was asked of him required courage. He didn't look the courageous type, but people will surprise you. If Gary had turned him down, O'Grady would not have blamed him.

In the ninety seconds it took for the fry cook to get the manager, O'Grady had spent the time sneaking looks around the wall. He searched the faces of the dozens of people waiting at the counter, looking for Kendall or McKinley or somebody who could the killer.

As he looked, a seed of panic grew.

Could he be wrong?

Maybe finding Trip *had* scrambled his mind. He thought through everything: the McKinley report, the fact McKinley had known about the anti-depressants taken by the killers, the dead youth in his house. No, he wasn't wrong.

Did he have the right venue?

What if this was a decoy, while somewhere across town an atrocity was occurring while he wasted his time here?

No, it all fit. He could just imagine the satisfaction McKinley would feel bringing this thing full circle, to where it all began.

He checked around the wall again. A fresh-faced, pony-tailed girl serving at the counter had noticed the kitchen emptying. She wandered back toward the area with a puzzled look on her face. O'Grady sunk back behind the wall. As she passed by, he grabbed her arm. A few words whispered in her ear, and she was out the side door as though exiting was an Olympic event.

Once he'd briefed the manager Gary, the clock in O'Grady's head began ticking again. Roughly, three minutes had elapsed since he'd entered the kitchen. A decision had to be made. Either he called in an alert and put out an A.P.B. on Kendall and McKinley, or he continued to clear this restaurant as though an event was about to occur.

He gave himself one last visual sweep of the restaurant, before he would make the call.

When O'Grady saw her, he was, at once, relieved, then puzzled. Then afraid.

Kendall stood near an external window just off to side of the people queued. She didn't look like the Kendall Jennings he'd met. The girl he'd met had a fire in her eyes and a persistent energy like a pesky bug that wouldn't leave you alone. *Or a beautiful woman who invaded your thoughts.*

This Kendall Jennings looked like a zombie. Her eyes, vacant and lost, stared toward the counter. Her feet shuffled back and forth on the spot as though she stood on hot stones.

While he watched, she stretched her neck stiffly, first to the left and then to the right as though she were performing warm-up exercises before a race. Her hand moved to her face and rubbed harshly across her forehead, rubbing as though she had a headache. A few seconds later, her hand dropped away. Again he noted the lifelessness in her eyes. No light, no animation. She was a sleepwalker.

She had to be drugged, which meant McKinley must be somewhere nearby. O'Grady didn't understand exactly what was happening. If they were here, and Kendall had ingested this Zombie's Breath, then, something *was* about to happen. He doubted it was a peaceful protest. He hadn't imagined he'd face this; He'd thought Kendall would be a hostage.

Now he needed to decide, was Kendall in danger or was *she* the danger? O'Grady looked past the crowd of diners to the restaurant's entry door.

The manager, Gary, had just walked in. He didn't look like a hero, but he was proving he had guts as he carried out O'Grady's request perfectly. Thank God, because nobody would blame him for taking off instead.

Quickly, Gary moved through the restaurant stopping by each table, crouching, spending a few moments before moving on to the next. Immediately after he'd leave, the seated patrons would rise and make their way to the side exit. The manager was informing the customers of a gas leak, assuring there was no need for panic. As directed, he'd begun on the opposite side of the L-shaped restaurant, out of direct view of Kendall. All was going well. People were escaping without Kendall realizing.

His other worry: he did not know McKinley's whereabouts and whether the man knew someone was intervening with his plans. He also didn't know if others had been programmed like Kendall. The entire scenario was truly frightening.

With nobody left in the kitchen, the lines had stopped moving. Unfortunately, he had no way to alert the counter servers without creating suspicion. The two employees, a shaggy-haired girl and a tall, gangly boy whose nickname surely was Stretch, had suddenly realized something *was* happening. Puzzled looks crossed between them as Stretch walked back into the kitchen, calling out to his manager

The customers at the counter had, also, begun to notice the problem. They, too, looked around and beyond the counter, restless and confused. A woman at the front of the line, furthest from Kendall, pointed and exclaimed, far too loudly for O'Grady's liking: "What's going on? Where's all the staff?"

Kendall looked at the woman and then where she'd pointed. Damn, he'd hoped for just a few more minutes. Far too many people remained in the dining room. The two young servers now faced terrible danger.

Despite the commotion, a beanie-headed kid wearing a headset swung away from the counter carrying a to go bag, his the last order filled. A customer behind him moved up to take his place. O'Grady's breath caught in his chest. He now knew his time was up.

CHAPTER 51

K ENDALL WATCHED DOUG McKINLEY STEP UP to the counter. Pale, ghostly colors shimmered about him, making him appear to glow like a muted rainbow, an angel of light. The voice began again as though a play button were pressed.

Take the gun.

A flood of emotions exploded. The greatness of the act; the peace she would bestow; the change she would bring to the world. She was born to this. Her mother's death had sealed this future. Now with this one act, they would be reunited. She could finally tell her mother: *sorry.*

Straight and true.

The words, the letters, the voice surrounded her, before her eyes, inside her head, a flood of syllables filling every cell of her body. She might explode with their energy. The pain in her neck licked at her mind, but she was so close now it didn't matter.

Over and over, she mouthed the words, "straight and true."

Slow and determined steps carried her forward. Small steps to a grand destiny. She maneuvered to the side of the counter and stopped.

Take the gun from inside your bag.

The old man had given her a knapsack, which she'd slung across her shoulder. She reached inside and felt around. Her fingertips found the cold hardness of the gun. She felt another gun; there were two small guns inside. *Just to be sure.*

A shudder ran up her arm. She felt her mother's warm smile. *Not long now, Mom.*

Her grasping hand wound around the barrel of the first weapon; her fingers sought and found the trigger.

Keep the guns hidden. Until it's time.

She held the gun inside the bag. Not afraid. She was ready.

Move toward the counter.

The gift of the voice was not thinking. She had only to listen and act. No decisions. No second-guessing. No questions. The voice spoke. She obeyed. Her conviction made steadfast by the overwhelming sense of purpose, of destiny.

Kendall stopped at the counter entry, a hinged door, which doubled as counter space but could be lifted for access. Blue plastic trays lay stacked to the side. With her free hand she reached down, flipped the door up, and moved behind the counter.

One of the servers, a tall boy with dark hair pulled back in a short ponytail, noticed her as he walked back to the counter from the kitchen.

"Hey, you can't come back here."

In response, Kendall pulled the gun from the bag. The gun said differently, she could travel wherever she chose. She released the safety clip like she'd done it a thousand times, though she couldn't remember ever handling a gun.

Raising the weapon, she extended her arm and pointed it at the tall boy. His arms flew above his head, fingers spread wide like they were spring-loaded. Suddenly he seemed to have shrunk six inches.

A girl employee next to him stopped serving a customer and turned. She began to shriek, but stopped mid-scream.

"Oh, my God. Oh, my God!" she said.

"Fuck. No," Tall Boy said, his tone piercingly high-pitched. His voice and the girl's scream, like the screech of a train derailing. Kendall fought a sudden urge to drop the gun and cover her ears.

She fought the urge. She needed to stay straight and true. Just a little longer.

You will pull the trigger. Do. Not. Hesitate.

Kendall didn't.

She felt her finger flex. Her hand snapped backward with the gun's recoil. A small throb bloomed in her wrist simultaneously with the crack of the shot. Then the world went breathlessly silent. As though she were watching a movie, Kendall stared, unmoved, as a red mark appeared on the shoulder of Tall Boy's shirt. The stain turned from deep red to dark purple as it mixed with the blue of his shirt and spread.

Tall Boy looked down, his eyes blinking wildly like an overworked ventriloquist dummy. His female co-worker screamed. He joined her, even louder, as though they were members of an a cappella Halloween group.

Behind Kendall the sounds of chaos erupted. People shouting, running, chairs and tables being overturned. A cacophony of panic.

As though he'd run out of breath from the screaming, Tall Boy collapsed to the floor and began crawling along the black, rubber mesh mat toward the kitchen. Pony Tail girl didn't hesitate. She jumped over him and ran without a backward glance to her injured workmate.

Kendall watched, keeping the gun trained on the girl, then swinging it back to the boy. It didn't matter, there were more in the dining room. She turned to face her terrified audience. She was reminded of a marathon, the gunshot a signal for the competitors to run. Those who'd been in line had become a mob running for the door. A young woman, business skirt, perfectly straightened hair, had been knocked to the floor. Others trampled her, until a man leaned down to help her up.

Four. Take Four.

Yes, that was right. She needed to send four on their journey, four, the magical number today. Two guns, twelve bullets, and at least four deaths.

She held the gun straight from her body, aimed toward the retreating crowd. Those at the back were frantic, shoving and pushing their way to a door that would only feed two through at a time. She took aim, but didn't shoot. One other thing she needed to do first.

Take Doug McKinley. Help him find peace.

He waited for her at the counter. As though standing before an altar, the old man leaned forward, his hands clasped and resting heavily against the surface. His eyes were closed, while his lips moved, mouthing words she couldn't hear.

She moved to the center of the counter.

Help Doug be with his son.

Kendall clasped the gun with both hands and held it before her body. Again, the weight felt good. Yes, she would deliver him to his son. Then she would be free to continue with those who remained.

Her finger squeezed back on the trigger.

Doug McKinley maybe sensed her there. He smiled. When the gun exploded, he didn't even flinch.

CHAPTER 52

O'GRADY HAD MOVED ALONG THE back of the kitchen, so he could be closer to where Kendall stood. He'd moved swiftly, not taking his eyes off her or McKinley. As fate would have it, just as he rounded behind the kitchen workbenches, (the one spot where he'd lost sight of the pair for a few seconds) that's when he heard the gunshot. In that split second, he saw nothing, but heard it all go to hell. Pandemonium had erupted in the restaurant.

"Shit," he said, dropping to a crouch behind the prep shelf. He stretched his neck and body around the bench, until he glimpsed the counter. Adrenaline fired into his limbs. He'd seen Kendall move behind the counter and, if she'd started shooting, he didn't know how he would save her.

Where he was, he had no angle to see anything in the dining area and only had a glimpse of the serving area. One of the warming units for the food ran horizontal, blocking his view.

"Shit. Shit," he swore under his breath.

He *should* have called for back-up. A stupid mistake, but his thoughts were clouded because of Kendall. Now everything had gone to shit. Not only was she in danger, so was everyone else. He didn't know whether Kendall or McKinley had the gun. They were both near the counter where the gunshot had sounded.

His breath caught in his throat, as he braced himself for more gunshots to follow in the next seconds.

Damn, he had been a fool. He'd made a bad call, allowed this to happen. Right now, he needed to move and move fast.

O'Grady pulled his gun up to chest height and held it before him. Still squatting, he maneuvered along the side of the counter, his thigh muscles burning as he balanced on his toes. On the other side of the deep fryers, he caught sight of the upper body of a girl running toward the exit. He prayed she'd make it. That would be one less person in danger.

He'd made it to the warming unit, which separated the kitchen from the serving area and concealed him from view of the serving area. Rivulets of sweat rolled down his face, a few drops falling into his eyes, momentarily stinging them shut. He brushed other hanging droplets from his brow.

Thirty seconds had passed since the gunshot, and there'd been no more gunfire. The lack of it didn't encourage him. In fact, as each second passed, his gut wound ever tighter as though attached to a giant key. His instinct told him this wasn't over.

Keep moving. That was all he could do.

He was up, not squatting anymore, crouching, as he prepared to round the corner of the warming unit, his gun at the ready. That's when he saw Stretch, the tall employee he'd spied before. Stretch was on his stomach flat to the floor, crawling. Smeared blood trailed him, dark and rich on the white-gray tiles. The poor kid. From the position of the exit wound on his shoulder though, he'd live.

Stretch hadn't seen O'Grady, his focus only on escape. Shock would be propelling him. He reached out and placed a hand on Stretch's leg. The boy stopped, his head snapping toward O'Grady, his pupils dilated and his eyes moving wildly.

O'Grady lowered his gun. "It's okay. You're okay. Keep going. Get to the door and get out."

The boy simply nodded, before crawling away at a greater speed, his hips moving up and down as he worked his body along the tiles. As if suddenly gaining strength, Stretch climbed to his feet and took off around the bench, heading for the exit.

Good, another life saved.

Now it was O'Grady's turn to move. If anyone died, the fault would lie directly at his feet. He pushed up to a half stand, the thump of his heart loud in his ears. He glanced above the warmer—, still filled with fries and abandoned burgers—into the serving area.

In that glance, he saw everything.

Kendall Jennings only six feet away. Doug McKinley at the counter. People bottlenecked at the door trying to escape. This close he smelled the sulfur odor of the discharged weapon. Now there was no mistake. Kendall had the gun. A gun now aimed at McKinley, her intention clear.

O'Grady had only two moves, neither of them good.

Then the gun fired.

CHAPTER 53

KENDALL FELT THE MOVEMENT FROM behind her, even before she saw him. The rushing of a dark figure, close, just to her right.

Kill anyone who will stop you.

Instinctively, she knew this shadow did want to halt her mission. She began to turn toward the figure. Her feet were suddenly sluggish, her coordination off, her body mired in thick air. One hand came free from the weapon at the moment she fired, swinging the aim of the gun to the side.

Her finger had been paused on the trigger. The rush of air had thrown her concentration. She fired toward the flying figure—yes, it felt like he was flying—but she missed. She recovered herself enough to correct her aim. Maybe two seconds was all she'd lost. Long enough, though, for the shadow to disappear behind a wall to the side of a preparation counter. She went to follow, but the voice stopped her.

The mission is all that matters.

She spun back to the old man. He, a statue at the counter, his eyes still closed, his mouth continuing to move as in prayer. She needed to hurry.

Four. You must deliver four.

Kendall raised the gun. This time she took a moment, her aim more careful. The word *hurry* rang in her ears.

CHAPTER 54

O'GRADY SAW KENDALL RAISE HER arm and swing the gun in his direction. He'd begun acting on option one: rush her like he was Tom Cruise in *Mission Impossible*. With the element of surprise, he'd calculated he could overpower her before she got off a shot.

She'd heard him, though, and had begun to turn when he was only halfway to her. He'd realized he wasn't going to make it. Fortunately, his momentum enabled him to hurl himself behind the wall jutting out from the drive-thru window.

He'd skidded into a hollow under the window, immediately swinging about in readiness. Such a close call. He sucked down several lungfuls of air before he felt steady again, his gun aimed at where he expected she'd appear.

Moments before his failed move, he'd discarded his second and safest option: to shoot Kendall from his previous hiding position. He could only take an upper-body shot from that vantage. Chances were that could prove fatal.

Seconds ticked by, as he brandished his gun, his hand tight around the grip, his body quivering from the adrenaline. She hadn't seemed to follow him.

Now he was left with option two from this new position. All he could do was hope he could place the bullet in her shoulder or arm and wing her. The danger of fatally wounding her was high, but the life of every person in this restaurant was his responsibility. He'd already risked so much for Kendall Jennings. If he was honest, feelings he still didn't understand were the cause of his lapse in judgment. Anyone else, he would have done what his training demanded.

Time was running out either way. Any second, a swarm of police would arrive. Shots were fired and every available uniform would have already been diverted to this location. The crazy shit fight he'd hoped to avoid was about to happen. Kendall Jennings was probably dead either way. It was now his job to ensure she didn't take anyone with her.

His initial relief that she hadn't followed him might mean she'd returned to complete whatever insanity she was programmed to deliver.

O'Grady ran through his next viable move. He repeated the steps in his head, ran his mind through the actions. His life would depend upon precision and luck.

Step out, aim, and fire.

She wasn't trained to use a gun. He was. He had a better chance of hitting her than she hitting him. Still he hesitated. Lives could be lost because of that hesitation, but damn, if something about her hadn't wound its way inside his heart. The thought of shooting her pierced his soul as though a bullet had already found its mark in a soft, deep spot inside.

The sound of sirens shattered his thoughts.

Time had run out. While it was just he and Kendall, there was still a chance to save her. Once more police arrived it was out of his hands. She *would* die. That was how McKinley programmed them. No survivor. No answers.

Then he thought about the drug, this Zombie's Breath. He'd read up about it in detail. Those under its influence had killed of their own volition, but it wasn't truly them. Toby Benson, Benito Tavell, and Kate Wilker. Deep down Kendall wasn't a killer. Doug McKinley was the killer. He'd given them the drug and programmed them—

Programmed to kill.

Wait a minute! If Kendall could be programmed, could she also be deprogrammed? Could he redirect her to stop? Could the plan be undone?

It was a risk. If it failed, he would be ready. He could stop her with a bullet, a last, final resort.

Somewhere on the other side of the wall, he felt her. The melee he'd heard after the crack of the second gunshot had quieted. Hopefully that meant most customers had escaped.

He reached down and pushed himself back to standing, keeping his back pressed hard against the wall. His stomach clenched like he'd eaten something rotten. He knew what he had to do. *Could he do it?*

O'Grady raised his gun. His hands couldn't grip the weapon any tighter as he stepped out from the safety of the wall.

CHAPTER 55

KENDALL PUSHED AT THE FINGER resting on the trigger. Suddenly it required an enormous amount of energy to move that single digit, as though thick half-set glue had coated the firing mechanism.

The voice continued to whisper to her as she stared at the old man, the one called Doug McKinley. She trained the gun on him and imagined the bullet patiently waiting to complete its mission.

Send him to his son.

Kendall. Kendall. Stop.

Something about the voice, the warm honey voice she trusted and loved had changed. It was now distant, faded, replaced by this harsher one, frantic and insistent. This voice didn't make her feel wonderful and safe. It made her feel off kilter as though there was an echo in her head that didn't fit, an off note on a musical scale.

She *did* have a memory of this voice, though. She pulled at that memory, deep in the recesses of her mind like tugging at a forgotten dream. Its familiarity stopped her. Deep inside, it evoked a feeling of something like love or hope, and then of being saved. She saw her mother in the car and a shadow calling to her, explaining everything would be okay. The owner of the voice would save her.

Please, Kendall, put down the gun. It'll be okay. I'm trying to protect you.

She felt herself lower the gun. She *wanted* protection.

Then the other voice rose, the one she would follow anywhere.

You must deliver the message.

Yes, she must deliver the message if she wanted her mother.

The other voice came back. *Kendall, we haven't much time. Please.*

An eternity passed as her mind swayed back and forth. What should she do? Her mind filled with swirling mist, both voices calling for her from somewhere she couldn't reach.

Her mother's face hung before her. The image was all she needed to remind her why she was here. This was her gift to her mother. She was the messenger.

Kendall's wrist moved as suddenly and smoothly as the flick of a tail. She brought her aim back to Doug McKinley. He opened his mouth and spoke in the voice that commanded her heart and her mind.

"Hurry," he said. "Hurry. Now. Do it now."

Their eyes met. It was like a dance, his head nodding slowly as though listening to a silent beat. He wanted his peace. He awaited deliverance.

Kendall bowed her head in a final goodbye. The time had come. He would see his son. She didn't feel the trigger compress, only heard the explosion of the gun and the terrified shouts still in the room attempting their escape.

The old man took the hit in the chest. For a moment, he didn't move, didn't clutch at his wound. Though his head stopped moving and his mouth had stilled. He looked down at his chest, then his eyes found hers, and he sent a *thank you* with the flicker of his lids.

From the far corner of the restaurant, a scream and sudden movement drew her attention. She twisted her head toward the sound. Five people huddled beneath a table. A woman wearing jeans and a t-shirt leaped up and, despite the others pulling at her, made a run for the door. She tracked the woman with her gun, before her attention was drawn back to the old man, to McKinley.

His hands reached for his wound, but before they'd moved to the growing red spot on his shirt, he began to fall. McKinley's upper body landed on the counter with a thud. He lay there for a moment, slumped, glued to the surface at an awkward angle, then he slowly slid to the floor and was lost to her sight.

Now he would find his son.

And she must continue and complete her mission.

You must deliver four.

She reached inside her bag to retrieve the second gun.

The other voice came again: *Kendall, you must stop.*

Suddenly, she realized, this voice wasn't in her head. Not like the warm, good voice. This voice came from behind her. She turned in its direction.

Confusion engulfed her mind. Should she finish the mission first and then follow this voice? *Which one came first?*

Panic gripped her mind, a wild fury turning what had been clear, into shadows and valleys of doubt.

Kendall. Stop. This is not you. There's a drug. In your system. KENDALL, put down the gun."

But she already had her plan. She needed to finish the mission.

She followed the direction of the voice and turned to see the man. She recognized him. He meant something to her. His name was deep in her memory, but she couldn't find it. His words, they didn't make sense. They seemed wrong. Her mind felt torn apart.

She wanted to fire the gun. She wanted to give these people their peace. She wanted to see her mother. She wanted to deliver the message. She wanted to follow the voice.

Kill anyone who will stop you.

Straight and true was what she knew.

"Kendall. It's me. Lance O'Grady. Come on, remember."

The man held a gun. He would stop her. That's all she knew. That's what she remembered.

Feelings coursed through her. Anger. Fear. Frustration Another, deeper emotion, alien to her—desire. *Who was he?*

Then she understood.

It came to her like a clear and beautiful sunrise, so bright she closed her eyes at the pure thought. He was there to receive her peace, to help her deliver the message. If Tall Boy was number one, the old man McKinley was number two, that would make the man with the gun number three.

CHAPTER 56

"**K**ENDALL. IT'S ME. LANCE O'GRADY. Remember? Listen to me carefully. Shortly a police will arrive. Then I can't help you. Put down the gun. This isn't you. It's the drug."

His gun remained on her. Kendall watched curiously as rivulets of sweat trickled down his face. The droplets looked too big as though he were an actor on a large screen, part of a slow-motion film.

"You don't want this, Kendall."

She did, though. She really *did* want this. Her mission was not over. More needed to be done. One more, after him.

Kendall twisted her neck, easing the long tendons left, and then right. The ache had returned, along with the throb at the base of her skull.

This man's fault. His words filled her head, confusing her. They'd merged with the good voice and now turmoil reigned inside her brain. What she had known for sure was diluted and fuzzy.

You need to hurry. Deliver the message.

Delivering the message was all that mattered. Her time was almost done. This man had taken her focus from what she was sent here to do. Soon there would be nobody left to make the four. The mission would fail. Then what of her mother?

Who was this man?

She stared at the gun he aimed at her, her mind faltering at her next move. He held up a hand, signaling her to wait. Surely, he knew she couldn't stop. Surely, he wasn't a friend.

"Listen to me, please. You're Kendall Jennings. You write articles. You don't kill people. Put down the gun. Please, Kendall, I don't want to do what I must if you don't put down the gun."

Kendall studied his face looking for a sign or a clue as to what to do. Doug McKinley was gone, but the good, strong voice remained, only faded and indistinct as though fed through cotton balls. Something in this man's words, something in the tone of those words, made her pause. She checked through her memories. What was he to her? *What?*

His eyes stared into hers, dark and piercing, and something else. *Afraid? Desperate?*

"Something you need to know, Kendall. Okay?"

His gun was still on her, but his face had softened, his jawline relaxing, though his shoulders remained tense.

"You and I need to work out something. There's something between us. In the coffee shop, remember? I know you felt it. Your hand, my hand, when we touched. Think, Kendall. Remember?"

The murky bubble in her mind felt as though it were bending and reshaping. A memory was attempting to pry its way out. She felt drawn to him, as though he was a magnet and she, metal. His eyes so warm, so brown.

Yes, she did know him. She felt a touch. From him. Feelings for him. A tingle on the back of her hand. Yes, something there. It wasn't clear, though. As much as she prodded at the memory, she couldn't fit that feeling in with the mission. The pieces seemed misaligned.

He moved toward her, cautious, one slow step following the other until only a few yards separated them. His gun still aimed at her. His head tilted to the side and he smiled. A hand reached for her.

She thought it through.

Another messenger, perhaps? Or did he want to stop her?

Kill anyone who will stop you.

His eyes: they were brown, deep brown. She had a sense of those eyes looking at her before today, before the mission.

An idea swam toward her conscious mind, like a shark swimming through the murk of a storm-whipped ocean. Suddenly she understood who he was. He was the man who would deliver her. He wasn't part of the message. This man was her test, the final assessment of her capacity to change the world, to win her mother back.

A light flicker became a beam of certainty, indecision gone.

Straight and true her only choice.

The gun in her hand felt warm again, reminding her of destiny.

She raised her arm and took aim.

"Kendall. No, please."

Somehow, she found her voice. For the first time since this began, she heard herself. This showed her commitment, how much she deserved the reward. She wanted him to understand her, understand the message, so she'd fought to find her voice.

When it came her voice didn't sound like her own.

"I must deliver the message."

"No, Kendall, you *must* put down the gun. Please. The drug's talking. That's him. That's McKinley's warped ideas in your head. *Listen, to* my voice. *Follow* my voice. Put. Down. The. Gun."

Kill anyone who will stop you. If you're stopped, deliver yourself.

He would stop her. She saw that now. She needed to pull the trigger. She needed to finish the mission. She was born to deliver the message.

But something was staying her finger.

She pushed with her mind, willed her hand to move, to stretch the muscles, for the tendons to pull back her finger. Another mind was inside her, stopping her, taking control of her body. She wanted to scream. She wanted to do what needed to be done.

She ignored the man and turned her focus on the gun in her hand. What to do next?

Deliver your own message, Kendall.

Yes, that she could do.

Her arm moved even before she thought to move it. The action, the most certain thing she'd ever done. This was *her* message. Delivered perfectly, she would have her mother again and the world would be changed forever.

She brought the gun toward her head. A smile moved her lips as she stared into his eyes, the one who would stop her. She liked his eyes. Eyes that suddenly looked stripped bare and afraid.

His gun was on her, still. His palm rose flat in the air toward her, as she pushed the gun into her temple; the barrel felt hard and round against her skin. The smile now stretched across her face.

It would be a beautiful message.

"Oh, my God. Kendall. Stop! I don't want to—"

An explosion in her ear. A searing pain in her head. So sharp. As though thunder had exploded inside her skull. Where was the blackness? Where was her peace?

Fear burst in her mind.

Where was she? What had she done?

A screaming, unbearable pain filled her body. Then falling ... falling ... falling. Forever.

The floor reached up to her. As though with hands, it pulled her downward, faster and faster. She fell into the feeling, and, as she did, suddenly she was no longer falling but afloat, amid beautiful, iridescent colored lights. Here was her destiny. Somewhere here, her mother waited. She wanted to live in the lights, forever, more than she'd ever wanted anything.

The good, warm voice came one last time: *You are the messenger. You will deliver peace.*

Then she was alone, completely alone, in the darkness. Her final thoughts were not of her mother or of herself or of anything or anyone in her life. As she touched the light, was welcomed by its gloriously warm embrace, it was a simple thought that engulfed her. She thought of her message and, with all her heart, she hoped she'd delivered it right.

CHAPTER 57

K ENDALL WOULD NEVER GROW ACCUSTOMED to the bright lights of television studios and rooms used for interviews. They reminded her of the bright colored lights, the only thing she'd remembered from that day.

When she'd awoken, she'd sobbed uncontrollably after realizing her mother wasn't there, that she was still gone. For some reason, she felt even more bereft than she had when her mother was first murdered. It felt as though a second chance had been stolen from her.

A girl with a black-and-white-spotted bandanna about her head and bold, ruby lipstick painted on her full lips stood in Kendall's personal space holding a makeup puff. She powdered Kendall's face meticulously like she was painting a work of art.

Sixty Minutes' host Dana Masters sat across from Kendall, glancing down at the pad on her lap, then back at the ceiling. Each time, she mouthed words, and then looked back down again, to practice another question. Most of the journalists who'd interviewed her seemed to do the same thing. Nothing in television journalism was impromptu, she'd learned.

Two cameramen and a boom mic operator stood patiently by for the veteran journalist to give the go-ahead. At the back of the rented hotel suite, the producer and an assistant producer, a man in jeans and a torn t-shirt—who'd taken casual dress to the next level—stood holding clipboards and quietly talking.

Dana Masters suddenly stopped mouthing and memorizing as though a silent whistle had been blown to ready competitors for a race. She looked around the room, nodded to her team, and said, "Are we set to go?"

A chorus of "yes" echoed back like a roll call.

Dana looked over to Kendall and nodded.

"And you, Kendall? Are you ready?"

Kendall bit her lip and nodded. She was never ready, had never become comfortable with the interviews.

She had no memory of that day. No memory of the events in the restaurant. She could, though, talk to the motivation behind how they could occur.

The memory of how it felt to awaken in a hospital to discover she had killed two people and had tried to kill others would never leave her. The disbelief came first, the shock and the shame, later. Even though it was repeatedly explained to her she was never in control and had never formed any intent to hurt anyone, the guilt still filled her nightmares.

The thought a killer lived inside her sometimes clawed at her very sanity. Even if a drug had drawn out that killer, she wondered why she had no power to stop. *If she'd just been stronger? Maybe?*

The assistant snapped a clapperboard between the few feet separating Kendall and Dana's chairs. Dana was like a wind up doll, snapping to attention, talking, welcoming Kendall, and thanking her for agreeing to be interviewed.

"Kendall, over the past year, you've become a well-known advocate for greater investigation into the correlation between anti-depressants and violence. Some people have suggested you are probably the *last* person who should spearhead such a push, considering your involvement in the injury and death at the Burger Boy's Restaurant, as well as the death of Detective Trip Lindsay."

The large lights perched on their tripod stands felt mid-summer hot, reminding her of one of the few things she did remember from that day ... the warmth inside her body and her mind.

Kendall cleared her throat, a nervous response she'd developed in the past few months, although she was getting it under control. She was always nervous at the start of interviews.

"Yes," she said, haltingly. "But I wasn't responsible. I was under the influence of a powerful drug. That, Dana, is what makes me the perfect person to talk about these drugs, the SSRIs, anti-depressants, which are still being prescribed as though they're just headache tablets."

Dana nodded slowly as Kendall spoke, as though she were agreeing with her answer, but then asked, "But these drugs weren't the ones found in your system after you shot and killed sixty-nine-year-old Doug McKinley and Detective Trip Lindsay. So why would you then take on the drug companies and the F.D.A. regarding them?"

"Because, like everyone else, I did take them. That's how I was targeted. Doug McKinley believed those drugs carried a side effect risk of violence. It wasn't something I fully understood before. That particular risk was never explained to me when they were prescribed. These drugs can influence non-violent people, like you or me. It's like a lottery. You don't know what impact they might have. They don't tell you at the drugstore or at the doctor's. These drugs have snuck in and become an acceptable part of our lives. Little friends to help us get through the day. Or the night."

A door opened to Kendall's right. She looked over for a moment as Dana bowed to her notes. Lance O'Grady entered the room, moving quietly to the side to stand against the wall next to the producers.

He caught her attention and smiled. Kendall smiled back, and suddenly felt more relaxed, more confident. Those brown eyes always had that effect on her. His eyes were the only other thing she remembered from that day.

Even the scar high on her shoulder, the bullet entry wound, provided no memory prompt. She remembered awakening in the hospital and feeling the pain of the wound. How she was injured was forever gone from her memory, a byproduct of the drug given her by Doug McKinley.

Lance O'Grady was the last person she'd expected to see sitting by her bed the day she awoke. He looked terrible, as though he'd hardly slept. Turned out, he hadn't. He'd been by her bedside for most of the three days she'd been unconscious.

When she thought of Trip, she only thought of his smiling face. Then the guilt quickly closed in on her. She worked on that daily. Therapy helped. Lance helped her, too. When the nightmares grabbed her by the throat in the night, when she awoke screaming and crying, he held her until she fell back to sleep.

Sometimes, although she'd never tell Lance this, she believed there should have been a full trial, that she should pay a price for what she'd done.

The medical reports were thorough, though; the law was on her side. You couldn't be convicted of a crime if you weren't in your right mind. At the indictment, her lawyer argued it would be the equivalent of accusing a person of promiscuity when they had been slipped the date rape drug rohipinol. With all the scientific evidence presented along with Lance O'Grady's testimony, the grand jury agreed.

It still didn't stop her from blaming herself.

Dana fixed Kendall with one of her famous piercing, cold, journalist stares.

"Kendall, you've constantly claimed you have no memory of the murders. A year later, is that still true?"

Kendall raised her chin, held her head higher. Lance constantly told her, she had nothing of which to be ashamed.

"Yes, that's still true. I live with it every day, and I'm constantly reminded I've taken two lives. That's a terrible thing to know. Every time I do an interview or talk about it, I'm forced to face the same question."

"So why do you do it, then? Why do you continue to remain in the public eye and agree to do interviews like this one?"

Kendall glanced over at Lance. He gave her *the* smile, the Mark Ruffalo smile, the one that gave her the strength to go on, the *I'm with you and you're doing good, baby* smile. That smile gave her courage to keep facing the public and keep confronting her own demons.

Kendall looked back to Dana, her posture stiffened, her jaw more squared, and replied, "You do know a senate committee has been appointed to look more closely at multiple pharmaceutical companies' research, showing a correlation between SSRI's and increased aggression, suicide, and mass killings. These companies hadn't made the dangers clear to prescribing doctors or the public?"

"Yes, I did see that," said Dana as she looked down at her notes.

"Dana, this is progress. This came as a fallout from what happened to me, from all the news and magazine articles and current affairs shows. As crazy as Doug McKinley was, he *had* a point. These drugs *are* dangerous. I guess, because of everything that's happened, fate dragged me into this, and I've found my purpose in life."

Kendall paused and looked directly into the camera, understanding the impact it would have on a viewer. She'd practiced it enough. She drew in a quiet breath, settling and calming herself. Knowing she spoke for all those people who'd died, not just on that day but all the years before, Kendall's voice held conviction.

"Dana, I do this because I have a message to deliver, and I will not stop until somebody listens. Think of me as a messenger."

THE END

FROM THE IMAGINATION VAULT

Hi, it's Susan may here. I thought you might enjoy a behind the scenes look at the writing of *Deadly Messengers*.

Sometimes authors enjoy challenging themselves, so they do something crazy they've never before attempted. I say *enjoy* loosely, because, occasionally, it works out to be tough at times more than fun. Count me as one of those authors.

I'd just sent *Back Again* off to the editors and was musing on how much I enjoyed writing the antagonist Kylie from that story. In a moment of inspiration (or madness), I thought: *why don't I write a book filled with evil antagonists and really have a party?*

So for the three weeks *Back Again* was away at my editors, I tasked myself with crafting a story about a series of seemingly unconnected mass killings which were, in reality, connected.

That was all I had. No plotting. No months of thinking about it. The next day I started *Deadly Messengers* with the first massacre scene. Then the rest came quite easily, until half way through, I found I was in trouble. I still hadn't worked out how my mass killers were being controlled (which is what happens when you don't plot).

I believe, though, for those who are in the writing arena and fighting those lions, a muse watches over. You often feel tested as to whether you're worthy to be granted the answer to your plot problem. This was one of those testing moments.

The answer came from a surprising source—my twelve-year-old son Harry. We were driving back from his soccer practice one night and my mind was with my story, thinking this must be how writers' block feels.

He said: "Mom, did you know there's a drug which can make people do whatever you want them to do and they won't remember. You just blow it in their face."

Well hit me over the head with a muse. I was so surprised I pulled the car over to quiz him. He didn't know I needed that drug as a plot device for my story. My son is a mad Youtube watcher—aren't all kids these days?—and he'd found a video entitled The 10 Craziest Drugs You Never Knew Existed.

It can't be true, I thought, even as my mind was playing *push it around and see if it fits* with the idea.

Sure enough, when I checked, there it was as he'd said: *Devil's Breath*, from which a drug called Scopolamine is derived. I changed the name of the plant to *Zombie's Breath* and the drug to Seratolamine in the story. The properties of *Zombie's Breath* are the same as the real drug, but I've nudged them a little further in their ability to control human behavior. However, the real drug is one scary chemical, and its effects are pretty close to my fictional creation.

Even now, with the book published, I can't believe my son delivered the solution to me. Nowadays, I'm not so quick to tell him to get off YouTube. Who knows what else I might need him to tell me in the future?

You may be surprised to find the idea regarding the relationship between SSRIs and violence is based on some fact. I know, scary! During research, I found many articles discussing this relationship. If you are interested, read some of the reports on this website: http://www.ssristories.org and http://www.corbettreport.com/medicated-to-death-ssris-and-mass-killings/.

This book is the story of the characters and is fictional. It doesn't represent my opinion on these drugs. In no way do I mean to create a negative view of anyone who takes or prescribes anti-depressants. Many people do benefit greatly from their use. Although I'm not advocating those who need them shouldn't have them, I wonder if there should be a little more awareness of their potential to cause harm for _some_ people. The advances we've made in society with our more sympathetic acceptance and understanding of mental disorders is a very good thing.

In the end, *Deadly Messengers* became mostly fiction with a little bit of science woven in. I know it's a little different to anything else I've written, but I can only travel where my stories take me. I do hope, wonderful reader, you've enjoyed this unplanned journey as much as I did.

I will leave you with a final thought: Should you find yourself in South America and feeling weary, don't fall asleep under any trees with beautiful, trumpet-shaped flowers. You never know where you'll wake up.

THANK YOU

This novel would not exist in its present form if not for the help of a few brilliant people who play on my team.

My husband Franco has been my staunch supporter since day one. Thank you my most loved best friend and soulmate. Every writer should be blessed with a friend or family member like him. When I'm feeling disheartened that I've lost the plot—literally lost the plot, it happens—he's there assuring me I'll work it out.

Thank you goes to my children, Bailey and Harry, who go away when I tell them to go away because I'm finishing something. They drive me mental many times, but I love their brave hearts.

This book would be riddled with silly errors and inconsistencies if not for Christie Giraud at EbookEditingPro.com, the best editor a writer could have. She's tough and blunt, but she has a great sense of humor. Christie makes me feel as though I have an advocate for my characters riding on my shoulder as I run through the edits.

Late hour thanks go to Paul Litherland of www.surfonlinesafe.com.au. I'd just finished the final edits of this book, when I attended a presentation of Paul's at my sons' high school college. Paul is an ex-policeman and passionate about Internet safety for kids (and adults). The small part about how Doug McKinley geo-tracked his potential subjects was already there but not in the detail it now enjoys. Until I saw Paul's presentation, I had no idea how easy it was to track and locate people from the metadata contained in an uploaded photograph. Nor did I understand clearly all the dangers of social media and the Internet for my children and myself. My recommendation is that no matter where you live, visit his site and read everything there. It's a cautionary tale.

You'll also find several pages included, front and back, filled with amazing and humbling praise for this book from my early readers on GoodReads. They deserve to be part of this book forever as their comments and reviews have put the wind beneath my fingers on the keyboard on the final edits of Deadly Messengers and in writing future books. A very special thanks goes out to a few hawk-eyed readers who caught typos and little mistakes and were good enough to let me know, Chris Terrell, Carrie Glover, Amanda Gillie, James Hayward, Vicki Tyley, and Jan Graham.

Last but not least, thank you, wonderful reader, for taking the time to read my book. If you enjoyed *Deadly Messengers*, please leave a review wherever you purchased and/or Good Reads. Reviews really help an author. If nothing else, it brightens my day to know somebody is enjoying my work.

Remember to register at my Wonderful Readers' newsletter to stay up-to-date with my new books and happenings. I release a book about every six months. My wonderful subscribers always receive an offer of a FREE copy in exchange for an honest review. When you sign up, you'll receive two short stories absolutely FREE.

I hope to see you again. It's been my pleasure to entertain you.

BONUS SHORT STORY

For seventy years, World War II veteran Jack Baker has endured vivid flashbacks to that horrific June day on Omaha Beach. But tonight, the flashback will be terrifyingly different. Tonight it becomes real. Tonight, Jack's seventy-year-old secret will come back to claim him.

THE WAR VETERAN
CHAPTER 1

When I close my eyes, I can still hear the sound of it. Then the vibrations follow, like a dozen trees felled and fallen at the exact same time, landing only feet from my head.

It was always hard to tell whether the flashes of light—red, orange, and blinding white—came before or after the sound; a kaleidoscope of color, which if it had been fireworks would have brought delight instead of chaos and fear.

I recognized the sound immediately.

It was 2:23 a.m.

I was never asleep between two and three.

Never asleep at four. Or six.

I barely slept at all these days. When I did, the nightmares came. Always. I would awaken with my bed wet with cold sweat and my chest aching as I struggled for breath. In the short moments before I opened my eyes, I'd feel myself clawing at some unknown assailant, his hands twisting around my neck.

Then, fully awake, I would realize it was just a nightmare; it was the night, and the life I now led, that was asphyxiating me. I was safe and alive.

But only half-alive.

When the sound buffeted my consciousness, I presumed, as I always did, this was just another one of those "flashes" where I was back there on that beach among the other soldiers. Knowing I was about to die. If I did survive, the human being who'd entered the torrid waters that morning would not survive, even if I were still breathing when the sun set.

So when I heard the sound, I merely turned my head toward the window and counted to fifty. If it came again, I would get up and take a look. It was rare I needed to count beyond thirty. On a bad night, it would take the whole fifty.

Tonight was different from other nights. Nearly seventy years of what I called "my flashes," often visited upon me when the guilt became overwhelming.

I waited and counted, watching the blur of the television, the sound muted because I didn't need to hear the details of whatever they were selling at 2:30 in the morning.

I lay there, the pain in my right hip feeling as if someone were playing "dig the dagger in and twist." Osteoporosis. Doctors informed me my milk intake when I was younger was inadequate—as if we worried about milk and aging when the chances of keeping your legs were pretty much against you. Getting old wasn't a problem. Living with getting old was the problem, especially when you hadn't expected to live.

When the familiar sound came again, I seriously considered whether it was worth my while to pull my complaining body off the couch and shuffle it to the window.

At eighty-eight years, this small movement was akin to sprinting a mile. Since I knew what I would find when I peered out the window, there wasn't much incentive to move.

Oh, it beckoned vaguely. Sometimes I enjoyed looking at them. If you weren't in the middle of the shit-fight; if, around you, your buddies and strangers (still kindreds) weren't dropping like flies—their lives' value only the claiming of a few inches of beach—then it was actually quite entertaining.

Most of the time the explosive sounds and blinding lights were an annoying intrusion into my day-to-day life. A life which was nothing more than interlinked moments of mundane shuffling from the couch to the bathroom to the door to family get-togethers that I "must attend to keep my spirits up."

The last thing I ever needed was a damning reminder that, by some kind of divine joke, I was one of the unfortunates to land on that Normandy beach on June 6, 1944.

I glanced at the rooster clock—a ridiculous piece of bric-a-brac that Mavis had purchased at a thrift shop, on our honeymoon in 'Frisco back in '52. I'd always hated the thing, but it had been fifteen years since she'd passed, and now it served as a reminder of her ability to see the beauty in things that were nothing more than junk. Probably why someone as full of life as Mavis wound up with a broken soul like me.

The rooster clock's hands showed 2:45. I figured I could sit there another hour and watch some idiot try to sell me something on the shopping channel, or I could pull this creaky body up and answer the call of the flashes. Then I could stand there and enjoy the wonderful vista of mortar shells raining down on my front lawn. And wait.

Eventually, the switch in my head would flick off and the twisted part of my mind that played this history reel would be satisfied with its daily quota of reminiscence.

Tonight, even my knees had joined the cacophony of pain, and I wondered if losing my legs—as so many of my compatriots had done— would have prevented the aches that plagued me daily. If, in losing limbs, they were the lucky ones. A splutter of laughter escaped my lips at the thought. Those complaining legs, with the addition of will and patience, were still capable of getting me across the room to watch the fireworks. So I pointed them in the right direction and willed my body forward.

I knew by the time I reached the window the shelling would have all but stopped. It rarely lasted longer than the time it took for my heart to begin the familiar pounding and my mouth to dry to a parchedness that no amount of water could quench. It would stop because it had achieved its goal. It had reminded me and proved its power over time. It could rest, knowing I was still its puppet, still its slave, and that still I feared it.

Tonight it was a persistent tormentor. As I reached for the lace curtains, and brushed them aside to peer outside, I wondered if tonight it had a point to prove. It had called me to the window, when most nights it was content to hurl its nightmare intrusion into my living room, my kitchen, my bedroom.

Tonight it wanted me to follow it.

I'm coming. You bastards, I'm coming.

The curtains felt dry and brittle in my hands, the lace catching on my rough, furrowed fingers. The coolness of the night leached through the glass, and as I pushed my face to the window, the cold kissed my skin.

A flash exploded.

My image reflected in the glass as the flares flickered and flashed beyond it. I looked like some kind of ghost arisen from the battleground. Sparse white hair sprouting out at I-don't-care angles, a nose twice the length it once was. Eyes dark and hollow, and tired, so very tired. It was a face infested with lines, not of a life lived, but a life experienced through a veil of memories that hung so thick that only the strongest emotions struggled through.

There it was, beyond my reflection … a seventy-year-old war looking as fresh and real as the day it was lived. Damn, if the vision wasn't brighter and even more vivid tonight.

Across the road, the snipers sat in their bunkers, their guns unmoving: deadly black sticks poking over the sandbags, waiting to strike with a near-silent *phht*. Behind the stoop of Patrick Smith's house—a single man with a penchant for blondes with big hips—perched the machine gun battalion. Yes, those bastards didn't miss a trick, and neither did Patrick, from what he'd shared—which I didn't care to know, but still he shared.

Pinpoints of red flared from the stoop, lighting up like a hundred angry eyes. The bullets smacked into the garden wall, the front door, and the bushes near the mailbox. Dirt flew up, exploding into the air in an arabesque of green and dark brown, spraying grains of sand and soil upon my driveway.

Thanks for the aeration of the lawn, you kraut devils.

I could feel the momentum of the assault building, just as I had that 1944 June morning.

I was in the 2nd Ranger Battalion. They sent us into Omaha Beach as a distraction, so that the Dog, Easy, and Fox Companies could take them out from inland. They hadn't told us that before; we only learned of it later in the history books.

Old Dwight's meteorologist gave the okay, when the tides, the moon, and the weather would be our allies. It was a good plan, except the weather just wouldn't play ball. So you lose a few men because overcast skies means the air support can't get through. Five thousand is a good number, isn't it, folks? That's acceptable, unless you're one of the five thousand. It's acceptable, unless you're one of the forty-five thousand who lived, but waded past the bodies, past your friends dying around you, past the horror. It's all very acceptable from a room with a map and names that end in Company, Battalion and Squadron.

Often when the flashes visited me, I wondered how Eisenhower made that choice: throwing us, and the 1st, and the 29th Division to those devils in order to claim that beach. Did he put the numbers in a hat? What was it for? Now we drive their cars and visit their beer festivals.

A grenade landed just below my window. It wouldn't explode while I watched it. They never do. Too much detail. I don't get all the detail. These experiences: fugues, Dr. Clarke tells me. My version of post-traumatic stress disorder doesn't supply the detail. That's normal for me. I don't get faces or direct explosions, just distant visions of gun flares, flashes, and buzzing bullets, and an inescapable hell.

I thank my brain for that small mercy. If I'd had to watch my buddies die over and over, see the pain on their faces, hear their cries, and look into their pleading eyes, I couldn't have taken it.

I looked down through the glass; the grenade sat there, nestled just next to the rose bush, black and waiting. Waiting for me to react, to run, to allow it to win, to allow it to impact my life.

I stood still, watching it. It would disappear in a moment, unable to withstand the assault of my stare.

Ten, nine, eight, seven, six ...

It'll be gone by three.

Five, four —

When the flash came, followed by an explosion that pierced my ears like the smashing of a thick glass wall, it was so unexpected that it threw me back across the room. I staggered, reeling, both arms swirling in mad circles as I fought to gain my balance. My hand caught the arm of the lounge chair and immediately I grabbed for its solidness, falling backward to half-land on it, my ass embedded in the cushion, my legs hanging over the arm.

That was new.

I pushed my body back up, my heart solid and thick in my chest as if the blood had pooled there, forcing the muscle to work overtime to shunt it out.

My feet shuffled beneath me toward the window. *Move faster, you bastards.*

The flashes had dulled, though the sounds were still there, cracking and banging. When I reached the window, I pushed my nose to the glass and looked down.

The grenade was gone. As it should be. As I knew it would be. The rose bush was alone in all its floral glory. In the moonlight, the white petals shone as if kissed by the sun and not its darker sister.

Across the way, the snipers were still sending their zinging bullets toward me. From the top of the street, I could hear the rumble of the trucks and the tanks.

It was almost over. The tanks only invaded when this thing had worn its way down, when the hallucination had run out of steam, as if they were the final resort of the battle.

That's when I saw him. His face was clear as day, as if he were here, now, instead of reaching across seven decades of time and memories.

Young Charlie O'Shea stood near the elm tree at the edge of the property. He held his gun before him, clenched between hands shaking with the knowledge that he had only minutes to live, or maybe one chance in ten of survival. His helmet hung back over his head—it never fit him right. Even at this distance, I could see the sweat slicked across his brow, the whites of his eyes as he swung his head left to right, frantically looking for a way through the melee.

Then he turned to me, and our gazes met. *That never happened before. I never saw the eyes. I never saw the faces.*

Our eyes met as if we were only feet apart. He mouthed some words, really tried to send me a message, but all that hit me was the surprise at seeing him there, and curiosity at why.

Then the bullet struck. If his damn helmet had fit him right, he might have been okay. Those helmets could take a hit sometimes. But it was back on his head, with his forehead standing out like a shining, white target.

In a slow second, during which I felt I could see the bullet move through the air, his head disappeared in an eruption of red and white matter, and his body collapsed like a rag doll.

For the second time that night, I staggered backward to the arm of the chair and fell into the welcoming cushions. Charlie shouldn't be there. I didn't see faces, especially his. My head felt heavy, as if filled to overflowing with a thousand pounds of sand from that beach.

My breath came in short, sharp gasps, and I grabbed at my chest. If I didn't get myself under control, my heart could give out. I didn't want Charlie O'Shea's exploding face to be the last thing I ever saw on this earth.

As I stared down at the worn, intricate design of coiled gold and brown vine carpet, from my periphery came the realization that the flashes had stopped. All that remained was a distant murmur of crackling and pops. I kept my head bowed until I felt sure it was over.

When curiosity enticed me to look up, I was again alone with the empty night. Pulling myself up, I moved back to the window.

It was then that I saw it.

If I hadn't run my hand over it, felt its jaggedness against my palm, I wouldn't have believed it. "Another illusion," I imagined Doctor Clarke saying. This was no illusion or mirage. This was real.

My fingers smoothed over the glass and followed the trail of cracks. One stretched from the base of the frame to the mid-section, and then fractured off into four lines of pure white. They were strong and solid, as if to say: "This is our window. We claim it as our territory."

It wasn't that which caused my heart to pound, it was the cracks in the wall, the jagged lines running up from the window into the ceiling in splintering roadmaps of damage. I hadn't registered them when I saw Charlie, but now I had a vague memory of seeing them there. I'd thought they were part of it, part of the craziness.

Now I remembered: they were there before Charlie's appearance, and after the grenade exploded. The grenade that should have disappeared, the grenade that couldn't be real. Yet, somehow…

CHAPTER 2

"Mr. Baker, what's happened? Mr. Baker."

Claire's voice sounded distant, tinny, as if captured in a box. It filtered through the thick darkness, pulling me awake long before I was ready to face whatever awaited in the world.

"You've hurt yourself? Are you all right?"

Unwillingly, I opened my eyes to find Claire's round face and curly brown hair bobbing in and out of my vision. Uninvited, her arms reached under me, pulling and pushing my complaining body upright.

Her tutting and fussing sent my mood spiraling further downward. A five-foot-nothing, thirty-something woman having enough strength to maneuver a six-foot man so easily bemused and annoyed me in equal measures. My weight, though, was forty pounds less now than it was ten years ago—not skin and bone yet, but certainly more bone. I'd stiffen my body to ensure she didn't have an easy time of it.

After last night, today was not a good-mood day. I grunted a reply. Once she'd propped me up sufficiently, as if I were an oversized doll, with pillows tucked between the bed's headboard and my head, she stood back and examined my face.

"What have you done here?" Her hand reached out and brushed across my forehead. "You've cut yourself?"

A sudden throb of dull pain brought back the memory of the cracked window. I must have hit my head on something when the grenade exploded. In the confusion, with everything going on, it must not have registered.

I waved Claire's hand away, none too gently. Why did she keep coming here? I didn't make her job easy. Over the years, many health workers had come and gone, spending only their allotted fifty minutes, but this one lingered.

And she talked. Constantly.

She prattled on about her children—two boys in school, middle school or something. She talked about her husband, her thoughts on the health system, her weather predictions, her beliefs on manners, and a repetitive exposition on the real reason for the fluctuating cost of gas. She shared her views on anything and everything, whether I wanted to hear them or not.

I didn't try to be good company—had given up on civil manners years ago. Didn't share thoughts, and didn't offer her anything to suggest I cared a whit about her life. Yet, every day she turned up and cleaned and cooked, and, of course, talked.

When I asked her once—more out of annoyance than curiosity—why she bothered, she only replied with a smile. I knew why she really came: the goddamn government paid her to check and see if I'd died yet. That was her real job. One day she would come and complete the task.

Now she stood there staring, hands on hips, as I wiggled my feet off the side of the bed. They made a clopping sound as they found the floor.

Claire leaned into me to offer assistance, and received my best *don't help me* look. *Still* she swooped.

"I'm fine," I said, waving her away, my voice cracked and whisper-weak. Sleep offered so little benefits these days, except a brief reprieve from thought.

"You are not fine. I want to know how you cut yourself."

Ignoring her, I moved to the dresser, faster than I would have had she not been there.

I stared into the mirror. The gash across my right eye was two, maybe three inches, but shallow. Dried blood trailed across my forehead in thin red smears. Ribbons of it had run into my eyebrows, transforming them from snow white to pink.

My unchanged clothes from the night before hung on me like a sack of gray-blue rags. I shambled out the bedroom door, leaving Claire staring after me. I needed to check that window. And the wall.

It had to be a dream, part of the hallucination. I expected to find nothing. The thought pervaded my mind. Perhaps the head injury was the answer. There I was seeing Charlie and grenades and wilder things than I'd ever seen before, when I was actually out cold, fallen on a chair or table.

My feet followed the treaded path from the bedroom to the living room, and then to the window, my back complaining as it always did upon first arising.

"Where are you going, Mr. Baker?" Claire called from behind me.

The words bounced off, just like the shells and flashes of memory that invaded my life. The window. I needed to see the window.

It would be whole. It had to be. No cracks. No damage. The faded yellow and green flower-patterned wallpaper would be all that I would see. There would be no fissures sliding upward scarring it. It would be perfect, smooth, and right, because a seventy-year-old armament had not exploded in my flowerbed. And Charlie hadn't been there. He was dead, and he was gone, just like all the rest. What happened on Omaha Beach that day, well, it had died with him.

Yet, last nigh, the way he looked at me, it was as real as that day. The words he'd mouthed, just like then, I couldn't hear them; would never hear them. He was dead. I was alive.

My fingers dragged across the wall's surface. What was real and what was not had merged. My tongue rolled around, dry and desperate, in a mouth that felt as parched as a noonday beach. A drone as loud as a dozen overhead planes filled my ears. They were there.

In the daylight, the pattern of cracks in the glass, feathered and fine, stood out in etched detail. Alongside the window, a two-inch-thick breach ran up the wall from floor to ceiling. Through it daylight streaked, leaving gold and silver lines on the mottled carpet.

In comparison to the night before, the fissure in the window appeared to have enlarged. Maybe the coldness of the air, the shrinking and expanding of the wooden frame, had worked on it overnight. Or perhaps I simply hadn't taken it all in.

"What's happened here?" said Claire, moving alongside me. She, too, reached out to place her palm against the wall, her skin light pink against the dirge-green floral pattern Carmen had so loved.

What should I tell her? An explosion had drifted across time, damaged the wall, and knocked me on my ass? By the way, the ghost of Charlie O'Shea came by just to cap it all off?

"Settling," I said, turning back to the kitchen. Claire would leave soon. Then I would come back and study it. Attempt to fathom its meaning.

"Settling? That's not settling."

She followed me.

"Houses don't settle like that. It wasn't there yesterday. You can fit your fingers through that gap. It's dangerous. The house may be unstable."

I'd made it to the stove—in good time, for me. Normally, it took me twice the time to travel the distance. The lack of normal was lessening the boundaries of age.

"I'm only worrying about coffee," I said, as I pulled the kettle from the stove and swung it toward the kitchen sink. Before I'd completed the maneuver, Claire intercepted me.

"I'll make that for you." She pulled the kettle from me and pushed it under the tap. "You just sit down, Mr. Baker."

Usually I would have argued, if only to see the way her lip quivered when I went too far. Today I obeyed. The quicker I convinced her all was fine, the quicker she would go.

She didn't go. Instead, she made two coffees and put both on the table along with a plate of sugar cookies. She pushed a steaming cup toward me, and instead of flitting off to the recesses of the house to do her "straightening," she plonked herself down opposite me. Then she continued to talk, as if the cracks were a conspiracy in which we had both collaborated.

"What will we do with you, Mr. Baker? I want a doctor to check you. We'll need to get that wall and window repaired—immediately."

She sipped her coffee and continued. "In fact, that window is dangerous. Promise me you won't go near it?"

She set down her cup, staring at it. Then she stopped, as if suddenly remembering something, and looked up.

"Is that how you hurt yourself? Did you fall against the window?"

I shrugged my shoulders, the only true answer I had for her.

"No, you couldn't have done that, could you? Maybe the window, but not the wall... no." Her lips pursed, and she tutted and shook her head. "Maybe the local kids. Vandals? Do you think, Mr. Baker? Did you see anything?"

Oh, I saw plenty. But I'm not telling you.

She picked up her coffee cup, and stared at the yellowed melamine table between us. "Vandals. I bet that's it. Little so-and-sos."

I stared at her and sighed loud enough to catch her attention, hoping she'd interpret it as a sign of exhaustion. *Please just go,* I willed.

She looked up from her headshaking, and her face softened. Here was my chance.

"Can you help me back to the bedroom? I think I need to rest."

"You need a doctor," she said, nodding her head with each word.

"I need to rest," I firmly repeated. "Really, that's all. I bumped my head. I don't remember. It's nothing."

She took a deep breath and slowly expelled it, as she tilted her head sideways and back.

"I don't think I should—"

"Please. I'm just tired."

She breathed another "tsk," as if I were now part of the vandal's gang.

"Please," I said, as an ache behind my eyes began to build.

She chewed her bottom lip, staring at a point behind me. Then her face relaxed. "Okay. One proviso. You call me the instant you feel lightheaded, or if a bad headache comes on, or you feel unbalanced. Anything not normal. All right?"

My head bobbed up and down.

She herded me into the bedroom, changed me into my pajamas, and tucked my body in as if I were a weary five-year-old returned from a big day out.

"I'll make you something to eat and pop it in the refrigerator. I want you to eat all of it when you get up again. Do you hear me?" She patted my hand.

Her tenacity would have impressed Mavis. She would be my wife's version of "a keeper." I called her "a keeper" too, but I was thinking more of animals in a zoo imprisoned until the day they died. Yes, she was "a keeper," Mavis.

And more.

I wouldn't know that until later.

CHAPTER 3

An explosive rumble, followed by the sound of cracking and splintering wood, jolted me awake. It was dark when my eyes opened, my senses immediately alert.

Flickering light lit the slit below my bedroom door. For a moment, I thought Claire was playing games with the light switches.

Now I faced a familiar choice. Go watch the spectacle, which always seemed to shorten it—some kind of strange reward for my attendance—or stay here and wait. They would eventually go; they always did. Except for last night, the anomaly. That made this a different choice, one that was uncertain and somehow—

A flash again.

The vibrations of this explosion I felt through the bedclothes. My hand shook as much from the tremors as from my shock. Normally I could control my emotions. It had taken decades of familiarity with fear, but eventually we'd become bedfellows in life. Tonight my heart leaped like a trapped animal.

Then I heard the voice.

At first, I thought it was just another new part of it, just like the grenade and Charlie O'Shea and his silent mouthing. After another tremor and another flash from beneath the door, it came again. The muffled words were indiscernible and muted, but the terror in them resonated loud and clear.

My neatly folded dressing gown lay at the foot of the bed, courtesy of Claire. The chaos I heard propelled me to my feet; I threw the gown on more quickly than my eighty-eight years usually allowed. The only thing slowing me down was the complexity of forcing arthritic fingers to knot the sash while panicked. Intermittent flashes, like rapid fireworks, continued outside the door as my hands slipped and contorted around the material.

Was I mistaken, or were the explosions growing louder?

Finally I'd tied the damn knot and gathered my faculties, and I was in the hall. From here, I had a straight view to the living room and the cracked window. The cracks now reflected a fiery light playing through from the front yard.

There was Claire at the window, staring out, a silhouette against the illuminations, an intruder in the drama.

"Claire?"

She swung about, her eyes saucers in her pale face, her hand cupped to her mouth. When she saw me, her hand dropped, and she cried out, "What is it? What's happening?"

She saw it.

How? These were *my* nightmares. They belonged to my past. They couldn't be here for her to see. What would that make them?

I used everything in my trick bag to stay calm and steady, my heart beating like that of a startled animal. Reds, yellows, and brilliant whites burst in from outside, dappling the darkened walls like grains of brilliant sand thrown against them.

"You see it?"

Claire nodded, and then seeing me move toward her, she swung back to face the window, where the filament cracks had multiplied, urged on by the proximity of this night's explosions.

When I moved beside her, she didn't turn to me, but continued to stare out, bewildered, hypnotized. She stuttered barely recognizable words, "I ... I s-s-see some ... What's—?"

A loud bang sounded, followed by a crack. It came from a tree near the perimeter of my property. Then a boom, and a second later the hissing of sand and dirt spraying against the window.

Claire screamed and took a step back, one shaking hand pressed against her mouth. The reflection of my creased, strained face looked back at me from the glass. How could she and I both view a scene that didn't exist?

Mist surged and swirled in a sweeping wave of gray. Through the smoke, red-gold flares shot upward, only to fade in moments, then fall back to earth fifty feet away, exploding on impact. Glowing remnants lit the ground like scattered embers, except these were not of warmth but of destruction, of killing.

Shrill, sharp gunshots echoed in the street, until the whir of a machine gun spilling its rounds drowned out the lesser sound.

My hand found its way to the glass again, as if touching it might cause the mirage to disappear. At first touch, as if my fingers were electrified, the glass shattered with an ear-splitting crack. Glistening shards and splinters exploded into the air, raining down on Claire and me. Cold air and smoke rushed in, laden with the smell of gunpowder and the wretched stench of death.

Instantly our arms flew up in an attempt to deflect the glass. I caught sight of my hands and saw blood seeping out through cuts in the creases. I felt nothing.

The destruction of the window must be another part of the illusion. Damn, it was so vivid, I could taste the air.

My instinct was to move away from the window, but I was drawn to the vision outside of it. The wind had kicked up, clearing patches in the smoke, just as it had back in '44.

Through the hollows in the curling gray-white, I saw them. Poor wretched souls they were. Bodies toppled upon bodies in piles of anonymous death. Men dropped so rapidly that they still clutched their guns, eyes blank, staring at comrades who battled forward only to be cut down themselves a few feet farther on. The sand ran red with their life, terrible crimson rivers straight from hell.

As the mist retreated, I saw their eyes. Eyes I'd never before seen in the visions. Open eyes, hundreds of them, all turned toward me. Unseeing, unmoving—but knowing. So knowing.

A low *phht* zinged past my face, close enough that I felt the air move and the heat of it. *Phht*—another. *Phht*—and another. I ducked down below the windowsill. Claire quickly moved beside me. I wanted to turn to her and explain. Whatever it was that she saw, it was not what she thought. It couldn't be.

Yet the room glowed with the color of exploding armaments, the smell so strong I was beginning to gag.

I knew I should move, do something. Get Claire out of there. I was frozen, afraid, and weak, just as I had been seventy years before. Just as I had done at eighteen, so I did at eighty-eight: I lay there, and I prayed for it to end.

CHAPTER 4

The memory of that morning was so vivid that I could still taste the salt of the sand in my mouth and feel the grit between my teeth. I lay on Omaha Beach, on June 6, 1944. I'd made it under the machine gun bunkers.

By then, five hundred men had already died so that some of us—the lucky few—could make it there to the overhang of the salt cliffs. In its shadow, we would be safe. When enough of us were there, we would climb up and over and overrun the gunners. More would die, but it was our best chance.

So I waited as instructed, gathering my breath in short, hurried gulps, not daring to look back down the beach toward the sea. I didn't want to the see those left behind. Hearing them was bad enough.

I'd been there ten minutes when I saw, under the shadows of the cliffs, a man moving sideways toward me, crawling on his arms and knees. For one terrifying moment, I thought it was a Jerry bastard.

I struggled frantically with my gun, trying to heave it around and level it up before me, ready to fire. My hands shook so much that if it *had* been the enemy, I would have been dead.

Turned out it was our reedy platoon sergeant, Bill Black—an ex-jockey we called Blacky.

He took one look at me and whispered through gritted teeth, "Calm down, Baker."

"How?" would have been my answer if I could have spoken, but my teeth were chattering too much. My body was rigid; the only part of me moving was my shaking hands, and I had no control over that. We'd fallen into hell, or more accurately, been offloaded into hell. No amount of training could prepare a fresh-faced eighteen-year-old for this.

I tried to follow Blacky's orders, tried to still my hands, my jaw. Reaching for a chain around my neck, I pulled at the Saint Christopher's medal my mother had given me the day we shipped out.

Then I took five deep breaths.

Between the second and the third, I felt my heart slow a little.

Somehow, by the fifth, I'd brought my panic under some kind of control.

Blacky saw it in my face, that I'd come back from the edge. I've often wondered, if I'd succumbed to my hysteria, if he hadn't picked me, if he had moved on to some other hapless soul, how would my life have turned out?

I did calm down, and when he saw that I was quiet, he began to speak in a clear, frighteningly calm voice, his gaze never leaving my face. His dark brown eyes bored into me as each word left his mouth and sank into my brain.

"That's right ... Breathe, son. Okay? Good. Now listen, Baker. I need you to do something. It's very important. Do you understand?"

My head nodded automatically. He was my superior; even if I didn't agree, I would do whatever he commanded. They'd trained us well, and explained in detail what would happen if we disobeyed or abandoned our post in combat.

"Right. Now stay with me, Baker. For some reason, we can't get through on the radios to the landing vessels."

He paused, letting that sink in, though I couldn't understand why he was telling me. I wasn't a radio operator, so I couldn't help him with that. I was still trying to comprehend why he was talking to me, thinking maybe he'd mistaken me for someone else. In fact, I was about to set him straight when he continued.

"I need you to go back down the beach, back to the landing crafts, and find Colonel Ryan. Tell him to stop the landings and to retreat. Able and Baker Companies and the 5th Rangers radioed us ten minutes ago. They're inland and moving forward. They're certain they can take this bluff from the rear. This beach assault is suicide. We need to send the landing troops back to avoid unacceptable casualties. Each minute we lose hundreds—in an hour, thousands."

He raised his voice to almost a shout. "Understand, soldier?"

My head moved as if encased in Jell-O; I nodded before I fully understood his words, before it had sunk in that he wanted me to go *back down that beach*, face the gunfire and the grenades, crawl through the broken bodies, and do what—save the day?

I wouldn't make it. I knew that in my heart. He was asking me to die. Sending me to die, when I'd only just made it here to safety. Here, where they'd told me to wait for the others. Here, where I wouldn't die just yet—where I had a chance.

"Soldier! You understand? You go now. Every second counts."

He reached out and tapped my helmet, as you might pat an obedient hound. "Good man, Baker." Then, assured by my nodding, he was off, traveling back the way he had come.

I was alone.

I swiveled my head around to look down the beach, through the smoke of the battle and the mist of the morning. The combination was so heavy that I could barely see twenty feet.

I turned back to look for Blacky, to tell him "no," that I couldn't do it. He'd already disappeared behind the curves of the dunes.

Panic overwhelmed me. With each beat of my heart, it spread through my body like an immobilizing poison. Every breath I took echoed in my head so loudly that I imagined the enemy would hear me, peer over the top of their dugout, and lay a stream of machine gun fire into my position.

I burrowed my cheek into the cool grains of sand and held it there. The sand formed a perfect pillow, calling to me like a siren to stay in the shadows, in the safety.

There were men back there; "thousands," Blacky had said, who needed me to go down the beach and send them back to safety. I was one man, and yet, somehow, this enormous responsibility had fallen upon me. Eighteen years old and asked to be a hero, when twelve months ago I had been nothing more than an insurance company clerk.

I rolled over and stood against the sandbank, propped straight up by my backpack. The sun was moving higher in the sky, lifting the gray cloak of mist, and the vista of the beach lay before me. Bodies in green and tan splattered with red dotted the cream landscape. Large crossed planks of wood and steel—"Rommel's Asparagus" we called them—some with barbed wire, obstruction barriers against our landing parties, lay scattered along the beach like a giant game of jacks.

Even over the ceaseless gunfire, I could hear the moaning. Multitudes of injured and dying, sounding more like animals than men. Just listening to it was agonizing.

The unnaturalness of it all—me, on this foreign land, staring at this scene beyond anyone's wildest imagination—overwhelmed me.

Every second counts.

I checked my gun, the feel of the cold metal in my palm really of little comfort. Much good the gun would do me. When the bullet came, I wouldn't see it. It would hit me in the back of my head or my body. My only chance was to weave and crouch. And pray.

That was a lot to remember.

A hum, growing stronger every second, built in my head. Every breath I took sounded so loud it felt as if an airtight bubble had settled over my head. My heart banged into my ribs.

Thu-ump. Thu-ump. Thu-ump. It beat so hard it hurt.

I took a step. then another. I twisted my head at an unnatural angle to peer up at the bunkers.

Thu-ump. Thu-ump.

I knew I couldn't stop now. If I stopped, I wouldn't have the strength— no, the courage—to keep going.

Another two steps and I'd left the shade. A few more, and I'd be in the line of sight of the gunners. The rushing of blood through my temples, now an accompaniment to my heart.

Thu-ump. Thu-ump.

Two more steps and I'd be there.

The kill zone.

Something took over at that point: legs that felt like jelly, muscles behaving like loose strings of fiber, were suddenly filled with steel. My body, pumping adrenaline, took off of its own accord, with me along for the ride. A silent, terrified passenger.

Without thinking, I ran left five paces. Then fell to the ground.

Breathe. Breathe.

Thu-ump. Thu-ump.

Then up again. Springing like a cat.

My legs pumping, driving into the sand.

Another five paces to the left. Then three to the right.

Longer strides, stretching. If they were scoping me, they couldn't anticipate how far I would travel.

Then down. Flat on my stomach, near a barrier.

Breathe. Thu-ump. Breathe.

Mouth in the sand, eating grit, my body nestled against other bodies—dead, motionless, bloody bodies. Sucking in oxygen, as if I'd just surfaced from a deep-water dive.

God, my chest ached.

Don't panic, Jack.

Thu-ump. Breathe!

And pray. Remember to pray.

God, please save me.

Tilting my head up from where I lay, I looked back up the beach. I'd only traveled fifteen feet. This zigzagging was getting me nowhere. I had to hurry. Get out of here. Keep moving. That's what they'd drilled into us.

Breathe. Breathe. Breathe.

Stand up, Jack.

As I jumped up, I heard the zing. Then a sharp sting. It caught me in the right calf, sending me toppling over. It hurt for a second; then there was little pain. That shocked me more than the hit. When something enters your body at that speed, you expect something more. It just felt hot, like the worst bee sting you've ever had.

I lay facedown in the sand, waiting. Seconds became minutes of just breathing, containing the panic.

Nothing.

They hadn't targeted me. It was a random bullet.

Slowly sliding my leg up along the sand, I reached around and touched the wound. There was an entry and an exit. That was good. Tentatively, I pushed my right foot into the sand, checking to see if it still had strength to bear me. It felt solid. It still didn't hurt too badly, though it was beginning to throb, as if I'd banged it against the side of a door.

From my dropped position, I surveyed my immediate surroundings. Bodies of the fallen were everywhere. Now I was in the middle of it.

Three feet to my left, one poor fellow had lost half his head, the eyeball socket empty except for a dark red cave which I could see light shining through. The other eye stared at me—a gentle brown eye that had once looked upon the hills of California, or the Brooklyn Bridge, or the skyscrapers of Chicago, or even some small country town, a whistle-stop on the way to the city. That eye was seeing nothing ever again. It was a hideous, frightening sight, but I had to ignore my revulsion, or that would be me soon enough.

A black army boot lay on its own above the head, abandoned and missing its partner. It didn't belong to the man with the eye. He still wore both of his.

What a strange place to kick off a boot, I thought, until I realized that within the boot nestled a foot and part of a leg. Above the bloodied calf, with its jagged white bone protruding through the torn and pulped muscle and sinew, was nothing. A quick scan revealed no owner nearby. Abandoned, forever lost to its owner who must have somehow staggered away. It left me with only one question. How far had he gotten?

Beyond these two horrors were many more bodies, more parts of bodies. It was a slaughterhouse gone crazy. Pieces of men thrown everywhere. I could hear some men farther away still alive, still calling for help or screaming in a hideous, hysterical pitch, but there was not a soul left alive near me.

The idea hit me like a chiming bell at the exact same moment a bullet whizzed past. It hit the sand inches from my face, flicking up sharp grains that stung my eyes.

I tried to dismiss the idea, but each time I did, my mind dragged it back and stubbornly held it before me. My instinct to survive just wouldn't let it go.

If I stood up and kept running—no matter how much I zigzagged—those gunners would get me. No doubt in my mind. I might make it to the landing parties, but what would be left of me? The image of my leg or my arm lying somewhere farther down the beach, while I crawled away in agony, filled my imagination.

This injury, which I'd thought was a terrible piece of bad luck, was perhaps my salvation. Here was my plausible excuse.

It was, wasn't it?

I took the story out for a spin—ran it through my mind. Backward. Forward. It *was* reasonable. Nobody could ever say any different. I was hit, and I blacked out. What happened after that, I couldn't say.

If it weren't for the other brave soldiers' bodies falling on me, covering me, I would have died, too. I tried to get through, I would tell them. If it weren't for that bullet…Yes, if the bullet hadn't found me, I would have carried out my orders. I wanted to be a hero, but it was terrible bad luck. Blackey had said that the beach would shortly be ours. I only needed to wait it out.

Who would know?

Another bullet skimmed overhead, only inches away. That was all the encouragement I needed. Pushing my gun away, I crawled the few feet toward "One-Eye." Stretching my neck up, just over his waist, I peered over. There was the owner of the boot. He hadn't gotten very far. His body lay in a shallow trench at a crazy angle just a few feet away. Thank God his face was turned in the other direction.

With all the strength I could muster, I half-dived, half-crawled over One-Eye to land between the two bodies. Then I pulled One-Eye inward, trying to keep his face out of my sight. I couldn't bear to look at his face for too long. I cursed the weight of the body. It was heavier than it looked. It only needed to be moved a foot at the most. The sand gave a little with the force of my tugging and that made the job of pulling it toward me easier.

Once he was in place, I turned my attention to the other body, grabbing it by the belt. This was more difficult because I couldn't move around too much or I would dislodge One-Eye. After several sharp tugs, I managed it.

Now I was sandwiched between the two, and all I needed was to snuggle beneath them and lay still. The overpowering smell of blood and gunpowder, combined with the exertion and the heat, made me feel sick. I turned my head into the sand and retched violently, as I'd never vomited before. The heaving didn't stop until the only thing left in my stomach was bile, and still it came.

It surprised me how calm I had become. The thought of surviving was a balm to my terror. My leg, though, had started to throb and itch. I reached down to scratch at it, gritting my teeth against pain that was increasing with every second. Each movement I made was slow and careful, even though I wanted to scratch the hell out of it. I thought the bodies would provide protection, but I was uncertain how much.

Tears ran down my cheeks, as much as I tried to hold them back. I didn't sob; they were silent tears. If I cried, my chest might heave, and I couldn't risk the movement.

I closed my eyes in an effort to stem the flow. With my eyes closed, my hearing became more acute. The whistling of the bullets, the punch and crack of the explosions in the distance, the shouts from both sides, the screaming of nearby men mortally wounded. *Hell on Earth. Hell on Earth and beyond.*

A string of bullets laced through One-Eye, the soft *thwack* sound and the slight jump of the body as each one found its mark. I was terrified. I wanted to jump up and run. Once it stopped, I realized no bullets had found me.

My heart took off again.

Thu-ump. Thu-ump. Thu-ump.

It beat so hard I thought it would lift me off the ground.

I held my body rigid, hardly daring to breathe. Playing dead was easier when death surrounded you.

I counted to one hundred, not breathing until I reached fifteen, and then each ten after that. Then I would take a shallow breath through my nose, just in case a sniper had seen me and was waiting for my movement. I imagined him patiently watching through his scope. When he saw no movement, he would blink and then swing his rifle to another unfortunate target.

After one hundred, I opened my eyes, the only part of my body I dared allow to move. Another minute passed as I lay there, breathing every count of ten, only my eyes moving as I scanned the immediate area.

I realized that when the bullets had struck my savior's body, the force had moved him slightly off of me. My legs were now exposed. I needed to get him back over me, and again burrow myself into the cave created by the two corpses. Again, I began the strenuous process of moving the body. As I half-twisted around, pulling at the belt of One-Eye, prodding at him, trying to maneuver his body over mine, he came upon me—almost stepped on me.

I saw him at the same moment that he saw me.

Charlie O'Shea was in the 5th Ranger Battalion. I knew him because, in the previous week, we had shared training games with them. We weren't friends, but we knew each other enough to nod and say hello. It had gotten around that he was one of the best lightweight boxers they had in the company. They'd said when he got home—if he got home—he had a future in the sport. World class, apparently.

Now Charlie O'Shea, champion boxer and soldier, was staring at me. He stood there, facing up the beach, his rifle clutched in his hands. His face, though, turned in my direction, revealing by just the lift of his eyebrow that he'd recognized me for sure.

It dawned on me if I'd kept going, followed my orders, and made it to Colonel Ryan, Charlie O'Shea wouldn't be heading up to the bluff and facing the gunfire. Instead, he'd be on an assault boat, motoring back to safety.

I could tell by the way he stared he'd seen what I was doing. It was obvious. My story of my injury being too serious, of passing out—well, it wouldn't stand now. He saw me for what I was: a coward, hiding under two brave men who'd given their lives.

His face changed as he looked at me, as the realization dawned. His eyebrows furrowed, his lips tightened, the muscles in his neck stiffened and stood rigidly. He began to shake his head.

I knew what he was thinking.

Suddenly I saw me through his eyes, and the scalding shame burned through me and colored my cheeks. He started to mouth something, but the whip of the wind and the explosions carried away his words.

A thick ball of emotion filled my chest. In my mind, I began a reply to his accusations. He would report me, and I would be court-martialed or worse. Until then, I'd had an exemplary record. Until then, I was a hero to my family.

I thought to get up, face him, and explain that it was the fear, the death, the horrors. That I'd never expected them. I'd even begun to push myself up, moving through the bodies that, as the sun rose higher, had already begun to stink of rot—when he was suddenly gone.

One moment he was there, mouthing, staring, accusing me with his eyes, and in the next his head was gone. Exploded. Thick, wet drops landed upon the exposed parts of my body, my arms, my face. A piece of flesh hit me just above the eye, along with splatters of blood. For a moment, it blinded me, and I felt a wild panic erupt. My heart raced off again. *Thu-ump. Thu-ump.*

It was instinct that caused me to dive back under the bodies again. I couldn't help him; I could only help *me*. Hell, I could have *been* him, if I'd followed my orders. That was my alternate fate, played out before me in all its Technicolor horror.

With the gore thick in my hair and upper body, I lay there praying, looking as much like a corpse as did the bodies on top of me.

I lay there crying, not worrying if the sobs caused my chest to rise, with the sand cradling me, the fallen men protecting me, and the weight of what I had done forever frozen at the moment when Charlie O'Shea shook his head and mouthed those words. His words that I would never hear and never know would forever haunt me.

Five thousand would die on the beach that day. Every day after I would wish I were one of them.

CHAPTER 5

When I looked out the window again, they were still there: the soldiers, the gunfire, and the hellish battle. This couldn't be real.

I shook my head, which made the world spin like a slot machine. Cursed vertigo had set in ever since that day. Always striking me at its convenience, never mine.

Even as the vertigo slowed, I saw nothing had changed. They were still out there. Now advancing toward me. They *never* did that. It was always as if I had a side-window view of the battle. Tonight's vision seemed even realer than last night's. I slumped back down under the window, my breath coming in short, sharp pants. I twisted around so my legs lay out straight before me, my back pressed into the wall.

The room was a wreck, torn to shreds by the bullets. The sofa stuffing floated in the air like clumps of snow. Mavis would have been devastated. She loved that sofa. The desk lamp across the room lay shattered on the floor. All around me was the glass from the room's windows. It sparkled orange and red from the flares outside, and it was almost beautiful.

At some point while my mind traveled back to that beach, the lights had gone out. Of course, they'd *taken* them out. That would be protocol. Blind the enemy.

I needed to get away. If I could get through the kitchen to the back door, there was a gate out the back to the neighboring property. Surely, they wouldn't dare follow us.

A moan came from beside me. Small like a child's.

Caught up in my memories, I had forgotten Claire. I'd turned a blind eye to the human being right beside me. The poor girl must be terrified.

I turned to her and leaned over, anxious to reassure her that it would all soon end. The sight of her was as shocking to me as the specter of Charlie O'Shea next to my mailbox had been.

Claire sat only two feet away, and like me, her back was against the wall. She looked, at first glance, as if she were resting, as if the two of us were playing hide-and-seek together.

Except for the blood.

Down the front of her lemon-yellow blouse, near her collarbone, a patch of red expanded as I watched. Her face was pale as a sheet, and her hand dabbed disjointedly at the material. After a few jabs, she held it out before her, her eyes saucer-wide at the sight of the blood. A bullet had ripped into her. I thought it was my touch that had broken the window earlier, but I saw now that it had been a bullet.

Her breath came in hiccups. As she pulled air into her lungs, her stomach, beneath her skirt, sharply expanded and contracted as if manipulated by a machine.

She rolled her head to look at me. My immediate thought was to reassure her. "Don't worry. It will go. It's just some serious guilt haunting me. You'll be okay. It's me it wants."

This wasn't a mere vision or manifestation of post-traumatic stress. This was us, somehow, in a war that had already been fought. Claire—with the two children and the husband and the opinionated views—the health worker who loved to talk, whose only mistake was to come back to check on me, had become a casualty of that war.

I pushed myself to my knees and crawled the few feet to the sofa. A ghastly multi-colored wool headrest, crocheted by Mavis while watching *Mod Squad* in the seventies, hung over the arm. Yanking it away, I clutched it in my hand, carrying it back to Claire.

Bunching an end of it into a ball, I pushed it into the wound. Claire cried out. It hurt me to hurt her, but I had to stop the blood flow.

"Claire… here." I held the cloth to her chest. "Can you hold this? Push it in. It will help to stem the bleeding. Pressure. You need pressure on it."

She attempted to take the bunched cloth in her hand. Due to either the shock or the loss of blood, she lacked the strength to hold it. A pool of red formed on the floor. Tears streamed down her face and slipped into her open mouth. She kept repeating only one word. "How? How? How?"

"I don't know how," I said. "It's in my mind."

I patted her hair as my own tears traveled down my cheeks. What could I do? How could I prevent this thing from happening to her? This had nothing to do with her.

She looked down again at her chest, then back at me, and said, "What have you done? Not in your—mind." Her eyes looked lost and worn.

Her words tugged at me. She was right.

I had done something, and it had come to claim me. All the guilt I couldn't shake, the guilt that had piled up—day after day, year after year— filling my heart, filling my subconscious, until I couldn't hold it anymore, and it spilled out into this world.

One mistake under terrible circumstances. How could I know that my one act of cowardice would never be forgiven? How could I know that even though no one would ever know—except for Charlie O'Shea—I would still be condemned? That my own conscience would mete out a justice far greater than my superiors of the day? I had become both judge and defendant; prisoner and jailer.

I leaned toward Claire, my hand outstretched. She met my eyes, and I could see the same look I had seen on so many dying men in that war. That look never left you. I couldn't take another person looking at me that way, dying in front of me, dying *because* of me.

The cloth had fallen into her lap. I grabbed at it and pushed it again into the wound. She winced, but she was so weak now, she barely made a sound.

"Claire. Claire! Look at me. Hold this." I grabbed her wrist and forced her to take hold of the cloth. "You must hold this to stop the bleeding. It will be over in a minute. I promise. Do you hear me?"

She barely nodded, but her eyes, which had been frantically moving between half-open lids, slowed. A whispered "yes" escaped her lips.

I leaned forward and kissed her on the forehead. "Claire, thank you for always caring about me. I didn't deserve you. I haven't deserved anyone."

Crawling backward a few feet, away from the window and the line of fire, I stood up, far more quickly than I could remember having done in the past decade. It was as if the years had bled from my body. My muscles, no longer withered, had now grown stronger.

It took only five strides to reach the front door. I paused for a moment, gathering my thoughts, thinking back over the years I'd enjoyed. Years I hadn't deserved.

There was Mavis's sweet face when she'd said "I do," quickly replaced by the guilt of knowing that all those men would never hear these words from their sweethearts.

There were the children and the grandchildren. How tall and proud they stood whenever I marched in the remembrance parades, my purple heart and all the other awards proudly displayed on my jacket. Awards I was sure I had never earned.

These images filled my mind, the emotions traveling through my body, fueling my resolve. My hand reached for the doorknob, and with the flick of my wrist, it turned. In that instant, it was as if I'd turned the off switch on a radio. Suddenly the air was empty of sound; my mind was clear.

I flung open the door, expecting the vision to be gone. I'd finally had the courage to face it, and, in return, it would dissolve to nothing, and Claire would be fine.

The scene before me was exactly as I remembered from 1944. I quickly glanced back at Claire: she hadn't moved, still sat in a pool of her own blood, her tiny body heaving with the exhaustion of each breath.

I turned back to the door, and stepped outside.

As I walked down the steps, the odor of gunpowder and death assaulted me. The gray cloying mist swirled below my knees, and I heard the crunch and squelch of sand beneath my feet.

Across the way, I noted the sniper's sight trained on me, as he awaited his order from God-knows-who. By Mavis's favorite elm—whose dropping autumn leaves I cursed every year—the machine gun battlements spat out their stinging rounds. Dirt and grass flew up around my feet, spraying my pants and dressing gown. Still I walked. No zigzagging this time.

Just as before, I heard the bullet before I felt it, in the millisecond before the slug pulped my calf muscle and shattered the bone. Still I kept walking, limping as I went, and ignoring the pain, even glad for the pain.

Under my breath, I began to chant, "I understand, sir. They're counting on me." The men. Poor Claire."

I dragged my injured leg behind, each step now causing sharp, shooting pains to travel to my brain. This time I missed nothing. My penance, no doubt.

He was at the end of my path, just where he'd been the night before.

Charlie O'Shea was waiting for me.

He'd always been waiting. As had all the men, who'd pointlessly lost their lives. Because of me.

His lips moved, as they had done that terrible morning. He mouthed words. Seventy-year-old words I had never heard. Words that had haunted me and destroyed any true happiness I might have enjoyed in my life. My life always and forever colored by those unheard words.

Now I was only feet from him. This time I was standing. This time I faced him. Whatever he would say, I was ready to hear it. So very ready, and so very, very tired of waiting.

He lowered his gun and held out his hand. I didn't expect that. In another time, I would have made a joke. *So, you want a dance, Charlie?* He was saying the words again, and now I was close enough to hear.

The pain in my forehead was sudden.

At first, I thought it was a rock kicked up by the gunfire. Then blood dripped into my eyes. In the split second between life and death, I understood it all. This bullet was the one that should have been mine. On that beach. On that day.

As I lay on the ground, the sounds and lights fading to a pale pink, then a gray, then a deep, beautiful black, I felt Charlie lean over me, and whisper in my ear. His voice so clear, so close, it was as though it was inside my head.

"Baker, we're clearing the beach. Stay where you are. Stay down. Stay alive."

© 2013 Susan May

FROM THE IMAGINATION VAULT

The idea for "The War Veteran" came from *Salinger*, a fascinating documentary on the late, great author of *Catcher in the Rye*. One of the interviewees (who had served in WW2 with Salinger) talked of the horror flashbacks he still experienced. He shared that, to this day, the mortars and gunfire still erupted in his home, and were just as terrifying as they had been when he'd experienced them in real life. You can view the excerpt here: https://youtu.be/YHnQVmuWVqY

He didn't preface the statement with the words "imagined" or "visions"; he spoke as if the armaments were actually real. The idea of that haunted me. How horrific must it be to live with that for all those decades? There was no choice then. I had to write the story of "Jack Baker," to put myself in the shoes of a man in this position.

In researching the story, I read and listened to firsthand accounts of surviving WW2 veterans. Nothing I could write can ever totally capture the experience, so my apologies to anyone who has witnessed war firsthand. I know my description pales.

Behind More Dark Doors

I hope you enjoyed *Deadly Messengers* and *War Veteran*. *War Veteran* also appears in *Behind Dark Doors* (one).

You might like to venture through some more dark doors with my collections of short stories with a twist.

Behind Dark Doors collections are each six thrilling short stories per book, which will delight fans of **Twilight Zone** and **Outer Limits** and any lovers of genius twists you won't see coming. By the author (that's me), readers are naming **the next Gillian Flynn (Gone Girl)** and the **female Stephen King.**

Partake of these exciting story morsels of six short stories of **suspense, horror**, and **supernatural**. They promise to thrill with their clever twists and wicked irony.

BEHIND DARK DOORS (One)
BEHIND DARK DOORS (Two)
BEHIND DARK DOORS (Three)

Now turn the page to read the first five chapters
of Susan May's best selling novel *Back Again*.

Between life and death lies Fate.

A fast-paced time travel thriller with a mind-bending plot and an ending you won't see coming. A story of hope, forgiveness, and the serendipity of Fate. By the author readers are naming **the next Gillian Flynn (Gone Girl)** and the **female Stephen King.**

What would you do if the thing most precious is taken from you in a terrible moment? What would *you* do to change fate?

A tragic accident takes everything from Dawn. The following surreal days are filled with soul-destroying grief and moments she never wants to live again until, inexplicably, Dawn finds herself back again, living *that* day. It's a second chance. But changing fate is not as simple as it first appears. Time is not Dawn's ally.

Kylie's life hasn't turned out quite as she'd planned. At twenty, she's over her dead-end supermarket job, and her life is a mess. Her boss is on her case, her ex-boyfriend won't stop harassing her, and all she wants today is to drive across town and cry on her best friend's shoulder. As she leaves the supermarket parking lot, she picks up her cell to send a message. It's a decision that will change her life forever.

A **thrilling** story of **hope, forgiveness, and the mysterious journey** of two people whom Fate has destined should meet. Only on the last page will you know everything. This thought provoking book will stay with you long after you close the covers.

Fans of **The Time Traveler's Wife,** the film **Sliding Doors, Timebound (The Chronos Files),** and any **fast-paced thriller with a mind-twisting**

plot will enjoy this clever, poignant, and satisfying read. You've never read a time travel story quite like this. It's science fiction fantasy with heart.

She'd lost count of the number of times she'd lived through this. Every time it hurt as much as the time before. Eventually, she thought that she must become immune to the events, and that her heart wouldn't shatter into a thousand, million pieces ...
But it always did.

Praise for Back Again
"Compelling and masterfully written." **Anne Frasier NY Times bestselling author**

"From the very first chapter you know you're in the hands of a real written." *Sarah Kernochan, Best selling author & Academy Award Winning Screenwriter*

"Compelling off the first page. You can feel the pulse!" *Caroline Kepnes, NY Times Best Selling author of 'YOU'*

CHAPTER 1

4:29PM

4 MINUTES TO THEN

Fourteen seconds.

Dawn counted them down in her mind. On any other day, what difference would fourteen seconds make?

Today, they would be the difference between life and death.

Tommy would leave his music lesson any minute now. No, that was too vague. She knew the time. He would leave his music lesson at *4:33* and fourteen seconds. The seconds were what mattered. Fourteen increments of time that could—and would—change everything.

She checked the car clock. Dawn always glanced at it—she couldn't help herself—though there was no need to note the time. She knew it.

4:29

Her hands twisted together in her lap before pausing to pull at a stray thread on her skirt. She wrapped it around her finger and pulled. The thread was always there. It came away from the material, but she kept it twisted on her finger like a ring, as if she were married to the moment.

Married. That was a few years ago. She didn't think about Richard so much anymore. She used to, but there wasn't the time to care and fuss about inconsequential things like a broken marriage since this.

How many times had she checked that clock? How many seconds had she counted down? Still, the beat echoed in her head as if she herself were a ticking time bomb.

Her mouth felt dry, not a normal dry but the draining thirst that no amount of water can quench. Without looking down at it, she pawed at the drink bottle sitting in the center console. Flicking the lid open, she raised it to her lips and sipped. As she did, the digital clock changed numbers.

4.33

She lowered the bottle, her fingers gripping the cylinder, as if it were the last rung of a ladder hovering over a long drop. The metal felt as cold as her heart in those times when it all seemed pointless.

The door of the music studio flew open. Tommy's guitar, a large black case that seemed too big for his ten-year-old body, preceded him through the doorway. He paused and looked across the cars parked outside.

Catching sight of her, a smile erupted across his face and he waved. It was a small wave, one of those waves where you barely lift your hand. A wave that simply said *I see you—you're there*. Not a wave to say *I love you, you're special* or *I am so happy to see you*. Certainly, it wasn't a wave to say goodbye.

Internally, she coughed back a sob as her hand raised to wave back. *Her* wave said more. It said *I love you. I'm sorry. I will find a way to get you back.*

Fourteen seconds to go.

CHAPTER 2

8:10AM

8 HOURS 23 MINUTES TO THEN

Today was not the best day of Dawn's life. She'd had very little sleep thanks
to last night's phone call with Richard, her prick of an ex-husband. She
tossed and turned most of the night, churning about his request.

He and that woman wanted to take Tommy to Disneyland for a week.
He'd never suggested that kind of trip while he was with *her*, so why he'd
suddenly decided to do it now, she couldn't understand. *Well, she could.* It
was his way of winning Tommy over to thinking that his new wife, the
"everything's awesome," curly-haired, husband-thief was better mother
material than her.

She remembered when he'd first courted her. It was fifteen years ago,
but still so fresh in her mind. Richard had been such a charmer, tall,
square-shouldered, confident, mesmerizing deep-brown eyes—the same
eyes Tommy had inherited. He'd made her feel as if she was the most
beautiful, exciting woman in the world, and marrying him seemed like a
dream come true. Even her mother, who'd disliked every other boyfriend
she'd brought home, was in love with him.

So she could almost understand why husband-thief Miranda ignored the
fact that he was married with a child and stole him away. That notion was

little comfort and, certainly, it was no excuse for her to break up their family. She blamed him just as much—not the correct apportion of blame, according to Dawn's best friend, Gail. In Gail's opinion he was totally to blame.

Sometimes, like last night, her thoughts swung like a pendulum from anger at them, to a deep guilt that somehow she was responsible for it happening. That it was her punishment for spending more time worrying about Tommy than their marriage.

Then there were the slips—that's what she called them, anyway. It wasn't like she'd kept them a secret with Richard; he knew about them *before* they were married.

So what if sometimes she lost a little time and forgot what she'd been doing and where she'd been? Didn't everyone have forgetful moments? Before the other night, she hadn't had a slip for years. With the medications and the relaxation techniques they had dwindled in frequency and duration. None was ever as bad as that first time with her sister on the mountain when she was a kid.

Why was she even thinking about him? She must stop blaming herself. He met a woman, whom he found more attractive than her, who would pay him more attention, and who didn't have the welfare of a child to consider. The End.

She needed to get her head back into today and stop thinking about the past.

This morning was the usual rush, their son being an average ten-year-old dawdler. On days like this, parenting him was a tricky job. When they were married, Richard just hadn't been up to the task of managing the day-to-day organization of Tommy's life. If Dawn were honest, some days neither was she.

Today Tommy was on a go-slow. He could be charming, delightful, loving, and beyond enthusiastic about life and particular topics that interested him—like soccer and YouTube stars. On some days, though, like today, she would get the other Tommy. The ten-year-old that ate his breakfast—always Coco-Pops because of the monkey on the box—so slowly that it could easily become lunch before he'd finished.

She looked over the counter at him, drew in a deep lungful of air, and exhaled a long, frustrated breath.

"Tommy, if you could hurry it up, Mommy would appreciate it."

He looked up and gave her his cheeky smile. That boy knew how to work her.

"Mom, you want me to get indigestion? I'm going as fast as I can."

"Not fast enough, if you want to get to school on time. And I don't think you can get indigestion from Coco-Pops. Come on. Hurry it up."

Tommy went back to eating, now shoveling the cereal from the bowl to his mouth so quickly that little brown beads of over-processed rice, or wheat, or whatever the stuff was made from, fell all over the counter. It lay there, scattered around the bowl, like mini brown rocks.

Dawn saw the amusing side, but she'd learned that if she let him get away with these antics he would think he had the go-ahead to clown around any time. He never understood when it was a good or a bad time to be a funny little guy.

"You can clean up that mess you're making as well, buddy."

"What mess?"

Dawn put on her stern mother look and said, "Very funny... Not! In one minute, you are putting that spoon down and we're walking out the door, mister. I don't want you to be late. Again!"

Dawn checked the clock on the microwave. If she had one dollar for every time she glanced at those glowing digits and thought, *I'm going to be late,* she'd be rich. About every third time, she would think about Richard, and how if he hadn't done what he did, she wouldn't be running from one thing to the next, and have a better chance of being on time.

Forget. Him. Dawn.

Her mother had told her regularly that she needed to move on. She knew she did. Maybe tomorrow she would make a resolution. Today she just wanted to be angry as hell with him.

She looked at Tommy again. He'd slowed back down to the snail pace, as if she hadn't spoken. She wanted to remind him that they were a team, and he was letting the side down. Gail told her that she said that to her children in these situations, and that sometimes it worked. Dawn couldn't say those words. They seemed kind of... well, false. "*Yahoo*, aren't we the perfect *Brady Bunch* family. We're a team. Yippee-yi-ay."

Truth was, she didn't believe Gail acted like that all the time. How could she? It seemed impossible to keep your cool when, often, children seemed like an opposing force in your life, put there simply to test you.

Dawn grabbed a cloth from the sink, wet it, then wiped around Tommy's bowl. He was mid spoon-to-the-mouth when she decided she'd had enough. Swiping the spoon from his hand and grabbing the bowl from beneath him, she pulled them away and put them in the sink.

"Enough. We're going."

Tommy looked shocked, affronted. He gave her one of those looks that said, "You're *not* part of the team, I hate you." That look in his eyes always hurt her. He'd been giving it to her more often lately. Perhaps in response to her waning patience.

Damn Richard.

Now the day had started badly. Tommy's annoyance always faded quickly, soon replaced by his charming chatterbox self, while Dawn would spend the next few hours riddled with the type of mother-guilt that ate into her mood all day. Her inability to control herself with Tommy activated a nagging self-doubt about her power to take control of her own life. She couldn't afford that, because as much as she dismissed the slips, it was always in her mind that one might happen at any moment.

When people told you that parenthood was the hardest job in the world, it wasn't the truth. Being a single mother was the toughest, most demanding job in the world. At some point every day she felt like a miserable failure. The person paying the price: Tommy. That just didn't seem fair.

Tomorrow, she decided, she would make a change and begin the day with a renewed determination to be patient. She just knew she had it in her. Today, she was tired and cranky. Tomorrow, she would start again. Surely, tomorrow she could find it in herself to be a better mother.

She checked the time on her phone as she grabbed Tommy's bag and hustled them both out the door.

8:20 a.m.

Chapter 3

8:20AM

8 HOURS 13 MINUTES TO THEN

Kylie dawdled out her front door. Late again. She was always late. Late to meet her friends, late home for dinner, late in making her car payment and, at least twice a week, late for work.

Being late never bothered her. It bothered everybody else, she noted, but that was *their* problem. It was her thing. Part of her personality, part of what made her unique, like the blackness of her hair or the green hue of her eyes, or the way her nose tipped down a little at the end.

That tip was the reason she'd had the single nose ring pierced through each nostril. *The mom*—as she called her—said she looked like a cow, but Kylie thought it drew the attention away from her nose; she hated her nose. As soon as she had enough money she would have plastic surgery like all the actresses did and have it fixed.

To her mind, the ring camouflaged the flaw using reverse-psychology. Everyone noticed the ring and nobody really looked hard at her nose. It gave her face a daring look. Like *mess with me and I could get wild and dangerous*, just like those cannibal pygmy people with the bones through their noses. Mess with them and you'd get eaten. Mess with her and you'd wish you *had* been eaten.

Perpetual lateness was her other way of showing her true self. Time did not control her like it controlled her parents, her brother, and all those other losers who wanted to be part of the mind-numbing world of clones. She was an individual, and the rest of the world could just suck on that.

Although, today, concern did tingle at the back of her mind that this was the third time this week she would be late to work. Mr. Ramello, her boss at the shithole IGA supermarket, where she was slowly being bored to death, was constantly at her to show pride in her work. Every time he said it, she wanted to reply: "Yeah, well give me something worthy of pride and I will." She'd been close to quitting so many times.

Her little, red baby stopped her.

The first thing she'd done when she'd gotten the job was to buy a beautiful red Ford coupe. Complete with sunroof. Only five years old, it was perfect for her. The minute she saw it she fell in love. Driving it gave her a sense of freedom she'd never experienced before. It *was* her baby, and she took better care of it than herself.

She hadn't saved any money since she'd started this job five months, three weeks, and two days ago. (That's how much she hated it; she counted the days, marked the number up there on her calendar.) She'd given herself two years to pay off the car and set herself up to move out of home.

That plan wasn't going so well. All the Main Street clothes stores were too tempting. She'd also found an addiction that had surprised her at first, but that she found growing increasingly important to her. Tattoos.

The bluebird on her ankle was the first and meant to be the only one. After she got it, though, she couldn't stop examining it whenever she was sitting on the couch, or lying on her bed, or any time when her ankle was exposed.

It added something to her, improved her life in a way that makeup and changing her hair color didn't. So she went back for another, never telling her parents, knowing they wouldn't approve of even one, let alone a collection of them.

The next one, an entwining of stars and vines and hearts, was larger, and ran from the back of her waist to spread out just above her bottom. Every few months she added another tattoo to the collection. Her star-sign Gemini on her right breast, a bloom of rose buds springing from a vine up her left wrist, a dolphin jumping through a crescent of the moon on her stomach. Next month she was planning another for her left leg: a beautiful owl, wings spread, hovering over mystical symbols.

It hurt like hell to have a tattoo done, taking hours of pain that she could barely stand, but she endured it for a good reason. Right from when she got the bluebird, each tattoo filled a hole in her she hadn't known existed. Every night before she went to bed, she would hold up her shirt, twist her neck to catch a glimpse of her back, examine her breast, her wrist, and her stomach.

They were beautiful, just like her red baby. She deserved them, needed them and, as much as the mom was on her case about scarring herself once she saw her bluebird and rosebuds, she wasn't about to stop collecting them any time soon.

Continuing to work at Ramello's IGA was the biggest pain in the ass; sometimes it even got her down. Lately he'd issued even more threats about firing her, but he never followed through. She couldn't leave this job just yet, because then she might lose her car, the installments taking a big chunk out of her pay. And the owl, which she'd set her heart on and couldn't stop thinking about, would have to be put on hold.

No, she was stuck at this dead-end job, putting up with her idiot boss and the stupid parade of customers she was forced to serve every day. Eventually, she'd find something else, and if he got on her back today, maybe she'd start looking sooner than later. Maybe as soon as she'd gotten the owl tattoo.

As she turned the key in her car, her gaze fell upon the painted rose bud daintily resting on her wrist, while the vine travelled up and under her sleeve. She suddenly imagined herself a rose stuck in an ugly weed garden. She thought, *Even another year of this and I'll wilt and die.*

Her decision was made in that instant. Tomorrow she would change her life, look for a new job. She was not a wilting flower and she wasn't going to stand for the cosmic unfairness of working at this mind-numbing job.

Tomorrow would be the beginning of her new life.

CHAPTER 4

Thursday 10:40AM
5 HOURS 53 MINUTES TO THEN

This was Dawn's day off. That was quite the joke. As if she ever had a day off. Sometimes going to her part-time secretarial job seemed like more of a holiday than the chores that waited at home.

Stop with the bad attitude, she told herself as she hung out the washing. She was still smarting from the look Tommy gave her that morning. Pressing a peg over the arm of his T-shirt, she thought about all that she should be grateful for in her life. She had Tommy, a few good friends, a job she liked. If she was going to be a better mom for Tommy starting tomorrow, she needed to change the way she thought.

So what if Richard ran off with that woman? Since the divorce, she had always begrudged Richard being too busy with his work, leaving her to take Tommy all week and every second weekend. If she were being honest, though, that *did* suit her fine. At least, she never had a chance to feel too lonely. Perhaps one day she'd even meet a good man and they would be a complete family again. Gail kept telling her that, but her best friend *was* the eternal optimist. Gail had a good marriage, two lovely children, and as the manager of a travel company, she travelled to fabulous holiday places for free.

In comparison, Dawn's share job as a secretary at an accounting firm was less exciting, but the firm offered part-time three days a week school-work-hours, and those were the magic words for her.

The sound of the phone ringing interrupted Dawn's hanging of the washing. She turned and ran the few steps through the small terrace garden into the house, almost falling over Tommy's scooter lying across the entrance to the back door. A tingle of annoyance entered her thoughts, but she brushed it away.

A new positive you, remember?

She snatched up the phone and realized she was still carrying Tommy's blue and yellow soccer socks she'd been hanging.

It was her mother.

"Sweetheart. It's a quick call…" They were rarely quick. "Are you coming over on Sunday? I need to know. I'll get something special to cook."

Dawn knew the reason for the invitation. Tommy was with Richard this weekend and she knew that her mother was worrying about her. Her mother thought Dawn needed to be occupied every second of the days Tommy was gone, so that she didn't fret about Tommy being with Richard and his new wife.

"I will let you know, Mom."

The pitch of her mother's voice rose slightly. "I really think it would be good if you came, Dawn. We could go shopping, or have lunch. Whatever you wanted."

"Mom, I'm quite busy. Please, can I let you know on Saturday? And if you get a better offer, just go with that."

"I'd like you to come over. When you get too stressed, that can bring on your turns." *Here it came.* Dawn hated the fuss. It didn't matter how long since the last slip, her mother acted as if it was yesterday.

"They're not turns. And I haven't had one in years."

"But are you making sure you take the medication when you should?"

Dawn wasn't taking the tablets anymore, hadn't been for over eighteen months, but she wasn't about to share that information.

"Yes, of course. I'm not a child anymore, Mom. You really don't have to worry so much."

"It's just the last time we saw you with Tommy, your father and I thought you looked, well, exhausted. And we worry that if you're driving and it happens..." Her voice trailed off, then she began again with gusto.

"There was that woman on the news the other night. Did you see the story? In Denver? She walked out her front door and six months later, they found her living in Pasadena, unable to even remember her own husband. When they took her back to her home, she suddenly remembered everything, but then had no memory of the six months she'd lived as the other woman."

Another story from the news. Dawn's mother always beat her over the head with these. Yes, she did have a strange slip episode when she was a child, and then a couple more as a teenager. Since then, she'd had only a few short slips, and only one major one two years ago just after Richard told her he was leaving. She wasn't counting that one a few weeks ago. She wasn't even sure what it was, because it was different. Normally she would have little memory of the passing time, left with just a strange dream. Even though it was a terrible memory, the most recent one she recalled unusually well. And she'd been driving at the time. So she absolutely wasn't sharing that with her mom.

The doctors had always told her there was no guarantee with the medication anyway. The specialists felt as she grew older, and the time between slips increased, the chance of them disappearing forever grew better. Dawn chose to look on the bright side, and hope that they were behind her—a product of hormones, or stress, or whatever imbalance had occurred in her brain. Dawn called them slips. Her mother called them turns, and the doctors called them fugues. There were no definitive answers.

At the moment, with everything on her plate, she didn't need her mother constantly stressing her out about it, so she firmly answered: "I didn't see that news story, but I don't think that will happen to me. Please stop calling them turns, too. That makes me sound like an old, hysterical woman. Now, can we please change the subject? Tommy wants you and Dad to come to his concert. It's a week away, next Thursday night."

"Of course, darling." Her mother hesitated. "Is Richard coming?"

"Possibly. I've told him, and that's all I can do. He's always *so* busy." She fought down another twinge of anger. The way he prioritized his life over Tommy still pushed her button.

Then, as if her mother hadn't heard anything Dawn had just said, she began pestering her again. "We really want to see you this weekend. In fact, after you drop Tommy off at Richard's come and stay the weekend. What do you say, darling? You have to forgive a mother for worrying."

Dawn had to get off the phone or she would give in and agree. The last thing she wanted to do was spend the weekend with her parents. She loved them, but thanks to those childhood slips—she was never going to call them turns—her mother had smothered her, and she wasn't letting up any time soon.

"Mom, I've must go. I've some errands to run and I haven't got a lot of spare time today before I pick up Tommy."

"Just consider it, Dawn. Even for a few hours."

Dawn sighed, not loud enough for her mother to hear, but just enough to release the tension that was building within her. When her mother got like this, the only thing to do was agree. She hated doing that, because later she would have to come up with an excuse and endure a repeat of this conversation. Right now, though, she just needed to get off the phone.

"Yes. I'll see how I feel and what happens. I've got today and tomorrow to get through before the weekend. Maybe a tall, dark, handsome stranger will invite me on a date."

They both laughed and Dawn was glad that the phone call was ending on a better note than where it had begun to head. *See? She could become a new person.*

Dawn hung up and studied the sock still clutched in her hand. Somehow, she'd managed to twist it around her wrist without realizing. She possessed absolutely no memory of having done it. She'd been preoccupied with controlling her annoyance; it was like when your mind wanders sometimes when driving, and you arrive at your destination with no memory of driving there.

Concern entered Dawn's mind, but she pushed it away. No, it wasn't a sign that a slip was coming. It was simply a sock, and a phone call, and her mother nagging her.

Her mind wandered back to the first time. She still felt a chill when she thought about it. She'd been only a year or two older than Tommy then, and she still remembered it as if it was yesterday. What she actually remembered, she could never be sure. Was it a dream? Or an hallucination? Who knows?

It was the first and the worst of the slips. So really, on a positive note, she'd been getting better ever since. Other than that strange event last week, and she was ignoring that. She simply refused to live in fear. And it might never happen again. She was determined to never allow it. For Tommy's sake.

Of course, that wasn't her choice.

CHAPTER 5

1990

Sunshine was like an energy source to Dawn and her sister, Anna. When the warm rays touched their skin, it was as if they super charged cells deep within their being. Long ago, their mother gave up asking them to come home for lunch on the weekends. They would take off on their bikes after breakfast, loaded up with snacks, to return only after darkness crept across the mountain.

Their mother fussed too much, according to Anna who, at fourteen, was the oldest of the two by eighteen months. If they came home for lunch, she argued, it would eat into their exploring time.

Even more than the sunshine fuelling their adventures, their escapades were the release they needed after five days of being cooped up at school—learning what adults felt important. Living on a ridge above the town, the mountain gave them the opportunity to stretch their legs and learn something for themselves.

They spent these days cycling along the dusty, gravel walking paths on the canyon road whose access was, conveniently, only a hundred yards from their front door. The myriad paths had come to exist through various means: natural breaks in the foliage, trails molded by the Parks and Recreation Department when budget permitted, and some by the constant assault of dirt bikes, bicycles, joggers, walkers and their dogs. The pathways closest to the houses had been groomed by residents who'd taken it upon themselves to create access to their local treasure of natural beauty that was Elk Canyon. It was a mixture of green-gray brush, trees, and rugged volcanic rock, but in spring, it came alive as a postcard scene of blooming wild flowers in glorious hues of pinks, purples, and whites.

Every year at the end of winter, a "working bee" was organized, and the residents took to the pathways, tidying and clearing them for the summer months. The working bee also doubled as a necessary fire prevention strategy for the dozens of houses perched along the escarpment.

Held over two weekends, Dawn and Anna's parents hosted one of the two after-work barbecue parties occurring on each Sunday. These would carry on into the night, long after the two girls went to bed. They would hear the adults laughing and talking as if the clearing was the fun part of the trails. For the girls, though, it was a means to an end. The pathways were their ticket to adventure.

The entry to the trails was a checkpoint between the street of perfectly manicured gardens and architecturally striking homes of glass and wood, and a wild, dusty, gray-brown pebble-strewn passageway. Beside the trails, clumps of straggly bushes and patches of wild flowers created a vista of a beautiful, but harsh landscape. Trees clung precariously to the edges of rises and sheer faces.

This summer, the girls had gradually begun to travel farther past the cleared tracks. After all, what was the fun in exploring the homogenized version of an adventure? Travelling where others hadn't gone, that was the true exhilaration. Sliding down embankments. Stringing rope between trees growing at odd, crazy angles, so they could climb around them, and pushing through thick scrub that lay higher up the hill and fought their every step.

They were adventurers in strange lands, imaginary characters shipwrecked on a wild, desolate island, and inter-galactic explorers left stranded on a distant planet. In their fantasy landscapes, they would fend off attacks from the wildest, most dangerous creatures. Sometimes they wouldn't survive, and they would then invoke their superpowers to be resurrected again to explore another day.

Anna was the imaginative one, all brown, shaggy hair and dark, mischievous eyes, and a good head taller than Dawn. At fourteen, Anna seemed a lifetime older than her sister. She created the scenarios, decided who would play villain and hero and, if Dawn didn't play her part to the best of her ability because she was tired or bored, Anna would mete out the punishment. This would usually involve giving up some of her treats, which their mother had packed in their supplies, or carry Anna's backpack to a certain marker point of their trek.

Instead of feeling the normal sibling outrage, Dawn found Anna so charismatic and wise that she rarely argued. She was happy that her older sister took control—Dawn, always the quieter one.

When it came down to it, on an unconscious level, Dawn understood that without Anna her own life would be so much less colorful. She didn't have the imagination or the drive to reach beyond their childhood vision of the world. So Anna would drag Dawn into her thrilling realms. Dawn didn't like an argument or fuss, so she happily followed.

Today, though, *following* her sister would not take Dawn on a wonderful adventure. This day would not become another glorious day where the sisters returned home tired, but brimming with excitement from all they'd discovered. Today was the day that Anna's exploits took them too far out on a limb. Today was the day everything changed.

Read *Back Again* now.
Available exclusively at Amazon
Read for FREE with Kindle Prime and Kindle Unlimited
http://amzn.com/B00P10J7HG

A Favor

If you've enjoyed this story or any of my stories, can I ask you a favor please?

An author needs help to sell their books and grow their career. They need you, the wonderful reader, to spread the word. If you've loved this story and want other people to experience it, please let them know. It would mean so much to me.

And if you have a spare few minutes, could you please go to Good Reads or where you bought this book and leave a short review (a long one if you like) and let me and the world know what you thought of the story.

Get in touch with me, too, if you like and let me know by emailing susanmay21@iinet.net.au or finding me on Facebook or Twitter. I would love to hear from you. You will absolutely make this author's day.

Other Works by Susan May

NOVELS
BACK AGAIN
DEADLY MESSENGERS

NOVELETTE
BEHIND THE FIRE

COLLECTIONS
BEHIND DARK DOORS (One)
BEHIND DARK DOORS (Two)
BEHIND DARK DOORS (Three)

BEHIND DARK DOORS (The Complete Collection)

ANTHOLOGIES
FROM THE INDIE SIDE

SHORT STORIES
THE WAR VETERAN
SCENIC ROUTE
BACK AGAIN (SHORT STORY)

Contact Susan May

Connect with Susan May

http://susanmaywriter.com

Join Susan May's Wonderful Reader's Club
for news and updates

http://www.susanmaywriter.com/p/loading.html

Favorite social media hang out:
Good Reads

https://www.goodreads.com/author/show/173617.Susan_May

Twitter

@susanmaywriter

Facebook

https://www.facebook.com/susanmaywriter

Made in the USA
Middletown, DE
05 December 2016